I0658144

CRUSHER

in

Wonderland

The second book in the "Geronimo's Revenge" trilogy

by Mike Palecek

To Zacarias Moussaoui, the "20th hijacker,"
now in federal supermax prison in Florence, Colorado.

There were no hijackers.

CWG PRESS

Published by CWG Press, 1517 NE 5th Ter #1, Fort Lauderdale, FL 33304
www.cwgpress.com

Cover art by Lisa Rouleau and Damara Jean Rose Allen

ISBN 13: 978-0-9906714-6-6

Printed in the U.S.A.

Also by Mike Palecek

Fiction:

SWEAT: Global Warming in a small town, and other tales from the great
American Westerly Midwest
Joe Coffee's Revolution
The Truth
The American Dream
Johnny Moon
KGB
Terror Nation
Speak English
The Last Liberal Outlaw
The Progrrressive Avenger
Camp America
Twins
Iowa Terror
Guests of the Nation
Looking For Bigfoot
A Perfect Duluth Day
American History 101: Conspiracy Nation
Revolution
One Day In The Life of Herbert Wisniewski
Operation Northwoods: the patsy
Red White & Blue
Welcome to Sugar Creek
CRUSHER vs. The Empire

Non-fiction:

Cost of Freedom (with Whitney Trettien and Michael Annis)
Prophets Without Honor (with William Strabala)
The Dynamic Duo: White Rose Blooms in Wisconsin, Kevin Barrett, Jim
Fetzer & the American Resistance
Nobody Died At Sandy Hook (with Jim Fetzer)
And I Suppose We Didn't Go To The Moon, Either! (with Jim Fetzer)
Nobody Died At Boston, Either (with Jim Fetzer)
America Nuked on 9/11 (with Jim Fetzer)

Of course, the whole idea is to create as much confusion as possible, so that people are not quite sure what to believe.
— Colin Wallace, former MI6 intelligence officer

"That's two to the fighting eighth power," *Yossarian pointed out*, "if you're thinking of writing a symbolic poem about our squadron."
— Joseph Heller, *Catch-22*

Imagination is the only weapon in the war against reality.
— Lewis Carroll, *Alice in Wonderland*

I will splinter the C.I.A. into a thousand pieces and scatter it into the winds.
— John Kennedy

How intelligent our guts are, making us know the scheme of this all, right when it happened.
— Unknown

ONE

"You can't execute him. He's got intel."

"He blew up a market in Roomabudi."

"I know, but he's got intel. When a nightclub in Florida goes up in smoke it won't be on me."

"What are those?"

"His 3D glasses. They were in his pocket when we picked him up."

"What are you doing?"

"You reach out and touch and it's almost real. That's what I've heard."

"Bless your heart. You take my breath away. You've never been to a 3D movie?"

"Not really."

"One hundred people died in Roomabudi."

"I know, right? But he's got intel."

My Land.

TV.

That's a professional job, I'm just me, acting, writing, production and it ends up right there, big time on TV, in every living room. Me, I'm just me. They fake that and they can fake this. Fake history, fake lives. At least mine is. I assume yours is as well. Anywho.

1

I s'pose you heard about Korey?

Do you know about ADHD, what it stands for, what it means, what it does? I don't know, I just have all these things I want to talk about. Shit.

I used to be so obsessed with electricity.

That is with electricity or power or the completion of a circuit, magical, to me. I was never diagnosed with autism in the day, that was way back when it wasn't so popular. Who knows? But I'm over the electricity thing not really. But now I am also obsessed with aliens. They are real and we've known about it since 1947, that's a long time and they have covered it up, in a way, in a clever way they put it out into culture but they have also made it into a sort of a joke.

The C.I.A. is nothing if not inventive and creative.

Also that brings to mind and let's not forget aliens from Mexico, the poor people who walk across the desert to try to make a home, get their kids on a school bus route. Amazing people those aliens.

I was talking about Korey.

Nexus Lexus Dallas Texas. Korey said that to me one time, that he heard Max say that when Max was trying to make up a song, but Max was really only a writer and I said it sounded like the lyrics to a John Prine song. Korey said he never heard of Prine.

Patriots Day, Wahlberg, traitors, Stalin, Goebbels. Actually? Really? Seriously. Those are my notes here that I scribbled while driving. That's all I wrote. There might be more somewhere. I'll look in the back seat in the spring.

I was talking to this one woman about the moon. I said we never went there because we never went back for about fifty years now. If we did go there, there would be at least one McDonalds on the moon, a gas station, maybe a bar, a church, a grain elevator.

But there's nothing. I asked the woman why? And I answered my own question quickly probably because I needed to be right. I said maybe it's because Carl retired. Carl? Oh, yeah, Carl. He knew how to get to the moon, but he retired. None of us know how. She said, maybe we don't need to go there. Maybe that's why we haven't gone since. I said maybe you're right and I sat down.

I think I need to talk about those who died. There was Skylar and Rick, Morgan, Mollie, umm, Joe, no, not Joe, yes, Joe, and Ariel, uh, Rachel. I think that's it. There were more, but those are the ones you know. Can you think of anyone else? I think that's it.

Korey. I'll get back to Korey.

Can you imagine how great it would be to be in a band. I was thinking that the other day. First of all you can play an instrument, wow, like knowing another language, special, not many people can do that, well, a lot, but in relation to the whole population is what I mean. And you've got at least that many friends, and you create something, and the music, that's at least one more language. Just wow.

Disparate thoughts, looking for connections, that's me, to a T. I get these panic attacks where my thoughts just keep going, on a straight line, into space, infinity, finding nothing, connecting with nothing, they just keep going. I just float in space. So dark I can't see and it's cold.

Cue the crickets. That's in my notes too. Sometimes I have these notes and later I look at them and think what is this? I think this means something with conspiracy theories.

Doesn't everything? I know. It's like there is all this happening, but right here, nothin'. And I think that's what they want you to think. I wonder who they are. That's what I wonder. I know, right?

Top of the mind. You know what that is? Once I was driving this group home van and the radio didn't work only when it wanted to. Well boom! I'm on the freeway and it's early morning and dark and it comes on blasting, classical music and my immediate thought was that I just thought something that the F.B.I. didn't like and I was in trouble. Top of the mind.

The general population uses a lot of military lingo.

The next false flag attack should have magicians, fireworks, and laser shows. I read that in the comments section for an article on the internet.

Once I was picking up someone in the van at a group home to take him to the workshop and the group home worker comes out talking about the Green Bay Packers and said he knew I would be happy because they won. And when I got back in the driver's seat after using the wheelchair lift I thought.

How did he know I was a Packers fan?

There were bigfoots spotted at Old Faithful on closed circuit TV. Six.

I like aliens. I don't even know for sure they exist, but they do. I think they give us hope. This isn't all there is. There's more than uncle Franz talking mean, stupid conservative American stuff at Thanksgiving and more than I see on TV, more than *Gunsmoke* and more than *Price Is Right*.

Dorothy Kilgallen, the reporter who knew too much. If there were one Dorothy Kilgallen these days the world would shift so much everyone would have to move over to keep it from tipping, and then They would kill her to make it shift back.

I've never been as upset about anything in my whole life. Not really, about what's happening with Korey. Not really. But I do care.

Well, if you want to know who They are, they are Carroll, Marv, Trevor (Troy? Brad?), and Alexa, that's who They are, if it helps to put a name on them. They do exist. They walk. They poop.

Looks like we've got a traitor in the house. I was watching, no, not really, but I was thinking what if I was watching this big football game and everyone stands up for the military and the national anthem and there's this one guy who won't stand up.

Do you know there is such a thing as C.I.A. karma foreshadowing? I guess they have this thing where if they are supposed to kill someone they have to go to that person first and tell them they are going to do whatever they are planning to do and in doing that sort of warning the C.I.A. killer is not responsible.

It's like they put it on the killee. That stuff, with The Simpsons? The Lone Gunmen? With that Batman movie? The Big Lebowski, lots of that stuff out there.

Well, anyway, I wanted to get to Korey and finally I have.

Note from the narrator ...

Well, once Evey was sitting outside by her home on that bench by the trees while I was visiting. I think it was after supper and I had just helped Maria with the dishes before I came outside to sit.

Evey was making some notes and I was always looking for something to write about, so I asked her what's that.

She handed it over and went on to something else.

What it was, was a list of homework, reading assignments, study, for the CRUSHERS during the time of planning way back then, during the overnight sessions.

It said, "Read about these and learn. Remember when you were a kid and during the summer reading program they told you that you could travel anywhere through books? Well, if you read these you will leave America. You will no longer be an American. We don't know quite where you will go, but one thing is for certain. You can never come back."

And then there was this list: Gladio, Bernays, Operation Northwoods, Phoenix Program, MK Ultra, COINTELPRO, JFK, MLK, RFK, Aurora, Boston, Sandy Hook, LAX, Orlando, Chatanooga, 7/7, 9/11.

Did you hear the one about the C.I.A. agent
who went to heaven?
That's funny.

You get so used to lying that after awhile
it's hard to remember what the truth is.

— Philip Agee

Take it back, take it back, oh, no, you can't say that.

— John Prine

TWO

There's one thing I didn't mention in that last bit, from my notes. I just found this in the manila folder file I keep for Max. It just says "Bernays Bernays Sirhan Sirhan." Max. I miss Max. I hope he's watching over us. We're gonna need it in this yarn I'm about to unfold for you.

It's not plagiarism if that's what you're thinking. It's living in the culture, being surrounded by all this new shit, letting, actually, you have no choice, having it flow through you like a current, a circuit, being a part of you and then you provide your part, you have no choice, and coming up with *a yarn*: Fibre. Natural or synthetic, for example wool, nylon. Often found as one continuous thread bound into a ball, used for knitting. Throw in portion of ADHD, autism spectrum, too much Diet Coke and other petro-chemicals in the water and food, a human brain not nearly understood, salt, cumin, beer as needed and voila.

Korey was in that group as we recall that left the Bumfuck battlefield in the night, escaped to live another day. Korey left under protest but followed the order of Lara. The others who left were the scouts who guided the group, Evey, Blake, Reuben, Hector and various wounded CRUSHER soldats.

I am planning to have fewer swear words in this installment but you never know about those CRUSHERS if you know what I mean.

They made their way through the perilous no moon Iowa night to relative safety and to learn the next day about the capture of Lara, Jim, Kaitylyn along with the rest of the CRUSHER troops, those who did not perish in the morning battle.

Well, when Korey heard what happened he couldn't take it. He could not stand being safe while his friends were captured and dead. He ripped his clothes and screamed. He threw things and he felt it deep in his stomach, cracked his knees and put his forehead to the floor. His face was so red.

He got up wiping away tears and snot with his sleeve. (I really had no idea he had this within him. I actually thought he was kind of a slug. Sometimes a bit clever, but for the most part … oh, well.)

He heard where Jim, Lara and Kaitylyn were being held and he went there, stood outside the facility, his hands in his pockets, wondering what to do. He was filthy, wearing a dirty orange CRUSHER T-shirt, camo, an empty sheath on his belt, his hair littered with brush from the long walk. He paced slowly back and forth on the sidewalk knowing his friends were locked up inside. He was tired, had not slept, fueled by rage and confusion, coffee and one whole package of rolls stolen from the C-store. He found crushed cigarettes in his jacket pocket and smoked, not seeming to notice the looks from the windows and from the cars slowing as they passed.

Soon three large men in suits stalked purposefully out of the building, headed across the lawn toward Korey.

This is not what Lara wanted, the thought might have crossed Korey's mind at this moment. She wanted Korey to be on the outside working to rebuild CRUSHER, keep it going, attack Mayfield and the home of Beaver Cleaver.

"Sir!"

The first big man shouted while still a ways away, a black man, apparently in charge, carrying something in one hand, a club or rolled-up newspaper, followed by the other two, perhaps symbolically or not, a white man and the last one, Hispanic, looking.

This was observed from across the street so we don't know exactly what was said, but Korey stopped his pacing to face the sudden onslaught of the three large men in suits they did not look quite comfortable in, if you have seen the same sort around here and there.

Korey raised his hands while talking, not in surrender but in exclamation. He stomped a period foot, and pointed a finger at the ground, again and again, commas in his sentences.

It began to drizzle as it does.

One of the large men spotted our observer across the street and waved to make the observer move along, but that did not happen.

They surrounded Korey, close-in, and our watcher could not see what was happening, but cars were slowing down even more and at least one stopped.

Korey broke through the men and appeared to be walking away having had his fill of whatever was happening. This made them rush after him, throw him belly first to the ground, not the sidewalk cement, I don't think, pull out handcuffs and handguns, secure the area, haul him to his feet and hustle him into the building.

So there you have it.

Korey is now captured.

He had warrants out for the Stone Arch Bridge event, for one thing, probably half a dozen others, and when they find out who he is, he will be theirs. They will own him. He does use the alias Kory rather than Korey, which he told me once would save him sometime and I wanted to tell him maybe not, but I didn't, and what good would it have done anyway. He wasn't going to listen to me.

Well, I guess we'll find out.

I've got a lot I need to cover.

What more can I say about the dead? Yes, Morgan, Mollie. Did I mention them. God rest their souls. And Bow. Okay, I'll go there. Is it worth it? You tell me. I'm just a reporter, not really even that, a … forget it. This is not about me.

And there are those in prison, they will keep. Not going anywhere as they say.

Prince Hope is dealing with his own sorrow. I'll talk about him later.

Joe and Ariel are still alive, having escaped from Mayberry. No, they're not. I keep forgetting. And Zima. Shit.

And Evey and her brothers up there on The Range. Yes. I know.

But first there is this TV show I am just obsessed with. I watch it on Netflix. The writing is actually good, so good. They probably have six writers, twelve maybe, in one room for days and they have years of experience doing this kind of thing. They are very smart, well-educated, witty. They are good. And I am just me. Shit.

One time I picked up a hitchhiker. Yep, I'll get back to the TV show, *My Land*, it's called. I just can't concentrate on one thing for all that long, please excuse. Too much coffee, but I haven't had all that much this morning … this hitchhiker. And bear in mind I wasn't meant to have this knowledge, this insight, but some light leaks through.

He was barely coherent, said he could kill quickly with his hands if he heard this one commercial. I turned down the radio. Said he was taken from a California orphanage when he was very young, some mumbling, bad things, went to Vietnam, Phoenix? I thought. And then some bible thumping that made me turn off and I left him where I was going the other way. Now years later I wish I had learned more from him, but still he gave me something, something I was not supposed to have. Anyway, this show, I just can't stop watching it.

Note from the narrator ...

More of the CRUSHER Reading List:

A Funny Thing Happened On The Way To The Moon, Apollo Astronauts Press Conference, Danny Casolero, Gary Webb, Michael Hastings, Jim Fetzer, Kevin Barrett, James Tracy.

At the time of Robert Kennedy's assassination, the C.I.A. was conducting mind control experiments. Experts think that Sirhan Sirhan was one of those under the C.I.A.'s control. This would explain why Sirhan Sirhan has no memory of the event.
Anyone who thinks that democratic governments would not kill their own citizens is uninformed beyond belief.
If you are one of these gullible people, please go to the Internet and become familiar, for example, with Operation Northwoods and Operation Gladio.

— Paul Craig Roberts

I would love to trust you buddy,
but you are clearly keeping secrets from me.

— Todd Snider

THREE

FADE IN:

INT. [office in C.I.A. HQ, Langley, Virginia]

Two agents meeting in the room. One, AGENT 001, is the older, the other is in his 20s.

AGENT 001

You heard of them? Well … Where's she?

AGENT 002

Yeah. On her way, I guess.

AGENT 003

(Quickly enters the room.)

What'd I miss?

AGENT 001

Lighting cigarette, opening a window slightly.

Terr'rists.

AGENT 002

So, yeah, we've got assets there, why us?

AGENT 001

OO4 says, okay, well, speak of the devil.

(He whispers last part.)

(Another man enters and takes charge. He turns off the lights on the way in as AGENT 001 flicks his cigarette out the window, shuts it and waves his hands at the remaining smoke in the room.)

AGENT 004

(Operates computer, shows images on screen on wall. Goes through images of suspected terrorists, landing on one and bringing the picture to full screen.)

That's your mission.

AGENT 003

Mission?

AGENT 002

Should we choose to accept?

AGENT 003

Don't do that.

AGENT 002

It's a long ways.

AGENT 003

We have planes, please stop.

AGENT 004

(To AGENT 001)

Open that window. It's smoky in here.

… The guards removed the handcuffs in the hall so that when he walked into the cement block room his hands were free. He messaged his wrists as the door was opened for him, then closed behind him and he was left facing the stone room.

Korey's stomach actually hurt immediately upon seeing that classic torture chamber setting, the lone chair, the bare bright light.

Trevor and Alexa (in the dictionary, under "Alexa," there is her picture) stood there, at the metal table talking casually and looked at Korey critically, as if he had interrupted them.

"Oh, I suppose then," said Alexa, pulling out a metal folding chair for Korey to sit at the table, with a full ashtray and cigarettes littered around.

Korey sat, an awkward distance from the table. Trevor (Troy? Brad?) perched bravely with one hip on the table while Alexa paced, patrolled, slowly in the backward.

Trevor and Alexa wore suits. Korey wore his same clothes from the street, from the Bumfuck battlefield, some of Rick's blood staining his pants leg.

"So, how's it been?" said Trevor.

He offered a cigarette, set it on the table.

Korey let it be. He stared at it.

"I said, how's it been? How's it going?"

Korey studied the table top, the mess of the ashtray, ashes, cigarette butts.

Alexa stopped her pacing, turned and faced Korey and the table with her hands folded at her waist.

"Lara sends her love," she said.

"Kate as well."

Korey looked up.

"Jim?" said Alexa.

"He's fine."

Korey resumed his table study.

Alexa walked, slowly clicking, head down, a contemplative monk in a black suit, nice shoes.

Trevor stood.

"So, you're from Minneapolis then?" he said.

"Listen, fuck, this can go easy or this can go very hard."

"Don't do that," said Alexa.

She moved close to the table. They both smelled of perfume, cologne.

She invited Korey to move his chair closer. Korey did and folded his hands on the table. Alexa worked to clear the debris.

With both hands she recommended the overflowing ashtray to Trevor. Trevor looked at her incredulously as she nodded toward the door. He took the ashtray, spilling ashes, and left.

Alexa leaned over the table so Korey could see her bosom and he saw.

She paged lightly through some papers.

"Korey Miller," she droned.

"K-O-R-Y, M-I."

"K-O-R-*E*-Y," he said. "You must got the wrong guy. That's not me. K-O-R-*E*-Y."

She glanced at him, then back to her papers.

"We can let you, and your friends, go," she hummed.

She rested a hand on his.

"Listen, I understand what you guys are doing. It's amazing. You have a lot of fans."

"They wouldn't let you," said Korey, nodding toward the hallway where he supposed the guards waited.

"Who do you think we are?" she said, standing straight, folding her arms at her chest.

Trevor returned. His eyes asked Alexa where they were now.

She stared back hawk-like down at Korey.

He tried to stare right back at her.

She looked at the floor, shook her head in disgust, as a teacher or parent disappointed.

"Take him back," she said, and Trevor went to the door for the guards.

Again Korey was brought to the room. He couldn't tell if it was night or day. There were no windows in his cell or in the hallway or in the room. He remained in the same clothes, had not showered, had only eaten and drank but a bit.

This time he took the cigarette when it was offered, accepted the light from Trevor.

"You are a murderer," Alexa began.

This time she sat at a chair at the table as Trevor stood at the wall, watching.

"They will hang you for treason. Any idea how that feels?"

"Electric chair," said Trevor and Korey caught a hint of Alexa glaring briefly over her shoulder at Trevor.

"Your friends, too," she said matter of factly.

"You could change that, man," said Trevor.

His speaking from the far side of that mostly empty room made the small room seem so large, like an empty gymnasium, and Korey recalled his after school job working with the school janitor and how he liked that guy, *but he's probly dead now.*

"Korey," said Alexa, scooting her chair closer to the table, making a screech sound that she seemed to apologize for with her mouth and eyes in an instant.

"We're not from around here. You understand that, right?"

He smoked and ashed into his cupped hand in his lap.

She did nothing to search for an ashtray.

"We're from Washington."

Trevor walked over slowly and as he walked he said, "Korey Miller."

Korey looked up at him while wondering what to do with the cigarette butt that was still hot.

Trevor produced a manila envelope from behind his back and tossed it on the table.

Alexa relayed it to Korey, pushing it within his reach.

Korey opened it and saw black and white and color photos of himself on the Stone Arch Bridge holding a rifle. He saw photos of various CRUSHERs in their T-shirts: Santa: He Knows; The Many Faces of Darth Vader; Walter Sobchak, Nothing Is Fucked; and finally the orange T-shirt with CRUSHER. He turned the photos over slowly, coming to Lara, Kaitylyn, Jim in their cells, looking bad. He quickly closed the folder.

"You can make that go away, man," said Trevor.

"You want to do that?"

Korey pushed the folder away and stared into the ashes in his hands. He curled his toes and looked at himself, his clothes, his hands.

"You are fucked, man," said Trevor.

"*Fucked* big-time."

Just then a big, older man barged in, like Kramer, thought Korey for a moment. Marv, also dressed in a suit, but his was rumply.

He is smiling, seemingly in a hurry, assured that the three have gotten things figured out and they are ready to proceed.

"So," said Marv.

"We ready to get this show on the road? Get this young man out in the fresh air where he belongs enjoying this wonderful day?"

Alexa and Trevor looked glum, disappointed.

"Not quite," said Alexa.

"Korey doesn't really *want* to help his friends, I guess," said Trevor, turning his back, returning to his wall to stand.

"You gotta be kidding me!" said Marv, pulling a pack of cigarettes from his jacket, beginning to smoke, offering one to Korey. Korey put up his hand and shook his head no.

"That true?" Marv said to Korey.

"It's so nice out there, today. You like baseball? Do you?"

Korey shook his head and said softly, yes.

Marv grabbed a chair, sat on it backwards and got up close to Korey as Alexa removed herself to stand behind the prisoner.

"Listen, bud," Marv said, sounding intimate, in close to Korey, implying Alexa and Trevor couldn't do their job right.

"This shouldn't be that hard," he whispered.

Korey smelled his breath, heard his labored breathing. He tried to make eye contact and stare into Marv's face as they had practiced way back in the time of planning, but Marv's face had too much going on, the nascent baldness, the wrinkles from his eyes all the way around his face, the yellow teeth, the breath, the hair on the end of the nose, the eyes. He looked down.

He heard the loud screech of Marv's chair scooting back and looked up just to see the door close.

Alexa walked to the door to get the guards.

The guards assisted Korey under his arms, setting him down in the chair.

He barely noticed, but the room now had a rope hung wall to wall, other implements placed around on the floor, some sort of sound system, and Trevor, Alexa and Marv wore blue scrubs over street clothes, face shields, rubber gloves, disposable shoe covers.

They set to work as soon as the guards pressed Korey into the chair. They raised his hands up over the rope, zip-tied his wrists with black plastic, had him stand, took away the chair and shoved a black plastic hood over his head, pulled it tight and tied it like a garbage bag.

"You can hear me bud?" said Marv.

Korey said nothing.

Trevor wound up and punched Korey hard in the stomach. Korey dropped to his knees, as far as the rope would allow. He gagged, tried not to vomit inside the bag. He fought to breath and to stand, to relieve the tight pressure and pulling on his arms, but the rope swayed back and forth. Finally he stood.

"Do you hear me now, Korey?" said Marv, getting in close to Korey.

Korey nodded one time.

They made Korey stand in that position with his hands raised and they made him stand there a long time. Each time that he felt he had to lower his arms he was punched in the stomach by one of the three. He came to know them by the size of their fists and how deep the fist went into his stomach and how weak it made his knees feel and whether he almost puked.

They poured ice cold water from a jug down the back of his shirt and down the front of his pants and he thought they were pouring fire.

Korey lost track of time.

After awhile he felt he had been born in this room and had been here all his life.

He felt Alexa's face right next to his.

"I ain't talkin' to you," Korey managed to get the words out.

"Go fuck yourself."

"No Kor-eee," said Alexa.

"I'm gonna fuck *you*," she said as she kneed him in the genitals, twice.

Korey tried to fake feinting and was hauled to his feet with many hands and demeaning epithets.

He felt a weight, a dumbbell being placed into his hand and his fingers squeezed around it. He was told to raise the weight above his head.

"You are the Statue of Liberty, fuckhead!" Trevor screamed.

"Don't bring the fucking torch down! KO-REE!!"

"Where's the fucking ticket man!" Trevor yelled and Korey wondered if Trevor was real.

"The golden ticket," Korey mumbled and received a backhand slap across the face.

"We want the ticket."

"I can't give it to you."

"Why not?"

"It's not mine."

Again Korey found himself being pulled to his feet and his arms raised by the rope and the rope going away leaving his arms and hands to stay up by themselves and they didn't want to.

Then it stopped. All at once and in a hurry and right now.

A chair was pushed against his legs for him to sit. His bag was removed and a headset was strapped to his head, earphones. The headset had a chin strap like a football helmet. He jumped when loud, loud music blasted on, pulsing back and forth, all around inside his head.

The bag was shoved back on, his arms raised, the chair taken away and someone punched him full-on in the mouth, sending a tooth flying, trapped inside the bag. Korey heard the tooth rolling whenever he moved, sometimes felt it sitting right next to his cheek wondering why it could not be inside the mouth anymore.

Korey stood on the hard cement, his arms in the air, the loud, loud music and his head inside the bag, trying to put his chin to his chest whenever he could to get the precious air from the tiny opening where the bag was tied around his neck.

The tooth rolled out the little hole and Korey felt like he'd lost the only friend he'd ever had and he cried, glad to be inside the bag, away from the world, away from everybody, and then a punch exploded in his stomach and in his brain and snot flew from his nose and ran down into his mouth.

With the music he could not hear them, so the punches in the stomach were a complete surprise, but not really.

Sometimes he felt them right next to him, perhaps listening to make sure the music still blared loud enough.

One time Korey felt the presence and even though he did not know if it was real he licked his lips, tasted blood and snot and swollen lips and attempted to talk, not knowing if his voice still worked.

"So, yeah," he said, out loud, over the sound of the music, inside the bag, inside the cement room, in America.

"What do you want me to do?"

Note from the narrator ...

From "Not Exactly a Radio Show," a live podcast that traveled the circuit of Twins Cities bars for about six months, produced by former members of The Prince Hope Show:

This *just in again* ... *The Not Exactly a Radio Show* newsroom has received word that the "Homeland Security Obscene Statue Removal Team" — taking part in "Operation Bad Guys" — after they finished the Joe Paterno job at Penn State, has now taken their bulldozers and cranes and chains and torches, ropes and dynamite on six flatbed trucks and four semi-trucks, with lead pickup with lights flashing, headed for the other jobs that will need to be completed before the end of the coming spring and summer.

Right now the caravan is headed for the Ronald Reagan Statue at the National Airport in Arlington, Virginia, then on to the George W. Bush statue at Hamilton High School in Hamilton, Ohio.

They will then cruise on down to the George H. W. Bush monument in Houston, Texas, then out to the Black Hills to the Gerald Ford statue in Rapid City, South Dakota.

And this just in some more ... plans are underway to take out the Bill Clinton statue in Pristina, Kosovo, and the Barack Obama statue in Jakarta, Indonesia with drone airplane attacks.

Eight years old with a flour sack cape tied around his neck. He climbed up on the garage, figuring what the heck, screwed his courage up so tight, the whole thing come unwound. He got a runnin' start and bless his heart, he headed for the ground.

… So he licked his finger and checked the wind, it's gonna be do or die. He wasn't scared of nothin'. He's pretty sure he could fly.

… he did not know he could not fly … so he did.

— Guy Clark

FOUR

Korey stopped for a moment to think.

Why can't you put the fake bomb in the bus and then have your drill? Why me?

Thought Korey as he made his way to the school bus.

It's got to appear real.

Appear real, what's that mean?

Korey carried the duffle bag that had the bomb that Trevor, Alexa and Marv had given him, and he had the music still blaring in his ears, the same words repeating over and over and over it never stopped. They told him it would stop.

Yep, the hood was up and he had practiced with the three agents to know just how to put it. He scanned around quickly, hopped onto the bumper and bent over his work, feeling his heart pump way too much whatever and hoping he did not pass out. He licked his swollen lips and worked by the light of the strong little flashlight on the strap thing around his head.

Korey hopped down, gave an oomph to close the hood, scanned again and walked away.

He was done.

He was free of the agents and that cement room.

His friends were in prison.

He was a wanted man.

He was so hungry.

Korey was supposed to wait there when he got done, until the other people who were doing the drill that was supposed to train the police how to save the kids in the bus when there's a bomb planted by terrorists.

He felt eyes on his shoulders and on his back, like a laser beam pointed right in the middle of the back of his orange CRUSHER T-shirt they said he was supposed to wear. They even found a clean-one-owner one for him.

He was s'posed to wait, so he sat on the curb, not a curb, a cement thing where cars park.

"So, I'm going to plant this, umm, bomb, in a school bus?"

Korey recalled his practice training with Marv and Alexa and Trevor.

"Why would anyone do that?"

"It's just training," said Trevor.

"That is vitally needed," said Alexa.

"We appreciate your help, bud," said Marv.

"What about Lara, Jim, Kaitylyn?" said Korey.

"No problem," said Marv.

"Not a problem."

Korey felt his head and did not feel the headphones, but they were still there.

"The children will arrive after you have attached the training device," said Alexa.

Korey sat on the curb and heard the children chattering, herded by their teachers, onto the bus. A driver parked a pickup on the street and walked to his bus, staring hard at Korey. Korey got up and attempted to look *not-weird*.

The driver got in, got situated, all ready.

The teachers counted their children. And then counted them again.

Korey heard them telling the children how they should act on their field trip.

He remembered he was supposed to stand on the orange X. He looked for it, saw it, headed toward it.

"Yes, Mrs. Finley-Newberry!" said the children as one.

The bus driver started his bus just as a bang! went off and Korey felt a piece of cement bounce off his stomach not as hard as a fist.

Emergency vehicles screamed out up and down the street, lights flashing.

TV station vans parked sideways in the street.

Men and women poured from unmarked cars and SUVs.

Korey ran.

He fucking ran.

Into the crush of people rushing toward the bus he sprinted as the bus driver honked and honked his horn at the people to get out of the way, he was on a special trip to take these children to the zoo. Goddammit.

Korey made his way to a café, a coffee shop, through many people excited to be so close to some real action. He sat at the counter and watched the news. He hid out for a while in the restroom.

He sat for a couple of hours in the library. He returned to the café where his old chair at the counter waited. He sipped hot coffee with both hands and listened hard over the chatter to the TV where they were still talking about the bomb in the school bus.

"Authorities say a bomb was found in the bus. It did not go off as planned by the terrorist group CRUSHER, because as authorities say, it lacked a detonator fuse."

Korey fingered the piece of hard red plastic in his pocket and asked the counter guy for a refill on his coffee.

"Wash down the rest of this muffin," Korey tried to smile.

The reporter moved to the side and put a microphone to Marv's mouth.

Marv told how this had been a training exercise for school and emergency personnel that had somehow been infiltrated by the CRUSHER rebel group and an attempt to "cause significant human damage and destruction, pain and suffering."

"CRUSHER," said the reporter. "What can we do?"

"We ask citizens to be especially vigilant and watchful and close their doors," said Marv.

"Develop a password system with their friends and neighbors?" said the reporter.

"Nah, not really," said Marv.

The screen then showed a photo.

Korey felt his stomach and his knees and in his head he remembered everything in his whole life and in his mind the music blared louder than ever.

The counter guy walked over with Korey's coffee, shook his head, began to wipe the counter where Korey had sat and scooped up a piece of hard red plastic with the muffin crumbs.

Note from the narrator ...

From "Not Exactly a Radio Show," a live podcast that traveled the circuit of Twins Cities bars for about six months, produced by former members of The Prince Hope Show:

And now for another episode of "Waterboarding Anderson Cooper," sponsored by Mr. Bubble.

If we are going to torture people who we say we think are terrorists but we know are not really terrorists because we did 911, there are no terrorists, no Al Queda, no reason for war, and really no information we can gain, other than to perpetuate the lie, go deeper into the story of the lie, build and embellish the lie fable — then why not also waterboard people who we know are terrorists, who were in fact our terrorists, who helped us to lie a long time ago and overturn our own country — And! And!
This terrorist is one of those who really is there, who really knows the truth — and what he knows is actually real — no need to fake kill him and fake bury him at sea —One or two or maybe three quick sessions — which are not really such a big deal anyway, right? Would change the course of this whole country.
Just one little Goon Afternoon live on national TV.

The Committee To Waterboard Anderson Cooper — CIA agent fake reporter, who knows what is really happening.

... Reporters used to be on our side, like Penn Jones Jr. and the little Texas weekly he operated. They are not anymore. The CIA has money and they figured it out. Money sells, it works, that's how things operate.
Bob Woodward, from the office of naval intelligence, Dan Rather, Tom Brokaw, Peter Jennings: pour a bucket of water on his grave, that son of a bitch; Peter Mathiessen, started the Paris Review to spy on Americans in France for the CIA, it likely goes on much further than we dare to imagine. Read Carl Bernstein's article in Rolling Stone, Google Operation Mockingbird. ... etc. etc.

We are The Committee To Waterboard Anderson Cooper — it's not really that bad anyway — endorsed by Allen Dulles, Dick Cheney, George Bush, George Bush, John Yoo, Barrack Obama, four dental hygienists, and millions of folks like you.

Sponsored by Mr. Bubble ... gets you so clean your mother won't know you.

All the writer has to do is write in the bare description of what's going on around them and not try to over describe something and it leaves space for the reader or the listener to fill in their experience and they become part of it.

— John Prine

They're gonna go to jail with you as part of the crime.

— John Prine

FIVE

I just can't stop watching. I know I probly shouldn't, I know it's probably not good for me. The writing, with all that dramaturge, it works, it draws you in, the characters ... I know, I know, but I just like it. *Recruit them – defect them – capture them – kill them ... the Cold War was really to disguise the effort to develop weapons to fight the alien threat ... fascinating stuff.*

I suppose you know, by now, that Prince Hope hired Danny on Craigslist to get rid of Jim because he thought Jim was getting too close to Lara. And Prince Hope hired, formed The Special Team to take care of Brooke. Well, I didn't know. Sometimes I don't know how much you know. By the way, I found this YouTube link. They pop up on my computer and often they turn out to be just what I need. I don't know how it happens, but it's pretty cool.

We are what we are and we ain't what we ain't. John Prine words to live by. You gotta trust the you of that time to have done the right thing. It's over. I got a John Prine question: Why peaches? Not gouda?

I rip my fingernails, have my whole life. Probly torn to the nub when I was born. Lately I only do one, let the others grow. It's insane.

I leave one fingernail to tear. If I'm famous that's a story, gives depth and background to the life of the successful writer person. If I'm not famous, then I'm very crazy. I've got a feeling to quit this project, not sure where that comes from, the mercy of heaven, perhaps. Simple logic.

I've got a violin, a banjo, two harmonicas in the basement and plenty of books, a tool for tuning. I feel I need to learn Spanish, too. Learn it for someone, and quit these books. I feel it strongly some mornings.

So far I've done it a couple of times, but then come back upstairs. The last time I told myself there are like a billion people in India who can play violin, probably five-ten million who play banjo in southeast West Virginia and maybe at least that many who play harmonica and shit how many people can speak Spanish. There's just one me writing this one book. If it's not good when it's done, then okay. If it is good when it's done, then good, rather great, I can't believe it. If I don't do it, we'll never know. Ever. And maybe if there are dead people listening to what we think, one morning I'll be one of those and whispering, hissing-whispering to some strange guy telling him to do what I did not do, and that won't work. And so. I s'pose.

Talking w. the dead on a winter's Saturday afternoon.

That's in my notes.

So, do you want to talk to me, can you? if you can't hear me I think that's incredible … what if … and so … that's why I wanted to talk to the dead, nobody living could help me. I listened and heard nothing.

I also remember Bobby Kennedy coming to town and sitting on my banana seat listening to him and wanting some words to live by, getting them and telling my sister and she didn't care of course, and then the night he was shot … and that's a hell of a life, a hell of a life to live. Pisses me off.

Dreamer, Supertramp, *Father and Son*, Cat Stevens, to discover something like that amid your own turmoil, that your feelings are felt by someone else?

You kneel in the hard gravel in the alley behind your parents home puking up beer from a night spent trying to forget and to feel normal and you hear someone singing. How can this be? I am not uniquely criminal? I am not the worst? How can *that* be?

Note from the narrator ...

More of the CRUSHER Reading List:

Penn Jones Jr., Fletcher Prouty, Sirhan Sirhan, Lee Harvey Oswald, James Earl Ray, Terrance Yeakey, Kenneth Trentadue, Barry Jennings, The Church Committee, D.B. Cooper, Splitting The Sky.

It was a primary election day in New York and the start of Fashion Week, and the new President had gone out for a jog in the early Florida morning, and the smiling crowd had dutifully gathered outside the *Today* show. Babyface had a new haircut. Sarah the Duchess of York was promoting a new book.

But in a number of moments throughout the morning, anchors, stories, and promos carried eerie foreshadows of the events about to unfold.

•An American spy drone was shot down over Iraq, Ann Curry reports at the top of the Today newscast, "for the second time in two weeks."

•"There is something in the air," says a CNN anchor at the top of the hour. (He is referring to Michael Jordan's rumored comeback.)

•In a promo for the evening news, Tom Brokaw reports on "three numbers that could save your life — 9-1-1."

•An anchor on an NYC local newscast reports that in a Fashion Week pop quiz, most of the models failed to answer the question "what happened on December 7, 1941."

•"Whatever you do, *do not open that door*!" says weatherman Mark McEwen, quoting a Gene Wilder bit, just before he mentions that Ray Romano is in the studio, and says he watched *Everybody Loves Raymond* "while flying out here on American Airlines."

•At the end of his weather report, McEwen adds, "It's kind of quiet around the country. We like quiet. It's too quiet."

— Alex Pasternack, *Motherboard*, "The Surreal Early Morning TV of 9/11, Just Before The Attacks"

SIX

Prince Hope looked out the window of his upstairs office above The Lonely Lutheran bookstore.

It was summer in Saint Paul, Minnesota with everything up in the air: baseball, hiking, all sorts of outdoor, fun stuff.

Hope wore a yellow T-shirt showing a big orange image of the moon and below it the image of a spacecraft and "Fake It 'Til You Make It."

He stood and put on his white sport jacket. He wore white pants and red tennis shoes. He also grabbed his straw hat, reached for the pipe and decided to leave it there.

He went down the steps, through the bookstore, out to the street, walking slowly by himself in his immaculate white suit, yellow shirt, red shoes, straw hat, so tall and so straight, except for the slump around the shoulders, like a walking vulture one week into a new vegan diet, his hair in his eyes.

He used a walking cane, perhaps for affect, did not pause at the alley. He has not seen anything come out of there ever 'cept pigeons 'n delivery trucks.

Barely checking traffic he crossed in the middle of the block, walked past the next alley where he could have gone to enter by the actor's door, but he proceeded farther, past the people waiting for the show.

He stopped to talk to one person and a crowd gathered. He stayed longer than he should have and had to excuse himself and hurry away.

Prince Hope sidled through the crowded lobby, resisting the popcorn aroma, down the west side aisle, right up the steps, on a little jog, on to the stage. He carried his hat at his side as he moved toward the middle.

He began to talk, his hat and cane in his hands at his waist, even as the crowd was organizing itself, finding seats, collecting parties, toting drinks, taking phone pictures for Facebook.

"My son," he said.

"My son … is dead."

The people stopped where they were, dropped to a knee in the aisle, in the wrong seats, stopped talking in the lobby, shooshing any new people coming in.

"Bobby was killed at The Battle of Bumfuck … Iowa.

"He was a member of CRUSHER, a rebel, someone we are not supposed to mention, to admit is real. He did exist."

Prince Hope turned and walked to the wings. In a few minutes the curtain opened and the show began.

Note from the narrator ...

> From "Not Exactly A Radio Show," a live podcast that traveled the circuit of Twins Cities bars for about six months, produced by former members of The Prince Hope Show:

Now a word from a new sponsor, American Dream Memory Blockers. It's the big blue pill.

Don't worry about the American Indian genocide, El Salvador or Iraq. You are an American.
American Dream Memory Blockers put your mind a little out of focus, just like you like it, with no peripheral vision.
Put those blinders on, keep moving straight ahead. Manifest Destiny.
Just watch out for the California cliff and that deep drop-off.

American Dream Memory Blockers.
It's the big blue pill.

It's embarrassing, Americans have wasted so much money on this agency that's done nothing but graft and corruption, destabilize decent countries all over the world and now attempting to do the same thing right here in the USA. [Jim Fetzer]

It's been a problem since 1948 from its inception from the OSS. It should have been disbanded almost immediately. And the only reason it hasn't gone away is every sitting and standing President is fearful of it because they know the power that it wields. It is the de facto shadow government that controls the United States of America. We do not see the people that rule this country, they occupy a place in Langley, Virginia, an obsidian black building, and that's where the real power's at. [Dennis Cimino]

The Real Deal Radio Show
Jim Fetzer & Dennis Cimino

That sounds like a lot of crap to me. — General Dreedle
It is a lot of crap, sir. — Yossarian

SEVEN

"**U**R rong, T—h—e—l."

Lara looked at the writing on her own palm. Her hands were always sweaty so it was easy to erase it by just a little rubbing.

She had taken down the message from Kaitylyn tapped out on the metal toilet from her cell somewhere in the prison. They had taken to calling each other Thelma and Louise to maybe confuse anyone listening.

Lara got her tapping toothbrush, anxious to fire right back at Kaitylyn, but stopped short of the commode. She didn't want to say something she might regret.

Lara and Kaitylyn fought all the time these days in prison. They never saw each other or knew quite where the other was, but having been taught how by the other prisoners, they could communicate by tapping out a Morse code, thanks Actually, delivered through the plumbing pipes.

Jim was in a separate part of the prison, ad seg or something like that. They never heard from him or about him.

Lara wanted to "kill them all."

Kaitylyn had become something closer to a pacifist, or at least was questioning guns, it seems.

There is really nothing much to add about their situation at this time. You know what a prison is, and they are not the only ones there, there is noise, deceit, mistrust, and hate, there is food, there is sleep, some push-ups, some sit-ups. You have your thoughts, your regrets, your plans, your fears, all amplified by a hundred or a thousand because that is how you do it.

Note from the Narrator

More of the CRUSHER Reading List:

Karen Silkwood, Julia Butterfly Hill, Lori Berenson, Karen Woodson, Carl Kabat, Paul Kabat, Larry Cloud-Morgan, Ken O'Keefe, William Pepper, Dorothy Kilgallen, Mae Brussell.

… the problem is, if no planes hit the buildings then the media had to be an accomplice, had to be a direct involved accomplice.

— *9/11 Taboo* No-Plane Documentary

EIGHT

It was Evey, her mother, Reuben, Hector and the toddler Rachel, all in the house. The father was still in the nursing home.

Evey and her mother worked together on the dishes while together they watched Rachel, out the kitchen window, playing in the sandbox.

Reuben and Hector were already outside down the lane, at the road waiting for their ride. Reuben, recovering from his injury at The Battle of Bumfuck, stood on one crutch. It was his arm that was damaged, but he found the crutch inside the house and wanted to use it. Hector held both their sack lunches.

They waited for America Joe, A.J., to come pick them up in his camouflage Toyota Tercel.

A.J. had the car before he went to Afghanistan and when he came back he got the custom desert camo paint job from his cousin who had a shop.

After Bumfuck, Reuben and Hector had come to live with their mother in her home, Reuben to heal and Hector to come along. Right away they wished to continue working in their underground, telling Evey they wanted to keep working on the CRUSHER vision of having the underground cover the whole United States.

Evey knew they liked getting out of the house and having something to do, some place to take a sack lunch, and said that soon they would run into the space alien underground and the underground cities of the government, but, yeah, go ahead. It got them out of the house.

But what Hector and Reuben wanted, yes, to get out of the house, but to find the treasure. They still had the map and before Bumfuck had made what they liked to call significant progress.

So, yeah, they hitchhiked to the underground, back and forth, each day.

Until one day they got a ride from America Joe, which is the name his friends had given him when he announced he was going to Afghanistan, and when he returned and went to work in the mine with the rest of them he became A.J.

"We used to know a Joe!" Reuben had said that first time, referring to the Joe killed at The Battle of Mayberry, and was hushed quickly by Hector because they were underground, secret.

A.J. was kind of a little guy, active, hyper kind of, with tattoos, cigarettes, freckles and kind of a big smile.

He said he could give them a ride every day if they wanted and Reuben and Hector said yeah.

For a few days he dropped them in the middle of the country with no mine around and they told him it was just a little walk over the hill, you can't see it from here, but if you get out and walk up the hill you can see … no, just stay there.

Finally they told him the truth because they needed cigarettes.

A.J. said yes, he had two cigarettes to borrow to them, but first they had to take him up the hill to see their mine.

And they did, and the rest is history, not history in books, but history anyway, where they had no choice but to show him the opening and the rest of the underground and all about CRUSHER because they were out of cigarettes and might be for a long time because they really had no money. None.

"Hey," said Reuben as he got in the passenger door and climbed over the seat to the back.

"Hey," said A.J.

It was so early, not even nine in the morning yet and they did not talk much at first. A.J. had quit his real job to join the CRUSHER rebellion and now had no money for cigarettes so that was another reason they did not talk.

Well, this morning, yes, Reuben got in and then Hector got in the front seat, first sweeping away cigarette package wrappers and it made him sad. His feet instinctively kicked away the plastic pop containers, remembrance of The Glorious Days Of Pop. In his lap he held the brown paper bags that held the peanut butter and jelly sandwiches and chips and juice boxes that they would share with A.J. because probly he had no lunch.

"How fuckin' goddamn long we gonna do this?"

(Okay, here we go.)

Reuben hollered at Hector or it could have been the other way around because just fifteen minutes ago Hector said the exact same thing to Reuben.

A.J. sweated and jammed his shovel against some pretty hard rocky stuff. It was dark in there. Their head lamps were all they could see by and Reuben and Hector spent a lot of the time raising their chins or lowering their chins just a little to shine their lights in the other guy's eyes and then saying, "What?"

So, yeah, they got there about ten usually and then worked 'til about ten-forty-five, when it could be reasonably called lunch time.

"It's ten-forty-five somewhere," said Reuben.

"It's ten-forty-five here," said Hector.

A.J. quit digging, sat on the hard dirt floor, his knees to his chest, his head on his knees like he was just going to sleep here for a while, you guys go ahead and have lunch. And, sure, they shared all their stuff and spent a lot of time looking around for cigarette butts.

The afternoon went on like that, lots of scraping, scuffling, bitching about it being too cold or too hot and dusty, dark, too. Sometimes there were bats and that didn't help things a fucking bit.

They got out the map for the fourth time that day, put the two parts together where Reuben and Hector each owned half, spread it out on the dirt floor and said, yeah, yeah, uh, huh, ran their fingers along the lines on the map and then dug all the harder, encouraged, in the same spots they had been digging before.

And once in a while, for no reason A.J. could see, Reuben and Hector just took swings at each other, usually slipping on the rock and missing, but once Reuben caught Hector good in the back and then they talked Spanish back and forth and pretty soon they were laughing back and forth, for no good fucking reason that A.J. could tell.

"Hey," said A.J., taking both hands on his short shovel to peck at the ground.

"What a buncha shit. Who fuckin' put this here. You did it, Hector. Why you mess wi' me like that. Why you gotta be like 'at, man."

Note from the narrator ...

From "Not Exactly A Radio Show," a live podcast that traveled the circuit of Twins Cities bars for about six months, produced by former members of The Prince Hope Show:

And now for another episode of "Waterboarding Mount Rushmore," sponsored by Mr. Bubble.

If we are going to torture people who we say we think are terrorists but we know are not really terrorists because we did 911, there are no terrorists, no Al Queda, no reason for war, and really no information we can gain, other than to perpetuate the lie, go deeper into the story of the lie, build and embellish the lie fable — then why not also waterboard people or figureheads who we know are terrorists, who were in fact our terrorists, who helped us to lie a long time ago and overturn our own country — And! And!

These terrorists really know the truth — and what he knows is actually real. One or two or maybe three quick sessions — which are not really such a big deal anyway, right? Would change the course of this whole country.

Just one little Goon Afternoon live on national TV in the Rose Garden. The Committee To Waterboard Mount Rushmore – and let's start with the four last rock-head President's: Barack Obama, George W. Bush, William Jefferson Clinton, and George H.W. Bush, who have been instrumental — monumental — in implementing fascist America. Without them and their handlers where would we be in the war to expand poverty, war, secrecy, lies – deception, camo hats on baseball teams and just a general unraveling of the fabric that is America. We are The Committee To Waterboard Barack Obama, George Bush Jr., Bill Clinton and George Bush Sr. — it's not really that bad anyway — endorsed by Allen Dulles, Dick Cheney, George Bush Jr., George Bush Sr., John Yoo, Barrack Obama, two dental assistants, four Wal Mart produce managers, and millions of folks like you.

Sponsored by Mr. Bubble ... gets you so clean your mother won't know you.

… I feel bad for those guys. Talk to anyone on earth that has traveled anyplace of significance and you will see their faces light up as they remember their trip. So why aren't these boys happy? What an amazing journey it must have been!!! Their lack of enthusiasm tells the truth.

…The greatest achievement in human history and they act like they just ran over someone's dog. The Apollo-gists tell me they were pilots who didn't have good communication skills or they spent 3 weeks in quarantine and were grumpy. … I remember Collins once saying that "he felt the immensity of space" when the module was on the far side of the moon. So, when he was orbiting the moon, waiting for Buzz and Neil, on the far side of the moon, out of the glare of the sun, in the moon's shadow, he would have had a fucking grandstand view of the cosmos... "can't recall..."

… You just have to watch the body language of all three men. Two of these men supposedly were the first humans to walk on the Moon, the greatest and most exciting human achievement in modern times. So, do they look at all happy, excited, enthusiastic or proud of what they had achieved. No they don't. Instead, they appear awkward, embarrassed, miserable, very uncomfortable and somewhat ashamed. They certainly do not look like three men who had just made Space history...

… yup, they look like the C.I.A. just showed them some pics of those who don't play by their rules and keep quiet.

…Why did Collins make his comment? He didn't even land on the moon! His gaffe only showed it was all fake.
That's why Armstrong gave him the nudge.

… I guess if I had a loaded gun pointed at my head and dared not to follow the script, I wouldn't remember seeing shit either. Well, NASA took out two of the original liars that did the movie in AREA 51. Buzz you better watch your ass, burning people up isn't the only thing that NASA does when you don't follow their script ...

… If the moon landing was fake then that means that America itself is a fake and nothing more than a wet dream and in most cases a nightmare.

— *From the comments section*

NINE

"And he dug and he dug, and the strongbox rang out like a bell in that deep dark crevice in the earth."

Prince Hope sat backwards on his wooden chair at the edge of the stage. The big room lay dark as a cave in front of him and behind:

"… turned the stone and looked beneath it … Confederate Army … was all it said.

"I dint do nothin'," said his friend, who had stopped his digging to come have a look.

The three of them stared into the little hole. They shined their head lamps on it, what looked like metal, maybe a metal box. Each one of them wondered to himself why would anyone put a metal box way down there. They looked at each other, shining their lights in each other's faces.

They turned back to the hole and dived at it, all three of them.

Their fingers clawed the dirt and the metal.

They stopped for short breaks. They picked at the dirt around the metal with their shovels for hours until finally they had it, uncovered, sitting there in the open, a metal box with a lock on it.

One of them knelt and wiped away the last dirt and clay and rubbed his hand over the raised letters on the box: CSA.

They talked about what to do.

One raised his shovel to break it open right there.

"No," another said.

"We'll take it home, open it there."

"I'm goin' with you, then," said the third.

"You ain't takin' that home without me."

When the other two turned their backs to think, Reuben raised his shovel high and brought it down flush, clank! right on the lock, cutting it. The lid flew open and away, released, finally, of its burden, like a genie after all these years.

The three fell to their knees in front of the open box shining on the stage lit by their head lamps.

A.J. picked up one of the pieces, held it up for the others to see, still on their knees, hands folded as if the box were the cradle in the manger.

"Gold!" said A.J., showing them, front, back, the coin in the dirty hand.

"Gold," he said, setting it back reverently on the pile.

The rented desert camo Hummer with the rear window 1st Cavalry stickers managed the turn at the mailbox onto the lane, going slow over the bumps. It stopped at the front steps, the Virgin Mary and Pancho Villa shrines.

Prince Hope got out, climbed down, stretching a toe searching for the moon surface. He was alone. That was a requirement, they'd said.

He wore casual camo as he thought that would be something the rebels would like.

So, yeah, apparently it was Confederate gold, packed away by train by President Jefferson Davis from Richmond in front of the advancing Union army, somehow ending up on a map, stolen by Lutherans from the train? and in the dirt where Reuben, Hector and A.J. could find it, from how many years ago was it? Or not.

Prince Hope had come to the farm to talk to Evey, Reuben, Hector and maybe A.J. if he was there, about the gold.

He had an idea.

They didn't like his idea.

They had no idea what his idea was.

Prince Hope held his camo jungle hat in his hands as he stood in the weedy grass with one foot and the cement steps with the other, admiring the Virgin Mary and Pancho Villa and the neat garden surrounding them on both sides of the cement front steps.

Evey came to the front door, opening it just enough as she does.

"Come in," she said.

"Entrez vou-ez," she said, grinning this time.

She got Prince Hope seated in the front room.

They gathered around him, kind of staring, kind of not.

Evey showed Prince Hope the palm of her hand, the note that said don't talk until we go outside.

As they slipped through the house, through the kitchen, past the mother and the child, Hope nodded, as they examined closely his boots, pants, shirt, hat.

Outside they sat on the stone and wooden benches. The mother let the child loose out the kitchen door and she ran straight for the woods and they had to catch her.

"I think we can get Lara and Kaitylyn out of prison," said Hope.

"With your gold."

He received some seriously focused "dude we never asked you what to do with our gold" looks from the three gold discoverers in the pirate hats they had found in the trunk of the Tercel while stashing the treasure box and almost blowing out the springs, according to A.J. (Not even close.)

Hope continued.

He told how a woman who worked in his bookstore has a niece whose husband is a guard at the prison.

"They love shiny things," said Hope.

"The bookstore workers?" said Evey.

"The niece?" said Reuben.

"The guards," said Prince Hope.

It sounds unlikely, I get that. But I have known people like that, who love shiny things. You may not yet in your life have met the people you will, those who love shiny things. And gold is shiny, or could be made so with a little rubbing, maybe with some soap and water solution or oil.

And so, yeah, they talked it to death.

They stayed out by the chairs and benches, all of them smoking except for Rachel. They took walks in two's and three's and one's down the dirt road. They tried to forget about it for a while and played with Rachel. Let her loose for a moment from her tether to watch her run like she had a lottery ticket to cash.

They had supper with the mother, whose name was Maria, of course. They talked a lot about the father, Jorge, still in the nursing home and hoping to get to come home again, but the prospects were not good. They talked about Maria and Jorge coming to Minnesota. They didn't talk about CRUSHER or gold, though how could Maria not know about all of this.

"Who will fight if you do not."

Said Maria softly out of the blue, putting her head down, adjusting the napkin in her lap.

And, okay, guess that's up for grabs now.

And then all of them talked about CRUSHER and the gold and they were happy, smiling, moving around the kitchen, helping with shit.

"Where's Rachel?" someone said.

They all stopped talking, stood motionless, like one of those group things they have in malls.

"There!" Maria, standing at the sink pointed out the window at Rachel scooting along in the grass like a prisoner escaped, short fat arms and legs pumping.

They got her back in and Hector rubbed her tummy and they all giggled.

"That one," said Maria.

They talked late, sat on the small cement front steps to talk and smoke, watched the moon and stars, went to sleep, on the sofa, the floor, the chairs, and in the morning began talking right away as the coffee pot worked its magic.

After breakfast Maria tied Rachel to the kitchen table with a dish towel and the rest of them went outside.

"We just don't see it, man," said Hector to Prince Hope as they were still getting settled into their spots in the sitting place under the trees, rocks, chairs, hard ground.

"We got other plans for the gold," said A.J.

"I need a new transmission. Hector wants a horse. Ruby wants dynamite to dig faster. I don't even know what Evey wants. She never says nothin' to me."

"Evey's not in it," said Hector quickly.

"We *all* need cig'rettes," added A.J.

"Yeah, buuut ..." said Hope.

Prince Hope tried to explain that it wouldn't take all the gold, just some, and didn't they want to do whatever they could to get their friends out of prison, keep the CRUSHER meme if not the real thing going?

"Jim?" said Evey.

"What about Jim?"

"Oh," said Prince Hope.

And Evey at once knew it was true. Prince Hope did not like Jim. He thought, for no reason, at least to her, that Jim and Lara were a couple. Prince Hope had wanted Danny the sniper to kill Jim.

"He's in another part of the prison," said Hope.

"Not easy to get in there."

"But it could be done?" said Evey. "Even if it's not easy?"

"I don't know," said Hope. "I just don't know. Not sure about that."

"Maybe you should ask someone in another section of your bookstore," said Evey, calmly but seriously, with eye contact while lighting a cigarette. It was her last cigarette, ever, just saying. She had smoked like a russian race horse, as A.J. put it, all day yesterday, and now this one this morning, to highlight the taste of the eggs and hashbrowns and coffee, as cigarettes can do, but as far as anyone knows, that was it.

The scenery was so nice. I think it was spring, or fall, but there was a breeze. Well, it if was spring in northern Minnesota, I'm wrong. Spring sucks there, so maybe fall. But that's a lot of words to waste anyway because they didn't even see the scenery, so locked in the drama of the gold and the prisoners.

"Got-damn!"

A.J. was the one who spotted her this time.

He spiked his cigarette in the ground and took off after Rachel, who had almost made it past the barn. He was skinny and ran good, high steps over the shortgrass. Maria noticed this as she watched out the kitchen window. She liked having A.J. around. The others seemed lost in their own thoughts and if they ran they did not put their whole heart into it.

Just before noon Hope began saying his goodbye's, adios', getting his stuff, tossing his shit up into the open driver's door of the Hummer. Leaving the door open he went along inside to eat after Maria said he must.

Once during lunch even Hope got Rachel.

Maria watched and saw that Hope could hardly run at all and when he came in with Rachel, she laughing and he maybe having a heart attack, with sweats and a numb ear, Maria agreed it was time to go. (Don't die here, she thought. You never get that smell out of a house once it's there. Not ever.)

So, she began picking up dishes, waving her hands to scoot them along, gave hugs and side kisses and waved and put Rachel down for a nap with the gold box and chain tied to one leg, Hope's idea and she would try it.

The others walked Hope to his Hummer in the bright sun, slowly on Hope's part, not so slowly with the three pirates.

"We will do it," said Evey.

"Que?" Hector leaned in.

"What'd she say?" said A.J.

Reuben put an arm on Prince Hope and moved him toward his vehicle door.

Evey stood straight and said they would do it.

Some shiny things will be taken from the gold treasure box now attached to Rachel's leg in order to free Lara and Kaitylyn.

"And you will talk to some nieces and others to try to get Jim, too," she looked straight up at Hope and he said nothing.

Both Hector and Reuben turned their backs, threw up their hands, kicked at whatever was handy and cursed in Spanish as A.J. asked what was happening.

Prince Hope backed out, waving. Evey followed him, waving, too. She continued to wave as he got onto the road and roared away, the dust following him to Saint Paul, presumably.

She turned to go to the house as Reuben and Hector threw things. A.J. picked up a stone and fired it into the grass, hit a tree by pure luck and searched for another rock of similar size.

Note from the narrator…

More of the CRUSHER Reading List:

Lee Bowers, Mary Pinchot Meyer, Frank Wisner, Tom Brokaw, Dan Rather, Peter Jennings, William Colby, Gulf of Tonkin.

According to the official story it [the plane] went completely underground and yet, there must have been an open window, somehow the bandana and passport jumped out. — David Ray Griffin

Americans don't want to know that the official government explanation of the attacks of 9-11-01 is perhaps the greatest fairytale since "Alice in Wonderland". Don't tell them that Osama bin Laden's death a couple months after 9-11 was widely reported in Pakistan. Don't even whisper that the USA is a fascist empire, even though it's obvious to anyone who's even half awake that corporations own the government on every level, and that fascism by Mussolini's own definition is the merger of state and corporate power. Most Americans don't even realize that their country is an empire. Go and figure.

— John R. Hall

TEN

Korey was on the loose, but not free, pursued, in danger, excited, scared, hungry, cold. He ran, walked, tried to walk quickly, not too fast, just like normal. Head down, head up, looking all around, looking only straight ahead.

He found himself at the entrance to the pauper's cemetery that held Geronimo captive. Ha. He grinned to himself as he put both feet down for a stop. He had thought of how Gerry and his friends had tried once to fart into balloons and then tie them up and send them off into the air to try to fart bomb people a long ways away. He looked inside, saw a familiar lone car parked on a crest, behind a tree. He kept going just as it started to rain.

For a while it drizzled, then it poured, just like they say, it's true, clichés are just amazing writing that everyone wants to copy, in buckets.

Korey, drenched through to soggy, kept going, head down, at least now feeling a bit free, as if he could not be seen. He put his head up, walked slower, put his head way up and tasted the water on his tongue, like waffles he pretended.

He walked past the old workshop, then the old group home, the lights in everything glowing so cozy and warm from where he stood.

He didn't see, all jammed in tight, Marv, Trevor, and Alexa go by, throwing up waves in the street, humming past in their electric

Volkswagen e-Golf, rented, thinking they might be able to spot Korey on the street.

Trevor was bored, and it was raining. They couldn't see shit. And, they were just riding around with not much idea where Korey could be.

"This thing got a radio?" he said.

Marv flipped it on.

"Couldn't somebody else be doing this?" said Alexa.

"We are highly trained agents after all."

"Matter of opinion," Marv mumbled under the radio.

The radio played a song Trevor and Alexa liked a lot, so much they sometimes did a skit in the office.

Trevor smiled in anticipation.

"War!" he sang bass.

"Hoooh!" said Alexa. "Yeah!"

"I mean," she said, "anyone could do this, actually."

"Good god y'all!," said Trevor.

Marv's head bobbed with the beat.

"What is it good for!" said Trevor, also playing air drums.

"Nothin'!" said Alexa.

"But, of course, I'll do whatever, you know, but still. You wonder if anyone's paying attention, ya know?"

Korey found his way to the Science Museum, past the Twins stadium, past all the bums out on the street waiting for the meal at the Dorothy Day Center. He walked way down Summit, all the way to St. Thomas, and by this time he was dry. He went down Lake, another fucking long way, through neighborhoods to Minneapolis downtown, past where they put the Mary Tyler Moore statue back after they had stolen it. That song ran through his head, the one for that show and it made him sad to think they took the statue, but they had to. He had to make himself trust the "him" of that time to have done the right thing. Didn't feel like it right now.

Korey went and stood on the Stone Arch Bridge, right over the spot where he had sat that one day and told the truth to everybody and now it didn't matter. Everybody was stupid again by now, probly.

He wondered about the other CRUSHERS. No doubt they'd heard all about him and how he, well, maybe not. But for sure Evey and Hector and Reuben knew all about him and were trying to do everything they could to help him, right now.

Jim, Kaitylyn, Lara ... why had *he* been told to do that? Damn, he could have gotten them out, but the kids.

He looked around and saw only a couple people watching him, so he climbed up on the railing and let himself down the other side, down the bridge to his spot. He sat there with his feet dangling.

His fingers found little cement chips and rocks and he leaned over to look down and drop them into the water. He tried to figure out what had just happened. The three in the suits, the torture sessions, the cigarettes ... the test bomb. I think I got shot at ... his picture on TV ... now ... what ...

Korey didn't see the e-Golf, light blue, whiz past his spot up on the bridge.

"Cool bridge," said Alexa.

Marv had his chest right up to the steering wheel and Trevor's knees in his back. Marv's phone buzzed to remind him of the calls from Carroll.

"Go back," said Alexa.

"Why?" said Trevor.

"I think I saw something," said Alexa.

So Marv slowed right there, whipped it around.

"Here," she said and they parked right there and got out.

The three stood with their arms on the railing like tourists looking out on the river, the city, right over Korey.

Without looking Trevor formed a spit bubble and let it drop before he saw Korey.

"Shit!"

The spit wad dropped right past Korey's head, but he saw it. For some reason he didn't look up. If it was kids spitting at a bum well what was he gonna do against three of them.

He felt them still up there.

A phone buzzed and Korey reached for his even though he knew he didn't have it. He did find a soggy hunk of muffin. He checked a little for lint and stuffed it in his mouth.

"What'd you see?" asked Trevor.

"Nothing," said Alexa. "My legs were losing circulation."

Marv walked a little to take the call.

Trevor and Alexa followed, their hands stuffed into the pockets of their long black coats, same as Marv's.

"Yeah," said Marv.

"Yeah."

"Yeah," said Trevor, grinning.

"Yeah," said Marv.

"Yeah," said Trevor, trying to keep from laughing as Alexa looked away, wishing she could fly.

A big truck honked.

And then it fucking honked.

Like a garbage truck or something because their little car was blocking the road. They could see the driver all mad.

Trevor and Alexa walked back, holding up their badges from a hundred feet away, so, yeah, I'm sure the driver could tell right who they were. Then they put the badges away when they got right up to the truck.

"Official business," said Alexa.

"You will have to go around, sir."

"Government!" said Trevor.

"Whose government?" said the driver, his head out his window.

Trevor began coming around the truck fast and ran into Alexa's hand.

"Easy, sport," she said.

Marv walked up behind, still on his phone, walking down the middle of the road, stopping traffic on the other side as well, unaware, didn't care.

The truck backed up, the driver still hot.

Alexa, Trevor, and Marv stood in the middle of the street, a long line behind them and now other vehicles having to back up, onto curbs and lawns to get out of the way of the retreating truck. Horns beeped and blared. Feelings were injured.

"What's up, chief?" said Trevor.

"Oh, just some updates from clandestine (he pronounced it cland'stein). Stuff we don't need to know that they think we should know."

"But we don't," said Trevor.

"Exactly," said Marv.

"And that fucking airplane ... shred ... ticket? What's that about?"

"Not one fucking clue," said Trevor.

"Shred ... ticket ... airplane."

Trevor fired out fingers from his fist and shook his head at each one.

"Geronimo," said Alexa.

"We have to meet with a Mike Braxton, special agent," said Marv.

"Or, I do."

"F.B.I.?" said Trevor.

"Yu-up," said Marv.

"Why?" said Alexa.

"No fucking clue," said Marv.

"Ah something about the bus, CRUSHER, Korey Miller. They want to be briefed, I guess. Somebody's not happy."

"Fuck them," said Alexa.

Korey hunched behind the railing on the ledge, listening. He had climbed up when the truck started honking.

He raised up and pointed at the three in black coats standing in the middle of the little road on the Stone Arch Bridge blocking traffic.

"You're the C.I.A.!" Korey shouted.

"You are the fucking C.I.A.!"

Alexa drew her gun and moved toward Korey.

Trevor drew his gun, bent his knees, and aimed with both hands.

Marv cursed and threw up his hands and turned away as his phone rang again.

Korey turned and hopped as he had done a dozen and more times, one spot, another, step, hop, to the ledge.

And he jumped.

He fucking jumped.

He hit the water feet-first, straight, arms at his sides, as bullets pelted the water, everywhere.

Poor people gonna rise up and get what's theirs.
Poor people gonna rise up and take their share.

— Tracy Chapman

ELEVEN

I had a dream. I don't have a dream, but I had a dream.

It contained the letters BIM, also Sam Stone, Russian racehorse, The Beagles, and the Actually Basement Tapes. I remember it because right when I woke up I quick wrote it all down on the pad I keep next to my bed. It means about nothing. It turns out the pad is a stupid idea.

And the usual, Sirhan Sirhan Bernays Bernays … electricity.

And, and, this part I really remember. I was in a rebel group and it turns out we were fighting invading aliens, not Mexicans.

And I was captured, and they did things to me and then they put this thing on me and they shot me into space, no, rather, one of them kind of nodded up, intimating that I could/should go.

And so I went. And I tell you, I still remember it, being in outer space, all the stars, it was amazing. I've never had a dream like that. I still remember it.

You should have round characters, they say, understand the "other side." What is there to say? I don't care what the other side feels. I simply don't care.

Once when my dad and I were coming back to our town the fifteen or so miles from the town that had the little horse racing track, I counted all the middle stripes between and was able to report to dad at home.

He was unimpressed. Neurologically imprinted depression in my brain. It feels good, felt good and now I'm stuck with it. So I drink. I didn't write all that down. I just remember it.

I'm actually kind of glad I have this story, this reporting assignment to work on. I don't know what I'd do otherwise.

Just not sure.

How do I do this? Write this story? And how do I know what I know? Or think I know? Well, think about it. Or don't. I don't give a fuck.

But I do know that by writing, about evil, exposing it to the fresh air, you destroy it. Maybe not today, but it's done, toast. You believe that? I think it's true or I wouldn't do this, no matter who paid me or asked me to do this story.

At first I thought it was just interesting, these young kids and I needed the money, and I knew I was the best person for the job. If you let the truth out of the bag, it will seek out, inherently, the cancerous evil and destroy it. Eventually. The truth is a bulldog.

The world fell over. Did you feel it. You felt it, right? The world turning over? Maybe it was just me. But one time or several times or so many times I can't count, it felt like out of the blue I got jacked, knocked down and the world was totally different than a second ago. You probably didn't feel it, it was just my world.

Anyway, that's all I got for now.

Note from the narrator ...

From "Not Exactly A Radio Show," a live podcast that traveled the circuit of Twins Cities bars for about six months, produced by former members of The Prince Hope Show:

If you are a good American, then with all the poking and probing going on in airplanes, trains, ballgames, schools, the mall, you might well be asking yourself: Am I A Terrorist?

Well, the Center For American Studies has put together a handy brochure, now available in most U.S.A. interstate rest areas, called: *"Mommy, Am I A Terrorist?"*

A few samples:

"If you are driving, past a policeman, in the United States ... you might be a terrorist.

If your Readers Digest subscription is expired... you might be a terrorist.

If you order a salad ... you might be a terrorist.

If you are walking ... down the street ... you might be a terrorist.

If your American flag on your front porch, flapping in the spring breeze, is not larger than a circus tent ... you might be a terrorist.

If you are directing by remote control, from the portico off the Rose Garden,... a drone airplane ... that hits the home of a family in a small town ... in Pakistan and rips their arms and legs from their bodies, their heads from their shoulders ... and forever destroys the lives of their extended family ... you might be a terrorist.

Scott Creighton:

•VP Biden just did a little stunt on The View yesterday morning and when he mentioned the "intel agencies" the gaggle of hens on-stage swooned at the mere mention of them and the audience, undoubtedly triggered by the "applause" sign, went WILD for them.

•Fascinating isn't it? In the wake of the fake intel of the Iraq WMDs and the illegal wars of aggression and all the lies our various intel chiefs told congress and the press about spying on congress and the rest of the country, the Dems are stupid enough to buy into this latest "GO BIG BROTHER!" propaganda coming out from the Mockingbird press and the puppet politicians.

•…There is certainly a war on for your mind.
It's not the ebil commies verses the Shining City on the Hill, but it is there and it is very, very real.

•Yes, the last thing they want is for the average U.S. citizen to know there is a gang war taking place in post intel industry coup America. In all likelihood, Hillary Clinton was one of the first casualties. It had nothing to do with Russia or Donald Trump getting hookers to pee on a bed somewhere in Moscow. If you believe that, it's because you want to believe it because, quite frankly, it's about as dumb as the Magic Bullet theory or office fires bringing down skyscrapers.

•Gee, when you think about it, the intel industry comes up with some mighty stupid shit don't they?

TWELVE

Rachel went as far as she could, tied to Maria's waist in the garden by a clothesline rope.

The rest crowded in the Tercel, the strongbox under a many shades of purple afghan on the backseat floor, headed down 53 toward Duluth and the Twin Cities.

Lara and Kaitylyn, in their separate cells, both sensed a different attitude among the guards, a look here, a whisper there.

Jim sat alone in his cell, still hearing the new wood creak in the thing that had been constructed, taking up almost the whole little recreation area for those in the hole. When prisoners in the hole were let out for their hour into the rectangle with the high walls that only showed clouds and blue sky and sometimes the sun, they had to walk around the new big thing. Jim, too, was allowed that hour and he could either sit for his time against the wall or parade around. The smell of the wood, however, was nice, something different, to be enjoyed, as long as it wasn't meant for you.

He sat and he thought as he watched up to the open sky. If it rained while he was out there the guards might let him back in before his hour was up, or they might not. They might be busy. But it wasn't raining. No reason to worry about that now. Jim counted the steps up to the platform. He wouldn't have wanted to be the one. And they better take this down after it's over. Or, yeah, more likely, it's permanent. They can do their shit in total privacy and the prisoners just have to walk around it and it's a perfect addition to the whole great experience of prison.

"Come out."

The guard said to Lara as her door broke.

Lara got up slowly, not trusting. This was not the normal time. The guard looked at the floor as Lara passed into the hall, then locked the cage behind her. She nodded for Lara to go ahead and they passed down the narrow passage into the brightness that Lara never went to. Lara saw the guard station where so many sounds that she heard originated. She saw on the desk coins, gold coins, bright, several of them, glittering in the low light of the guard station like nice stones under water.

The guard did not speak, but motioned with her head and arm for Lara to proceed. She too had heard the building of the thing and she wondered, not only wondered, but she began to think, to worry. In the middle of the wider hall they walked, the one guard and Lara. They were joined by Kaitylyn at a certain point, from another hallway. Kaitylyn moved in close to Lara and they held sweaty hands, flanked by the two woman guards.

In the prison there is one hallway with a few windows, a narrow hallway that passes between units where you can look down into the recreation area for the hole, (and on the other side for shoplifters) for segregation, the punishment unit. This is where they must walk to get to where they are going, apparently. One guard led the way. There would have been no room for someone to come from the opposite door.

The windows passed quickly and maybe you were not supposed to, but Lara and Kaitylyn looked. There it was, the big new thing with new wood. And there sat Jim! Down there, against the wall, in a corner, his head down on his knees. Kaitylyn stopped and banged her open hand on the window.

"Jim! Jim!" Lara hurried to the next window, but that guard was quicker and cut her off while the rear guard took Kaitylyn and moved her away, past the windows, to the next heavy door. It closed behind them with a permanent thud.

Another hallway, another guard station, down steps, grey steps, grey railings, break rooms, vending machines with exotic food.

Until they ran out of steps and railings. Another door, this one led to a lighted, not unhappy place.

They recognized the intake-customer service area where they had been so long ago. Behind the counter was a man who had just been smiling at something and now that the prisoners had been brought in, he was still smiling, remembering, but not as much.

He went to work after speaking briefly with the two female unit guards to bring out manila envelopes and baskets of clothes and little property to the old wooden counter.

Quickly Lara and Kaitylyn were taken by their guards to the changing area where they were weighed and told to change into their old clothes.

"What's going on?" said Kaitylyn.

One guard shrugged her shoulders, the other did nothing.

"We're being freed," said Kaitylyn to Lara as if the guards were not there.

"Why?" said Lara.

"I don't know," said Kaitylyn.

"Why? Is that right? We're getting cut loose?" she said to the guards.

The guards worked slowly with the baskets and clothing and manila envelopes. It would be a long shift and this would not nearly kill the whole day.

"We're not going," said Lara.

"Not without Jim."

Now the other guard shrugged while the first did nothing at all.

Outside on the street Prince Hope walked up just as A.J. pulled the Tercel to the curb.

Hector leaned out the passenger window.

"This it?" he said.

"I think so," said Hope.

Hope asked about Rachel as they climbed out of the car, sat against the car, paced back and forth and stared straight up at the grey wall and the big sign and asked how high was that.

First Reuben asked it and they all looked, then Hope asked it again, just as they all looked up again.

Nobody seemed to know.

They smoked, sat on the curb and the car and on the sidewalk, against the wall, watching the cars, the bikes and the people, everything tense around the Tercel to the nth degree, the concomitant normalcy shrouded by the steady cigarette smoke haze.

"But that's high," said A.J., looking up.

"Yes, it is," said Evey, looking up.

Is this the right door? S'posed to be. I don't think it's the right door.

A.J. and Reuben walked down the street, turned right and walked all around the block.

"Got to be," they said as they returned, from still forty yards away, just as the side grey door opened, pulled inward.

Kaitylyn moved out, slowly, barely getting onto the walk, just enough room for Lara to edge out as the door silently shut behind them.

The others moved slowly toward the two until they got pretty close then they rushed and hugged and laughed and kissed.

Hope offered to take them all out for breakfast so that's what they did.

Note from the narrator ...

From "Not Exactly A Radio Show," a live podcast that traveled the circuit of Twins Cities bars for about six months, produced by former members of The Prince Hope Show:

America Will Soon End and Nature Will Live, Have The Last Word.
Nature Bats Last, as the saying goes.
Some Famous Last Words.

Apollo 11 astronauts at a press conference three weeks after they were supposed to have been on the moon: Neil Armstrong: We were never able to see stars without looking through the optics. ... Michael Collins: I don't remember seeing any.

Neil Armstrong, speech at 25th anniversary of Apollo 11: There are great ideas undiscovered, breakthroughs available to those who can remove one of the truth's protective layers.

Janet Reno on burning children alive at Waco: "Our concern was for the children."

Ronald Reagan: "What we have found in this country, and maybe we're more aware of it now, is one problem that we've had, even in the best of times, and that is the people who are sleeping on the grates, the homeless, who are homeless, you might say, by choice.

Larry Silverstein: "We've had such terrible loss of life, maybe the smartest thing to do is pull it. And they made that decision to pull and then we watched the building collapse."

America Will Soon End and Nature Will Live, Have The Last Word.
Nature Bats Last, as the saying goes.
Some Famous Last Words.

Poor kid probably never had a chance to give a fuck

Wouldn't know good luck from a debutante

He's gotta find a way to be Steve McNair or young buck

Or it's tough luck looking for a prison to haunt
And you can fuck getting any kind of job you want
Unless you really want to work in a fast food restaurant
And who wants to do that?
Do you want to do that?
I wouldn't trade that for my crooked hat
Or my gang or my gun or my waist full of pagers
For a job deep frying shit, for richer teenagers
If that's where it's at and no one's gonna help
How you gonna blame a man for helping himself?
There's a war going on the poor can't win
Helicopters over the house again

— Todd Snider

THIRTEEN

They came into the busy, happy restaurant kind of happy and kind of weirdly.

Someone dived into the open semi-circle booth in the corner by the window and they all followed like geese into the lake spreading around at about the same time as three guards entered the recreation rectangle for the dungeon where Jim still sat in the corner, his head on his knees, eyes perhaps closed.

He was on again off again dreaming, of his father's pet bear he'd named Poochie, probly because of the neighbor with the dog named Bear.

Poochie wasn't really a pet, but he did come 'round sometimes to eat what was put out for him around the house. Jim then saw someone being brought up the steps, arms tied behind their back, black hood over the head.

He even thought it while inside the dream that what he was seeing had come from a novel that Kaitylyn had made them read. He heard a sound like the swinging of the drop door.

He opened his eyes, did not move his head, realized where he was and felt three men standing by the door because perhaps one had not been enough on a previous occasion. He raised his head and there they were.

71

"What happened with Jim?" said Kaitylyn.

"And Korey."

"They're coming later?" said Lara, looking at Hope.

"Jim's in another part of the prison," said Hope.

"We know, we saw him!" said Kaitylyn.

"They had to be promised more gold in order to bring you two out," said Hope.

With an open hand he fended off the wide eyes and mouths of Reuben, Hector and A.J.

"I'll see what I can do," said Hope.

"Gold?" said Lara and Kaitylyn.

They drank coffee, ordered food and talked about the finding of the gold and how the two had been freed.

The food came, mounds of scrambled eggs, waffles, pancakes, sausage and gravy.

Prince Hope said his goodbye's and went to the counter to pay for whatever they would eat. The waitress at the counter spread her white jacket to show him her T-shirt that said "CRUSHER Rocks." Hope thought she was showing him her boobs, did not notice the words, smiled just briefly and continued signing for the bill.

Lara and Kaitylyn both picked at their food, not ready yet as freedom had been thrust upon them very suddenly.

Rather, Lara got a pen from someone and grabbed a handful of napkins.

She shot her elbows out for room and began a list.

First on the list was "JIM AND KOREY."

"We're getting them out," said Lara.

"Ducks fly together."

"We're doing Mighty Ducks now?" said Kaitylyn.

"Korey's not in jail," Evey reminded them.

"He walked out with us that night. Remember?"

Lara explained that the only movie they had seen on the TV that was wheeled into the unit and left in the hall for them to watch from their various cells on Friday movie night was "Mighty Ducks." The other movie nights had been cancelled for various reasons.

BROOKE.

"Brooke?"

"Bill?"

"Who's Bill?"

"He's the prison guy. The reason we invaded Iowa. Remember? We will get him out of prison, too."

"We're gonna be busy."

Lara started a new list on a fresh napkin:

Morgan, Actually, Sandara, Skylar, Rick, Zima, Joe, Ariel, Max, Ty, Pete.

"Anybody else?" she said softly, as Evey shoved over a napkin with names of others.

"Who's this?" she said, nodding toward A.J. with her head down writing.

"A.J.," said Reuben. "America Joe."

"Really?"

She looked up.

"Can somebody get him a T-shirt?" said Lara.

Kaitylyn found her own napkins and begged a pen from the waitress.

Lara put her hand in the middle of the table, over the remaining pancakes as if to bless them. She nodded and the rest put their hands on hers.

She did not say "ducks fly together," which would not have caused a stir. She said "WE ARE CRUSHER!"

Which made the restaurant go stone silent as everyone looked at them.

"What the fuck?" Lara whispered as they sat with their hands together, gazing into each others puzzled faces, seeing all the stares from practically everyone in the world.

"You guys are famous," said A.J.

Somewhere one piece of silverware dropped, while on the TV above the counter the news story continued about how Korey Miller of the rebel group CRUSHER had attempted to blow up a school bus of local elementary children and was being sought by the F.B.I.

They slowly pulled their hands back to their laps.

"There's Korey," Evey whispered and nodded toward the napkins in front of Lara that she should put an asterisk by Korey.

Rather, Lara underlined KOREY three times.

"To believe in CRUSHER was like believing in Narnia, foolish, forbidden, not done, like talking about IT," Kaitylyn hissed so that all at the table and nearby could hear her.

"To utter the name CRUSHER."

"That's from the Chronicles of Nunya," Lara said plenty loud enough for all to hear as she stared down the people looking at them from the next door booth and the booth after that.

Lara leaned over the table and gathered them in like a quarterback.

A.J. interrupted.

"Everyone can hear us."

Lara looked at him like who are you.

She sat back up to address A.J.

"Maybe we should all speak Spanish, and then only half of these people would understand us," she said.

"You go first," she said to A.J.

"Hola," he said.

"Hola to you too," she said.

She looked at Evey and said "Hola."

"Hola, como estas," said Evey, "y tu?" she looked at Kaitylyn, who shrugged.

Lara put up a hand and said, "shut it."

Lara brought them in again.

"We can do this," she said, looking each one in the eye.

"It sure as fuck (here we go) doesn't seem like that now, but that's how all the best legends are made. We are in perfect position."

"Surrounded," said Evey.

"Exactly," said Lara.

"We need a little review. I've been thinking. Close your eyes and hold hands or touch fingers or as close as you can get. Really. Please.

"And just imagine. Everything, movies, books, newspapers, is a lie in this culture. History is a lie. It's so damn hard to imagine, but try.

"Also. You ever notice how nice guys, gals, just kill the vibe in the room.

"Also. Do all fat people know each other? That's nothing, just some shit I been thinking 'bout. *Long days.*

"Okay. Keep those eyes closed. Feel the people around us, hear them breathing, talking, looking right at us. Don't open your eyes, just absorb it all. You have to. This isn't going to be easy. This is good practice.

"Everything in the world is either the best or the worst that is has ever been in history. Why? Because it is our time. We are special.

"Special ed," Hector mumbled.

"Open your fuckin' eyes," said Lara.

"Okay," said Lara, returning to her napkin notes, finding her pen again.

"We have some housekeeping business to attend to.

"Recently Kaitylyn and I have had a discussion regarding what CRUSHER will be about. I say fuck it, kill them all. Kaitylyn wants to be all non-violent now."

"Woah," said Evey.

"Yeah," said Lara, "I know, right?"

"And we need to plan Mayfield," said Kaitylyn.

"We need to get that going, I mean A-S-A-P."

"Leave It To Beaver?" said A.J.

Black and blue cars that nobody would really buy pulled up outside, like two in a row, then two more and then one more.

Men in sunglasses, some no sunglasses, some in dark suits and ties, some just in F.B.I. windbreakers got out of the cars and sort of stood around when you would think they would be charging in somewhere, but maybe they were there for food, you really could not tell at that point for certain.

The waitress with the CRUSHER T-shirt appeared at their table.

She nodded to Lara to look the fuck out the window.

Lara noticed Mike Braxton and thought a hundred thoughts at once. Was everyone in on the shiny things release? Prolly not. Didn't Evey and Reuben and Hector have a dozen or more warrants out for them? She looked at A.J. and for some reason thought he had "deserter" now written on his forehead in sweat.

The waitress subtly, very cooly, expertly perhaps, nodded to Lara to follow her.

And they did, remembering their training without really remembering it, which is how it should be: *Slowissmoothandsmoothisfast.* All one word, like that. Really.

As the waitress and the remaining CRUSHER rebels walked discreetly into the next room and the back room and toward the back door, about six or seven F.B.I. agents entered the restaurant, looking around.

Special Agent Mike Braxton sucked on a toothpick, looked around, kind of pissed, kind of not. Braxton, though not a big man, was a local high school star and small college somebody, possessing the air of slight vanity that goes with good looks, a trained body and a high IQ. He was pretty used to being the center of attention when entering a restaurant during high traffic breakfast time.

He walked all around, found the back door, said "smells good in here," to the waitress with the CRUSHER T-shirt stuffing a napkin holder on a back table, then walked back to the front. He checked his watch against the clock on the wall, thought about telling everyone breakfast was going to be right here, but then remembered the fucking meeting he had with Marv and said, "fuck it," and walked out.

Note from the narrator ...

From "Not Exactly A Radio Show," a live podcast that traveled the circuit of Twins Cities bars for about six months, produced by former members of The Prince Hope Show:

America Will Soon End and Nature Will Live, Have The Last Word.
Nature Bats Last, as the saying goes.
Some Famous Last Words.

Christine Todd Whitman, head of the Environmental Protection Agency, speaking about downtown Manhattan in the days after 9/11: The air is safe to breathe.

Colin Powell at the U.N.: My colleagues, every statement I make today is backed up by sources, solid sources. These are not assertions. What we're giving you are facts and conclusions based on solid intelligence.

George W. Bush: The same folks that are bombing innocent people in Iraq were the ones who attacked us in America on September the 11th.

U.S. Secretary of State, Madeline Albright, speaking about the millions of deaths caused in Iraq by the sanctions during the Clinton administration: We think it's worth it.

America Will Soon End and Nature Will Live, Have The Last Word.
Nature Bats Last, as the saying goes.
Some Famous Last Words.

Motherland, cradle me, close my eyes, lullaby me to sleep, keep me safe, lie with me, stay beside me don't go. — Natalie Merchant

The Kennedy assassination has demonstrated that most of the major events of world significance are masterfully planned and orchestrated by an elite coterie of enormously powerful people who are not of one nation, one ethnic grouping, or one overridingly important business group. They are a power unto themselves for whom those others work. Neither is this power elite of recent origin. Its roots go deep into the past. — L. Fletcher Prouty

In what I believe was an accidental slip of the tongue, McVeigh revealed the identity of a high-ranking F.B.I. official who was apparently directing McVeigh in the bomb plot. The name McVeigh let slip was Larry Potts, lead F.B.I. agent at Ruby Ridge. — Terry Nichols

FOURTEEN

M arv strolled into Murray's looking for Carroll, his boss. Carroll waved, Marv went over, a booth in the interior of the restaurant.

They didn't talk much, just how's the family. They had already had their talk about the school bus and shooting into the river on The Stone Arch Bridge.

Marv and Carroll were both tall, seemingly fit, at least not fat. Marv was going bald. Carroll was greying and if his looks and confidence and people skills got any greater he would soon be sitting on a white horse on Saturday morning at his home in Georgetown with his neighbors looking out from behind the curtains. When he spoke to someone he looked them right in the eye and smiled intently, shook their hand with both of his and smiled until he broke the smile meter. His voice would have made him a rich man in radio. He grabbed your hand to shake with his undergrip, bored deep into your soul with his intent gaze as if you were the only person in the world, and then he moved on.

They fiddled with the menus, studying the drink list even though.

"Mike!"

Carroll spotted Braxton and half stood to wave him over.

Braxton and another agent took the opposite side of the booth.

They ordered waters, coffee, V-8 juice for Braxton. Marv offered he had never been there. Braxton had been coming here since he was a child. Carroll said it had been recommended to him. The other agent said he was "ready for some decent chow" after eating alone for so long since he was new to the area.

They talked about the weather, the local pro sports, and then Braxton asked Carroll "what the fuck you guys doin' here, you mind tellin' me?"

The waiter appeared, and another with water, another with the other drinks. They ordered.

"Official business," said Carroll.

"Such as," said Braxton.

"Government."

"*Fuck* you."

Carroll asked Braxton what he knew about CRUSHER.

"Enough," said Braxton.

"They're pretty much over anyway."

"How so?" said Carroll.

"How … so … what?" said Braxton, "you wouldn't mind fillin' us in on the school bus side show now would ya?"

He jerked the tab on his juice and filled a small glass.

Note from the narrator ...

From "Not Exactly A Radio Show," a live podcast that traveled the circuit of Twins Cities bars for about six months, produced by former members of The Prince Hope Show:

America Will Soon End and Nature Will Live, Have The Last Word.
Nature Bats Last, as the saying goes.
Some Famous Last Words.

George W. Bush:

"My fellow citizens, at this hour American and coalition forces are in the early stages of military operations to disarm Iraq, to free its people and to defend the world from grave danger.

... every effort will be made to spare the lives of innocent civilians,

... the campaign will be 'broad and concerted' and will use 'decisive force.'

...no outcome but victory will be accepted, ...America's freedom will be defended, and freedom will be brought to others."

America Will Soon End and Nature Will Live, Have The Last Word.
Nature Bats Last, as the saying goes.
Some Famous Last Words.

From the internet, comments section:

…Recent reports on the Donald Trump, C.I.A., Russia, Home Depot Shower front … show that U.S. Intelligence has jumped the shark. Desperate times for desperate folks.
The Russians did not hack the U.S. election, but just think about it. If they had … we are complaining?
Read William Blum and find out how for decades and decades the U.S.A. C.I.A. has done nothing but meddle in other countries' elections, and doing much more than hacking, hacking off heads perhaps. It's something like complaining that Iran or other countries develop nuclear weapons. Really? Seriously?

… And, in honor of Martin Luther King Jr. we are planning a national holiday for Monday, which is weird because this country, at least its government, which organized the national holiday, also murdered Martin Luther King Jr. You can find out pretty much everything about it in William Pepper's most recent book,
"The Plot To Kill King."

… And also, it is reported that in Iowa, the license plates that now say "VETERAN," to distinguish the driver as a veteran of America's military — because of the wars fought for U.S. imperialism over the decades and the willingness of Americans to go along with that atrocity — beginning in the coming year
… those license plates will now say "IDIOT."

FIFTEEN

They crowded into A.J.'s car.

"T-shirts," said Lara as she snapped-in.

"We usually have CRUSHER on the back and then something on the front, for different stuff," she explained to A.J.

"What should we have for The Battle of Mayfield?"

Now she asked everybody.

"The Beagles," said Kaitylyn.

"Yeah," said Lara, "that's not really a thing."

"It's the Beatles and Eagles combined," said Evey.

"I've heard about it. It's a meme. There is and there isn't."

"Yeah, I like it," said Lara.

"Okay, The Beagles. CRUSHER. The Battle of Mayfield. Beaver Cleaver. The New American Revolution. Makes perfect sense after you take a half hour to explain it. Perfect."

"So yeah, where do Narnia and The Big Lebowski fit in?" asked A.J. as he looked into the rearview mirror to make a right-hand turn and he wasn't really from the city and the others, or most of the others, all reached a little ways for the steering wheel.

"Ho-la!" said Evey, in making her move for the wheel.

Lara sat right behind A.J. and reached to feel his shoulders, his back.

"Where's the wire, A.J. American Joe?"

"Huh?" said A.J.

"Oh, c'mon, Lara," said Hector while Reuben fucking punched A.J. in the shoulder.

"Where exactly are we going?" Lara said.

"Because if we don't know, I got a few ideas."

Note from the narrator ...

> From "Not Exactly A Radio Show," a live podcast that traveled the circuit of Twins Cities bars for about six months, produced by former members of The Prince Hope Show:

This message brought to you by The Foundation For A New American Dream:

Did we go to the moon?
Maybe.
Maybe not.
But just like Voldemort and so many discussions that are prohibited in America, it is one that cannot be named.
Was 911 an inside job?
"Stop!"
See? Like that.
You can't talk about that.
Was Paul Wellstone assassinated?
A roll of the eyes.
You are sent to Siberia by your brother, your mother and your cousin, disaparated from the Thanksgiving dinner table.
Poof!
No one can now see you or talk to you.
You are a non-person. Might as well go smoke in the garage.
Did FDR provoke Pearl Harbor in order to get into WWII?
Did the government burn men women and children alive at Waco?
Was the government involved in the Oklahoma City bombing?
What are chemtrails?
What does the government know about UFOs?
Do those questions have merit or are they preposterous?
We will never know because Brian Williams and NBC and Amy Goodman and NPR are afraid of even the question.
Why? Why? ... Why?
Did Bush steal the elections of 2000 and 2004?
Ask these questions on any mainstream or so-called liberal website or TV show or newspaper or radio show and you will get laughed down.
Ask it on the so-called liberal, progressive Stephen Colbert and Jon Stewart.
They will try to humiliate you.
Why?
Is it because you are truly so hilariously pathetic?
Or is it because they are so, so afraid?

The more stupid one is, the closer one is to reality. The more stupid one is, the clearer one is. Stupidity is brief and artless, while intelligence squirms and hides itself. Intelligence is unprincipled, but stupidity is honest and straightforward.

— Fyodor Dostoyevsky, *The Brothers Karamazov*

SIXTEEN

Brooke by now had been in three or four different cities, working in various positions of local government, always followed by The Special Team, filming, recording.

She had gone rogue as it were, not being able to get in touch with any of her friends with CRUSHER since or before The Battle of Bumfuck.

She had been acting out her role, her assignment as a spy. Everywhere she went she kept notes about the government activity she witnessed, bills paid, ordinances passed. [She was calling it just in her own head *The Pothole Diaries*.]

Brooke sat in the city park having her sack lunch.

She got a text from Lara.

If we pull the camera back from our close-up we can see a winding sidewalk path through newly planted small trees and four red Suburbans parked in the small parking lot nearby, straight-in, facing the same way, with the tiny type on the front doors: PH Prods.

This from Scott Creighton:

The C.I.A. are the real terrorists. You don't know that? … You will.
During an interview Sen. Chuck Schumer let a little truth slip out
inadvertently when he told her President Elect Trump needs to be
careful when he criticizes the C.I.A. because they have ways to make
folks pay for doing that.

In a recent interview with Rachel Maddow, Schumer said that Donald
Trump is being "really dumb" to take an antagonistic approach to the
US intelligence community, because
"if you take on the intelligence community, they have six ways from
Sunday to get back at you."

He actually said that.

That's right. The leading senator from the Democratic Party just told
the world that the C.I.A. will punish a seated president if he dares
contradict the narrative they are trying to push about Russia.

Let's forget for a second the last time a seated president dared to
question the glorious C.I.A. …he actually fired its director for lying to
him and trying to start a world war … with Russia. He got shot by the
way and his successor appointed that same fired C.I.A. director to help
investigate the shooting of the president who fired him. Subsequently,
the Magic Bullet was found guilty by that commission.

SEVENTEEN

Korey swam, underwater, kicking, kicking, out of breath, out behind the next cement bridge support, where he found a bit of a ledge to pull himself out of the water. *Geezuz fuck! he hissed. Damn! What the hell! Are you fucking kidding me!*

Korey walked with a purpose down the sidewalk in downtown Minneapolis.

With his head down, his clothes and hair wet, still not breathing right, sucking down water, his focus intense and specific he watched the sidewalk scroll under his feet and he muttered as he walked — "Don't fucking shoot at me! Godamnit, I can't stand that" — not seeing anyone around him. It was just he and the buildings and the sidewalk, a northwoods dystopian sci-fi movie.

He stopped to lean over and cough, thinking he had water in his lungs.

"Don't fucking shoot at me! Godamnit, I can't stand that!"

He raised up, hands on hips, disgusted with everything and everybody around him, like a losing football coach on the sidelines who thinks he has greatness inside of him.

My notes, I didn't have time, or didn't take time to put them into sentences. Anyway.

Comes to Murray's. Recognizes Marv's voice. Comes to a stop. Nervous. Almost pukes. Ducks into a convenience store with a post office kiosk, sees …

On the wall of the post office kiosk corner of the tiny city convenience store, Korey spotted, in a frame, a black frame, the current, dated on the bottom that very day, The F.B.I. Ten Most Wanted List.

And there … Oh my God.

He about shit. He really had to steady himself by clutching the fucking kiosk.

He saw photos of Lara, Kaitylyn, Reuben, Evey, Hector, and himself.

Lara Frances McDonald
Kaitylyn Anne Bridge
Reuben Carlos Martinez
Hector Carlos Martinez
Evangelina Isabella Martinez
Kory Robert Miller

Korey asked the guy behind the counter for a marker to borrow. He gave him a pen. Korey walked all the way to the wall before he realized. He marched back.

"I need a marker, man."

"You gotta give it back."

"Yeah, man, I know."

Korey marked on the glass with a caret to change his name to KOREY, then gave the marker back, then came back to the kiosk.

Lara is first? He thought to himself? Kaitylyn second? Those fuckers.

Korey vowed right there, silently, to get back at the C.I.A. He stuck his head out the glass door and saw Marv and the other guy still out there smoking. He thought about charging, tackling, ramming Marv to the sidewalk. He coughed, probably river water. Marv looked and Korey jammed back inside the door, just nicking his head and it hurt a little.

He saw squirt guns and rifles for sale, many different colors. See how they like it.

"Hey, man, how much are those?"

"I don't know, look yourself."

"Can I have one?" asked Korey.

"Have one? It don't work that way, man, you know that, c'mon, man, what is this?"

"Yeah, I know, man.

"Hey, man," said Korey.

"This post office ain't workin. I can't get … stamps, or nothin' outa here. It must be fuckin' broke or something. You gotta help me. I gotta get to work. See?"

He pointed up at a tall building.

"That's my office, right there."

The guy looked as he walked slowly toward Korey and the kiosk.

"What?" he said.

He looked at Korey and his clothes as he passed him.

"I can't really fix …"

The guy just saw Korey's back as the other door closed.

Korey hid the yellow plastic water pistol on his right side as he ducked his head and walked right toward Marv and the other guy out smoking in front of Murray's.

The convenience store guy stepped out of the store. He couldn't really leave, so he hollered.

"That guy just stole a squirt gun!"

"Him!"

He pointed.

Korey was right there, right next to Marv.

He heard them talking in official tones.

"My game's not been that ... I don't get time to practice."

"Yeah."

"That guy!" yelled the convenience store guy again.

Marv and the F.B.I. agent looked back at the convenience store guy just as Korey crossed the street, through heavy traffic, ducking low.

Marv and the other guy looked around, fired their cigarettes at the sidewalk and headed back inside. Korey ducked low behind the cars parked on the opposite curb, fighting with the plastic to get at the yellow gun.

"Shit!"

He should have taken the fuckin' AR. Goddamnit! Shit!

Sometimes you climb out of bed in the morning and you think, I'm not going to make it, but you laugh inside — remembering all the times you've felt that way.

We're all going to die, all of us, what a circus! That alone should make us love each other but it doesn't. We are terrorized and flattened by trivialities, we are eaten up by nothing.

— Charles Bukowski

EIGHTEEN

Bill sat in the locked ward on the top floor of the state hospital in Iowa, just outside the eponymous location of the so-called Battle of Bumfuck.

He looked out the window of his room, east, perhaps, facing the corn, which he would have been facing in any direction.

Bill was taking a break from the computer.

He was allowed access to Gmail, only to write to friends and relatives, nothing to news organs, as it said in his personal commitment plan.

On his screen was displayed his most recent letter to the editor, the one that had gotten him in trouble, apparently.

"... we spend the money on this monument rather than on our schools so that we might further tell lies to our children? Bush, no WMD, attacked Iraq and Afghanistan based on lies, and the lies continue, daily. The Bush government itself did it. The troops went to Iraq for no reason whatsoever except to steal oil and conquer. It was not to protect freedom. It was not heroic. We put up monuments to fools and murderers. ... Just make sure to leave room for the next one."

He wondered about that one thing that one day, all the police, all the guns, those people with their hands raised, apparently being arrested. He didn't get the paper, not allowed, or the radio, or TV. It kind of sucked.

93

When the guard, or rather, officially, the "attendant," came with his next meal, Bill asked about his getting out.

"How's that all coming along?" he said.

Note from the narrator ...

From "Not Exactly A Radio Show," a live podcast that traveled the circuit of Twins Cities bars for about six months, produced by former members of The Prince Hope Show:

And now for another episode of
"On Babushka Kalashnikov's Korner"
"The View From My Piroshki Kart."

Grandma Kalashnikov writes on her website her most recent column:
"Get used to it and live your life"

... And on the other side of the globe, we now get the view from Uncle Bill's Front Porch:
Sponsored tonight by All American Apple Pie, in the big red can.

I do think it's worth noting the social and political function of these attacks. They certainly fit the profile of the strategy of tension, contemporary Gladio exercise that's meant to terrorize people and make them that much more likely to submit to authority. This type of terror has a corrosive affect on Democracy, to put it mildly. So the fact that all these things have happened, since 9/11 is something I think we're obliged to think critically about.

— Mark Crispin Miller

NINETEEN

Marv and the other F.B.I. agent sat back into the booth, pushing Braxton and Carroll to the inside wall.

By now it was heated. Marv saw some notes on napkins in the middle of the table. He reached for one, almost had it, then without looking Carroll snatched it back, continued to lock stares with Braxton, the veins in his temples bulging, his jaws doing pushups and pull ups.

"Loving is what we need," said Braxton and Marv thought what the fuck is this, reaching for the stainless steel coffee pot the waiter had left.

"No, really. Hear me. We got to have passion, you can't know everything," continued Braxton, who looked like someone to Marv.

"And it's that constant, incessant search, that will never end, that makes us loners, cynics, always finding the fault in someone else. You got to enjoy what you're doing, or what good is life anyway?"

Michael Scott, from *The Office*, that's it, smiled Marv.

Carroll smiled big and tilted his perfect grey head as he was wont to do. He leaned over the table. His hands were also perfect, Marv noted, sipping his coffee with both hands, can't spill in this fucking place. Carroll had brown spots on his face, maybe from a lifetime of trips to France, Italy, tennis and golf and boating in the sun, but somehow with him they were merely accents.

"So true," said Carroll.

Marv looked down into his coffee. Whenever Carroll started with "so true," he came back hard right at you with everything, both barrels, blazing.

"But don't you think loving comes from knowing, stems from understanding. If you don't understand, then from where does your passion spring? Really, please think about it."

"I am," said Braxton, locked-in.

"When you understand the world," Carroll continued, "then you just have to listen to your own heart, follow where it leads. If you understand football, it will lead you to the sofa. If you understand Dostoyevsky, somewhere else, wouldn't you agree."

"Everything, everybody is so fucking serious, that's all I'm saying," said Braxton.

"You need a drink," said Carroll.

He raised his hand for a waiter.

"It's not even noon," said Braxton.

"And what about The Enlightenment?" said the other F.B.I. agent. "What was that?"

"Yeah," said Marv.

"Sorry," the other F.B.I. agent said to Braxton, who just shrugged his shoulders like, no problem, man.

Marv saw his opening.

"It's four-thirty somewhere," he said.

"I know, right?" said the other F.B.I. agent.

"Exactly." Carroll pointed a perfect finger and smiled so big, his teeth so big, so white, like the keys on Beethoven's piano.

Note from the narrator ...

From "Not Exactly A Radio Show," a live podcast that traveled the circuit of Twins Cities bars for about six months, produced by former members of The Prince Hope Show:

We have heard from Randall from Stevens Point:

"I got my gun, my dog, my truck," Randall says.

I'm heading for the woods, then up the mountain. Tell Bubba Jean I always loved her.

Don't follow me. I got on my camo socks. You'd never find me.

When you hear about the big shoot-out and all that, then that'll probly be me.

To my relatives in Baraboo I just got one thing to say:

"I'm really not talking to any a you, 'cause you know why."

Every minute of every day, through the national security mechanisms outlined in this book, the oligarchs that own America and through it seek to own the world symbolically transform themselves from murderous beasts into a force for good that protects us from them. They call it "America," but what does that word represent: a shining city on a hill above a fruited plain, or a segregated oligarchy with a murderous dark side?

The answer is obvious. You are the victim of a massive criminal enterprise, and the key to its success is its ability to keep its crimes and corruption secret.

— Douglas Valentine

TWENTY

The CRUSHER Rebellion crunched shoulder to shoulder inside America Joe's camo Tercel, smoke streaming out the loud muffler, pretty much keeping up with traffic on I-94.

"I could tell you, but then I would have to kill you."

Kaitylyn turned around to address Lara's question.

Lara smiled but Kaitylyn was not.

"I was just asking," said Lara.

I am every guy I've ever tried not to be,
I want everything as good as it gets.

— Todd Snider

TWENTY-ONE

That knowing vs. loving thing is interesting.

What do we really want? We want that feeling on Saturday morning after working hard and fitting in and being a part of the culture all week. We are safe, somewhat liked, we have a place. And, we get Saturday morning. That's what it's about, right? We may have also done our part somewhere in that week to expose the killing of children in the poor parts of the world, even by our own military, our own tax money, we've done something about it, wrote a letter, made a note to write a letter, and this is our time. *Aaah.*

Like the first moment of climbing into a hot tub or a hot sauna. Aaah. That first sip of that first beer. Aaah. Sex. Aaah. And, as Hofer miraculously noted in a televised interview, being on the job, but still thinking about your novel in your head while on that job and having something click in your head about your novel while actually having a conversation with a colleague, the feeling of that. Aaah. How he must have known that, he must have been in the same exact situation, and that is a miracle. And that is Aaah.

So there, the meaning of life is Aaah. And we incessantly seek our Aaah. And if we do not have Aaah, we want it, and are not happy until we find it, even though we feel kind of bad for people dying and being bombed, but if we get some Aaah the two can co-exist in the world,

103

bombed children and our Aaah, and if we are doing at least something for the bombed children, sending our prayers, writing a letter to the editor in a publication that our colleagues at work do not read so we can get Aaah *and* Aaah, all is good. It's all good. It's all Aaah.

"The need to constantly consume news," that was another thing that Braxton was talking about in his dinner with Carroll at Murray's. The thing that many of us do, it's our base, okay, go here, go there, not there. We're good, we know what's going on, we are up to date, and we understand, the world, our view is set, content, we feel good about our place in it.

Yes, but, as Carroll countered, isn't that required. If you had a cave man's view of today's world, if everyone did, what could be accomplished?

I know, but, said Special Agent Mike Braxton, who, we know has at least Molly's blood on his hands don't we, or was it the sheriff who shot Molly? Both rifles seemed to be smoking as they broke them down.

Anyway, yeah, so, oh, it's hard to concentrate on this … oh, he said, but it's almost like we have to remember to enjoy things, it's not on our list … enjoy sunset, sunrise … all that shit.

Anyway … oh, here it is. I'm on a bus and I've got my computer on my lap and of course there is Wi-Fi on the bus toasting my brain, but in the meantime, I think that Braxton and Carroll must stay up nights to make sure they know everything going on in the world no matter what Braxton says about too much reading going on, because I also read this by Vltchek:

These hundreds of millions of broken and idle people (some of them actually not stupid at all) *are tremendous loss to the world. Instead of erecting barricades, writing outraged novels or openly ridiculing this entire Western charade, they are mostly suffering in silence, some succumbing to substance abuse or contemplating suicide.*

If the opportunity to thoroughly change their lives really arrives, they cannot identify it, anymore; cannot grasp it. It is because they cannot fight; they were 'pacified' since early age, since the school.

That is exactly where the regime wants to have its citizens. It's where it got them!

That's it.

That's the article, a part of it. I have no idea what to do with it.

Here's my stop.

Braxton asked if the millions of Americans who "know" that what the government says is true, if their cognitive abilities are affected by "knowing" that.

Carroll looked at his watch. Marv sucked out the last of his coffee and I don't even know what else happened, that's all I heard.

This is my new bar. I like it here, nice people. I drink and I write my novel and they have Wi-Fi, so I can check all my sites.

Later.

Smell the roses, coffee, the cigarettes, feel the nachos, hear the hops.

Aaah.

… the movie *Pearl Harbor* came out, big-budget flop, didn't make any money, but it sure did put the Pearl Harbor meme into people's minds and then on 9/11 itself, endless reiterations, Pearl Harbor, Pearl Harbor. Predictive programming is something you find with all of these events.

— Dr. Kevin Barrett

TWENTY-TWO

She walked toward them, stood outside, stretching, this way, that, like a runner. She didn't run. A tall man, Ethan, the producer, stepped out of one of the four red Suburbans. He wore dress clothes, white shirt, black pants, the red tennis shoes, the uniform as Brooke called it, but his shirt was out on one side and stained with quick breakfast and one shoelace not tied. He was tall, so it didn't matter. On a short man it would have been defiling.

"How's that for today?" said Brooke.

"Yeah," he said, stretching as well, from the waist, reaching to the ground, as he was a runner, and he'd like to get out yet today.

"You guys had lunch?

"How about a drink?" she said.

Now all the doors on all the four red Suburbans pushed open and they all crawled out, squinting, blocking the sun with their hands, the Reality Show Crew Apocalypse.

... All this is never pronounced not even in fiction books anymore, unless you read in Russian or Spanish. The success of the Empire to produce obedient, scared and unimaginative beings is now complete!

Big corporations are thriving; elites are collecting enormous booty, while great majority of people in the West is gradually losing its ability to dream and to feel. Without those preconditions, no rebellion is possible. Lack of imagination, accompanied by emotional numbness, is the most effective formula for stagnation, even regression. That is why the West is finished. Grotesque obsession with science, with medical practices, and with 'facts', is helping to divert attention from the real and horrific issue. Constant debates, analyses, and 'looking at things from different angles', leads to nothing else but passivity. But taking action is too scary, and people are not used to making dramatic decisions, anymore, or even gestures.

This also leads to the fact that almost no one in the West is now ready to gather under any ideological banner, or to embrace full heartedly what is called derogatorily 'labels'. For millennia, people flocked intuitively into various movements, political parties and groups. No significant change was ever achieved by one single individual (although a strong leader at the head of a movement, party of even government could definitely achieve a lot).

To be part of something important and revolutionary was symbolizing often a true meaning of life. People were (and in many parts of the world still are) fully committed, dedicated to the important and heroic struggles.

Trying to build better world, fighting for better world, even dying for it: that was often considered the most glorious what a human being could achieve in his or her lifetime.

— Andre Vltchek

TWENTY-THREE

Korey hunched behind the cars across the street from the convenience store. He needed the AR-15 squirt gun if he was going to be able to do what needed doing.

He looked for a little opening in the traffic and still crouched low, he skittered across in front of a bus that did not slow even a little. The door jingled as he went inside, still hunched down low. He grabbed a yellow mop head for sale, ripped open the plastic and stuck it on his head.

He stood and nodded to the counter guy who was behind the counter on the phone in an animated discussion, telling someone about how he had just been robbed.

Korey set the yellow squirt gun pistol on the counter and swiped the yellow and red AR-15 rifle Super Soaker and headed for the door.

"Hey!" yelled the counter guy, racing for the door.

Korey hit the sidewalk and ran.

Like hell he ran.

One of those real issues is that the C.I.A. has consistently lied to the American people for many, many years. Why would Trump conclude that Brennan was spouting fake news? Well, in the past 15 years, the C.I.A. said that it was not torturing its prisoners.

That was a lie. The C.I.A. said that it had not created an archipelago of secret prisons where it was holding hundreds of people, including innocent civilians.

That was a lie. The C.I.A. said that it had not created and used a dungeon torture center called the "Salt Pit" in Afghanistan. That was a lie. The C.I.A. said that it was not sending prisoners to third world countries to undergo torture with a wink and a nod from the C.I.A.'s leadership. That was a lie.

The C.I.A. said that it had not hacked into computers belonging to investigators of the Senate Select Committee on Intelligence while they were writing the definitive report on the C.I.A. torture program. That was a lie.

— John Kiriakou, *former C.I.A. counterintelligence officer*

TWENTY-FOUR

Billy Blackbird sat in the window of the mental hospital in the Iowa corn land, looking out on his country.

Nobody knew where he was.

One day they came for him and here he was. They didn't really ask if he wanted to call anyone or tell anyone where he was going. Cars pulled up in the yard and he just kind of knew what this was. He gathered what he wanted, his computer, a jacket, and went out to meet them.

So now when he wrote to his friends and relatives he talked like he always did. They didn't need to know. It would worry them, for one thing, and this way he could try to pretend things were the same, he was the same ol' Billy, and then one day they would let him go and well, maybe he wouldn't say a thing, nobody would believe him anyway.

They took you where? For writing a letter to the editor? Yeah, right, Billy, tell us another one, why don't ya.

Ten gallons of gas and a bottle of propane
Electric igniter off my grill and I still can't
Say for certain if this thing'll blow,
But if it does I'm gonna be the first one to know.
I'm thinkin' 'bout burnin' it down, boys
Nothin's ever gonna be the same in this town
I'm thinkin' 'bout burnin' the Walmart down.

— Steve Earle

TWENTY-FIVE

FADE IN:

Two agents standing on sidewalk outside steakhouse in downtown Minneapolis, Minnesota.

AGENT 001:

Did you find the passport?

AGENT 002:

Of course. It tells us exactly who did the terrorist action.

AGENT 001:

And the manifesto, which tells why they did it, where they are from?

AGENT 002:

Exactly

AGENT 001:

Our country can now begin bombing, in order to stop them from doing such a despicable act against our great country, ever again.

AGENT 002:

(Lighting cigarette, offers cigarette to AGENT 001, who declines amicably)

God Bless the USA. Did you see the game?

AGENT 001:

You got that right.

No. The missus had a long honeydo list. Who won?

AGENT 002

(He pauses, looks around, then back to the other AGENT.)

Have you ever read Zorba The Greek, 001?

AGENT 001

I do not think so, boss. Is it on DVD?

AGENT 002

Yeah, I think so.

I'm home again now, for a while, just catching up a little on my show.

Okay, maybe time for a nut graf, which should follow the delayed lede, right?

Definition: *A paragraph in which the main points of a story are summarized. Nut graphs are often used in conjunction with delayed ledes on feature stories. A feature story may begin with a delayed lede, often featuring description or an anecdote, that can last several paragraphs. That is then followed by a nut graph that outlines the main points of the story.*

The thing is, and I s'pose some of you might have already figured, I don't really know what's going on either.

Who does these days? But it's all very important, I think we can agree, the essence of our world, whether we live or we die. Oh, yeah, we're gonna all die anyway, just, well, when we die, that has not yet been determined. I know, right?

Here's what I do know.

CRUSHER is wanting to launch a new offensive against Mayfield, the land of Beaver Cleaver, which, as they see it, is unreality, i.e. lies.

There's more, but it's like Joe Pesce in *JFK*, right? Hard to understand.

You ever had recurring dreams? Yeah, not those, the ones you have your whole life, but ones who come like days in a row or a few days out of a week. I know, that's kind of different.

… Gee, Wally. I don't understand.

That's because you're a kid, Beaver.

Note from the narrator ...

From "Not Exactly A Radio Show," a live podcast that traveled the circuit of Twins Cities bars for about six months, produced by former members of The Prince Hope Show:

And now for another episode of ...
"Sitting On The Floor At Ward Cleaver's Feet, Listening To Ward Cleaver."

Ward Cleaver speaks ...

Remember the peace dividend?
They didn't want peace.

Remember the first fake World Trade Center bombing?
That was our baptism ... to fear Muslims.

The Patriot Act.
Anthrax.
Wellstone.

The Dept. of Homeland Security.
Modeled on the East German Stasi.
A lot of thought has gone into all of this.

Manifest Destiny, the American Century, American exceptionalism, globalization, or, as Madeleine Albright put it, "the indispensable nation" ... while others less kind have used the term "imperialist."

My, oh, my, Beaver.

The print and TV media, which serve as propagandists for the ruling military/security complex and Wall Street elites, make certain that Americans have nothing but bogus orchestrated information. Every household and person who turns on TV or reads a newspaper is programed to live in a false orchestrated reality that serves the tiny few who comprise the ruling Establishment.

— Paul Craig Roberts

Pancho was a bandit boy. His horse was fast as polished steel. He wore his gun outside his pants, for all the honest world to feel.

— Townes Van Zandt

TWENTY-SIX

"**Y**ou guys had lunch?

"How about a drink?" she said.

Now all the doors on all the four red Suburbans pushed open and they all crawled out, shielding the sun with their hands, walking unsure of the earth, strangers in a strange land.

They decided to go to a bar to watch the big premier of their new Reality Show that Brooke had named "Oh My God." Her idea was that whenever someone heard the name of the new reality show they would say, oh my God, and it would travel like that person to person to practically everywhere.

They got there, found all the booths taken and sat at the bar.

Ethan got a text.

From Prince Hope.

"It's off," said Ethan to the others.

Ethan said that the pilot of "Oh My God," the reality show about Brooke the CRUSHER spy, was being pushed back.

"Something about a CRUSHER rebel blowing up a school bus in Minneapolis," said Ethan.

Brooke and the crew — named The Special Unit by Prince Hope or The Red Unit because he told them to wear red tennis shoes just because and he rented the red Suburbans, all the camera equipment, paid their salaries — they finished that first drink then turned around to look behind. They wanted a spot to camp out. They wanted to stay longer. They spotted a red cushion booth way in the back.

"Perfect," said Brooke, leading the way.

"He thought the time was right," said Ethan, "and he likes what you and your group is doing."

"And Lara," said Brooke.

"And Lara," said Ethan.

"There's a bit of an age difference," said Brooke.

"He's been eating more cabbage," said Ethan, "that's what I've heard."

"That should do it," said Brooke.

So, what are we gonna do now, that's what Brooke wanted to know, so she said, "what are we gonna do now?"

Some of the crew wanted to quit, go back to their regular jobs if they were still there.

"We could just keep filming," said Brooke, "things might work out."

"I'm pretty sure it would be volunteer from this point," said Ethan.

Brooke looked around at the faces around the booth, most of them avoiding her eyes in the low light.

"Okay," said one, "okay, I guess," said another.

"You guys are awesome!" said Brooke, standing in the booth to high-five all around.

"We're goin' to Mayfield!" she said, not knowing if she had the authority, but was going to try.

"Mayfield?" said Ethan.

"Beaver," said Brooke, "you know, Beaver Cleaver, Wally, Eddy Haskell."

"Is that still a thing?" somebody said.

"It's a thing. It is definitely a thing!" said Brooke.

She spotted reflection of low lights off teeth and oily skin around the booth as some of the crew were smiling and nodding in recognition.

Note from the narrator ...

From "Not Exactly A Radio Show," a live podcast that traveled the circuit of Twins Cities bars for about six months, produced by former members of The Prince Hope Show:

This program has in part been brought to you by the Iowa Ministry of Fear.

If you're not afraid, you're not trying.

Look.

Out your window.

Gold-finches.

Used by terrorists. Bird feeders are common drop-off areas.

... For terrorist stuff.

Have you seen slow drivers in your neighborhood, disguised as old ladies in white, blue or grey hair ... slouched down so low it looks like nobody is driving?

Terrorists.

Call Wal-Mart. ... Before it's too late.

... Be Afraid. Be Very Afraid.

We're your Iowa Ministry of Fear.

We already know enough of what the C.I.A. does to resolve to oppose it. The C.I.A. is one of the great forces promoting political repression in countries with minority regimes that serve a privileged and powerful elite.

… the key question is to pass beyond the facts of C.I.A.'s operations to the reasons they were established — which inexorably will lead to economic questions: preservation of property relations and other institutions on which rest the interests of our own wealthy and privileged minority. This, not the C.I.A., is the critical issue.

— Philip Agee

TWENTY-SEVEN

The fuck? thought Lara, rolling down a window to smoke. She rolled her own, Bugler, in her lap, shaking her head about Kaitylyn biting her head off.

Lara said they needed funding to get CRUSHER going again.

"What?"

The wind thundered through the car, and the muffler was loud.

"With what?" said Hector.

"What?" said Lara, rolling up her window.

"Where you getting' the money?" said Hector.

"Hope?" said Reuben.

"Possibly," said Lara.

She sat with Reuben and Evey in the back seat, their toes touching the gold box on the floor of the back seat, under the afghan.

"We should find Korey," said Evey.

Lara raised her napkin list to say, we're gonna.

"Where did you work before the group home?"

Lara directed her question to Kaitylyn riding shotgun. She had never really talked about that with Kaitylyn. They had just met at the group home and after that it was a fire spreading. You know that you can hear a fire? Yes, the crackles, but if you get close there is also a heartbeat to a fire, like a train way down the tracks, headed this way. Stunning.

Anyway, Lara's question.

You know how I know these things to tell this story. Just a brief interruption. There are CCTVs every fucking where, probly even in cars and on computers, you know that right? That's one thing. And microphones, people listening. It's really like that. Do you tape off that little hole above your computer screen. You might think about it. Anywho.

Kaitylyn turned and stared into Lara's eyes.

Lara thought, God she missed Actually. He would be able to do some real research for her, and Skylar, Rick, all them. They used to have such an organization, such great people. And now they were gone.

She tried to keep contact with Kaitylyn, but her stare was intense, and the blinking with those long eyelashes and the dark eyebrows, mesmerizing.

She just kept blinking, blinking, shit.

Morse Code, ohmygod, thought Lara and she smiled.

What the hell?

"You two gonna fight or fuck," said Reuben.

"We've got the gold, right here," said Evey, lifting the afghan off the old chest of gold.

Reuben and Hector swore in Spanish.

"There's an idea," said Lara as Kaitylyn turned back around.

Note from the narrator ...

From "Not Exactly A Radio Show," a live podcast that traveled the circuit of Twins Cities bars for about six months, produced by former members of The Prince Hope Show:

And now a word from the American Language Council, doing our best to combat inexactitude and shallowness.

On toughness, being tough. C'mon people. You need to get tough.

It's time for the NFL, training camps have opened up and it's getting exciting. The Vikings have a good team and a new stadium and the sports talk stations are in Mankato for training camp. And it's fun. It's a diversion. We'd all like to be tough like an NFL linebacker, right?

The NFL, military, cops, they are tough.

Tough. Tough. What is tough?

Bradley or Chelsea Manning ...

How about that? Is that tough? Going against all that everyone tells you that you should do, in order to tell the truth about our military killing people for fun?

How tough would it be to – not pay taxes, not sign up for military – to hold up a sign in your hometown where everybody knows you. ...

That's tough.

You're not going to find even one NFL player in any of those third and long yardage situations this year.

They are not tough ... enough, it seems.

A word from the American Language Council, doing our best to combat inexactitude and shallowness.
C'mon. Get with it people.

A colleague, R.R., was working on the Channel Four News program back in November 2001. Various well-known TV producers were sitting around, before the program went out, and sharing a good laugh over the absurd new 'fatty Bin Laden' tape the Pentagon had come up with. This was shortly after the bombing of Afghanistan had begun, and this tape was meant to corroborate Bin Laden's guilt.

It was the nearest thing to evidence, or a reason for bombing one of the poorest countries on earth, that America ever came up with. The character was meant to be a lookalike but could hardly compare with OBL's tall, wiry frame. He wore his ring on the wrong hand, got the month of Ramadan wrong, etc. After the Channel Four news team had all finished laughing, they put out the news report, deadpan — as if it were the real thing. Do we have any national media that can be trusted?

— Nick Kollerstrom

TWENTY-EIGHT

"Hey!" yelled the counter guy, racing for the door.

Korey felt the sidewalk and ran.

He was going to hit the C.I.A. where it hurts, a mouthful of water, see how they like it. He ran to find some place to fill it up, figuring Marv was still in the fancy restaurant. He'd come back and shoot him right in the mouth.

He opened the door to a restaurant right on the corner with lots of glass.

"Can I fill this somewhere?" Korey asked the first person he saw, a customer trying to pay his bill.

Korey went to the front desk, held up the red and yellow AR-15 SuperSoaker and asked again.

On the street he looked both ways, headed on down to what looked like the entrance to a parking ramp. Just before that entrance there was an alley, a narrow, shadowy path with weeds between the ramp and the restaurant building.

Way down there it looked like some sort of spout. Korey turned himself sideways, holding the squirt gun above his head and went for it.

The spigot was dry.

Korey had to piss and decided to piss in the squirt gun. He didn't want to get in trouble for pissing in public. He began.

"Hey, man!"

Korey was startled to find a couple guys squatting in the shadows and the weeds, with their belongings scattered down the path, passing a bottle between them that caught the sun at certain angles.

"What the fuck, man!"

"Hey, sorry," said Korey.

"You are right now pissing in a squirt gun, man."

One of them said to bring it to Korey's attention.

"You can't do that," said the other.

"Why not?" said Korey.

"You just caint."

"Why?" said the other guy.

"Just tell us why, that's all."

"I'm going to piss on the C.I.A.," said Korey.

"You are?"

"Yep."

"Can we piss on the C.I.A., too, sir?"

"Yeah, I guess."

And so Korey passed the stolen red and yellow AR-15 SuperSoaker to the other two guys, who had to stand to piss in the opening. They didn't hit the hole that great and it got all over themselves, the weeds and the gun.

The one handed it back, wiping off the gun and apologizing.

"We got doberman piss, too," one of the men said, trying to be helpful.

"Pit bull … somewhere," the other added.

He pointed at the cement, then walked farther down the little alleyway, pointing here and there.

"Pigeon piss, cat piss, not sure, could be."

"Yeah, but," said Korey, not understanding how to get the piss from the cement into the squirt gun. It just wasn't going to work.

He held up the gun in the light so they could all see where the level was.

"That's not quite enough," said one of the men.

Korey and the other guy frowned and agreed.

"We need more piss," said one of the men.

"Here, drink," he passed the bottle to Korey.

Korey took the forty and chugged.

"Anything?"

Korey looked down at himself.

"Not yet," said Korey.

"Drink."

Korey chugged again and again.

Through the afternoon Korey and the two guys in the alley drank beer from their stash of warm forties. They pissed in the plastic red and yellow AR-15, on the brick walls of the alley and the weeds and broken cement. They sang anti-C.I.A. songs and pro-piss songs and Christmas songs.

Korey held up the squirt gun.

"We got enough," he declared.

"We go with you?" said one of the guys.

Korey said sure and they headed off one way down the alley into a stone wall and then backed up, out toward the sunlight.

They decided the other two should also have squirt guns if they were going to go C.I.A. hunting in downtown Minneapolis.

At that, the other guys introduced themselves to Korey.

"Henry," said one as they stepped into the light of the sidewalk.

"I'm Patrick," said the other, reaching out his hand.

They all raised their hands against the bright sun. Korey held his squirt gun under one arm.

"This way," he said, heading off toward the convenience store and the kiosk. He wanted to show them the Most Wanted poster and get two more ARs.

On the way in they stopped quickly at the kiosk and the poster. Korey moved toward the counter where the same guy stood his hands already in the air.

Korey pointed the squirt gun at his head.

"That's piss," said the guy.

"Do not shoot me with piss."

"We need two more," said Korey in a calm deliberate voice.

The counter guy nodded toward the wire stand over by the Honey Buns and Bear Claws, that shit.

Henry and Patrick grabbed two, ripped them out of the plastic, held them at their chests, smiling, liking the substantial weight of their new weapons.

"Good guns," said Henry.

"Yeah, they're squirt guns, but," said the counter guy, his hands still raised.

Korey lowered his squirt gun loaded with warm piss.

The guy lowered his hands, too.

"What's your name, man?" said Korey.

"Washington."

"Washington, are you gonna tell on us?" said Korey.

He shook his head and said yes.

"As soon as you leave I'm callin' the cops," said Washington.

"For sure. The cameras are taking your pictures right now. They will arrest you before you go two blocks. You are fucking some kinda geniuses."

"Fair enough," said Korey.

Henry and Patrick nodded their approval, that sounded equitable to them as well.

"You could come with us, join us," said Patrick.

"Help us fill up these two," said Henry.

"You're all drunk, you mean me piss in your squirt guns?" said Washington.

"Yes, we're huntin' the C.I.A.," said Patrick.

"Yeah, really? Yeah, man, I don't know," said Washington.

"I got this job, [he nodded toward his bike stashed behind the counter] how can I just leave? The next guy don't come on for ..."

There ain't even no more Soakers left, just them little pistols, he added. You can have mine, I'll take a pistol, offered Patrick.

"You got red?"

"Yeah, but, nah, nah, you guys go ahead. I'm good."

You want beer? We got beer. We don't got none left. We can get some!

"Hey! Crazy dudes! I don't want no fucking beer! Go a-way! Take the fucking water guns and fill them with piss or shit or whatever you fucking crazy people do! Go hunt the fucking C.I.A.! Go fucking hunting for ducks with piss rifles! And the F.B.I. and the park rangers! Leave me ... the fuck ... alone! Go!"

"Woah," said Henry.

"We are just trying to involve you in your community, man, get out, immerse yourself. But I see someone doesn't want to be engaged."

"Hey, wait, man," said Patrick, "we're goin', we're goin', don't worry 'bout that, but first, let me ast you, what you wanna be doin' in five years, ten years, you still wanna be workin' in this here convenient store?

Maybe you be the manager? Woah, think 'bout it. That your hopes and dreams? Maybe they put in a metal pole outside that you can tie your bike, and give you every other Sat'day off? Now that be some livin' right?"

Henry stepped up.

"Or, do you wanna go wit' us right now and hunt down the C.I.A. with piss and make fuck'n hist'ry, his'try they gonna write in the his'try books."

"Why are you trying to talk all ghetto and bad, crazy guys? Fuck you, you fucking lying sacks a shit," said Washington.

"You fuckin' crackhead, drunk fucking losers."

He grabbed his jacket.

"I was gonna quit anyway, fuckin' dump."

Everyone went along to the metal rack to pick out a nice piece for Washington and everyone grabbed Honey Buns to stick into small-ass little jacket pockets.

And so, yeah, Washington went with them, got himself a pistol, full-on yellow, went into the restroom and filled it full himself, because, well, we don't, or at least I don't, exactly know why he went with them. He might not even know himself. And that is something left for scholars to determine in the coming years. We continue.

The Four stood outside for a bit, their heads bobbing because they were so bad, ripping the plastic from the Honey Buns with their bare teeth, wiping the frosting and stickiness from their lips with their bare sleeves.

They walked all over the downtown writing on the sidewalk with chalk and Magic Markers from the C-store.

They wrote on the backs of stop signs, on the sidewalk, in the middle of the street while the others blocked traffic: The C.I.A. Sucks... The C.I.A. Eats Shit ... Piss on the C.I.A. ... For A Bad Time Call The C.I.A.

The Four walked over to Murray's and stood outside, waiting for the C.I.A. to come out, then they walked down the sidewalk, kind of all stretched out across the sidewalk for a while, and for a while in single file, so bad.

A black and white police car seemed to notice them and Washington kept walking, but he looked back over his shoulder and the cop car was turning around in an alley, so he got all of The Four and they hurried around a corner. Patrick peeked back around the corner and yep, the cop was coming. They ran.

"Here. Here!" yelled Henry.

Note from the narrator ...

> From "Not Exactly A Radio Show," a live podcast that traveled the circuit of Twins Cities bars for about six months, produced by former members of The Prince Hope Show:

Don't Stop Thinking About Tomorrow.

Remember the night of the Bill Clinton inaugural balls?

The singing. The dancing. The persistently endless smiling. The dreams. The hopes. Remember how they gave up on health care?

Remember the Omnibus Crime Bill? The construction of dozens of new prisons? Remember the bombing of Yugoslavia for 70 days? Remember the Welfare Reform Act? The end of ADC? NAFTA, the end of jobs in America.

Does anyone remember the pardon of Leonard Peltier? **[pel-tier]**

Drug running by the CIA in Mena, Arkansas.

Gary Webb reports about that in the Mercury News and later he is murdered.

The sanctions on Iraq that killed one million people.

The reversal of Glass-Steagall, which is all about the 99% and the 1% in today's headlines.

I won't ask & please don't tell me if you voted for William Jefferson Clinton.

... Hope. Change. Elect Barack Obama.

Remember the Democratic Party?

John F. Kennedy. Robert F. Kennedy. We thought everything was possible, probable.

And then they blew it all away. Clinton and Obama got the message, wouldn't you say? Yesterday. All my troubles seemed so far away. Now it looks as though they're here to stay, oh, I believe, in yesterday.

A beast can never be as cruel as a human being,
so artistically, so picturesquely cruel.
— Fyodor Dostoyevsky, *The Brothers Karamazov*

TWENTY-NINE

Carroll had been brought to Minneapolis because of Korey Miller. *What the fuck!* The realization sat in Carroll's stomach like mud.

He shook Mike Braxton's hand at the Murray's front door then stayed in the foyer to visit with Marv, but he didn't want to talk to Marv.

He didn't want to talk to any-fucking-one right now.

This CRUSHER fucking thing was a joke. Mike Braxton was a joke and for sure Marv was a joke.

Jesus fucking Christ, he thought as he walked away, leaving Marv to stand alone. He could not even stand to stand by Marv. He smelled of cigarettes and he had never been to Paris, nor San Francisco, or even London. "Are you kidding me? Please tell me you are fucking kidding me," said Carroll to Marv when they were once driving alone together.

Carroll called his office and told his secretary to book him a flight back to Washington.

"Today," he said.

"Yes, today. Can you do that?

"Good."

Carroll was from Maryland, played football at Holy Cross, majored in psychology, had been an operations officer in Vietnam, the Phoenix program. He'd been in the Pentagon, had an office there, and now he was based in Virginia.

Whenever he travelled abroad he used the name Sam Stone and his favorite little tidbit, the thing that he knew that the world did not know that made his life interesting and worth living was not that he knew everything there was to know about CRUSHER and Prince Hope and any of these other fucking losers, but that the Cold War was not at all what it seemed to be, not even fucking close. And if he were here he would tell you just that, and leave it at that.

He used to like Minneapolis.

Plays and shit, lakes. They would rent a car, a boat, go up north, rent a cabin that was really a luxury home, fish and sit by the fire. He and the wife, the kids, when they were young. They were making memories, but that was gone, not coming back and so now he didn't even want to be here.

"You can handle this, right?" Carroll said to Marv when he returned to the foyer.

"Yep, sure," said Marv.

Carroll smiled wide and shook Marv's hand with both of his, got in close and asked about Marv's family.

"Alex, Brady," he said.

"They working out? Everything okay?"

"Alexa. Yeah, sure, yeah."

Carroll slapped Marv on the back and went out to the curb where his taxi waited.

Marv waved as he left and Carroll did not wave back, then Marv walked across the street to where Alexa and Trevor waited in the electric car.

"How's Carroll?" said Alexa.

"He's good."

"You get our raises?" asked Trevor.

"Oh, yeah," said Marv.

"All set, you're all set."

"Hey, you would not believe what we have been watching," said Trevor.

"We fucking found Korey, that's for sure. He's right now in that little C-store shit thing, right there."

"Where?" said Marv.

"Right there! Can't you see! There!"

"I don't think he's there anymore," said Alexa.

"He might not be.

"He was, but."

"Yeah, no, he's in there," said Trevor.

"We were watching."

"You were out walking around," said Alexa, "for a while."

"He's fucking in there, what are you talking about?"

So, Trevor pulled his knees way up into his face to get out of the electric car. He crossed against traffic, holding up his billfold that he didn't even bother to flip open.

Alexa and Marv followed, dodging traffic, bent low, leaning forward like they do, hands on sidearms.

Alexa and Marv entered the C-store with guns drawn, in both hands, pointed at the floor or the ceiling. They found Trevor staring at Honey Buns, scattered across the checkered tile, the little TV playing "The Price Is Right."

"Nobody here," said Marv.

"No shit, Sherlo …," Trevor began and caught himself, aided by a saving stare from Alexa.

They stood around for a while, checked out the bathrooms, the store room.

"Hey, look at this," said Trevor, standing at the post office kiosk.

"Fuckin' F.B.I.," he said, nodding toward the Most Wanted Poster in a frame, behind glass, on the wall.

Korey, Patrick, Washington followed Henry inside a door, a wooden door that led to the Minneapolis Downtown VFW where they were immediately standing in front of an entire room of metal folding chairs filled with grey- and-white-haired men in suspenders wearing hats that said "VETERAN," and were falling down into their heads to make them all appear to be melting.

Korey, Washington, Henry, and Patrick stood at the front of the room, holding AR-15s and Colt squirt guns filled with piss as the speaker stopped, thinking The Four are the Iraq and Afghanistan vets who were scheduled to speak that day.

The man in front in the "VETERAN" cap turned toward The Four and began to clap.

The men in the metal folding chairs put their hands on their knees to push off to half-squat and clap.

Through the window two policemen were visible from the shoulder up.

"Yo. Yo. What's up?"

Henry took the microphone from the master of ceremonies guy and stood in front of the podium while the others formed a scattered mess behind him, squirt guns dangling from trigger fingers.

Henry poked the air with his yellow and red AR-15 SuperSoaker filled with piss as he spoke.

"… An' you caint even sleep in the god-damn libary no more!" Henry shouted into the microphone. He paused to allow for the slight applause.

"What's up with THAT now! Who's mothafuckin' big idea was THAT!

"We need a re-vo-luuution in this country! They talk about regime change in other countries and what we really need is one right here! They talk about be all you can be! Bullshit! How can you be all you can be when you got some monkey ass fucker in your ear screaming at you to do push-ups. How many pushups you do during the course of a battle in one day, ballpark? Huh?

"God! Dammit! I am so sick and tired of wakin' up on the bench and standing right over my ass is the po-lice! Caint you even let a man sleep!"

Henry stalked back and forth on the little stage. He shot the squirt gun at the ceiling and it dripped now, from the ceiling to the floor, plopping each time right at the toes of the men in the front row. They moved their feet back.

"We are hunting the C.I.A.!" he yelled, his mouth too close to the microphone, to a smattering of applause.

The men in the hats and the chairs sat and stared, stomachs rumbling. They could eat.

"Have you ever tried to buy a decent tomato these days! They is either too damn hard or soft as mush.

"God! Dammit!

"How 'bout those Vikings! Next year!

"God! Dammit!

"America! Yeah!

"That's what I'm talking about!"

After Henry's keynote address at The Downtown Minneapolis VFW 65th Annual Patriot's Day Dinner And Luncheon Dance, The Four were guided to the front door.

Right there were Marv, Trevor, and Alexa in a tight black suit circle right in the middle of the sidewalk.

Korey drew up his SuperSoaker to his hip and fired. Patrick, Henry, and Washington formed a quick line and knelt on one knee or drew their weapon to their shoulder or put the pistol in both hands and aimed at the tight black-suit circle making all other foot traffic go around like a rock in the stream.

The piss hit the C.I.A. in the eyes, mouth, nose. The Four kept squeezing off stream after stream.

"Don't cross the streams!" yelled Henry.

"Don't worry 'bout it!" screamed Patrick.

"Don't worry about it?" screamed Henry.

"I don' want your suck ass piss in my piss!"

Marv, Alexa, and Trevor put up their hands, stumbled backwards, fell onto their backs, black shoes in the air.

The Four stood over them and squirted a few more times and ran.

Around the corner they ran.

Like the wind they ran, like a dream at morning, pursued for a while by three C.I.A. agents with piss burning in their eyes, like Theodore Cleaver, Whitey Whitney, Larry Mondello, Gilbert Bates, in and out of the sidewalk traffic, across the street, thump, thump, thump, thump into the side of a parked car and then on again, until they disappeared into the white picket fences, the bougainvilleas, the ram-a-lam-a-ding-dong, and the bop-she-bop-she-bop.

"Wait!"

Out of breath, Korey held up a hand and they all stopped, hands on knees, breathing hard.

"Guys, change of plans."

"What?" said Washington.

"Umm, nothing, I forgot," said Korey.

They started walking.

"No, wait, I remember, c'mere, got 'n idea. You want-ta-do something big? I mean big with your life? For your country?"

"Not really," said Washington. "I'm good."

"I don't know man, I'm hungry," said Patrick.

"Wait a damn minute," said Henry.

"Hear what the man's got to say."

"This always works for me."

Korey, Patrick, Washington, and Henry sat on the railing, their backs to the long drop and the water that Korey was so familiar with. Their weapons sat on the sidewalk, leaning against the bridge.

"Trust me. This is the spot."

They heard a buzz coming from a long ways off.

"Dude, man, where'd you get that tattoo?" said Washington, pointing to Korey's orange CRUSHER on his forearm.

"Oh, this?" said Korey.

"Yeah, man."

The robin's egg blue e-Car swerved across traffic, right on the sidewalk.

"Don't jump, guys," said Korey, the air whistling through his missing tooth.

Alexa, Trevor and Marv leaped out, guns drawn and already pointed.

"Do not jump! Do not fucking jump!"

Note from the narrator ...

> From "Not Exactly A Radio Show," a live podcast that traveled the
> circuit of Twins Cities bars for about six months, produced by former
> members of The Prince Hope Show:

Now it's time for the summer replacement series game show, "Whose
Country Is It Anyway?"

Welcome to "Whose Country Is It Anyway?" with our co-hosts, Matt
Lauer and Katie Couric.

Our contestants will be forced to register for the military, pay taxes to the
military, pay taxes for thousands of prisons, live in poverty and smile and
accept the obscene wealth of millions of their fellow countrymen all the
while.

Our contestants will be sealed inside a glass sound-proof box in the middle
of our stage while our studio audience sits all around in a tiny studio
stadium.

Our contestants will scream out and pound on the glass and try to make
our host and studio audience pay attention to them while working on their
personal telephones and eating the big hamburgers provided by our special
studio chef. They will remain in their glass cages, shouting, pounding,
until they can get one person to notice them.

"Whose Country Is It Anyway?"
Sponsored by Powder Milk Democrat Gonads, heavens, they're pasty.

… It's a very tough pill to swallow for Americans to consider that the media is controlled, that the government is not on our side. Americans believe in democratic elections, and we cherish the idea that we have a free press, and that we have a Democratic government.

We're taught since the time that we are kids that we live in the greatest democracy in the world.

And when you realize that your elections are controlled, the vote count is fraudulent, that the media is controlled, and that they're doing a 24/7 psy-ops against us day in and day out. Woah. It's too much for most people to handle. And they're not ready to leave those cherished beliefs.

So, they would rather say, oh, he's just a conspiracy theorist, everything's fine, don't worry.

As the country goes quickly down the hill into hell.

— Christopher Bollyn

THIRTY

The President, The POTUS, The Man With The Plan, The POS, The Chief Executive, The Chief Diplomat sat alone on the big plane.

He sat next to the window with the shade pulled. He did not like to look down and he really was not allowed. On the seat next to him were his extra hat and mittens and his story books.

He wore his gifted yarmulke.

The Pres'dent ate Skittles, not the green ones, and watched on the screen in front of him re-runs of "Leave It To Beaver." He mouthed along the words he knew by heart.

Big men and big women in suits sat all around him. They had electronic pieces in their ears and special watches and special guns and wore sunglasses. They communicated by hand signals and Morse Code blinking.

The plane flew over Minnesota, but the Head Of State did not like to know where they were or what was going on, anywhere, and he was not allowed.

The Commander in Chief smiled — popped an orange after letting a greenie klunk to the floor and roll all the way to the front, causing many agents to look, get on hands and knees and whisper on their earphones — and he talked, silently, along with the TV screen:

Beaver, your mother and I are very disappointed in you.

I wouldn't wanna do anything to hurt God. He's got enough trouble with the Russians and all.

Note from the narrator ...

From "Not Exactly A Radio Show," a live podcast that traveled the circuit of Twins Cities bars for about six months, produced by former members of The Prince Hope Show:

And also by a grant from ...
Warm & Fuzzy Small-Pox Blankets of Muncie, Indiana.
Made In The U.S.A.
Good ol' Mercan know-how.
Small-pox blankets, drone airplanes, anthrax and nuc-u-lur weapons.
Bombs, bullets, fighter planes.

Our products ...
Welcome to life in 21st Century America, where our products are death, destruction, low-paying jobs and the tossing overboard of the poor, sick and elderly, all to support the war racket.
Made in the U.S.A., making American strong, keeping our neighborhoods strong, and our churches strong, our car dealerships strong and our country clubs strong.

Warm and fuzzy.
Small-pox Blankets of Muncie.

The evidence that none of the "official plane crashes" actually took place is simply overwhelming, even if there are 9/11 Truth groups that want to avoid it. Not only did Flight 77 not hit the Pentagon, but Flight 93 did not crash in Shanksville and, even though we have all seen videos purporting to show Flight 11 hit the North Tower and Flight 175 hit the South, we know that those videos are faked or fabricated one way or another.

It has been astonishing to me to discover that the atrocities of 9/11 were not simply allowed to happen but come closer to having been produced as a Hollywood-style spectacle, with phantom flights, faked phone calls, and fabricated crash sites.

Anyone who wants to continue in a state of naive belief in their government as a nurturing institution that is dedicated to the best interests of the American people and to promoting their welfare should read no further, because 9/11 appears to have been a national security event that was approved at the highest levels of the Bush/Cheney administration, including the C.I.A., the Pentagon, the NSA and The White House itself.

When consideration is given the totality of the evidence, no alternative explanation is reasonable.

— Jim Fetzer

THIRTY-ONE

Well, here's the deal.

You like that better? Some people had been saying I've been saying so, yeah way too fucking much and swearing too much, but if you listen to what people really say, I'm just saying.

So, here's the deal-e-o.

We've got what's left of CRUSHER in A.J.'s Tercel, tricked-out camo, driving around Minneapolis and Saint Paul trying to basically figure out what to do with their lives, choosing what hill to die on, as Zima might say.

And they, as we have seen, decided that they would use the gold that Reuben, Hector and A.J. found in The Underground.

Reuben, Hector, Evey and A.J. said fine, yeah, okay, and were anxious to get home, to Maria and Rachel and the rented farm home and some rest and respite before the war would begin again, this time an attack on Mayfield.

Lara and Kaitylyn got the gold, some of it. They were not aware that Reuben and Hector had withdrawn a sizeable amount from the treasure chest in the back seat while they went to get food inside a McDonald's in Eagan.

So, they had money to buy cigarettes and a Russian Racehorse, which shocked the shit out of me when I first heard about it, because of, well, you know about my dream. Freaky thing, the human brain. The thing that weirds me out about dreams is that you have to come up with the script on the spot, all the actors, what everyone is going to do, right there, the scenery, speaking parts, the theme, your brain does that.

Anyway, that's just interesting to me, but yeah, they were relaxing on the farm while Lara and Kaitylyn were wondering how to turn gold into green paper and find food and a place to live and staplers.

The Russian Racehorse.

It was named Roswell, Triple R, triplets, not sure that matters, but I'm just sayin' you never know.

Roswell was owned by a KGB intelligence officer, which isn't as big a deal as you might think, more of an apparatchik type thing going on. Well, he married into money that came by way of the new soviet capitalism-ization and his wife.

He thought, a horse? Whaat? And so, when she moved to Paris with her sister he wanted to get rid of the horse asap and make enough to upgrade the dacha and buy a fishing boat, pointy claw attachments for shoes for walking on ice, and skis.

The horse was named Roswell, because the wife, also KGB, well, her mother, also KGB, had once received a tiny bit of the materiel from the Roswell crash and they had planned to reverse technology it and make invisible something and nothing ever came of that as happens more than you might think. Well, Yevgeny, not his real name.

His real name is Boris. Yevgeny, Boris, what's it matter, right? Well, I guess it mattered to him, he put the horse for sale on eBay and that's how it came to the attention of Reuben and Hector and to a lesser degree altogether, A.J.

He said the horse, Roswell, was an alien horse, just a young baby horse, only a cub, when it crash landed in the desert in New Mexico, which would make the horse too old, mostly dead, but he decided to go for it, hoping to catch the attention of some people like Reuben and Hector and probably not really A.J.

Okay, well. When they came back to the farm to relax they were playing war games on Evey's computer and they also had this gold so they went quick to eBay and they bought the damn horse and made Hector happy with the gold they had stolen from their own treasure chest as everyone else in the car took a nap while they were out cruising around Minneapolis and Saint Paul not knowing what else to do.

So, Maria said, go, go, I can take care of Rachel. You three go and buy a horse. Take a vacation.

So, they went to Kentucky in A.J.'s camo Tercel, which was quite a trip and quite a story itself, but anyway, yeah, in Kentucky because that is where it was shipped, Yevgeny having many stereotypes of America in his pretty large head.

How did they buy it with gold over the computer?

Actually, and god bless Actually wherever he is, got CRUSHER credit cards and made copies and they actually knew how to take the gold to the bank in Hibbing to put money on their account, which is exactly almost what they did, and this is also quite a story, but we do not have the time at this moment.

Because we have come to a solemn moment in our story, no quips, no fart gags, no poop jokes. "And then Korey pooped his pants." I could report that everywhere and to me it would never not be funny, but that is me and now is not the time for that. I know that. But still. Poop. Even just that ...

But not everything is funny or is supposed to be made fun of. I think I do that because everything is so serious. I do miss Max. He would understand. Or not.

Our scene:

Stay in the same town you grew up in your whole life and it's either a small town or kind of small town, or not do that.

Before we get to our scene I just want to say something about that scenario. Which would be worse? Which would be better? Are they the same? I don't know, but I think about it.

I took French in high school and did not realize the stupidity of that. Where the fuck did we think *we* were going? *Napoleon avait cinq cent soldats.* They might as well have taught Martian.

After being gone so long I try to imagine what it would have been like to live my whole life in my town. It would have been so great I could not handle it maybe, or so bad, so oppressive I could not have really been me. Me. ME. *Whatever.* Anyway, fuck it.

Our Scene/Part Deux:

Two cars parked on the dirt road outside the pretty old rental home in rural northern Minnesota. It's a nice day, still morning, birds chirping, little bit of breeze. One car is black, not one anyone would ever purchase, that kind.

The other is a robin's egg blue e-car with three people in suits packed tight. In the other car Special Agent Mike Braxton waited with three of his best F.B.I. men, all wearing sunglasses, gas tank full.

The two cars were not communicating. They had not means to do so, maybe cell phones, but nothing planned for talking. They faced each other, one on the north side of the drive, the other on the south side. How they got to where they were at the same time can only be guessed at, which I am willing to do. One of them had planned to be there and the other was listening as they do and so they decided the other would not get to do this alone.

The driver of the black F.B.I. car moved out, toward the mouth of the drive, and at the same time the robin's egg blue electric car started up, hummed like a microwave oven, and made its move to head off the black car and so they sat there going back and forth until finally the black car took the lead and they both moved slowly down the lane toward the quiet home with bees buzzing, birds chirping and in the back yard a small, black-haired girl tied to the clothesline pole by her leg, giggling as she played with her dolls under the watchful eye of her grandmother.

Maria, the grandmother, heard car doors and wondered why the triplets had returned already from the horse-buying vacation in Keentooky. She wiped her hands on the towel and was just pushing off to run to the front door when she saw them, from both sides of the house, men in sunglasses and suits with handguns at their chests, stalking toward Rachel in the backyard grass that it isn't until you see somebody walking out there do you realize you should mow.

Rachel spotted the men at the same time. She untied herself so quickly that it surprised even Maria, and she ran, little chubby arms and legs in perfect motion, like an Olympic sprinter, head up, bound for the deeper grass by the garage and beyond that the woods.

So now Maria had to do nine things at once and she had no doubt in her ability. She ran to the entry to the back door for the shotgun, knew it was loaded, returned to the kitchen, called Evey, got no answer and sent a text in the code they had long ago laid down.

She put the gun across her chest in both hands, kicked open the back screen door because the handle was broken intentionally to allow anyone to run after Rachel quickly, and stepped out onto the ruddy, broken cement back steps, letting the dog follow her out.

She set her back against the wall, seeing both sides of her by looking straight ahead. The men began talking to her in patronizing tones and then saw her weapon and the dog.

"Put down your weapon, ma'am!"

"Get down!"

There were six in all and four of them screaming.

Maria touched the metal cross on her neck with one finger and kept the shotgun where it was with her finger on the trigger. It was only a single shot, but 12-gauge. She felt the shells in her blouse pocket against her stomach.

In slow motion, but not, Maria pulled the shotgun away from her body and twisted it like you do if you are left-handed and are going to shoot the F.B.I. on your right.

In that quick move she did not aim, but fired at the group of three in sunglasses, as almost at the same time so many shots went off and the wood on the screen door flew and the glass erupted.

Maria's gun clattered on the cement steps and she bled from the mouth and the chest.

Her face hit flush on the edge of a cement step and she lay still, arms outstretched, her toes touching the top cement landing, the red tennis shoes that were good for chasing that Evey had found for her at Target on the recent trip to the cities.

Note from the narrator ...

From "Not Exactly A Radio Show," a live podcast that traveled the circuit of Twins Cities bars for about six months, produced by former members of The Prince Hope Show:

... Just in, this late-breaking news brief
The House Un-American Activities Committee will be re-convening next week.
The committee will be investigating Un-American Activities such as the murder of children in Iraq and Afghanistan and the restricting of personal freedoms through the so-called Patriot Act, as well as the infiltration of American organizations by members of clandestine Homeland Security terror groups.
Are you now or have you ever been, a member of the Central Intelligence Agency?
Appearing next week before the committee will be Dan Rather, Tom Brokaw, Matt Lauer, Katie Couric, Diane Sawyer, Brian Williams and Wolf Blitzer. ...

Note from the narrator ...

> From "Not Exactly A Radio Show," a live podcast that traveled the circuit of Twins Cities bars for about six months, produced by former members of The Prince Hope Show:

… Now, pull up close, some flannel and some pie and a Lutheran. …
It's again time for your "Lake Wobegon American Dream Naptime Story."
America is Nazi Germany and worse because we don't yet know it is and we have not yet hit bottom. But we persist in sleep-walking the American Dream all the same … as George Carlin said, you have to be asleep to believe it.
"The lawns are still looking green."
Garrison Keillor began his soporific monologue last Saturday, talking about the start of school, the end of summer, Lake Wobegon and Pastor Inquvist and Our Lady Of Perpetual Responsibility, The Hopeful Gospel Singers.
And why not? Why not lose oneself in fantasy in order to live one more happy day in America. Holding the door tight against reality with one hand while cutting the Thanksgiving turkey with the other.
But we can't help but ask why.
Why don't those with influence use that influence to tell us about what it is, what is real. Sure, they can do what they want with their cachet. [ka-shay]
Keillor has this immense talent and great idea and longevity. He can do what he wants. And he will. Well, of course.
As well as the movie producers, technicians, musicians, artists, novelists, screen writers. … They put in the long hours for decades and just barely make it and then when they do, why should they throw it away.
For heaven's sake.

A considerable proportion of the developed world's prosperity rests on paying the lowest possible prices for the poor countries' primary products and on exporting high-cost capital and finished goods to those countries. Continuation of this kind of prosperity requires continuation of the relative gap between developed and underdeveloped countries — it means keeping poor people poor. Increasingly, the impoverished masses are understanding that the prosperity of the developed countries and of the privileged minorities in their own countries is founded on their poverty.

— Philip Agee

THIRTY-TWO

Evey, Reuben and Hector returned immediately with A.J in the camo Tercel, leading a cloud of smoke down the gravel road all the way from the highway turn-off, yanking sharply into the little lane.

Even before the car plowed into the weeds Evey was out and sprinting around the house. She skid to a stop for a split-moment at the blood-stained back porch cement steps, then took off again, an older version of Rachel, heart racing in time with her pumping arms.

She paused short, shocked to see her father's dog lying in the weeds, a hole in its side. She touched it, pulled back her hand and surged on where she needed to go.

Reuben, Hector, in full camo with face paint and camo caps, jumped out of the car with rifles held high as A.J. moved the Tercel into a horizontal blocking position.

The three took up their posts, A.J. at the vehicle while Reuben and Hector ran left and right to the flanks and crouched in the brush, as the beasts sunning themselves in the grove across the road moved out.

Led by an armored vehicle, a cross between a jeep and a tank and grandma's metal gravy bowl.

A.J. and the others fire immediately on the armored car and the support vehicles.

153

Machine gun from the armored vehicle rips apart Tercel, other vehicles fire on Reuben and Hector, helicopter swoops over back yard. No known casualties at this point.

The armored vehicle continued to fire at the Tercel and A.J., throwing up bits and chunks of metal. A.J. attempted to shoot from his stomach underneath the vehicle. He tried over the top and around the back.

Reuben's shots tinked the armored car.

He switched to the cars and yelled out as loud as he could though no one heard as he was hit in the right shoulder, losing his balance and smacking his face into the earth and sucked in mud to breathe. He found his weapon and with one hand on one knee kept blasting away.

Hector found the stump where he sometimes went to sit and think and smoke marijuana because it was away from the house and he thought maybe his mother could not smell from there.

He rested his AR in a perfect slot and let out a string of shots at the armored car that was pummeling the poor Tercel.

Out of his peripheral vision he saw three figures to his right and switched his fire to them. He swore loud in Spanish as he ran out of ammo and told himself to go slow to reload, go smooth.

The following vehicles, three black unmarked cars, stopped in the lane and spilled their contents, a dozen men in full combat gear who began fire relentlessly on Reuben and on Hector in their basically unprotected positions in the brush.

A side door on the armored vehicle swung open. Special Agent Mike Braxton stood on the frame, raised his hand for the attack to cease.

The assault team formed into three teams, one man behind the other, crouching low.

Braxton led the team that found A.J. on his back behind the Tercel, arms and legs spread out, his chest bleeding and three neat holes in his face.

The other teams reported back to Braxton that the other two insurgents were also deceased.

"Search the home," said Braxton.

"Tag the gold, bring Evangelina and Rachel directly to me."

The helicopter continued to dive and hover over the woods as Braxton and his entire team conducted a slow step by step search of the area.

Braxton paused in front of the tree house or deer stand that Evey's father had built.

"Rachel!" he called up.

"How are you, dear? Come on out, hon'."

In the woods Evey opened her mouth to shout at the F.B.I. and others gathered around her father's stand to tell them to get the fuck out of here. Rachel gently, quickly put her hand over her mother's mouth.

With her little finger she motioned to her mother to follow her, down the little bank to the creek where they walked rock by rock all the way to the road and the little bridge where she had Snickers for them. They sat eating under the bridge and each jumped a little when the heavy guns blasted apart the tree stand.

Back at the armored vehicle, Braxton, Marv, Alexa, Trevor stood like football players with their helmets under their arms while others began the work of taking care of the scene and the bodies.

"There's no gold," Marv told Braxton.

"None that we could find."

"You searched the entire house?" said Braxton.

"No, we just looked in one little portion of the house and for the rest of it we used the law of probability, dickweed," said Trevor.

Alexa and Marv made their way casually back to their vehicle, leaving Trevor to pick himself up off his back as Braxton pounded up the steps to continue the search for the gold treasure box.

Note from the narrator ...

> From the assorted musings found by the cleaner, Jake the intern from St. Olaf, in the log book of Crawfish Cabin at Anderson's Resort on Lake June Bug in northern Saint Louis County, in the Minnesota Arrowhead.

June 4, 1947

We were out sitting on the dock tonight, watching the walleyes jump, at least we thought they were walleyes.

And we saw spaceships up by the stars, at least we thought they were spaceships. The newspaper says they found spaceships in New Mexico I think it was? These musta been them then.

AND! Two nights in a row Johnathan heard knocks on the wall by his bed. He whispered to Frederick and they crawled outside and saw a giant ape peeking in the window !!!

I am not kidding!

Nancy Nowazinski, from Hibbing

Note from the narrator ...

From the assorted musings found by the cleaner, Jake the intern from St. Olaf, in the log book of Crawfish Cabin at Anderson's Resort on Lake June Bug in northern Saint Louis County, in the Minnesota Arrowhead.

June 4, 1957

Someone from our family said they saw a family of apes down by the lake when he went outside to pee in the night. It was a full moon. Nobody is supposed to pee outside because there are bears and that is why we have a privy. I did not tell father yet, but I think I am gonna.

Anne Francis Broulliet
Chicago, Illinois

But what counter-insurgency really comes down to is the protection of the capitalists back in America, their property and their privileges. U.S. national security, as preached by U.S. leaders, is the security of the capitalist class in the U.S., not the security of the rest of the people.

— Philip Agee

THIRTY-THREE

Kaitylyn and Lara decided to take a little break from CRUSHER and from each other. Kaitylyn said she had a friend she could stay with for a few days, someone who didn't know anything about CRUSHER, didn't care, who just wanted to do hot yoga, watch Netflix, cook and put pictures of the food on Facebook, and Kaitylyn said she looked forward to it.

Lara went to Highland Park, her grandmother's cozy brick home with the apple trees in the back yard. Her grandmother was cool with the CRUSHER stuff, didn't ask many questions, but seemed to understand. So did her parents, really, so unusual, it seems.

It was the address Lara used for personal, business, contact type stuff.

After she got settled in her room her grandmother said she had some things in the basement that had arrived for her over several months.

Well, it wasn't the first thing she did, go down to that basement. She recalled hurrying down there once during a tornado warning and a Halloween blizzard, not THE Halloween blizzard, another one, when they had to huddle together in blankets with no electricity, but by now that was a really good memory, actually.

She found her stuff arranged neatly on an old sofa and sat down to get this done and get back to work. There was so much to do. She and

Kaitylyn had to turn the gold into real usable money (how the fuck?) and they had to get the whole recruiting, training, supplies procurement and re-supply network all moving again, not easy.

Well, she would try to relax, it might be the right thing to do, but she would not forgive herself if she got killed or captured again right here before they got the Mayfield operation going.

In the neat pile there were letters, some from people she did not know, some from high school friends, two from "PH." One said "United States District Court."

She wrapped the letters in a rubber band and put them aside and went for the box. It was wrapped kind of like professionally with tape with no bulges. It was addressed to her at this here and the return was SAC Braxton in downtown Saint Paul. (what the fuck?)

God damn! she thought. Wonder whose hands are in here! Shit! Lara went upstairs to find a scissors to cut the tape.

"I'm fine, gramma!" she responded to the query from somewhere in the house.

She danced down the steps, actually kind of happy to be back at work, not trying to "relax." That was so hard.

She cut the tape on all sides. It was a new box, didn't want to ruin it really. She stopped, started again. The F.B.I. wouldn't bomb her, would they? She slowly, smoothly reached both hands in and pulled out the neatly stacked pile that fit the space so perfect.

On top was a cover letter of sorts, in black magic marker, the kind the F.B.I. uses to black things out, but this was more of a fine line marker:

"The Actually Basement Tapes" – *maybe they will "actually" be in somebody's basement some day when you find these years and years from now and this will be cool. Or not."* — *Love, Actually*

God she missed Actually.

This must have been found by Braxton when they *fucking* literally destroyed CRUSHER at Cicely. *Wow.*

Lara started to think of Kaitylyn and that weird thing she was doing with her eyes, blinking, blinking, so weird. She's fucking crazy. Not really.

There was an envelope marked Fun Facts.

She opened it and took out the papers, scanned them quick, set them aside.

There was also a manila envelope and, shit, look at this, Morgan's diary.

What, the, fuck? *Woah.*

The manila envelope said "LARA ONLY."

Blink, blink, blink, blink.

Blink, blink.

Lara went for the envelope.

Morse Code, that's what Kaitylyn was doing! Wow. Let's see what exactly was she doing. Blink, blink ...

C .. I ...

She switched how she was sitting, put her feet up stretched out a bit, back to the Fun Facts and from the envelope tumbled a ticket from a Prince Hope show from 1974, and a Kirby Puckett rookie card.

Fun Facts: (I'm Just Sayin')

1) Actually, there's a town in Nevada, near Area 51, that is called Rachel. Just sayin'.

2) Terror is theatre... Theatre's a con trick. Do you know what that means? Con trick? You've been deceived. - John Le Carré, *The Little Drummer Girl*, 1983

3) CRUSHER ... "C.I.A. puts acronyms in all caps" - just sayin'.

4) There were no planes. — John Lear

5) The law of karma

And at the bottom was a fortune cookie.

Yeah, okay, she thought, that was weird.

She ripped into the envelope and found papers that Actually would have printed off. They showed something from the C.I.A. website, blah, blah, yeah, yeah ... and on the second page ... the third page ... a what?

A photo of Kaitylyn, all dressed up, her hair different. They put our pictures on their website?

Lara looked through the papers for her own photo.

She came back to Kaitylyn and began to read:

Kaitylyn Bridge: Criminal Investigator, Special Agent

I work to understand and criminal agents and target and figure out ways to exploit their vulnerabilities. I enjoy getting to try my hand at opportunities and endeavors to help the country stay safe. I am coming up on my fifth year at the Agency, and the C.I.A. always provides training to help me stay current in my field. Right now, I'm taking specialized courses ranging from interrogation techniques to countering urban terrorism. The opportunities at the C.I.A. are unmatched.

Lara dropped the papers. She scooted, hitting the floor she pushed away, away from the papers.

She charged up the wooden steps.

"What's the matter, dear!"

"Nothing!"

Note from the narrator ...

> From "Not Exactly A Radio Show," a live podcast that traveled the circuit of Twins Cities bars for about six months, produced by former members of The Prince Hope Show:

Hello. I'm Tom Brady from the New England Patriots.
And because I'm afraid that if I tell you the truth I won't be able to live my good life in America and be a pro football player on TV and rich and have a car and a house and a family in America.
If I tell you the truth about America and its soldiers and veterans I will be destroyed.

I'm Joseph, high school football coach.
I am a coward. I'm a co-conspirator in the raping and murdering and plundering of the world by America's military.

I'm Ann, emergency room nurse. I am an American. I'm afraid of other Americans. Really afraid.

Hi ! I'm Bill, your dentist. I want to be liked. I don't want to be an outcast. I <u>cannot</u> be.

Good morning. I'm Mrs. Thompson, your daughter's third-period English teacher.
I want to be able to exist. At least exist within a thin bubble.
I get one chance at living and I'm not going to waste it by telling you the truth.

So. We just want to all say ...
"Thank you to all of our nation's veterans and on-duty military for protecting us. You keep us free. You are heroes."

The world we live in is paper thin, the reality they have constructed with their fake news is paper thin. — *Scott Creighton*

… Facts are inspiring if they are true. It's impossible to tell truth from fiction if you don't practice telling the truth, and even then it's not easy when so many lies are purposely being propagated. We are awashed in lies, and therefore out of touch with reality. It's difficult to talk with people who are out of touch with reality, particularly when everyone believes they are in touch and everyone else isn't.

… There are many cures for our social malady offered by experts, all very dead suggestions and never stimulating of the imagination. Just one thing needs to be distilled out for the masses to follow, an action that would have the most impact, and I think that action could be to TURN OFF the Television. And I mean OFF. TV propaganda is subtle and pervasive and it's not worth the History channel or the nature films. A public smashing of a tv set should be performed in major cities.

… Another catalyst for change would be for the so-called left media to finally tackle an important homicide and out the perpetrators, for instance the F.B.I. killing of Martin Luther King. Living day by day with that festering cancer unacknowledged will kill us as sure as an ignored tumor in the colon. I can name others, but the point is that all other considerations are secondary to solving these crimes vigorously. All hell will break loose if we do, but at least it won't be a slow cancerous death we will suffer if we ignore it.

— *from the Comments Section*

THIRTY-FOUR

I'm just not sure about a lotta things anymore. I'm like you.

I thought I knew why I was writing this story which many have said is completely made up and others have said there is no way I know what I am talking about, that it all happened a completely different way.

Sometimes I feel like somebody else is writing. And so, yes, I went to Prince Hope, right up to the little office and over his shoulder I saw the people of Saint Paul walking around. He just looked at me like I was crazy.

I wanted him to give me some direction, was I doing what he had originally imagined.

"I never hired you. You are imagining that. What is wrong with you anyway?"

Woah.

Okay, dude.

So I just left and I was thinking, well, one of us is crazy. One of us doesn't remember a little thing called, oh, I don't know, CraigsList.

It is true that sometimes I lose my perspective. I get lost in my story. It's a little like bumping into a door, breaking out one lens of your glasses and walking around seeing the world through these two different sides, views, lenses.

I think of myself as writing something very important, even dangerous. I let myself think that. It's important that I think what I am doing is important even if I realize I personally am not so much.

And so, I also see myself as a revolutionary, with something on my hands on my computer that can bring down kings. And that is why I can do it.

If for more than a split moment I let myself realize that I am merely one of ten thousand and more just like myself, slinking in and out of coffee shops imagining I am being followed, that someone is trying to put the writing of the book into my head, that I am being watched and in danger of being arrested at any moment, then what good would it be.

If I sit by myself and realize that there are ten thousand just like me, who probably look almost like me and have almost the same historical background, who are living the same fantasy, lie actually, and then ten thousand more of the opposite gender doing the same exact thing, the bubble would burst, the whole dam, the water would rush in and I would drown.

So, what good does it do? I dunno. But what harm does it do that we go about our lives at least alive a little.

And by the way I often get depressed, well, by various things, but this particular thing is the criticism of the age of computers and phones, how we do not communicate in person but feel we are in touch by these machines, when in reality we are not and it is wrong. And it hits me because this current situation suits me. I actually like it. And usually I just take it and say, yes, I am bad, but for once, here I want to fight back and say yes, maybe in the "old days," people would sit and talk at the barbershop or at the hardware store or on the bench outside the ice cream parlor or on the cover of *The Saturday Evening Post*. But they still do those things, they talk, even me, I talk, we talk, you talk, all the conjugations and confederations.

Yeah, but that's all pre-arranged, nothing is ever going to be said, and it's not. They are scripted. You know your lines, they know theirs and you become very adept at your part in the play and it pleases you.

You are never going to hear/see what is said on computers. No fuck yous, no real information. Yeah, it can appear cowardly, but things get said, get out there.

And I like it. People, well, been there, done that. I have tried.

We have all tried. You have to, you have no choice, there are things, certain customs, traditions, rituals, ceremonies you go through and when you get to be my age, well, most of that is done and if you ask me it's a fucking relief.

All this to say I have gone to visit the workshop in Saint Paul where Geronimo worked and where many of his staff members from his group home also worked a second job. It was a day center, an activity center, they go by a few different names I guess.

I felt that I should do some investigating, finding out a few things for myself.

I had heard that Gerry/Geronimo, Napoleon Ulysses Custer, had a sister and she worked there. So I thought I should meet her while I was waiting for other things to happen.

Did you ever just say to someone, you are so beautiful? I never have, afraid what trouble I might get into. Maybe none, maybe it would be appreciated, but I have wanted to, said it in my head enough times.

The Beautiful Indian Maiden Heroine, The BIM(h), that's what she is to me now.

To call her Pocahontas would be a stereotype. But wow.

Just wow.

Her name is Josie, Josephine Custer. She is Ojibwe, I think.

I had made an appointment and so she had time to talk. She is tall, slender, long black hair, calf hide boots, all kinds of Indian shit dangling everywhere, even a goddamn tomahawk, Jesus H. Fucking Christ, and she carries with her, everywhere, a wry grin as if she just knows.

The BIM(h) works now in direct care, but she is studying to get her degree and would be eligible then for an office job if one came open and that is her plan.

"Gerry had an imaginary friend," she said, getting that right out there, in case, I don't know, she had to go do something or I died of a heart attack right there.

I write that down.

"Did the friend have a name?"

"It's weird," she says.

I look at her, pen touching pad.

(*Wry grin*)

"Marv," she said.

M-A-R-V.

"Okay, what else?"

"What else what?" she says.

Well, she said, she is working on a lawsuit that will point to her brother being murdered to keep the truth about "that day" from the public.

How would a plane ticket from "that day" do that? Tell "the truth" to the people about that day?

"That's just the beginning.

"We have to start somewhere," she said.

And I felt bad because I had burst her bubble maybe, already.

Sometimes I do that.

She took me on a tour and she showed me the shredding room where the clients shred documents.

"This is where they found it," she said.

"They?"

"I assume someone was with him, a staff," she said.

We have coffee in the lunch room.

"I like what you guys are doing," she said.

You guys? I say with just my eyes.

"I'm studying John Brown. Isn't the truth worth at least as much as that?"

I write it down not knowing what I'm writing.

She wants to talk about Pine Ridge, where she has visited, and poverty and genocide. I write it down, suppressing a yawn with the other hand and I do feel terrible. I was interested in what she was saying, why do things like that happen?

I called her "BIM" when we left and my face I'm sure was red.

What the fuck? What is wrong with me.

But, we did make a date to talk again about the lawsuit and I yelled out "Josie!" from the bus window as she waved from the door.

Jesus Fucking Christ.

Note from the narrator ...

> From the assorted musings found by the cleaner, Jake the intern from St. Olaf, in the log book of Crawfish Cabin at Anderson's Resort on Lake June Bug in northern Saint Louis County, in the Minnesota Arrowhead.

June 5, 1964

Lots of stars tonight. It is so beautiful.
Nobody believes me, so I'm writing it here.
Lee Harvey Oswalt did not kill President Kennedy. I just know it. I can't tell you how.
But I do. And I am going to get to the bottom of this.

Bud Nester, fourth grade
Spirit Lake, Iowa

And the eagle still flew in the sky
Hearts filled with national pride
Then you came along with your drug crazy songs
Goddamit you're all gonna die
How dare you sit there and drink all our beer
Oh it's made for us workers who sweat, spit and swear
The minds of our daughters are poisoned by you
With your communistic politics and them negro blues
— Elton John, "Texan Love Song"

THIRTY-FIVE

Caryl,
Had another poor night but have swept and showered and shaved and maybe can deal with less pollen, and be less surly or grim. Mike Blackbird came in from town and had picked me up more decongestants.

See above my note to James Kessler. I come from a blind family of the Democrat persuasion. Only with Obama had I cared about "politics," in as I wished to have a black president. As Steve put it: At least he is black. And, ho hum, as Debbie Lusignan put it, Obama followed the war mongering Bushies, and illegally jailed even more whistle blowers.

At this time nearly anyone I have known for years hates and fears Trump. But mostly all these folks believe Main Stream Media, which post 9/11 lies very much. They lie about Assad, Putin, Trump. I am grateful Trump is not altogether insane and will unlike the others talk with Putin.

I think Trump's belief in Israel's right to drop white phosphorous on hospitals in Palestine will do in him and Israel together, without he can jerk back into some reality in this case too. USA cannot arm Israel forever. Common sense.

Jim Kessler is hoping Trump can be independent enough or brave enough to question the official 9/11, and official 9/11 is a physical impossibility. That would also implicate Mossad. The Donald best decide fast and perhaps he cannot do it.

Oh, very funny piece you sent about Hillary's rampage about losing. I should not laugh at her illness maybe, but she does murder too. Too, had commanded the destruction of Libya. Had Khadafy suffer badly in his slow execution, so it appears. She did laugh, I saw this, her saying in glee: We came, we saw, he died....She is ill. Pity her.

Oh, I start to laugh. Drinking plenty wine, will try out these new decongestants. This little cow town or fake cow town, Cowboy Capital of the World or some nonsense is not well provided for in my own case. It is but a tourist town, charge about ten dollars more for a bottle of Skyy

Vodka. Madrea showed me how to make wine, my family take care of me. I wish I were a recognized novelist already. But am built to go down the road, if I want.

Coming off dog walk with Kelly and his dogs this morning Mike Blackbird asked me something about religions who believe in reincarnation. I should ask him why did he, but there we were crossing the cattle guard, entering our quarters. If you know, Bonnie and Mike do not believe in Spirit. What they see is to ever wonder how can Spirit be. What I see is how ever could Length, Width, Height, and Density of physical vibration be the all. Vibes between vibes be what. Rippling Infinity of the More. Spirit, nonphysical. Eternal. Spirit Memory is. Inclusive of bugs naturally. Germs, fungus. How can this not be?

Perhaps it is best I be out of vodka. Wine is healthful too.

Love,

Billy

Geoffrey,

Humans need their animals. I think you should bring the little family over here and get this extra plot of Bonnie's and teach in Prairie and bring in a trailer or build a house and find some guys to sink your well, consult Kelly and Janus. It is calming to sit at my window and see cows. Deer. A pair of skunks. A fox. Maybe Akiko would enjoy raising chickens, have plenty yard eggs, superior. Sell them should she care to, a market is local. Nina would like all this. Swim during warm weather and so on. I doubt teaching you would have such agitated kids as in Austin, or Japan.

Last night I slept unexpectedly very well, and tomorrow we go to one of these towns with an HEB, where I can stock up on what I need, and for less asthma. Part of the year here I do not use decongestants. I drink, for other causes. Very funny stuff. Grapes grow wild here, so I think if USA fails we with toil could have wine. Hopefully Mexican smugglers could bring in coffee. For venison or something. Oh, sounds like work, venison is my favorite. But I am only addicted to coffee. I hope this would not be warfare. We would need horses. Only got one now, Elsie. Out to pasture with a poor leg, lonely and more friendly having lost her friend. Mike gives her apples and Kelly gives her apples or carrots. She is more social now.

Funny, I was liking the white wine best then changed to red and am maybe out of red. The classical station from Dubuque is playing some Mexican. I can hear it. Usually in the day I get around to turning on the TV jazz station but have not today.

Further Out,
　Bill

Jim,
Thank you for interesting information.

My family have been Democrats, while I have been not interested, a misfit writer who age of 21 accepted 15 shock treatments, which naturally did not help me. I was amused.

It was not like in ONE FLEW OVER THE CUCKO'S NEST, while Ken Kesey was good friends of a couple of my friends. And I met Kesey. Knew William Burroughs, his son Bill III. Met Ginsberg. A couple of months older than yourself, I was a late beatnik. And an old hippie.

I had known from the sixties the USA used several fold more the Earth's raw goods than anyone else and had much more military. Like Jesse Ventura I have loved Mexico.

Though it scares me these days, for I stand out anywhere. In the sixties I knew wetbacks. It impressed me, their remarking that once you have crossed the river people are frowning, not laughing in the street like in Mexico. Probably, poor people these days are not laughing in the street in Mexico, or nothing like in the sixties.

I only have been attentive to anything that possibly can be called political since 9/11. Maybe mid or later 2006 I became certain it was inside, because, anything that tall falling down has to lean and fall to one side. That first propaganda of the weight of the floors gathering momentum is pathetic.

Maybe in 2007, 2008, a late writer friend of mine turned me onto Mike_Novak. And Mike sent me a couple of his Truther novels and turned me onto you. I cannot recall had you and I spoken by phone. Novak said you are the wise man, I paraphrase.

This of yours above I heard at your Raw Deal, and more. I remain uncertain of Trump. For me, his best case is he is smarter enough to talk with Putin. This leaves out the C.I.A. and Bushies and Clintons and Obamas who seem incredible. Want to nuke Russia first. I trust you, you may be wrong but say Russia has the better technology. Our fortune is we have Putin.

Past year I am digging The Sane Progressive, Debbie Lusignan. Nobody is any smarter, she is a phenomenon of Earth.

In a couple of her videos past month, she slammed in 9/11. Had not cared in first plans to speak of 9/11, be called Conspiracy Theorist.

She had not wished to distract from her subjects otherwise, rigged voting etc. Suddenly, she grasped it, to never call out 9/11 is to never free others from this hypnotism: "Our government could never do this to us." While, the 9/11 Wars go on, and on, daily bombings of livestock and poorest peoples.

Yours,

Bill

Caryl,

Thanks always, in such interesting times. Just then I posted you something, from Jon Rappoport: Is the NSA the Real President of the United States?

Caryl, at this date, 2,17, 2017, at Kessler's blog is another of his favorites, Paul Craig Roberts, who once worked in the Reagan administration and I keep forgetting what was his job then. James Kessler likes to call Paul Craig Roberts our greatest intellectual. So at this date Paul Craig who like Kessler would like to see Trump survive is speaking of the forces to kill Trump. I call this stuff more sociological, than political. It is war profiteering, entirely schizoid. Democrats / Republicans is camouflage. Why many have had hope in Trump is he early had said the official 9/11 made no sense being airplanes are too fragile to penetrate steel beamed modern skyscrapers.

In schizoid nation all roads lead to 9/11 and suddenly there be this international murderous devil worship pedophilia organized and it has been thus many decades and this outrageous entirely mad Merry Xmas from Pizzagate, pissants from Hell, hitting MSM.

Where are those Extraterrestrials. Uh, which ones?

Love,

Billy

The Americans Dream
of marshmallow clouds
and lollipop lanes
and TV towns
While the world wails,
fists clenched,
eyes blazing,
tears streaming.

The Americans Dream
of rocket ships,
fireworks,
freedom and alleluia,
While they sleep on
through the alarm,
the house afire. …

— *The American Dream*, CWG Press

THIRTY-SIX

Now we have Evey and Rachel, kind of having a horse, in Kentucky because that is where it was shipped, Yevgeny-Boris having many stereotypes of America in his large head.

And now Evey has put out a cry, a plea for help in alternative websites, saying how, speaking now from the voice of Rachel, the child who owns a Russian Racehorse that is an alien, a grey horse, a grey palomino, there are black spots on the hind, and they are going to try to win the Bourbon County Derby for to get to a bigger race maybe and they want to make enough money to attack Mayfield, if you know where that is.

And at about that time the C.I.A. and F.B.I. raided the farm and we know what happened there and they went back and again we have heard the story of that day.

And they are hoping through all of this that they will get on TV morning show with Rachel and horse and they will put Roswell in CRUSHER blanket and Rachel will wear CRUSHER T-shirt and they will get big lots attention of people for attacking America. That is how they talk sometimes now. It's funny. That's the plan.

And Evey has not talked to Lara or Kaitylyn about this. She doesn't know what to think about them these days.

And … we have gold from a buried treasure.

Do we have pirates in our story? Yes. I would have to say yes. Many pirates.

Well, yeah. Mike Braxton was given this assignment since he kind of knew something about it.

He decided to help with the publicity.

Note from the narrator ...

From "Not Exactly A Radio Show," a live podcast that traveled the circuit of Twins Cities bars for about six months, produced by former members of The Prince Hope Show:

Your car won't start and I know what you're thinking. ...
Kwik Trip doesn't carry your cigarettes anymore. They did it again.
Your toilet is plugged, and you know who did it.
Al Queda.

You have a flat tire on the freeway.
Yup, The Fucking Taliban.

You fall into a giant pothole as you turn off the freeway, disappear for days and who did it?
You got it, ISIS.

You can't find your keys as you head out the door.
There ya go. They strike again.
They are everywhere.
Sleeper Cells.
Caffeine Cells.
Amoeba Cells.
Al Queda. Bob Queda. ISIS. The Taliban.
Ninjas. Ghosts. Fairy tale characters.

You have never seen them, but they are everywhere.

This message brought to you by The United States of America, Dept. of Homeland Security.
Have a nice day.

Damn it boss, I like you too much not to say it.
You've got everything except one thing: madness!
A man needs a little madness, or else...
... he never dares cut the rope and be free. "

How could I, who loved life so intensely,
have let myself be entangled for so long
in that balderdash of books and paper blackened with ink!

Every man has his folly, but the greatest folly of all,
in my view, is not to have one.

Let people be, boss; don't open their eyes.
And supposing you did, what'd they see? Their misery!
Leave their eyes closed, boss, and let them go on dreaming!

While experiencing happiness,
we have difficulty in being conscious of it.

Only when the happiness is past and we look back on it
do we suddenly realize — sometimes with astonishment
— how happy we had been.

— Nikos Kazantzakis, *Zorba the Greek*

THIRTY-SEVEN

The teachers in our school, they never ever said anything about Vietnam, and we were destined to go, we all signed up for the draft, then the war ended and we didn't have to. When I think about those teachers I remember that. We would have died. We would have killed and nobody, not those teachers, our parents, priests, newspaper editors, they never said anything. That fucking sucks.

Of course we would have gone. We would have thought it was the right thing to do. There were hippies in our school, but we just thought they were weird.

Not us, we were the right stuff, cool, football players, basketball. Everybody wanted to be us. That's what we thought. We believed what was in the paper about the Gulf of Tonkin. We also thought Theodore Cleaver died in 'Nam. That's the level of our understanding.

That's Special Agent In Charge Michael R. Braxton, writing on Facebook as he receives a text on the phone sitting on the desk, by the computer.

He looks pretty young, but he's getting close enough to think about retirement. He works out, plays in a noon basketball league, coaches kids in the summer.

In the text he is given the "goddamn Russian Racehorse fucking shit" thing to look into.

So, that's where Evey and Rachel are. They are online.

Where are they? Back at farm?

Yes, as a matter of fact, with blood stains on the back steps, Pancho Villa and Virgin Mary with gun holes in front, crosses where A.J., Hector and Reuben fell and a crude wire gate with permanent Christmas lights now across the front lane.

Braxton went by himself, disguised as the mailman riding a bicycle.

And since Evey spent almost every second watching out the front window she was there to greet him and put her Glock barrel on the forehead of the silhouette as she opened the door, squinting into the sun.

She kicked opened the front screen and keeping the pistol on Braxton, reached out just as the screen was open and slapped him as hard as she could across the face. The screen door slapped and she kept her weapon trained on him.

She did it again.

He asked if he could come in.

She let him, told him to sit in the first chair.

She told him to put his handgun down on the floor, slowly.

"And the knife … on your leg.

"And the pistol on your shoulder."

"What else?" she said.

He shook his head, not mentioning the gun in the holster on his spine.

They sat and stared at each other, Braxton trying to talk and Evey sweating more and more, aiming the gun straighter and straighter at his face, wiping the sweat from her eyes with her shoulder.

He nodded at the computer on the dining room table.

He said he could get Evey the publicity she needed for Roswell's race.

"How?" she said, lowering her gun a bit to look him in the eyes.

Braxton said he would issue a press release to the newspapers. They will run it. That doesn't make sense, said Evey after she read it. Why would they run it. It says take no notice. Trust me, said Braxton. They are taking notice by putting this in the paper, she insisted. Yeah, well, said Braxton.

"The CRUSHER-owned racehorse Roswell, which they claim has connections to the actual crash in 1948, will be racing at Bourbon County

Racetrack in Kentucky, the winner of which will qualify for The Kentucky Derby, in order to make money to finance the coming CRUSHER attack on Mayfield, the home of Beaver and Wally Cleaver, Ward Cleaver, June Cleaver, Larry Mondello. The public is advised to take no notice of this event."

Braxton wrote it on Evey's computer while Evey trained the gun on his head while Rachel stared at him. Evey watched him send it to what he said was his newspaper, TV and radio list, then motioned for him toward the door. She stood in the doorway and aimed at his head as he waved and rode back down the lane, opened the gate, got off his bike, closed the gate, and rode away slowly down the dirt road on such a beautiful day.

The army has announced that a flying disc has been found and is now in the possession of the army. Army officers say the missile found sometime last week has been inspected at Roswell, New Mexico and sent to Wright Field, Ohio for further inspection.

— [Walter Winchell] ABC News

THIRTY-EIGHT

The BIM, The Beautiful Indian Maiden (h), Josie Marsha Marsha Marsha Custer, I know so much more about her after I barged back in on her and asked her to go to lunch with me. And she did. And I love her and I don't because she is who she is and I am who I am. I didn't say a word about "Marsha Marsha Marsha." I just feel there is a sense of humor with the Indians where they are fucking with white people and they know we feel uncomfortable and won't challenge them, and I didn't.

Lunch.

It was Indian rice, what is that? And other stuff and it was good, I think. I can't taste when I'm with someone else. I like it more when I can concentrate on the food, otherwise I'm just either nervous or thinking about other shit and then I look down and the food is gone and I don't remember eating it.

But she talked and that I remember.

THE BIM (h) was raised on the Fond du Lac reservation up around Duluth. She played soccer and basketball, mostly soccer and she set a scoring record against Ely, and then they played Eagan down in The Cities and they got obliterated, slaughtered, massacred, everyone was saying on the long bus ride home.

"Don't say that! Fight back!" she said, and she cried, her head bouncing along the freeway on the window.

She said, we'll beat them next time and there was no next time. Probably not ever, 'cause that's a long trip to just go and get killed.

They went because they thought they were good, but they weren't, not that good, not really.

She talked and I thought, she gets it, she would fit in with the CRUSHERS. I wish they could meet her.

The BIM (h) went to Pine Ridge one summer on a "Rez To Rez" sort of exchange program and she said it was so bad, so sad, Pine Ridge.

And when she was there she met a Lakota girl who told Josie she was reading about John Brown and how he freed the slaves by fighting and he got hanged and Josie thought, oh, well, there's an antelope, but now she thinks about it more, how her ancestors fought and how they were smart and no different than people today and she is angry they lost so terribly and how things are now.

And then the pie with ice cream came, and then the bill.

And then she went to junior college and was going to transfer to the university and somebody needed to be Geronimo's guardian after he turned a certain age and she thought she could not hardly be his guardian if she's not even in the same town, so.

So she stayed.

"And we are suing," she said, wiping her mouth with her napkin.

"Who?"

"Me and my lawyer."

"Suing who?"

"The government, for Geronimo, for setting him up, for maybe killing him, that whole airplane ticket, it's not right."

"Oh," I said as she turned way around to check the clock and we both got up because it was time to go.

Note from the narrator ...

From the assorted musings found by the cleaner, Jake the intern from St. Olaf, in the log book of Crawfish Cabin at Anderson's Resort on Lake June Bug in northern Saint Louis County, in the Minnesota Arrowhead.

July 5, 1968

I hate this year.
Poverty. Riots. Why are some people poor and others aren't.
Why did they kill Bobby Kennedy and Martin Luther King, Jr.
I really don't want to live anymore.
Not here. I want to move.
To Utah or Texas.

Jane Sonnegall
Age 15
Eau Claire, Wisc.

There were no planes on 9/11.
— John Lear

Elias Daviddson: There is no evidence whatsoever that these nineteen people boarded these aircraft.

People of ze wurl, relax!

All depression has its roots in self-pity, and all self-pity is rooted in people taking themselves too seriously.

— Tom Robbins, *Fierce Invalids Home from Hot Climates*

THIRTY-NINE

How about that Prince Hope, huh?

That's the TV talk show host getting his audience to clap one more time for the aging old song and dance man who is hobbling on his way out the door.

That might be how I'd like to see it, but it's not how it is.

Where he just gets old, karma gets him, keeps doing farewell shows, his reality show runs on Duluth/Superior Public Access TV.

"... and that's the news from Bumfuck, Iowa, where all the old fuckers go to die."

Actually, he's probably going strong, hiring more snipers, writing more books, staring down at the sidewalk with that intimidating look that grows more imposing with each passing year, that humiliates the people of Saint Paul because they know they did not study their vocab and grammar as they might have.

I suppose I was hoping what would happen to Prince Hope after my meeting with him. But those rich old tall Minnesotans with talent and connections and a certain cynical establishmentarianism acculturation don't go down quite that easily.

But what we really need to talk about now is Lara and Kaitylyn. I used to refer to them with an & sign, kind of like Mork & Mindy, Williams &

Ree, Cagney & Lacey, but now I think they are moving more toward "and."

"No, no, that's okay, no, that's fine, I'm fine."

Lara is speaking to Kaitylyn as they try to set up an office, try to make it all just like it was, a wonderful life.

Lara had tried to make a joke and it didn't go over.

She made these nameplates for them out of cardboard and black Magic Marker. One said CRUSHER and the other said C.I.A.

"We can do this," said Lara.

Kaitylyn wasn't saying much.

But they sat down, with legal pads, coffee brewing, woodsmoke scented candle that makes that fire noise and shit.

They each wrote "MAYFIELD" across the top of their pads and underlined it.

Okay, good.

"We were going to get Jim out of jail and that Billy guy in Bumfuck, too," said Kaitylyn.

"Ye-es, we're gonna do that, I think," said Lara.

It had turned out that Prince Hope didn't really want to have anything to do with turning the gold into dollars, so Kaitylyn went to a jewelry store and asked. She was advised to take their gold to a gold party which she found online. She did it and cashed in and they were set.

Remember how they had bickered in prison through the toilet about non-violence vs. violence? Lara had come to the point of "kill them all." She'd seen enough. Kaitylyn said maybe they should consider peaceful protest. Maybe she had seen enough as well. I dunno.

Well, I'm not sure how that all was going at this time. I'm not sure they had much time or energy to talk about much else than Kaitylyn being in the C.I.A., being undercover and not really being who she said she was.

So, yeah, after Lara stormed out of her grandmother's basement after discovering The Actually Basement Tapes she went for her jaunt, around Saint Paul, a nice section of Saint Paul and she walked and she walked, trying to understand what she had read. At first she would not believe it, but the Morse Code from Kaitylyn in the front seat to her in the back seat, if that's what it was. She hiked until after dark and all she was when she got back to her grandmother's was tired. She had tramped the angry out of her for a while.

And she had talked to Kaitylyn and they decided to meet in order to plan this new office and all of that. And over eggs and coffee Lara couldn't pull the trigger, couldn't do it. They figured things out, how much money they had, what they needed and they found a place, looked it over and got it.

They were sitting on the bench outside the new office digs and smoking even though they were both going to quit even though they both had smoked as much as they could in prison. Lara rolled Bugler in her lap.

"I'd like to just exist as an anonymous," said Kaitylyn. "I think that's good enough for me. I don't need to be famous."

"I want everyone to know my name," said Lara.

"Oh, really?" said Kaitylyn.

"You remember Trav Dudek?" said Kaitylyn.

Lara looked across the street to think.

"No."

"He looked just like Private Svec," said Kaitylyn. "You've read that right? I always thought of Svec when I saw Dudesky."

"I can't remember him," said Lara. "I didn't work at the center when you did, or did I?"

"Yeah, maybe not," said Kaitylyn.

"So, I got something from that F.B.I. agent in the mail," Lara said, not looking up.

"Oh? Brax …?"

"Braxton, yeah."

Lara handed a rollie to Kaitylyn and started on her own. A bus stopped and went on. People passed behind them. They smelled meat cooking.

"Yeah, and …"

Lara rolled and finished and lit them up with her lighter.

"So, you're a … C.I.A. agent, then, huh?"

Kaitylyn drew on the cigarette and let it out in a cough.

Lara kept talking, telling about the basement tapes and the printout from the C.I.A. website with her photo.

They watched traffic. Three more buses came and went.

Kaitylyn got up and walked away, down the sidewalk, east on Lake, toward Saint Paul.

Somehow they had managed to keep going, move into the new offices. They had already talked about The Battle of Mayfield many times, and had even begun the invasion in a way. They were buying up rental property in a poorer area of Cleveland, Cleveland Heights as a base for their sleeper cells, in order to be in close proximity to Mayfield, Ohio, which they assumed was the obvious location for *The Leave It To Beaver* television show of the 1950s and 1960s.

"Comfortable home to comfortable home fighting, backbiting, sarcasm, innuendo."

It would not be pretty or easy but they were going to do it.

With the success of Roswell and the Braxton memo to the press they had all these fucking recruits and all this fucking money. All that was to be done was to attack Mayfield and defeat America. It would be done.

But Kaitylyn was in the C.I.A., which they didn't talk about. One of those terrible things you have to live with and you know there is no amount of talking that will help, you just have to live it out, second by second.

"We are going to show them they should attack the real people they should attack when they have riots, not burn up their own neighborhoods this time," that was Lara's thinking and Kaitylyn went along.

That's condescending.

So be it.

And so, at this meeting they sat with their legal pads and MAYFIELD etched at the top.

"I have something I need to tell you," said Kaitylyn.

Lara doodled, waiting to hear, and then, this pissed her off so much lately. Kaitylyn would not just get on with it, she always had to be responded to before she continued.

"What!" said Lara.

"Oh, nothing."

"God-dammit."

"This isn't working," said Kaitylyn.

"You think?"

"Okay, okay, I'm not in the C.I.A."

"Yes, you are, you said."

"Okay, I am."

"No, you can't be!"

"I'm not then."

"Yes you are, you shit!"

"Yeah. Shit. I know, right?

"But that's not it."

"Not it what?"

"I shouldn't even tell you."

"Tell me!"

"It's not in Ohio. It's in L.A."

"What?"

"Yeah, I know. I Googled it. I didn't even check before. I miss Actually."

They spent some time going over what Kaitylyn had found about the filming of the *Leave It To Beaver Show* and found it was not made in Ohio at all, but actually produced in California on a Hollywood set.

"What should we do?" said Kaitylyn.

"Attack. Full force, right where we are. It's still Mayfield," said Lara. "We'll explain it all. We can make it make sense. What the fuck? We're all gonna die anyway maybe not you."

"What about reality vs. fake. I thought we were against fake, and yeah, that would be good for us, we're kinda good at that," said Kaitylyn.

"What do you mean?"

"I mean that when you attack by 'full force' that's what the military and police are good at. You literally cannot win, we can't.

"Tell people the truth. Just do that," said Kaitylyn.

"Oh, yeah, you'd like that," said Lara. "You are such a conspiracy theorist. I'm sick of that shit."

"I'm saying that as a friend," said Kaitylyn.

"What about before, Mayberry, all that?" said Lara. "What the fuck? What the fuck happened? The group home, the training, the books, that was all just a job you were doing? God!"

"That was before. That's all. That's all I can say," said Kaitylyn.

"We will attack," said Lara.

"I might be there, on the other side, I don't know, how that will all work," said Kaitylyn, looking down.

"Kill them all," says Lara.

"It just won't work. Who are we kidding?" said Kaitylyn.

Kaitylyn touched Lara's hand gently, pushed back her chair and padded softly out of the room, closed the office door on her way out.

Lara listened hard to hear her footsteps in the hall and really couldn't hear much.

She was gone.

Note from the narrator ...

From the assorted musings found by the cleaner, Jake the intern from St. Olaf, in the log book of Crawfish Cabin at Anderson's Resort on Lake June Bug in northern Saint Louis County, in the Minnesota Arrowhead.

Aug. 2, 1968

I can't tell anyone this, but I know about the Berrigans. PRIESTS. They burned draft papers in Maryland. PRIESTS!
I'm saying it here.

So many bugs, not just June bugs, every kind of bug. I caught three walleyes. We ate them tonight. So good. With potatoes.

Casey Thompson
Roanoke, Virginia

"The world is watching now what Trump says and listening very carefully. If he doesn't have confidence in the US intelligence community, what signal does that send to our partners and allies as well as our adversaries?" Brennan said.

Signal? Mr. Brennan, the signal was sent to our partners, allies, and adversaries decades ago: The C.I.A. is a criminal agency.

Is that clear enough?

Long ago, the C.I.A. criminally stepped outside its mandate, in order to shape world events it had no business participating in.

Is that clear enough?

In that regard, do these names and phrases mean anything to you, Mr. Brennan?

* The Gehlen Org. Operation Gladio. MKULTRA. Operation CHAOS. Nugan Hand Bank. BCCI Bank. Golden Triangle. Asian heroin. Air America. Central American cocaine. Mena. The Contras. Henry Luce. William Paley. Arthur Sulzberger. Operation Mockingbird. Overthrow of Mohammed Mossadegh (Iran). Overthrow of Jacobo Arbenz (Guatemala). Murder of Patrice Lumumba (Congo). Bay of Pigs. JFK. Diem assassination. Rafael Trujillo assassination. Sukarno. Suharto. East Timor genocide. Military coup, Greece. Allende. Gulf of Tonkin. Operation Phoenix. Laos bombing. Sihanouk. The Khmer Rouge. El Salvador death squads.

On and on it goes... Overthrow, assassination, regime change, mind control, covert war, mass destruction, drugs, financial theft, co-opting the press... Do you recall any of this, Mr. Brennan?

Trump is sending a negative signal about the US intelligence community to our friends, allies, and adversaries? Are you kidding, Mr. Brennan? Are you telling some kind of inside joke?

People all over the world have known, for decades, what the C.I.A. has been doing. And you're worried about the effect of a little tweak from Trump? The murderous history of the C.I.A. has been a cat out of the bag for a long, long time.

Professional amnesia may be your friend, Mr. Brennan, but it doesn't convince the victims and targets of your agency's actions since 1948.

— Jon Rappaport

FORTY

Billy Blackbird, in the mental hospital in the countryside somewhere in Iowa, well he kept looking out the window, writing to relatives, lying to them that he was back home, not wanting to tell them the truth.

Suddenly he thought, I got to get out of here.

He began to feel a panic, maybe the kind of rush of adrenaline that comes when you are on the bottom of a dog pile after your team has won the championship and you think, I am going to die here and nobody will know it.

One day when he was let out to walk around in the dayroom he decided to try the doors. The first one was open and so was the second, as well as the third and the fourth.

Only one door stood between he and heaven.

Billy hesitated with his hand on the knob. If it was locked he could not stand it. If it was not open and he could not walk out into the sun and the corn and the mud he would go crazy. If he didn't try the door it might mean that the door was really open but he just chose not to go, or it meant that it might be open, which was also good enough to convince his mind to live here inside this building, forever? He could say to his mind that he could go out whenever he wanted, but he just never would and he would die here and be taken out on a stretcher into the sun and heaven and down into the earth and that would have been his life and …

He twisted the old gold knob, tarnished like his grandmother's soup ladle, and shined from many hands. Would he join them now outside, or back up inside this three-or four-story hell house.

It rattlely clicked.

He pushed and it did not budge.

He pulled and squinted against the light. He stared out at the corn and the mud and the sun, leaning to see the better, feeling perhaps he had opened the door onto the moon, it felt so strange after having been inside the building for so long.

Something pushed him out, a hand on a shoulder. That is what he said he felt. Maybe a prisoner who died without ever having gone out? Maybe nothing. Maybe his metaphor for making himself go. Some things we will never know.

Billy for sure wanted to see the battlefield, where he had watched it from his window.

He walked across the lumpy lawn toward the open field that ran downhill between a cornfield and the road.

He found where Lara had told her troops they were going to live by surrendering, had lied to them that there were snipers on the roof of the hospital, because why? Maybe there were police, maybe someone shot from that area.

I don't know. Maybe she didn't want the story to end there, save the damsel in the tower and then what? There are not books called *Then What?* Because nobody knows.

He walked to the farm yard and the exploded house. There were lots of boards and sheets of plywood and shingles, a whole house deconstructed and laid about. He'd heard about the long tunnel but the wreckage had blocked it. He walked into the woods and found Kaitylyn's foxhole with her mirror pressed into the side wall. And a skull, Rick's head, with much of the hair, the teeth. Billy touched it with his toe, that's all.

There were also the paper mache Lion's heads but they didn't look like much now. He found the old Civil War cemetery where the CRUSHER skeletons lay atop the ground.

He found the exploded CRUSHER vehicle, Rick's command post, two, maybe three cow skeletons and a crashed helicopter where it looked like someone had been trying to salvage parts and some government stickers and tags that said don't do that.

He saw the mental hospital on the hill in the distance and nobody coming down the long lane road, so he just decided to keep going.

He would go, keep walking and where he came to that is where he would be, just like a young man escaping his home town, which Billy had never really done except for the weekend in the capital for the state basketball tournament, all the beer and staying in the college dorm. He had learned so much that weekend about life that when he got home that for a while he felt superior. That feeling did not last. And now he would "find America" and gain his rightly place in general lore.

For a mile, two miles he walked down a gravel road that became a dirt road that turned into a one lane road, which became a path. He found that in parts of Iowa there are woods and rolly hills.

Billy stopped at the top of a hill, judging if he can even keep going, if his search for America had come to an end because the path down the hill, well, he could slip and fall and break his leg and then what good would that do America?

He spied down and walked a bit to the side to find another way and saw through the trees, at the bottom, a bowl, a valley, very nice, hidden, with a little pond, like a park where nobody could go.

And down at the bottom was a round something, pretty big, grey and there were people walking around the round thing. Billy sat down in the weeds and the trees to watch for a while, except for one thing, he was getting hungry.

They were small people with big heads like The Callwell Boys and they seemed upset.

Billy plowed his way down through the brush and trees, sliding on his butt, stumbling, swearing, finally falling onto the ground in front of the grey round thing. The little guys were not around that he could see.

Pushing himself to stand, Billy approached the round grey thing that just kind of sat on its bottom with no legs. He walked around and around and could see inside the windows the little guys looking nervous and pacing and looking out at him. He found something on the ground, a rod, a piece to something maybe. It looked heavy but was light. He carried it at his side as he walked around.

He had not ever really been to this part of Iowa before so maybe this is the way things are here, he thought, but he could not remember these things back home.

Maybe this is a Hawkeye. Maybe the little big head guys are Hawkeyes.

He sat and leaned back on his hands outside one of the windows. The thing he had picked up sat next to him. He waved at the guys and the wave sent them into paroxysms of hand wringing it seemed.

Suddenly they were in front of him, three of the little guys with the big heads, The Callwell Boys, but they weren't. It was clear to Billy that these were space aliens now, with all the eyes and ears and mouths and hands you hear about.

And the feet. They wore space shoes, nothing else, no clothes, but shoes they had to have, that was weird, he thought. And big. My god. He tried not to stare.

One of them pointed at the thing by Billy's side that he had found. They wanted it. He handed it up to the guy and stood. They made him feel tall.

They were happy now they had their thing. They went inside, maybe they inserted the rod thing, but in any case now their spacecraft hummed and the lights worked.

Nice.

Billy felt good that he was able to do something for The Callwell Boys as he was now calling them in his head and it seems the aliens heard what Billy was calling them in his head because they said they were not The Callwell Boys, they were Fuck, Motherfucker, Shit-fuck, Fuck-Shit and Goddamn It Fuck, and there were others inside the craft as well, but he would not see them and trust them he did not want to.

Those are strange names, said Billy, in his head and also out loud, covering his bases, he figured.

The names were taken from having hovered over an Iowa house and listening in to what was being said and what the beings inside called each other. They liked the names and took them, because, let's just say, the other ones were not needing them anymore.

Fuck, Motherfucker, Shit-fuck, Fuck-Shit and Goddamn It Fuck said they were looking for a horse named Roswell that had just been an egg long ago and it was about time for that egg horse to be a real horse. They showed Billy some T-shirts they put on just for Billy: My Great-

Gramperdoodle Crash-Landed Here And All I Got Was This Lousy Shirt.

Nice.

"Where's Rachel?" asked Motherfucker.

"I dunno," said Billy.

They asked Billy if he wanted to go for a ride.

And he said, fuck yes, to which they explained that no, that was not their names. They were … and then they said their names, but that miscommunication didn't last long and did not get in the way of Billy taking a ride. He went all over Iowa and the whole United States and world and into space. Oh, my God, so many stars. And even Shit-Fuck and Goddamn It Fuck said oh my god, because it was just that fucking cool. They saw the moon and other space craft and all the stuff you have heard about but are not supposed to believe.

"We're making good time," Motherfucker said to Shit-Fuck and Shit-Fuck nodded.

And then Billy was again standing on the ground outside the spacecraft. It went up a little and he waved at Fuck, Motherfucker, Shit-fuck, Fuck-Shit and Goddamn It Fuck, they went up a little more, like a step and then in a bleep they rose to tree height, turned into an orange ball and were gone through a month or a year.

And the next thing Billy knew he was back in his bed in the mental hospital. He awoke for a moment and felt cozy with his coarse grey blanket and curled his knees to his chest and he smiled.

… At least that's the story I've gotten from unnamed sources. Some say that the aliens took Billy back to the hospital. That they are metaphors for the hospital staff, that Billy never left, that he should have kept that piece of the spacecraft, it would be worth money some day, that they took him to their own planet Lunatic, but all I know is that Billy wrote later to someone that the view from his window wasn't the worst in the world.

[And that doesn't tell us much, but sometimes we don't get the whole story. I am just sayin'.]

What If They Get Caught in Their Lies?

You may say "These hoax theories can't be correct as the persons
retailing them would be too afraid of being outed as liars."
Apparently that's not a problem. During Jahar's trial no one looked
ashamed at saying he was holding a black backpack when everyone
could see it was white.
Remember the fable of the Emperor's New Clothes?
It is enough that your neighbors all say they see something.
It makes you worry that you'd be called a mental case if you differ.
I even think the black white issue may have been built into the Jahar
scam in order for its egregiousness to be exemplary, and to frustrate
those who do see it's white.
This is so important to understand in Boston, too.
We grew up to think solutions could be found by tapping the
institutions: church, Congress, the prestigious press, but those
institutions are now filled with yes men. So is Academia, which is
pretty hilarious: Socratic yes men.

But let me walk you through my hypothesis by asking:
"What is needed for a bombing?"

A government would need:
-A team of experts in production and usage of bombs
-A story, believable to the public, of how a foreign group,
or ideologically motivated individuals, did it
-A set of media reporters to announce, some aspects of the event,
initially leaving a few questions unanswered
-A very compliant police administration to support "the story"
about the way the bombings were accomplished
-A national government agency that could see to it that
anyone arrested would be taken to the right place
-A collection of evidence against the arrestees, such as
receipts proving that they had purchased weapons material,
phone records showing that they conspired with others,
pals to declare that they had discussed their motives,
and videos of them attending the crime scene
-A control of all courts such that no judge would speak out, or allow
witness testimony to uncover the truth

— Mary Maxwell

FORTY-ONE

"You know, when you work in a group home you don't get paid much, you don't get benefits, you work evenings, nights, overnights, weekends, holidays, and you are also under a lot of fuckin' pressure. You have to give out meds and do it right. You have to be nice to people who might not be so nice. You have to wipe butts maybe, you might have to work with people who can't get out of bed and that's a killer on your back. You have to take them out to shop and out to eat and they can do things that could be embarrassing. There's a lot of shit, man. But it can also be a lot of fun."

When I got a chance to talk to Korey he told me that as a way I think of trying to give further motivation for why the CRUSHER group home workers might want to rebel and fight back. Also, he said, the owners of the group homes make a ton of money. They talk about all being in it together for the good of the people, but they don't exactly pass it down to the workers, who might have young kids or a shitty car, probably, work multiple jobs. They are not usually people who have much of a chance in life. They take the group home job because it's there.

So, anyway, Korey, Washington, Henry and Patrick, they got arrested by Trevor, Alexa and Marv at The Stone Arch Bridge, and taken to the grey concrete block room with which Korey was familiar.

"Don't torture us," Korey suggested.

203

"Just tell us what you want to know right off the bat."

So they put The Four around the table in the middle of the room, each with a yellow legal pad and pen.

"Tell us who are the biggest dipshit terrorists you know," said Trevor.

"What?" said Korey.

"Just fucking do it," said Trevor.

Korey began to doodle, draw and write.

Alexa watched over his shoulder as he drew a face and "I Love Big Brother."

Marv and Trevor now watched over the other shoulders as Alexa moved over to Washington.

On Henry's paper it said: Korey, Washington, Patrick.

On Washington's paper it said: Korey, Henry, Patrick.

On Patrick's paper it read: Korey, Henry, Washington.

"Perfect," said Trevor. "You guys are awesome."

After three days of torture on the wire running across the room The Four were let out of the grey room and the building.

They went where they were supposed to go, a yellow school bus outside a red brick elementary.

They opened the hood, crawled up on the bumper and all leaned in over the engine and took out all the shit they had tied around their waists under their coats.

The children came up, laughing, with their teacher, all happy to be going on a special trip for the day.

The special trip bus driver lumbered up, said hello to The Five standing there with the hood now down and everything looking like normal. The bus fired up, the gunshots rang out, the police cars rammed over the curbs along with the news media vans as The Four dodged the bullets and climbed the fence and ran down into the concrete river ravine and got away.

Note from the narrator ...

From the assorted musings found by the cleaner, Jake the intern from St. Olaf, in the log book of Crawfish Cabin at Anderson's Resort on Lake June Bug in northern Saint Louis County, in the Minnesota Arrowhead.

September 3, 1969

Did you see the Apollo Press Conference?
They look scared, not excited.

We heard a loon all day and even at night when we sat around the fire.

I love this place. I never want to leave.
Or I'm coming back always.

The moon is so big tonight, and the stars.
Love it.

Bryce Daniel
Mankato

The dramaturgists of 9/11 must have envisaged that the events, played out real time on television, would serve to unite the American people and rally the population behind the flag. This turned out to be the case.

— Dr. Ludwig Watzal

FORTY-TWO

"We still doing the Beagle T-shirts?"

Evey sat with Lara in a Caribou on Sixth Street.

"Yep, same band, different tour. That's always been the plan, you heard anything to the contrary?"

"Nope."

They had legal pads with "Battle of Mayfield" on top and underlined. Evey had Kaitylyn's old pad.

"We've got to find Mapleton Drive and/or Pine Street," said Lara.

"You know how many there are? In Ohio?"

Evey shook her head.

"A ton," said Lara.

Evey read from her computer screen: "Leave It To Beaver" *was filmed at Republic Studios in Studio City, Los Angeles, and the final four seasons at Universal Studios. The exteriors were filmed on studio back lots.*

"Blah, blah, blah," said Evey.

"Why am I just now learning this?" said Lara.

"It's *on* Wikipedia," said Evey.

"Oh ... my ... God," said Lara, smooshing the end of her pen into her yellow paper pad and watching a bike rider go by the window in the sun.

"What are we gonna do?"

She wrote for a while and Evey tried to interest Rachel in a Berenstain Bear book. She sat by the aisle, hemming Rachel against the wall.

"We've got our cells in place with the housing buyout. We are looking for Mapleton Drive and Pine Street in certain cities in Ohio and NONE of them have the right house number. Kill them all anyway. They're all guilty."

"Is that really what you want to do?" said Evey, tearing up Rachel's croissant with her hands.

"It's Hollywood, actually. That's who is responsible."

Lara stared out the window, seeing it all and also nothing, thought Evey, just in passing, thought in, thought gone as she felt delighted that Rachel was passing her fingers over the words in the book.

"You're right. That's where we should have gone first."

"Live and learn," said Evey, stuffing her bit of croissant into her cheek with her tongue to speak.

And then she had a thought, but should she go ahead and say it, things would get complicated, whatever.

"Or, Oz," she said.

"Oz?"

"Yes ..."

And so Evey asked Lara what she thought about maybe attacking Kansas, Oz, and linking it back to the whole reality vs. fiction meme they were trying to get going.

"I think it's a stretch," said Lara, going back to her writing on her pad.

They sat for a while more, they had time, after this both had nowhere to be or to go.

"Which do you think?" said Evey finally.

"Which what?"

"Hollywood, Oz, Kansas."

"I thought we decided that," said Lara.

Evey read from Wikipedia:

"Lee Sandlin, writes that L. Frank Baum read a disaster report of a tornado in Irving, Kansas, in May 1879 which included the name of a victim, Dorothy Gale, who was *found buried face down in a mud puddle.*"

"Yeah? So?"

"Irving, Kansas," said Evey.

"That's where the revolution continues. The truth is out there."

"Why?" said Lara.

"Why?

"Because why, because we're gonna look behind the curtain and see what's there. If you don't attack Kansas you can't get that story, that idea into the newspapers."

"We can't anyhow."

"Maybe, maybe not, but we're all gonna die anyway, right?" said Evey.

"Hmmm."

Lara actually hmmmed out loud it seems.

"How about, 'it seems we're not in Kansas, anymore,'" she said.

"What about that? We're not in Kansas anymore. Oz was not *in* Kansas, dude."

"Listen to it, *it seems*. It seeeeems," said Evey.

"It seems. Fiction versus reality. It can work."

"It's a stretch," said Lara.

"It can work," said Evey.

"There's no place like home," said Lara.

"Yeah, right" said Evey.

"There's so much there, courage, heart, all that shit. The problem will be keeping it simple. You can't get too complicated, people won't get it, and then you're just bombing Kansas, you die in prison and you did nothing."

She put her hands over Rachel's ears as she spoke. Rachel waved her arms and got Evey's hands off her head.

Evey gave Rachel a gold piece to play with.

"What the fuck?" said Lara.

"We've got lots," said Evey, "if she loses one, not a big deal."

"Yeah, but, in public?"

"So," said Lara.

"What do we do?"

"Hollywood," said Evey, "but Oz first, it's on the way."

Lara scratched out MAYFIELD and wrote underneath it: OZ as Evey scooped up Rachel and headed to the bathroom.

Note from the narrator ...

> From "Not Exactly A Radio Show," a live podcast that traveled the circuit of Twins Cities bars for about six months, produced by former members of The Prince Hope Show:

Now a shout-out to the U.S. Department of Homeland Security. See Something Say Something. What more inspiring words have ever been written. See Something Say Something ... think of Tom Paine, Ralph Waldo Emerson, Mark Twain. ... We at "Not Exactly a Radio Show" want to do our part in protecting the Homeland.

We realize the folks frisking chunky people coming into hockey games and Nascar races and those brave men and women on the frontlines of the airport scanner Maginot Line need our support.

So ... we are initiating program Neighborhood Watch.

We know that the FBI and CIA and local police are usually the ones bringing drugs into the USA from Central America. And we know that the FBI and CIA killed John F. Kennedy and Robert Kennedy.

So ... we know that it is the FBI and CIA and local police who we have to look out for.

So if you see these personalized government license plates in your neighborhood, call someone. If you see something, say something. Call a Wal-Mart department manager or maybe that one guy who checks ID's at the Eagles on Fridays.

Here are just a few license plates to watch out for, more as they come in to us:

WeBrndWCO
WiiDidOKC
WiiDid9/11

Note from the narrator ...

From the assorted musings found by the cleaner, Jake the intern from St. Olaf, in the log book of Crawfish Cabin at Anderson's Resort on Lake June Bug in northern Saint Louis County, in the Minnesota Arrowhead.

July 27, 1973

We danced disco around the firepit.

We caught two northerns and one walleye and one perch.

There are monkeys in the forest. I don't know why, maybe they escaped, but I heard them all night last night.

One of the members of the Torres Family

… Patriots Day the movie.
Mark Walhlberg, the director, anybody associated with the movie should be tried for treason.
This is Stalin stuff, Goebbels.
The real patriots are the ones who see through these lies. Think about it, please. They are calling these people patriots who lie, perpetuate the lie. … Nobody died in the fake bombing, but people have died, Tamerlan Tsarnaev. Ibrahim Todashev. … And Dzokhar Tsarnaev has had to endure the most mind-blowing experience anybody could ever have to go through and meanwhile is doing life in one of America's famous supermax torture chambers.

— Fucking Anonymous, *from the comments section*

FORTY-THREE

The Four, Korey, Washington, Patrick, Henry, on the run after failing to fulfill their mission and blow up a school bus with children inside, were on the run on the streets of Minneapolis, and for part of one afternoon, mid-town Anoka, which in itself is a whole story right there.

They checked the kiosk because Korey wanted to see if the standings had switched on the F.B.I. Ten Most Wanted list.

"Look man," he said.

He pointed and showed them where he had gone up, way up. Lara wasn't even on it anymore, so Korey had moved up a spot.

They went to Washington's old C-store, robbed the new counter guy, Jefferson, of Gooey rolls and squirt guns, filled the guns in the back alley, and went out hunting for the C.I.A. for a while.

They went back to the C-store and Jefferson asked if he could join them, and he could, so they were now The Five, in search of The C.I.A. They brought along all the cigarettes they could carry.

After awhile they got tired of the search and went to The Stone Arch Bridge to rest.

They sat on the stone top, their backs to the long drop and the water with which Korey was familiar. Their weapons perched on the sidewalk, leaning against the bridge.

"Trust me. This is the spot."

"We were down there, man," said Patrick.

They heard a buzz coming from a long ways off.

"Dude, man, where'd you get that tattoo?" said Jefferson, pointing to Korey's orange CRUSHER on his forearm.

"Oh, this?" said Korey.

"Yeah, man."

The robin's egg blue e-Car swerved across traffic, right on the sidewalk.

"Don't jump, Jefferson," said Korey, the air whistling through his missing tooth.

Alexa, Trevor and Marv leaped out, guns drawn and already pointed. "Do not jump! Do not fucking jump!"

After three days of torture on the wire running across the room The Five were let out of the grey room and the building.

They went where they were supposed to go, a yellow school bus outside a red brick elementary.

They opened the hood, crawled up on the bumper and all leaned in over the engine and took out all the shit they had tied around their waists under their coats.

The children came up, laughing, with their teacher, all happy to be going on a special trip for the day.

The special trip bus driver lumbered up, said blah, blah, blah, to The Four standing there with the hood now down and everything looking like normal.

The bus fired up, the gunshots rang out, the police cars rammed over the curbs along with the news media vans as The Five dodged the bullets and dashed across the street, dodging cars and screeching tires and ran into the mall and out the back door and got away.

Note from the narrator ...

From the assorted musings found by the cleaner, Jake the intern from St. Olaf, in the log book of Crawfish Cabin at Anderson's Resort on Lake June Bug in northern Saint Louis County, in the Minnesota Arrowhead.

August 1975

Where else can you write something like this?

At least some day someone might see it.

All those witnesses of the Kennedy murder, killed. Have you heard about it? And it's been how long and we still don't know what happened?

Dorothy Kilgallen, we watched her on TV, that's one of them.

Father listens to Mae Brussells on the little radio here late into the night, even here, at the wooden kitchen table. I think he loves listening to that program especially here.

Our brother died. And our car broke down on the highway. And we came here anyway this summer. He loved coming here. I put some dirt from his grave in the woods here. Did not tell anybody now I did, nobody will read this though.

Susan Nester
Spirit Lake, Iowa

And [he] sailed back over a year
and in and out of weeks
and through a day
and into the night of his very own room
where he found his supper waiting for him
and it was still hot.

— Maurice Sendak, *Where the Wild Things Are*

FORTY-FOUR

Jim sat in the recreation yard inside the prison. The rec yard is actually a rectangle inside the prison walls where a prisoner can walk around and around or back and forth. If the prisoner looks straight up he can see the sky. A big thing has been built inside the rectangle so the prisoner must now do his walking around the big thing.

Jim has sat down in a corner to rest, his head on his knees. That is where Kaitylyn and Lara saw him as they were being taken for release.

Jim felt the three enter the yard, the three guards where before one had been enough it seems.

With his head on his knees Jim is thinking that Korey and Lara and Kaitylyn are still in prison, and he really should wait for them longer, but he's got to start trying to escape, so he will try the window, he will try digging, he will try to hide in a laundry basket.

He will try jumping through the bars as the laundry wagon rattles past, dissaparating with meditation. He will try to make floo powder and use floo powder. He will try it all. Something has got to work. And what else has he got to do? He smiles as he lifts his head from his knees and turns his head toward the guards.

The appearance of the guards meant that his rec time was over, so he put a hand on the dusty concrete and one hand on the wall to stand. He walked, slowly toward them and the door. They wondering what sort of tricky prisoner thing he had in mind to kill them all.

He trying not to think of anything lest they read his mind with whatever devices were looking down on him from high on the walls. On the way he saw something shiny, two things. Both shiny.

He reached down to pick them up, wads of shiny wrapping for gum. On his way past the first guard in line he held up his hand. The guard held out his palm and Jim dropped the shiny gum wrapping into the fat guard hand.

That afternoon Jim heard keys clanking and did not know what to think because this was the wrong time. He tried to return to his dream in which he was not in prison, but the jangling grew louder.

It stopped at his door and then came the clunking, the clunking of the key inside the lock and then came the yank-clank, the yank-clank that always came with the opening of the door and then the "inmate report to the door," and he did and the guard told him to get his gear, and he had no gear and so he just stood there and the guard nodded like you might to an intelligent calf to come get out of the pen, and the calf won't go because nothing good ever comes from this.

But Jim really had no choice. He stepped into the shined hall.

The one guard, usually there were two or three, led him, did not follow him, actually led him down the hall where they passed the guard shack where Jim saw the shiny gum wrappers on the messy guard desk when they passed into a larger, wider, even shinier hallway, then down the narrow one-lane hallway that overlooked the rec yard.

The one guard went through more doors and hallways and Jim was thinking he was going to be moved to another part of the prison, which is something they do just to make you get used to something new all over again, and then they do that again and again. And after awhile you realize, they are fucking with me, but it doesn't matter. Oh, it matters to you, not to anyone else.

The guard stopped at a grey metal door and Jim heard cars on the other side of the door, honking, revving.

He heard talking and now he thought he was being taken to clean the guard movie theater, the legend that prisoners repeated, that's the thought that he had for that split-instant until the guard unlocked the door and opened it, put a hand on Jim's shoulder and pushed him out, into the sun.

Jim stepped backwards to the curb and looked straight up at the big grey wall and though the sun was in his eyes he saw some sort of advertising sign way up there. He shielded his eyes with his arm and just then a car honked loud and he leaped away from the street.

He walked all morning and dragged himself up a hill in downtown Saint Paul, across a very wide street with almost no traffic, on the other side of the street from The Lonely Lutheran Book Store & Lunch Club.

Jim sat down on the bus bench with the advertising that looked a little like the sign way up high on the prison wall.

Oh, man, it felt good to sit. The wood hurt his boney butt. He tried different positions, put his arm back and his head back to feel the sun, closed his eyes, opened his eyes.

Saw Prince Hope in the second or third story office window looking at him.

He flipped Hope the bird, now double bird.

Hope fired back with bird … bird-bird … bird-bird, bird … bird.

Hope's head disappeared from the window.

Jim concentrated hard on relaxing. He sucked his lips. He had begun to suck his lips when he was worried about something, he had recently noticed and he did not like it.

He squinted into the sun and saw a big, goofy figure gangling toward him, across the sparse traffic of the mile-wide street from the direction of The Lonely Lutheran with the silhouette sign of the man fishing alone in a rowboat, his head down as if working on his line, maybe asleep.

Prince Hope's flip-flops flip-flopped as he tried to run. He ran like a giraffe drinks from a pond. He wore all sorts of holiday, Hawaii, weird-shit clothes, shorts, button shirt, weird floppy hat and Jim thought someone would probably shoot him before he made it across because that was how fucking stupid he looked.

Prince Hope sat right down on Jim's bench, all long, white, old skinny legs and shit and few days beard. He held in his lap a book and explained as briefly as he could though some detail was necessary to get across the idea that it was his new book, "They Who LIVE In Hiding," with an original drawing of a Bigfoot wearing a CRUSHER T-shirt having coffee in Dunn Bros.

"Nice," said Jim, looking at the book and then away.

"Listen, about the sniper," said Hope.

"Forget it, man."

"No, I need to …"

"Fuckin' forget it."

"Well, will you let me do something," said Hope, "to make up for it?"

Jim thought about food, cigarettes, shower, clothes, sleep.

"How about if I read to you something from my new book?" said Hope as he began to find his spot.

People passing behind them noticed, a little, and some people driving past looked, a little. The people sitting in the window booths of The Double L did not notice at all. A bus wheezed to a stop, one long asthma attack, and then left and when it was gone Hope was still reading in that deep voice that had made him famous, everywhere.

Hope stopped, closed the book on his lap, closed his eyes, breathed deep and just sat, like a minister after his homily, to let Jim take it all in.

"So," said Hope.

"What do you think?"

"Yeah," said Jim.

"I don't really …"

"So, I heard you got out," said Hope.

"I'm right here."

"What are you going to do?"

"Not that much," said Jim.

Hope explained that he had been laying low lately, mostly concerned with getting out this new book. He had some more farewell shows planned and perhaps a full farewell tour and opening a new farewell season.

"Yeah," said Jim, "I could really give a fuck, man, just sayin'.

"I needa git Lara, Kaitylyn and I think Korey, too, outa prison. That's what I'm fucking worried about, ya know?"

"Yes," said Hope.

"They're out though, out of prison. They've been out for a while now. They wanted to get you out, but I guess they got busy. Say, are you people ever going to actually rescue that poor man from the mental hospital in Bumfuck?"

"I don't know, yeah," said Jim.

"Yeah, I'll …"

"Good," said Hope, "now, if you are interested …"

Hope explained that if Jim was interested he could buy him lunch at the Double L, get him some new clothes, whatever he needed, a new phone maybe? And then he'd be in touch with everyone again.

"First, let me read one more passage," said Hope.

"I think you'll find it interesting ... and important."

This crash was different.
There was no wreckage, no bodies, and no noise.
— Somerset County Coroner Wallace Miller

I was looking for anything that said tail, wing, plane, metal.
There was nothing.
— Photographer Scott Spangler

I was amazed because it did not, in any way, shape, or form,
look like a plane crash.
*— Patrick Madigan, commander of the Somerset barracks of the
Pennsylvania State Police,* regarding the crash at Shanksville

Soy un perdedor
I'm a loser baby, so why don't you kill me?
— Beck

Those are people who died, died
They were all my friends, and they died
— Jim Carroll

FORTY-FIVE

So, yeah, I don't know why The Five kept at it like they did, going through the whole ordeal of the torture and then the bombing and getting away and getting caught. I guess we must remember what they said themselves, they felt they were fighting the good fight. How often do you get to do that? And they were fucking with them. Fucking with the C.I.A. How often are you going to get to do that?

The law of pre-cognition karma, pre-programming, passport, manifesto, drill scenario, psycotronics: Those words just now came into my head and I wrote them down. It's kind of like this. When I write sometimes I just get ideas, words, phrases, that to me seem unique and universal at the same time and I write them down and then try to connect them in my story. It is weird. Right?

Well, the Five, Korey, Washington, Patrick, Henry, Jefferson, after once again failing to fulfill their mission and blow up a school bus with children inside, were on the run on the streets of Minneapolis.

They went back to Jefferson and Washington's old C-store, robbed the new counter guy, just matches, and so they were now smoking however fucking many cigarettes they fucking wanted, in search of The C.I.A. Which is nice.

They checked out the F.B.I. Ten Most Wanted List and found that Kaitylyn had dropped from the list. She was not most wanted anymore, and Hector and Reuben were also not on the list.

Evangelina Martinez was now F.B.I. Most Wanted The Most, a guy who was a member of The Bandidos and also a member of The Satans of Swing Elderly Motorcycle Gang was now Second Most Wanted and Korey had moved into a tie with the former mayor of Richfield.

After awhile they got tired of the search and went to The Stone Arch Bridge to rest.

They sat on the stone top, their backs to the long drop and the water that Korey was so familiar with. Their weapons sat on the sidewalk, leaning against the bridge.

"Trust me. This is the spot."

"We were down there, man," said Patrick.

They heard a buzz coming from a long ways off.

"Dude, man, where'd you get that tattoo?" said Jefferson, pointing to Korey's orange CRUSHER on his forearm.

"Oh, this?" said Korey.

"Yeah, man."

"You asked me that before."

"I know, man, you never answered."

The robin's egg blue e-Car swerved across traffic, right on the sidewalk.

"Jump, Jefferson," said Korey, the air whistling through his missing tooth.

Alexa, Trevor and Marv leaped out, guns drawn and already pointed at the jumping men.

"Do not jump! Do not fucking jump!"

The five went down straight as elevators, hands against their sides, feet first, bullets whizzing around. They hit the water, hard. You wouldn't think so, it's water, but it's fucking hard and it's a long jump, go check yourself.

So you go down a long way, dazed and confused and as they had planned, they swam in different directions to very specific different spots on shore where each would disembark the water and begin totally different lives and never see each other again.

And so they swam and they swam, dying for air, imagining all sorts of mean and nasty, ugly things above them and kept going, reaching, kicking, just dying down there.

Patrick's head burst out of the water, gasping, reaching, diving for the shore, sucking in air.

He lay there on his back, listening as Henry's head erupted out of the river, and then Washington, Jefferson, and finally Korey, all within twenty yards of each other.

Not having anything better to do, they decided to go rob the C-store and check the kiosk.

Korey ran his finger down the list and saw he was now No. 2. He high-fived all around and read the new fine print that said he and Evangelina were believed to be en route to Mayfield, Ohio and that residents of Ohio were to be on the lookout.

"It says you are dangerous," said Patrick.

"They must have seen you try to piss into a squirt gun, man," said Henry.

Korey wasn't laughing. He was thinking of how he was supposed to be on his way to Ohio and that he wanted to be a good outlaw and so he announced he was headed to Mayfield.

"Who's with me!"

He raised a fist into the air.

A little out of place
A little out of tune
Sorta lost in space
Racing the moon
Climbing the walls
Of this hurricane
Still overall, I can't complain

All I wanted was one chance
To let freedom ring
They said I had to get a permit
Tags and everything
I never made it through the red tape
I got this paper hat
I got a job working weekdays
You want fries with that?

— Todd Snider

FORTY-SIX

The Battle of Oz.
Is "actually" The Battle of Irving, Kansas.
Evey wrote that on her yellow legal pad under the heading The Battle of Oz, underneath the scratched-out heading The Battle of Mayfield.
Under that she wrote HOLLYWOOD, with a half-moon line for a hillside.
And under that she wrote nothing at all because she was busy chasing Rachel around the new WAR HQ as Lara called it.
Evey had found something on Wikipedia that she didn't want to show Lara.
"Irving was a town in Marshall County ..."
WAS.
It's a fucking ghost town she said out loud to herself and Rachel repeated, "fucking ghost town."
She read more and surmised it had been founded by a group of farmers from Iowa trying to escape the dust storms and the whole Grapes of Wrath thing. There were grasshoppers and draught and tornadoes, and then a flood, and it was still considered "as being located in one of the best settled and best cultivated portions of Marshall County," so that tells you what the rest of Kansas was like.

Then the people of Iowa went back home, perhaps and maybe some went on to California.

Well, some things don't change, thought Evey.

Irving the ghost town is in the northeast quadrant of Kansas.

"I'll bet the United States government is going to fight like hell to not lose Irving," Evey said out loud.

"Like hell," said Rachel.

The new WAR HQ was a used orange SUV in the same mode as the one blown up in Bumfuck.

They were in the Walmart parking lot, one of a thousand and more other vehicles, none orange.

They were on their way to Irving as were sixteen new recruits as well as Brooke and The Special Team, who had stopped in Ohio, looked for Mayfield and texted Lara "WTF!"

Lara, inside the store looking for the camo jeans damn aisle, sent a text to Prince Hope, one of ten that had not been returned.

Back at the WAR HQ Lara climbed into the driver's seat, her arms filled with stuff.

"They had specials," she said.

Lara: I got some good news and some bad news.

Evey: K, hit me …

"Well, we've got plenty of, oh, what did I buy?"

"What's the good news?"

"The bad news is, well, we're almost there and we have to go to war. I was kinda likin' this girls road trip."

"Yeah, me, too," said Evey.

"Me too!" said Rachel.

And then, as she had a dozen times by now, Rachel began to cry, big tears falling down her cheeks.

"She misses gramma, uncle Reuben, uncle Hector," said Evey.

"Aaah, baby," said Lara, taking Rachel into her arms.

"There's no Irving there," said Evey.

"No what?"

Evey explained.

"I've never seen a ghost town," said Lara, handing Rachel back to Evey.

"Well … we'll go there, take it over, occupy the buildings, make a stand. They will come to us. It's easy. They just cannot resist wanting to blow us the fuck up. They can't. We'll talk about our whole fantasy vs. reality thing. We'll put Brooke on YouTube, get millions of views, all that shit. And we'll talk about tax resistance and we'll talk about all kinds of shit. Actually, it's perfect, no worries.

"Shit I forgot something. Be right back."

She stuck her pointer into the air, put her head down and aimed back to the store.

Evey sat in the front passenger side trying to get Rachel interested in pattycake.

"Bakers man," said Rachel.

"Reuben, gramma."

Evey's eyes watered and she hugged Rachel close to her chest so she would not see.

"No cry, mamma. No cry."

A black and white police car moved slowly through the parking lot, going up and down the rows. Evey saw it. She kept her eye on it while keeping Rachel close.

The car edged up their lane, the driver checking every license plate, so slowly, not quite stopping.

The police car stopped in front of the orange CRUSHER WAR HQ SUV.

The driver was a woman. She looked at the vehicle, the license plate, straight up at Evey. Evey did not wave. She thought about it. She looked back, not averting her eyes. The police woman looked away first, down to something in her lap, a list perhaps.

Evey watched her get out and walk right up to the window.

Lara stormed up, all happy, with a bag full of goodies.

"I forgot it's Halloween!" she said, pulling out a plastic bag of suckers and a Fairy Princess costume for Rachel.

"Here, baby, excuse me," she handed it through the window past the cop.

The officer asked them where they were from.

"Minnesota."

"Yeah, I noticed your plates. Where you headed then?"

"We thought we might go to Kansas," said Lara.

"Do you have work there? What do you do?" Evey stared.

"We are in search of employment," said Lara, trying to put herself between Evey's hard glare and the police woman.

"You by yourselves?" Evey continued to stare, not taking her eyes off the police woman.

"What's wrong, mamma?"

"Do you have papers," she asked Evey.

"Papers? Is this Germany?"

"I'm afraid you will have to get out of the vehicle."

Lara spurted out, "wait a minute now, we are cooperating," thinking of the weapons and the pages and pages of CRUSHER plans, documents inside.

"Here is my license," said Evey, handing over her fake I.D., not knowing her face was No. 1 on the F.B.I. Ten Most Wanted List.

Lara had realized something in the aisles and the layout of the enormous prison-like Walmart. *You could literally go in there and never come out.* She wanted to tell someone, but not now.

The officer also took Lara's fake I.D. and began to go back to her car, saying she would be right back.

Rachel reached out the window, already wearing her Fairy Princess outfit, and touched the police woman's head with her wand.

"Let me tell *you* something …"

"No!" said Evey.

"No!" said Lara.

"… pendejo," said Rachel.

The officer turned and smiled, removed her cap and walked back to the window.

"I love that movie," she said.

"We watch it a lot," said Evey sheepishly, "too much."

"Cute costume," said the officer.

"You guys have a good trip," she said, handing back the fake IDs.

"Get lots of candy now," she said to Rachel.

"The bums will always lose," Rachel's high-pitched scream broadcast across the parking lot as the officer walked away, waving, smiling, getting into her car as Evey battled Rachel to get the damn window closed and Lara hurried around to the driver's side.

Note from the narrator ...

From the assorted musings found by the cleaner, Jake the intern from St. Olaf, in the log book of Crawfish Cabin at Anderson's Resort on Lake June Bug in northern Saint Louis County, in the Minnesota Arrowhead.

1980 October

If you are in the future this is what happened:
hostages released from Iran [FINALLY], Mt. St. Helens, John Lennon. I hate this year. Tomorrow, I mean next year should be better. I will be in high school!

So many mosquitoes here, all you can do is go swimming or stay in the cabin and read.

We had a great fire tonight. Best ever.

Stef Cook
Brainerd

The C.I.A. left behind inert explosives in a Virginia school bus
used for a canine training exercise and students were transported
in it before the materials were found, officials said.

The inactive explosives were discovered
in the engine compartment when the Loudoun County Virginia Public
Schools bus was undergoing maintenance, the Central Intelligence
Agency said in a statement on Thursday.

The school district in the Washington suburb
said the materials were aboard the bus on Monday and Tuesday when it
carried elementary and high school students.
— Reuters

The reason why 9/11 is so important is,
once exposed, everything is open to question.
— Morgan Reynolds, served as chief economist
for the U.S. Dept. of Labor 2001-2002

The orchestration of press, radio and television
to create a continuous, lasting and total environment
renders the influence of propaganda virtually unnoticed
precisely because it creates a constant environment.
— Jacques Ellul

FORTY-SEVEN

"**N**ice shot, Mr. C!"

Carroll's tee shot on No. 7 roared down the middle.

He and his group at Congressional Country Club strode down the fairway with a purpose.

Carroll took a call from his office, learning that CRUSHER had transferred its focus from Mayfield to Irving, Kansas. He was not surprised.

"It ties in perfectly with what we predicted in our Ghost Cities Panel two years ago," he told his secretary, who always agreed and said, yes, yes.

Carroll had been a presenter at GCP, where they had talked about how the military and intelligence agencies needed to find a way to cope with the coming, looming in fact, evidence that the abandoned towns of the United States would be the next theater of war. People would seek to live wherever they could and these tattered buildings offered at least some shelter and a place to start. If given that foothold who knows where it might spread.

"Right up the gut!" he shouted to his partners as he approached his ball, which had landed in the middle of the fairway perfectly aligned for his second shot to the green.

He was not surprised.

He smiled wide, spread his feet and put his head down then stroked the ball and continued smiling as it lofted lazily, knowing where it should go.

Have you heard of The Goldilocks Zone? Neither had I until somehow I found a reference to it by cruising almost aimlessly around the internet. It is the place in space where it is just perfect for life to exist, like earth. And probably elsewhere, I would think, would you?

Well, Josie Custer, The BIM (h), which if I ever call her that out loud you have my permission to shoot me, met with her lawyer then, not long after I talked to her last. They are proceeding with the wrongful death lawsuit I believe is what you call it, against the government and The C.I.A. specifically, charging that they intended to cause Geronimo's death.

Nothing will come of it, but I also realize they have to try.

In other news, Lara and Evey and Rachel have arrived in Irving, Kansas and found it a ghost town all right, with abandoned buildings, but a real main street, however abbreviated. They have declared it "just perfect" and gone to work making things ready for the new recruits they expect to be arriving soon.

Lara says they have a perfect view from the front porch, an old house in the middle of town, a nice hint of California and of New York.

And Jim has taken Prince Hope up on the offer of help to get him back on his feet as it were and he is just now climbing aboard a Greyhound out of the station on Hawthorne.

Korey and The Four have decided to hitchhike to Ohio, together, and that's gonna be tough.

While in another section of the Washington D.C. area, HE sits in a sandbox in an oval office, surrounded by scrubbed, polished, shined wood and his toy soldiers all around him and dump trucks and jeeps and he draws pictures, stick figures on a Big Chief tablet of dead soldiers, symbols of men he had sent to kill and they died.

The Pres'dent, The Most Powerful Man In The World (In The Universe) drew dot-dot-dot battles on his paper pad as he sat on the ground, getting sand all in his shoes and socks while his minder watched.

His babysitter worked his phone and sat with his feet on The Big Desk.

Director Robert S. Mueller, III has named A-Rod McGruff VIII special agent in charge of babysitting.

Mr. McGruff began his career as a special agent in November 1990 and reported to the Dallas Division. The next year, he was appointed to the Evidence Response Team and was involved in the management of a number of high-profile, major crime scene investigations, including the Oklahoma City bombing and the September 11, 2001 crash of United Air Lines Flight 93 in Shanksville, Pennsylvania.

Prior to joining the F.B.I., Mr. McGruff was a radio and television news reporter and an investigator for the state of Arkansas.

Special Agent In Charge Of The Pres'dent McGruff gets up quickly as he sees The Man With The Plan has fallen onto his side and can't get up. He sets him up and arranges again the trucks and soldiers and drawing pad around him, sweeps a little of the sand from The Pres'dent's booties, lifts him up and sighs.

This Chief Executive will need a bath.

Some paper items discovered at the crash scene played a role in supporting the official account of the 9/11 attacks and who was responsible for them.

For example, according to F.B.I. agents who were involved in the recovery effort, items made of paper and other fragile materials that belonged to the alleged hijackers were found.

These included driver's licenses, identification cards, passports, a credit card, receipts, tickets, a red bandana, pages from the Koran, and "a checklist reminding the terrorists to blend in when boarding planes and instructing them to 'shave their beards.'"

Referring to items found at the supposed crash site of Flight 93, F.B.I. agent A. Todd McCall said the hijackers "thought their identification would be destroyed during the attacks," but, he added, "They were wrong."

— TribTotal Media

FORTY-EIGHT

The days have gone by.

Do you know that they say the average age for an American male is way into the 70s? Geezuz fuck what are you supposed to do for all that time just sayin'.

The days move past sometimes like elderly golfers and sometimes like cows in a pasture who do not ever seem to move and sometimes the days go past like something really fast right past your face, maybe a bug, and you say what was that?

Well, shit.

Prince Hope is right now engaged in a reading from his new book in the cozy reading area in his own bookstore, with a fireplace, low lights, all that shit.

His book store manager has introduced him and the large crowd, squeezed in tight is applauding as Prince Hope, wearing a blue and white Saint Paul Saints ballcap and white Walter Sobchak T-shirt: Nothing Is Fucked, white shorts and red hightop tennis shoes, laces coming untied, no socks, has made his gangly way, somehow, through the walkers and canes, to the podium and microphone, deftly as a ghost through a minefield.

237

He doesn't give any opening remarks, figuring whatever he has said in the past will suffice as preface. He begins straight-away reading from "They Who LIVE In Hiding."

"There is a fat young lady turning left off Highway 9 right now headed toward Proctor, Minnesota. The agonized look on her face as she tries to comprehend why the car behind her might have wanted to honk loud at her tells it all.

"Her truck is plastered with stickers that tell how stupid she and her boyfriend are, that they have children who know practically literally nothing, and the fact is that almost no one reading this book knows much more than these unfortunate souls.

"There is no one who will understand this story, just sayin', except the core CRUSHERS with the tattoos, and that is why the C.I.A. wants and the F.B.I. wants to kill them. After that there will be not one. None.

"This book is dedicated to my son, who died as a CRUSHER at The Battle of Cicely, and will always be a CRUSHER and there is nothing I can do about it. The stark reality of seeing a crow astride the rump of a fawn in the ditch and you just have to accept it. It is.

"One of the earliest recollections I have is of being with two friends and they were holding tennis rackets, I think, and they were batting a frog back and forth. I grabbed that frog after awhile because I could not stand it any longer, and I suppose I ran and I imagine I was marked for life as some sort of a person. I don't know if I saved that frog, but even if I didn't I tried and I do not give one fuck if I ruined my life for it.

"Fuck you. Fuck you all. I am so happy to be here tonight, thank you all for coming.

"When I was growing up there was the music of Elton John, Tiny Dancer, Rocket Man, Texan Love Song, Daniel, Levon, Saturday Night. All right. What did they mean? No fucking idea but someday I will understand. We did not know it was genius that would not last. We didn't understand the lyrics, didn't understand the words, but it was our music.

"We thought it was us. We made it. We deserved it and it said that we were destined for great things. Super Tramp. Dreamer. Driving around in used cars from the '50s bought for us by parents who loved us, with beer we think we made ourselves on country roads we think we discovered. The magic music makers drizzle out and we get jobs at Sears. All this science I don't understand. So now I'm praying for the end of time.

"It is.

"Tom Brokaw, Matt Lauer, Katie Couric, Bryant Gum-ball, on TV on Sept. 11, 2001. But there were not planes, how could there be?

"How could there not be? We saw it. But we did not see a plane collide with a building. That so-called plane did not crash into the building, it melted into it.

"We saw Wiley Coyote smash into a rock wall and Road-Runner, getting away, beep-beep. And Brokaw, Gum-ball, Couric, Lauer in their ultra-offices telling us what happened, who did it and why.

"I had a so-called near death experience as a kid in a dental office. They gave me too much gas and I finally came out of it, but I saw things and I remember all the staff looking down at me when I woke up, saying my name. They were scared. I was not. But this might be the reason I have these thoughts. I still see these adult faces leaning over me with the dumb looks on their faces. The dumb looks are still there. I wave my arms. Get away from me. I am all right. It is you whom you should worry about.

"These kinds of people, the ones who have experienced certain things, have these things, these thoughts. And I suppose I passed them down to my son and he is dead.

"This is how you prepare a populace to accept a police state willingly, even gratefully.

"You don't scare them by making dramatic changes. Rather, you acclimate them slowly to their prison walls. Persuade the citizenry that their prison walls are merely intended to keep them safe and danger out.

"Desensitize them to violence, acclimate them to a military presence in their communities and persuade them that there is nothing they can do to alter the seemingly hopeless trajectory of the nation. ... as you also get them used to the idea of a friendly Walmart. That's John Whitehead, most of it.

"But, me, I've already been gassed and maybe I'm immune to this, or not.

"The American rebel group CRUSHER has waged war though you might not have heard of it in American towns, fake towns that are real in our hearts and minds because of television.

"Have you heard of Operation Enduring Freedom, The More Trees More Rivers More Oceans Act, No Child Left Behind, HealthCare For Practically Everyone, The Patriot Act ... non-violent extremists /

domestic terrorists / Cass Sunstein … John Le Carré, *The Little Drummer Girl*, 1983.

"Look at those and then get back to me. You have not done your homework. That is for certain. Someone said that freedom is for those who have been vigilant, but we have not been vigilant, we have been watching TV.

"The law of karma, is I suppose you get what you deserve. That can't be true. Look around you. But there is a weird thing with the C.I.A. and the F.B.I. where they think that they have to tell us when they are going to trick us because if we don't get it, then it's on us. Look around you. That's all I will tell you. It's all you deserve.

"And at the bottom of it all was a fortune cookie.

"They don't have fortune cookies when you do the all you can eat buffet, ever notice that? It's nothing. Not everything is something.

"If Bill Hicks were alive today would America be this much in trouble? How about John Lennon? How about if Robert Kennedy had not died in Los Angeles but would have lived for years and years in The White House. That might have happened if you had done your homework and that's true and that is on you. This is all on you.

"The hegelian dialectic. Create thesis & antithesis to control synthesis — to create, manage and perpetuate conflict. Look around you.

"You paid good money for this book and now you are not getting your answers. That is what you think, but you are wrong, as you have been for decades. I am helping you to be right for once in your life.

"Close Quarter Battle. CQB. It's like they use to destroy families in Iraq, Afghanistan, and what they will soon use on you, in Boise, Boston, Dubuque, Chanhassen, San Luis Obispo.

"Surprise, speed, violence of action.

"That's what it's about and it's gospel to them. And you don't say a word as you swipe milk and Captain Crunch from your chin with the back of your hand.

"Complete domination of battlefield, surprise, night, low noise, concealment, gaining initiative.

"Do you think when you experience this yourself some night in your pajamas with tears running down your son's and daughter's faces you will think of writing a letter to the editor in the morning?"

And that was that.

Prince Hope stepped back from the podium, dropped his new fucking book to the floor like the murder weapon and walked away down the middle aisle, through dozens of silent people, potential buyers of his book and well-wishers at the autograph table set up for him over there. He walked out into the sun, across the street, sat on the bus bench with the prison advertising, stretched one arm out and both feet and put his face into the light, pushed each shoe off with the toes of the other foot, without looking, let them drop and wiggled his toes in the sunshine.

Korey held out his thumb.
"It's a bus, dude," said Jefferson.
"Buses don't stop," said Washington.
Korey pitched his thumb higher into the air.
The bus passed.
And in one window he saw Jim's face, smooshed into the window, his nose, his mouth, his eyes closed. The mouth wide open.
"I just saw somebody I knew," said Korey.
"Of course you did," said Patrick.

Brooke and her reality show production crew, in all the red Suburbans, made their way around Cleveland, following GPS to "Mayfield." Nobody in the lead vehicle said shit because they would get yelled at for the producer not being able to hear the GPS woman.
Brooke couldn't take any more.
"Turn around as soon as you can," said Brooke. "You are surrounded."
"Back up, go sideways, shit yourself."
"Quiet!"
"You have arrived at your destination."
"Here?"
The sign said "Mayfield." They were at a four-way stop in the middle of a giant Walmart parking lot, a Wendy's, a C-store and a branch bank.

Jim's bus stopped on the far side of the Walmart parking lot. The door opened and by the look on the driver's face Jim figured he was supposed to get out.
The bus pulled away, leaving Jim by a bench and a sign that said bus stop.
He sat.

No luggage, little money. He had to pee. He could hold it.

He put one arm up on the bench and lifted his face into the sun and closed his eyes.

Inside the Walmart men's restroom Jim held his hands under the hand dryer and heard a big commotion behind him as several loud men entered the restroom.

"You couldn't hold it?"

"Geezuz!"

"I held it for three hundred miles."

"Well, you already fuckin' went then, right?"

"I'm just following you guys."

"God-dam-it!"

"Aaaah."

"Korey?" Jim said, looking over his shoulder.

"Hey, man."

Jim waited for them outside the restroom.

"I saw you, man," said Korey.

"We need …," he said.

"Huggies?" said Jim.

"No, squirt guns."

They all rounded the corner of one of the toy aisles, searching for squirt guns, SuperSoakers, hopefully.

At the far end of the aisle a group was gathered around the dolls, holding them in their plastic cases, examining them.

"Brooke?" said Korey.

"Brooke!"

"Korey?"

He ran to her, reached in around her waist and hugged her into the air.

"You were dead!" he said.

She just smiled, holding his head in her hands, tears running down her face. She pulled his head to her shoulder.

Jim moved in to join the hug.

Korey pushed away to look at her.

"They said you died," he said.

"Who said?" she said.

"I don't know, I just thought. You gotta tell Lara. She thinks you're dead."

"No," said Brooke. "I just talked to her. She told us to come here."

"Oh," said Korey.

"Whatcha doin'?" said Jim.

"Getting a doll for Evey's kid," said Brooke.

"Rachel, right?"

"Yeah," said Korey.

"What're you guys doin'?" said Brooke, "lookin' for the play dough?"

"Umm, no, yeah," said Korey.

"They must be all out."

Brooke pulled down a big box of play dough with play dough toys.

"Here," she said.

"Okay, great," said Korey.

At the checkout they paid for the play dough and doll and then stood around blocking traffic.

Let's go together. All units?

Just one. Leave the others parked here. People do that.

Road trip!

Wally World!

We've got a full tank, a half pack of cigarettes. It's dark and we're wearing sunglasses.

Hit it.

It don't matter to Jesus.

On a long trip you: try to sleep, think about pooping, eat, repeat, sometimes get out and stretch and wonder (a little) about where you are, but you are really too tired to care and you just want to go back to sleep.

It's supposed to be a fourteen-hour drive from Mayfield, Ohio to Marysville, Kansas, which is roughly the location of the Irving ghost town. You go width-wise through Ohio, Indiana, Illinois and Missouri. South Bend, Joliet, Springfield are some of the towns on your way. Also Normal, Pontiac, Jackson. You take Interstate 80 west a long fucking ways and then it goes south and becomes I-55 and you go on that pretty much forever until it becomes I-72 and you stay on that until you think you are gonna puke and finally at Hannibal you get all screwed up until you find your little highway connection and then you are in Kansas and just when you think you are gonna make it, you realize you came all this way and you are in Kansas. But at least you are off the god-damn Interstate. Geezuz *Fucking* H. Christ.

Well, as we said, we have all these folks in one of the red Suburbans, the ones that Prince Hope paid for the so-called special Unit to film Brooke as a spy and have that be a hit TV national reality show that would tell the world about CRUSHER and maybe Lara would like him or not, it didn't happen but they did send some footage back to Hope, and he edited it with some software he downloaded for free and sent it to the Duluth public access channel and so now it is running this month at one in the morning and also again at four in the morning, and we'll see, maybe it will spread across the nation and the world from there.

Well, now we have the producer and the crew. I lied. They had to take two of the red Suburbans and leave the other two in the Walmart parking lot in Mayfield, Ohio, which is technically called Mayfield Village, and they should be fine there. (I'm shaking my head.)

And in the lead red suburban we have Brooke, Jim, Korey, these CRUSHERS re-united after all this time and they have all this stuff to talk about and that gets old after not as long as you might think, and then we have Patrick, Henry, Washington, and Jefferson, so what's that, seven people, but it's a pretty big vehicle, with lots of cool stuff to mess with, but that gets old.

And then you have the highway.

They were stopped at a diner somewhere in Illinois not too far south of one of the great lakes.

Washington was reading a local newsletter while they waited for their food. The newsletter was put out each morning by the local radio show, birthdays, advertising, local sports, weather.

"CRUSHERs meet in Mayfield, public be advised."

Washington read and then read out loud to everyone else.

"Hey, we're goin' the wrong way," said Korey.

"We need to go back."

They argued about that back and forth and the food was really good, but they kept going and they changed drivers.

At the next stop, not the next stop, maybe two or three stops down the way, by now at about … Beverly Hill, Indiana, they stopped again, again at a restaurant just off the Interstate.

And as they got back onto the road after finishing their meal, not as good as others, not terrible, some said, on the digital directions sign that some roads departments put up here and there, well, this sign, said, "Stop, Go Back, You'll Never Make It."

And so, Jim, who was driving, pulled over.

"What are you doing!" said Brooke.

And they talked it over and kept going, but Jim made the decision, on his own, to go below the speed limit. He thought the others would not notice and for a while they did not, but later they did.

At the Elkart, Missouri stop they sat for a while on the benches at a roads department rest stop and just ate out of the machines.

Jefferson felt a pain all of a sudden in his chest, like a dart and he told somebody. He lay down on the bench while the others walked around and when they got back Jefferson was dead.

That was terrible. They felt terrible.

"What can we do?" said Brooke.

Jim asked what anyone knew about Jefferson and nobody knew anything, not a thing. Korey quick noticed, or maybe not, a robin's egg blue e-Car pull away, headed back toward heavy traffic just as Brooke decided for them that they would leave him right there. Think about it, she said, what else can we do? Korey had already forgotten about maybe or not seeing the e-Car, basically because he did not like the idea of just leaving somebody behind. Jefferson had joined them, signed off with their revolution, as it were, and now we just leave him here?

Brooke ran down the options, popping fingers out of a tight fist as visual aid as she did so:

Call 9-11 and in ten, fifteen minutes we will be all in a different vehicle because we have with us a member of the F.B.I. Top Ten List.

Korey smiled and a couple of people clapped, lightly.

Huh? Yeah. Bury him. Pick him up and set him over by the restrooms and then walk away from the dead body. Take him into town and say here is this dead young man.

They thought about that one for a while and then said no to that, too.

They pulled away, all staring at Jefferson, lying on the bench at the rest stop, wearing a Nothing Is Fucked T-shirt and a Twins cap over his face.

"Jesus Christ!" yelled Korey.

"This sucks, big-time."

They cried, some of them, and they didn't talk for a while, at all.

Well, by now the fun has gone out of the road trip, but it has become an adventure, exactly the same with any long trip by anybody in America. And that's the way you have to look at it. Or just bitch about it the whole way, but those are your two options.

The CRUSHER entourage, the two red Suburbans, went off course for their next bathroom break slash meal stop. They turned off in Missouri at the Pisgah sign because somebody had heard a song some time in the distant past and wanted to see the town.

Well, shit. Yeah.

Of course.

The waiter wore sunglasses and screwed up their orders, giving somebody someone else's hashbrowns and nobody really ordered eggs. Coffee? Oh, he said you didn't want coffee. And when the producer went to pay his bill the cashier, with sunglasses on a string, told him that Korey had said something about the producer. Like what? said the producer and the cashier acted like, I didn't say anything.

Pisgah.

Woah.

They pulled out of there in total silence.

Nobody said shit.

QUOTE REMOVED BY ORDER OF DHS, UNITED STATES DEPARTMENT OF HOMELAND SECURITY. [DHS US2FA]

… As Fitrakis and Wasserman point out, Trump is "actually (so far) a moderate compared to scores of murderous dictators the U.S. has installed in other countries throughout the world. Especially since World War II, our imperial apparatus has constantly subverted legitimate attempts by good people to elect decent leaders."

They present a partial list of "duly elected leaders the United States has had removed, disappeared and/or killed to make way for authoritarian pro-corporate regimes."
These leaders include: Patrice Lumumba of the Congo; Salvador Allende of Chile; Jean-Bertrand Aristide of Haiti; Mohammad Mossadegh of Iran; Jacobo Arbenz of Guatemala and many, many more. Their removals, and the installation of U.S.-friendly dictators, were accompanied by social chaos and mass killings.

Also included on the list were such names as Tecumseh, Sitting Bull, Chief Joseph — a few of the innumerable indigenous leaders who stood in the way of Europeans' conquest of the Western Hemisphere, the mentioning of which opens a chasm of largely unexamined and whitewashed America history.
Tens of millions of people died and numerous cultures were mocked and destroyed in this American holocaust spanning centuries.
— Robert C. Koehler

FORTY-NINE

Caryl,
   I think I have talked about all this, of your last two emails.
         Hitler or someone said if a lie is repeated enough people begin believing it.
         This flight 93 stuff cannot work because that plane was not busy that day. And at that time cell phone exchange aloft would not work, if it maybe can by now. But most of all, this plane forming this too narrow ditch outside Shanksville, Penn., is more absurd than Santa Cross and his flying reindeer. This is where official USA went nuts. It is in there somewhere! Must be in an abandoned mine shaft! Yeah, in there somewhere! Abandoned mine shaft!
         . Now, the other, later balderdash, is same old, same old, fakery. Uh.... And let both sides take some blame....Ah...
         Were Assad so evil as USA wants him to be, he has no reason to bomb his people, for he took three quarters of their vote. He is popular.
         ISIL created by C.I.A. killed Assad's civilians till there were refugees. Then Hillary came and gave these mercenaries poison gas to kill a batch of refugees, in order to say Assad did this.
         When I first heard of this, I had not heard James Kessler or anyone reasonable speak of this. Kelly who is so helpful was driving me and

mine to Madrea's, Ivanhoe, Texas, and I had told him I did not believe this crap. I asked him, why would Assad do this?

Kelly Blackbird: I dunno! He's crazy!

That is mindless. How can Bill respond to mindlessness.

What can I say? I am different. I never did respond to repetition.

Love,

Billy

Note from the narrator:

Discovered by the C.I.A. scratched with a fingernail into the green sidewall of a stall in the MEN's restroom at a diner somewhere in Illinois on Interstate 80 not too far south of one of the great lakes:

"From the real files of the F.B.I. and C.I.A., the ones without the black Magic Marker: 'We murdered Fred Hampton. And there's not one thing they can do about it.'"

/United States Government: Memorandum/CLASSIFIED

Signed: Washington

It is my belief that a much different profile of the 'serial killer' will emerge — a profile of the controlled assassin conditioned and programmed by a variety of intelligence fronts, including military entities, psychiatric institutions and Satanic cults. For while serial killers may well be driven by their own internal demons, they are likely not demons of their own making.

— Dave McGowan

Fear the time when the bombs stop falling while the bombers live — for every bomb is proof that the spirit has not died. And fear the time when the strikes stop while the great owners live — for every little beaten strike is proof that the step is being taken. And this you can know — fear the time when Manself will not suffer and die for a concept, for this one quality is the foundation of Manself, and this one quality is man, distinctive in the universe.

— John Steinbeck

Levon wears his war wound like a crown.
He calls his child Jesus, cuz he likes the name,
and he sends him to the finest school in town.

Levon, Levon like his money,
He makes a lot they say,
spends his days counting,
in the garage by the motorway.

And Jesus, he wants to go to Venus,
leaving Levon far behind,
take a balloon and go sailing,
while Levon slowly dies.

— Elton John

FIFTY

"L ittle more!"

Evey and Lara sweat, struggled and grunted, working to reach the chain on the porch swing to the metal hook in the porch ceiling. Rachel sat on the far side of the porch, watching.

"There!" said Evey.

"Ta da!" said Rachel holding up touchdown arms.

An old brown car pulled up, right to the front steps.

"Are we in Brooklyn anymore?" the driver leaned out and smiled.

"Camp America," said Lara pointing to the handmade sign nailed to the porch rail.

Lara stepped down to shake hands while Evey wiped Rachel's hands. She had gotten into the paint it looked like.

Lara told the new ones where to go sign in.

"They'll give you a camp assignment and brigade, T-shirt, let's see … CRUSHER, Nothing Is Fucked, The Beagles Same Band Different Tour, Moods Of Darth Vader, Santa He Knows …"

"Cool. That's what we were hoping. There's a few of them behind us too we saw 'em in the last rest stop. They were askin' for directions to Highway 9. I told them I thought what they were looking for was a little south of Highway 9, more like 9 ¾."

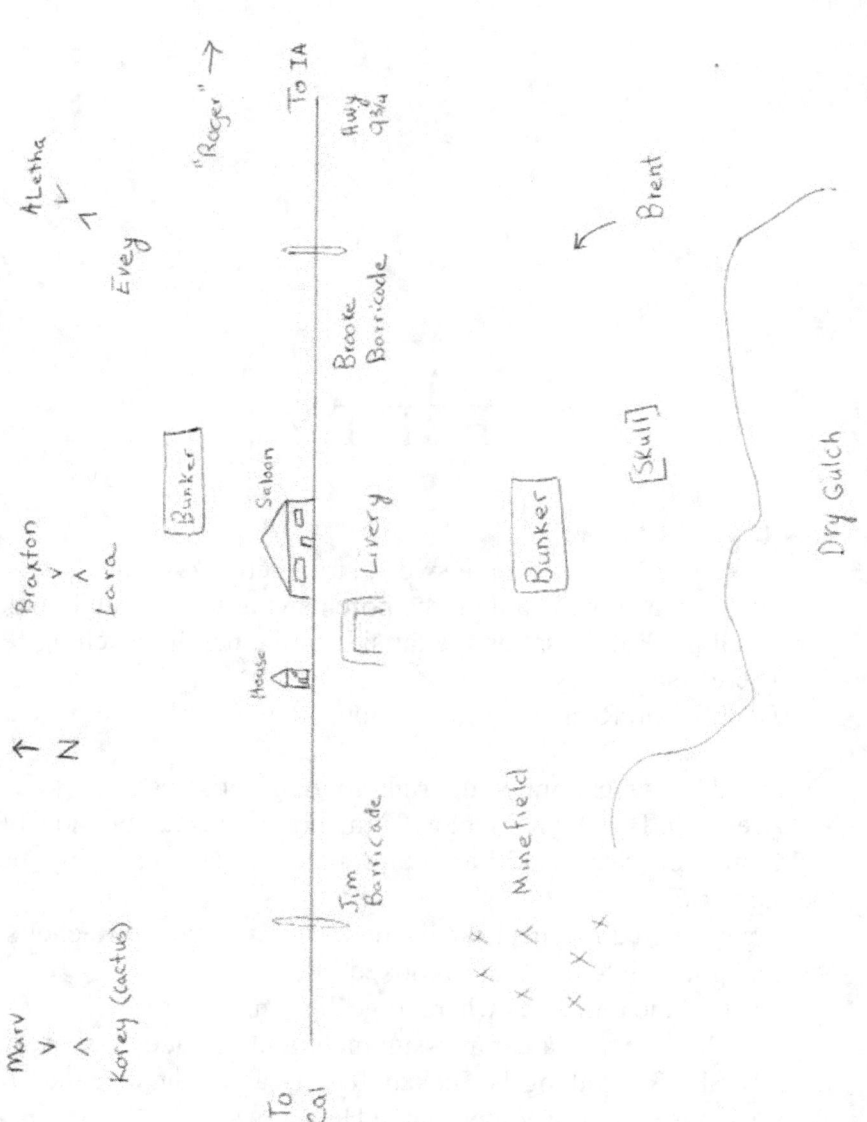

"

"Ha, that's good. I'm Evey."

"Ike. Nice to meet you."

"Yeah," said Lara, wanting to get back to fixing up the House slash Headquarters before she got way too busy with other stuff.

"And there's a church tent, hospital. I think we got it all covered. If there's anything you need let someone know."

"Any sign of the enemy?"

"Not yet," said Lara, looking out over the prairie.

"You should be able to see a tornado coming for a hundred miles out here," said the driver as Lara seemed not to hear.

"Or a tank," Lara mumbled, distracted.

That evening Lara and Evey tested the swing.

Evey went down a list of the new people in camp.

"Alice, Charlie, Cheryl, Dave ... froooom ... Rapid City, South Dakota.

"Andy, Hope, Harry, from ... Arcata, California.

...

"Ike, Frida, from Brooklyn.

...

"Beau, Alan, Ginny, Freddie, Gene, from North Carolina, uhhh, Asheville.

"Mandy, Greta, Cole from Austin, Texas."

"Frank and Addy from Des Moines."

"Gene, from Saint Paul."

"Saint Paul?" said Lara.

Each night they tried to have a campfire to talk, relax and continue planning and training from the day.

Evey, Lara, Jim, and Korey told about the founders of CRUSHER, about Geronimo, about the others, Morgan, Actually, Sandara, Skylar, Rick, Zima, Joe, Ariel, Max, Ty, Pete, Kaitylyn.

They sang songs about the founders of Irving, who came from Iowa during the dust bowl, depression, the grapes of wrath, and about Billy in prison in Bumfuck, Iowa, like Joe Hill.

One night at the fire Evey and Brooke were sitting in camp chairs wearing homemade tin foil hats.

"That's not funny," said Lara as she sat with them.

"What's that over there?"

Cole from Austin stood and pointed into the night.

"C'mere, look."

Cole led them all away from their fire.

"Ohh, man, look at all those stars," someone said.

"Wow."

They all looked up.

"No, man, not that," said Cole.

Lara walked away from the group and stood by herself, counting the campfires in the distance. She turned all the way around.

"We're surrounded," she whispered.

The next day was spent in not exactly frantic, but at least hectic last-minute preparations.

Right in the middle of it, Gene from Saint Paul found Lara and wanted to talk about them being from the same town and did they know any of the same people.

They stood right in the middle of the highway that ran through town.

"Yeah," said Lara, pointing.

"There's a bunker there, and one more over there, to our north. We can actually put everyone in those two. We're dug pretty far down. We have to have somewhere to go to survive the initial aerial bombardment. We do have two anti-aircraft guns, believe it or not."

"Where'd you get those?" he said.

"Don't ask," she said.

"Yeah," she continued.

"Just so you know, tell the others, I don't know if everyone has gotten the full tour. Brooke's team is on the east barricade, Jim's on the west.

"Don't go down there, that's the minefield. I'll be up north, Korey's brigade will cover our right and Evey's our left. No, that's not right, it's the other way around. I'm so dyslexic sometimes."

"I know, right?" he said.

"And what's way down there?" he said.

"South, down over that ridge. We haven't been allowed down there."

"That's the dry gulch, that's what we're calling it. Yeah, there's nothing there."

Two, maybe three days later Korey and Jim sat on wooden chairs out in front of the old livery stable, across from the saloon barracks and the house headquarters. The livery was the ER. They smoked cigarettes and looked into the sun, trying to feel like outlaws, desperadoes and feel good about that, but mostly they were nervous, probably even scared. They didn't talk about that, but they did talk about NASCAR and Korey said it was the stupidest thing, to watch cars go 'round a circle.

They wore full battle gear, T-shirts, jeans, tennis shoes or boots, bullet-proof vests, handguns, knives, bandolier, rifle. Jim wore a tattered cowboy hat he'd found in a gas station on the way. Korey wore a black ball cap with and orange "C".

"You try it then sometime," said Jim, cussing under his breath and shaking his head, looking around at their small city.

Korey started humming a song he'd heard in last night's campfire.

Jim grabbed Korey's arm.

"Listen," Jim said.

In the far distance they heard singing, chanting.

They both stood to hear.

Jim pointed to the east.

Korey pointed north.

They both shot around because it was definitely coming from the south.

"And so it begins," said Jim.

"Orcs."

"Don't fucking say that," said Korey.

And then it stopped.

Jim and Korey ran around to ask if anyone had heard the singing.

That night at the camp they did not have their own fire, but sat in a big circle turned outward, watching the campfires surrounding them.

Carroll, who was calling his post code-name "Roger," just to himself, sat in his command post SUV on an old dirt road northeast of Irving, on a ridge overlooking the town in the distance and what he saw as the entire coming battlefield.

He looked through binoculars: watching Lara stride across the street toward the hospital, Korey tossing rocks at a sign, Jim hammering a nail on the saloon-barracks, children chasing dogs with sticks.

In any case, he saw the little ghost town and he had prepared for this very thing years ago and so he had his best positioned to match the CRUSHER brigades and since the F.B.I. had insisted, SAC Michael Braxton was also included in the deployment. McConnell was to provide support, but that was a million miles away and Whiteman said they could be also counted upon and he had the Kansas National Guard and Nebraska out of Lincoln.

He still worried though. Things can go wrong. Men get killed. He wrote notes in his lap in pauses from watching. He was writing his memoirs, not that he would publish, he might, but that they would be there.

Serendipity, he wrote.

"It happens."

We think we planned all this, but we did not, but afterward, by some miracle we can make it make sense. Your day, your life.

He put parenthesis, underlined, crossed out.

God knows what I will do today. He has a plan for my life. We need that to be true. But what if God is an improviser? He gets up each day, puts on his boots, his pants one leg at a time and shoots from the hip?

Like with Star Wars. What if you just get new ideas or learn something new. Well, you add that to what you have done and voila, right?

In the binoculars he saw a person wearing a Cat In The Hat hat, some Vikings horns, and one with bunny ears, and another cap that said "Gone Squatchin".

"There must be a god-damned genius convention there at the same time," he said.

A sound, a dog barking a long way away. Carroll quickly crossed-out what he had written, then rolled down his window to hear better.

Lara had canceled the night fires and all daytime training. All troops were to be at their posts in full battle mode, 24/7.

She was hoping for more troops though. They needed people to stay in the saloon/barracks and also more for the day care center. At least Rachel had not run off yet. She seemed to know they could not chase her out here if she ran.

Korey's and Jim's teams were stationed pretty close so at night they sat out together and talked and smoked.

"Small Talk. What is it good for?" said Korey.

"I'm sorry, I wasn't listening," said Jim.

"I mean," said Korey, "why do we do that? The weather? That shit, you know. It drives me crazy."

"You are not good at it," said Jim.

"I know, it drives me crazy."

"Small people."

Jim said and put one pointer finger into the air that Korey did not see.

"Here's something," he said.

"Do small people have smaller lives than big people, you know, tall, big people. Do the small people feel things, think things, experience things as much as taller people?"

"Of course they do," said Korey.

"Yeah, just sayin'," said Jim.

Brooke stood at the eastward barricade, right on the highway with her team, which included the Austin group: Mandy, Greta, Cole.

She called their position Brooke's Barricades.

"Wouldn't that sound great on Sesame Street. And here's Brooke's Barricades, say the alphabet, Brooke.

"Lara said don't shoot the first vehicle that we see," said Brooke.

"She's still hoping for more troops.

"Me, I say, what a joke. Nobody's comin', nobody cares. Jim said don't forget to look up. Yeah, right, like that's happening."

Gene was in the headquarters house, the home of Lara and Evey that also had the computers, all the communications/organizational stuff, the secure server that he worked like an old-time operator, patching through messages from brigade to brigade so they did not have to just work by text.

Lara had begun calling him Actually Gene.

Carroll had stayed at his post through the day and now into the night, writing his memoirs and also watching the rebel town. It was not a perfect vantage, up there from the severe northeast, but he could see a lot.

He saw car lights headed up the road and put his binoculars on the lights and decided he could see more without them.

Lara sat on lawn chairs on the far side of the northern bunker with the Brooklyn group, Ike and Frida.

"We have the advantage of interior position," said Ida.

"I know, right?" said Lara.

"We should be in the bunkers for when they bomb," said Lara.

"But if we're all in the bunkers, they just walk right up and it's over. Right?"

Frida and Ike nodded and looked up at the stars, holding hands.

Lara looked at them, sitting so close to each other, and sighed.

She recalled a talk she had that same day with Evey.

"You just don't think we can win, really, do you?" Evey had said.

It must have been about something Lara had said about dying or something not very positive, but she had to admit. And she tried to make herself think like Evey. It lasted about two seconds.

Inside the car headed down Highway 9 ¾ in the middle of the night toward Brooke's Barricades, the driver punched his brights at someone at Brooke's Barricades shining a million-candle flashlight at them.

He was busy arguing with the other four.

"There's no such thing? What about Roswell, that other stuff?"

"All just government psy-ops of the testing they are doing. That's how we got the Stealth bomber."

"We got that from the ETs!"

"See, it's impossible to even talk with you people."

"You people?"

Evey, down below a ridge in the earth that you could not see without walking right up to it, sat not far from Carroll with her team, which included the Asheville Avengers, the CRUSHER group from Asheville, North Carolina: Beau, Ginny, Allan, and Freddy.

Evey had asked them to dream during watch.

Dream about what you want to do when this is over.

"Because it will be over, some day."

Alexa was opposed to Evey, physically, diametrically, geometrically, geographically.

Right opposite Evey in the northeast quadrant or whatever.

They were aware of each other. At times each group could hear the other talking, and sometimes they saw lights, campfires maybe, cigarettes being lit, car door lights.

Each member of each group tried to stay low and place all hope in the morning.

At three a.m., when the earth turns over, when if you are awake you know that things are different, different rules apply, different kings and queens are in control, well, not then, but a little later, about 3:20, Alexa was up on watch and maybe feeling a little loopy.

She sat on a high rock and carelessly lit a cigarette. She thought of a joke and because she was the only one awake on her side, she talked a little louder.

The singing the other night had been her idea.

Anyway, she thought, here goes.

"What's a scary cow, say?"

She waited.

She thought she heard something.

"What?" she yelled.

"Moo!"

"Just don't rain.

"Just don't fucking rain," said Trevor (Brent, Brad, Troy?), with his group on the southeast quadrant.

Special Agent in Charge Michael Braxton was stationed just opposite Lara on the immediate north. His troops did not wear joke T-shirts this time. They wore full military gear with helmets that said "F.B.I."

"The wind never stops, it just never stops," Braxton said to nobody as he watched into the night.

The vehicle stopped short, right at the barricade.

CRUSHERS aimed rifles, shouted, shined flashlights, approached the vehicle from all sides, shouting.

The five grey-and white-haired people inside put their hands straight up into the roof.

"… yeah, they're from the Twin Cities, they say," said Brooke to Lara. "It's your savior group. We are saved. They want to join, say they are the Prince Hope affinity group whatta think let 'em in?"

Lara said assign the old people to the daycare center and the saloon-barracks.

"Yeah, okay," said Brooke, "they want to give us T-shirts and they have some sample book copies they want us to pass around."

"Ten-four. Oh, wait, they say there's more, more coming."

"What?"

The Marv C.I.A. component post was on the northwest quadrant, out in the sticks, as Marv was saying.

"Yes," he said to the person standing next to him. "As you learn more about the real world you got to have something to ground you, you know, what you know is true. That's my bible," he said, thumping his shirt pocket.

The dawn showed itself about a million miles away.

Carroll thought if he decided they could all just go home. He had that power. Leave them here. What would they do? Sit, get hungry, sit some more. Take over what? The press, how long does that last? ... Yes, but, it could grow. They stay here, become a real town a county. Do they pay taxes? I don't think so. No. It stops here and now.

"We learned the lessons of Mayberry, Cicely," said Jim to Korey as they watched the sun sketch in the prairie.

"What lessons?" said Korey.

"Nobody tol' me."

"DFF," said Jim.

"Don't fucking die."

"That's DFD," said Korey.

"DFD," said Jim.

"DFD."

Behind the old people car came a U-Haul truck, the big kind, not the single family bullshit kind with the bullshit radio, and other vehicles, cars, pickups, and a horse trailer.

The U-Haul driver stopped at the barricade, right at Brooke.

Prince Hope leaned out the window and asked if this was the revolution.

"We want to televise it," Hope said.

Brooke smiled and stepped back to see the graffiti all over the side of the truck: CRUSHER UFO Show.

"You mean USO," said Brooke.

"Yeah, maybe you're right," said Hope.

"Can we come in?"

"Yes, please," said Brooke, stepping back, pointing to a way for all the vehicles to come around the barricade and into town.

Right away the rebels and the show workers, member of The Prince Hope Show production team, set to work on a stage right in the middle of town, stringing wires for sound. The Special Team Reality Show crew filmed everything.

"Roswell!" Rachel screamed and ran as her horse was walked out of the trailer. Someone helped her up and she sat proudly on the horse's neck.

That night the lights shined on the stage. Lara sat with the band. Prince Hope did his thing and the newspapers wrote about it, showing the world that CRUSHER was in Kansas.

The next morning, after breakfast it was time to go, Hope announced.

Evey asked if Roswell could stay, looking up at Hope and explaining that it would be a special treat for Rachel.

"It's dangerous here," said Hope, "are you sure?"

"I think it would be okay," said Evey, smiling, watching Rachel sitting on the dappled grey thoroughbred.

"Bye, bye!"

"Thank you for coming!"

They waved and hugged and said they'd be seeing each other soon.

Brooke stood at the barricade and waved way over her head after they were long gone.

Carroll put down his book notes and picked up his phone.

He prepared the group email text to Whiteman and to that other air base in Kansas, Marv, Alexa, Trevor or Brad, Gene, and Mike Braxton, in the agreed-upon code: LGTPS.

"Let's get this party started."

Two minutes, three minutes … Carroll wrote notes in his memoir, checked his watch, got out, scanned the sky, got back in.

He checked his watch again, four minutes, five minutes, seven minutes …

"You hear that?" said Lara.

She stood.

"No, really. Just listen!"

Finally heard it, aircraft buzz, closer, closer …

And then it was right overhead and he hoped for a moment that he would not be bombed. He was pretty close, but these guys were supposed to be good, three of the best.

Lara leaped as something loud headed her way.

Korey and Jim ran to their positions. Evey and Alexa ducked as a fighter streaked over their heads.

The rebel anti-aircraft guns opened up, firing into the sky as if the operators had never touched a gun before, which is conceivable.

In a flash the fighters flared over the town, dropping their bombs. One exploded in the middle of the highway, another right, another left.

The early morning erupted.

The jets scattered and gathered for return.

"Shit! Go! Go! Now!"

Lara screamed to her team, pointing to the nearest bunker. She commanded Gene to "direct all personnel to the bunkers."

All over the town people sprinted to safety underground. Brooke's team stayed at the east barricade. Jim stayed. Korey commanded his people to "hug the ground," because he thought it was too far to make it.

The fighters returned, spraying machine gun fire and launching their rockets. One hit near the north bunker and the lighted explosion showed three bodies in somersaults.

"We should go, now! Now!"

Trevor's text to Carroll screamed.

"I mean sir, go now!"

"No," replied Carroll.

"Let them do their work."

Inside the bunkers chaos reigned king with panic his queen.

The dead bodies had to be left.

The injured screamed in pain and the others cried out because they mostly did not know how to help.

In the north bunker Evey and Lara shouted to be heard, working hard to set up a system, first of dealing with the wounded and then of how to repel the coming ground attack under the air onslaught. Everything smelled of gunpowder and paper towels and soap, shit.

It began to rain. First lightly, then working up to a straight-down soaker that made it impossible to see ten feet. Under the cover of the rain the rebels darted about the town, taking care of horrific chores and work that needed to be done, transferring of equipment and people, getting dogs and children into the saloon-barracks if they would go.

"Epic," Korey texted Evey.

At the far-far end of the eastward highway the press corps sprinted for their vans and SUVs.

Evey's father, wearing his TWINS ballcap, watched it on TV in the nursing home, in his dark room with binoculars borrowed from a guy who brought them back from Germany, from his bed, looking for Evey.

It rained for a day and the night was powered by pulsating stars and pounding hearts.

The next day the Prince Hope Brigade served a quick lunch in the saloon barracks in the middle of a windstorm. Gene visited with Lara about their communications and logistics.

The following morning, fighters zoomed over, back and forth and around, low, high, for an hour, without firing any weapons, no rockets, just noise.

Carroll's Log, "Day One": Air assault successful, continue. Rain. We maintain our positions. More to come.

Lara's Journal, "First Day": We lost four people today: Frank from Des Moines, decapitated, I can't hardly even write that, and Andy and Harry from Arcata. I can't fucking believe it. Anti-aircraft guns for shit. Everyone is scared. We'll never make it. They're all around us. It is so loud. Where the fuck is Kaitylyn. What the fuck was I thinking. I want out of here. I want to sit in my grandma's house and drink coffee and watch it rain.

In the morning Lara sat on a sandbag with a metal coffee cup on her knee watching the humidity melt the rainbow.

She grabbed her gun and rang the bell.

"Dingdingding! Dingdingding!"

Everybody ran.

Lara leaped into her team bunker and listened, trying to catch her breath, she'd hit the sandbags hard with her chest and took her breath.

She didn't want to be right, but she'd heard it.

"There it is."

It was chanting, like Zulus and rhythmic pounding.

She felt it in her feet, the pounding, the beat, louder, closer.

From the barracks she heard the old people, as loud as they could: "All we are saaaaying … is give peace a chance!"

"Oh my *God!*" someone said from another post and someone began singing fuck the police and someone else something else and then there were competing songs from all the rebel positions, and the chanting of the invaders grew stronger.

And she saw them.

Like Indians on the high ridge, or the cavalry, or Orcs, they stretched the goddamn horizon, the sun glinting on their shields.

Ooo-rah. … Hooh!. … Hoooooh!

Then foot stomping, cadence.

One of the old people's head exploded like it'd been packed with C-4, covering her friends with blood. Cole from Austin saw that and fired, pttt-pttt-pttt, dropping two feds in line to their knees, replaced by two others.

Those sparks set off the box of fireworks.

Both sides commenced, smoke rising from the ridge and the bunkers and barricades like civil war pickets.

The government troops dressed like riot police, with full face shields, truncheons, rifles, frontal shields, armor wrapped around their chest, their arms, their legs, everything in black and deep shades of green, and behind them a full line of United States flags on high poles.

We forgot the lions, thought Lara, ducking low, telling herself to remember to breathe.

Now the government troops allowed gaps in their lines and through those lines came the tanks, shined and reflecting the morning sun like Easter Jesus, and the armored cars and the riot vehicles, everything rolling slowly, smoothly, advancing over the Kansas ground from the north and the south, the east and the west — toward the rebel hodge-podge resistance, around still smoking fighter wreckage from the days before.

Carroll watched, troops rushed past his SUV giving hand signals to each other, eyes, up there, over there, down there. He saw the excited shots and then the whole circle erupting and everywhere with his binoculars, smoke signals saying it had begun.

Evey watched Alexa, seeing her with long blonde hair under her helmet … Alexa looked at Evey … seeing … Evey in tears. Alexa wanted to look away and could not.

Trevor stood in the front line of his fully armored troops, bent at the waist, kicking at the cactus, walking out of his way to avoid the skull.

Marv faced off with Korey, from fifty yards, forty-five yards … thirty-five yards. Neither saw the other or wanted to, concerned with straight lines and cover and it was not easy, especially for Marv who did not have sandbags, or for some reason, any armored support way over on the far side of the northerly government formation.

Gene worked the phones, relaying messages, giving out constant map images, troop positions by GPS, drinking coffee, listening to his own music.

Lara ignored thirty messages and eight other things she wanted to attend to ... and aimed her rifle at the front and center soldier ... his head, his forehead. She thought of school and she didn't know why.

Korey wondered what Brooke was doing right now ... and then, not really, as his sandbags began receiving heavy arms fire, tearing, spilling, hitting people in the eyes and thighs ... as Marv's line began to find its voice.

Carroll took a deep breath and let it out, another. He lit a cigar ... puffed, held it out to look at it.

Brooke aimed over the barricade not wanting to explode the head of the soldier. She knew she was a good shot ... but ... she pulled the trigger ... the head erupted.

The sound of the metal gears of the anti-aircraft guns ratcheting down provided another layer, and then hand grenades, *Mr. Molotov, here's to you Mr. Molotov, Jesus loves you more than you will know.*

The armored vehicles, tanks, riot trucks with the troops right by them stopped.

All stop.

The anti-aircraft guns began to find their mark, blowing up one tank, everything inside of the tank coming outside the tank and into the air. The fighting seemed to stop while everyone watched ... and thousand-one, thousand two, thousand three, the debris and the bodies thumped and clunked back to earth.

Jesus Christ, somebody said, from one side or the other.

The anti-aircraft guns swiveled and fired, smoking, the whoever it was who had decided to give it a try having learned their craft quickly or they were gun experts from the military, but it was like a video game it seemed. Boom! ... swivel ... Boom! sweep ... there! ... spotter ... *Fire!* Boom! ... wow ... swivel, fire ... load.

Evey fired in Alexa's direction and missed over her head, and ducked as Alexa returned with a short burst into the ground.

Trevor advanced on the south rebel bunker.

Marv's group crawled on bellies, getting so close to Korey and his team.

"Yeah, no, yeah, yeah, go," Marv waved his arm over his head.

Carroll crawled out of his vehicle and took his time climbing from the door to the roof, down again to the hood to watch with his glass.

He let it go on for ten minutes, twenty, twenty-five and gave the order to withdraw. He didn't want it to end today, and it didn't look like they were going to be able to easily do it this day anyway.

"What?" said Lara as she saw it happening. She looked right, left, behind her and everywhere saw the government troops retreating with their wounded and their big armor, piling the corpses on the trucks where they could and leaving the other dead and the smoking hulks where they lay.

Carroll's Log: Made significant progress, flags impressive. Need to take out minefield with air power. Nice touch, whichever pilot dropped the red shoes in the middle of town.

Lara's Journal: I can't believe we made it another day. Old people awesome, some were nurses, one doctor even. They brought supplies, my God. The saloon is a hospital now, no room for barracks. Everybody hanging in there, it seems.

Evey's father, Jorge, now had a regular routine, and watched the evening coverage of "The Battle of Oz" on TV with the binoculars and his dinner on a tray. The TWINS cap sat on the bed stand. He now wore his VIKINGS cap, with horns and yellow pigtails.

He could tell by the sounds outside that the kids were heading back to school. The leaves were changing. The nurses talked about fall things. He ached to hold his own daughter and grand-daughter. He searched for them on the little screen.

The scouts were out, along with the electronic motion detectors and the spotlight scanning the perimeter constantly.

Brooke had organized a talent contest for the night meeting in the south bunker. In fact a tunnel had been built now connecting the bunkers and also the bunkers with the house headquarters and the saloon barracks hospital. The talent show was kind of a celebration of that.

They had organized into teams for the talent show, into towns.

Ike and Frida from Brooklyn told jokes. The Texans sang country, had guitars and harmonica.

South Dakota got everybody up and jitterbugging.

Gene read a short story written "by a Max," that he had found in the CRUSHER files, cardboard boxes.

North Carolina, Ginny, Freddy, Beau, read poetry.

The Twin Cities team was Jim and Lara doing "Paradise By The Dashboard Lights." Brooke and Korey sat close, watching, holding hands.

After the talent show there was Texas chili and California tea, and a meeting.

Hope from Arcata and Dave from Rapid City burst into the room, sweating, breathing hard, smiling.

The two hugged and everyone cheered as Dave held up the U.S. flag they had just captured from behind the government lines.

Evey led everyone in a prayer. She passed out pieces of paper and asked folks to write down the name of one person who had gone before them as Jim and Korey made the fire.

"Geronimo I," said Lara as she got up and dropped her piece into the blaze.

"Geronimo II," said Evey.

"John Brown."

"Fred Hampton."

Phil Berrigan. Joe. Ariel ... Skylar, Rick ... AIM, Che, George Washington, Villa, Sophie Scholl ... Rueben, Hector, and so it went, for an hour, people walking up one by one, tossing their paper into the fire, going back, doing it again.

Patrick wrote "Davey Crocket," crumpled it in his fist and tossed it into the blaze.

"And now," said Evey, standing up, brushing crumbs from her jeans and beginning to again hand out the little ripped paper pieces.

"Write your name on this and toss your name ... into the fire."

Evey and Lara and Brooke, Jim, Korey, passed out coffee and tea and cupcakes on napkins as everyone sat on the ground, against a dirt wall, on metal folding chairs, on bean bags.

Lara walked to the middle.

"It's over," she announced.

"We have won and we are going to live to fight another day. That is a victory."

"No fucking way!" said Cole from Austin.

"You have to believe that with me," Lara continued, standing in the middle of them, one side of her face lit by the fire, the other in shadow.

"We are not running away. We are going to another place. To continue to fight."

"Where are we going?" asked Gene.

"Wouldn't you fucking like to know," said Jim, standing, walking right up nose to nose.

"I say string 'im up," said Jim, holding a noose he had made himself inches from Gene's face.

"Let's not get into that, shall we," said Lara.

"We know there are agents among us."

"What?" said Gene, "are you saying I'm ..."

Lara motioned for everyone to be calm, to back away, stand down.

"One more day," she said.

"Tomorrow morning's battle will be merely to cover our retreat."

She nodded for Korey, Jim and the other men to take hold of Gene.

She explained that the government troops would be expecting them to try to leave in the dark and they had The Dry Gulch filled with soldiers every night.

"That's our only hope," she said.

"They know that pretty clearly. The only way is to go during the chaos of a battle. And so ..."

She asked for volunteers to stay with her to fight to put on a show while the others attempted to leave through The Dry Gulch.

"All the others, the old-timers," said Lara, "you guys are leaving, that's an order. We need people to carry on the next step."

All the old people raised their hands, along with Patrick and Henry, sitting in back.

"We'll stay," said Cole of the Texas group.

"Y'all get outa here. We got this."

"We're not leaving if you're not comin'," said Jim.

"That's right," said Korey.

Brooke and Evey walked up and said they weren't going either.

In the morning, before dawn, everyone gathered in the two bunkers with Evey and Lara. They dipped their fingers into jars of paint left over from their being artists in the first battle, at Lake Wobegon, and painted each others faces. They made themselves clowns, warriors, camouflaged.

The ones who were leaving hugged the others. They all cried.

"Later, bro," Jim shook Cole's hand.

Korey, Patrick and Henry walked away together to sit and smoke in the dark.

Ike and Frida from Brooklyn were joining the escape group, along with Hope from Arcata and Alice, Charlie, Cheryl and Dave from Rapid City.

Beau and Ginny from Asheville chugged their coffee and climbed up to their spots in the anti-aircraft guns. Addy from Des Moines and Greta from Austin took their posts as their helpers. Mandy and Cole from Austin headed out to the north bunker after many fist bumps.

Freddy and Alan from Asheville split to take the east and west barricades. The old people finished lining up their canisters and launchers for their fireworks palooza.

The old people walked up to the ones leaving, the traditional CRUSHERS, with the tattoos, who were not feeling very great about leaving the others behind.

The old people placed leis they had made over night from plastic flowers they had found in the saloon around the necks of Brooke, Evey, Rachel, Lara, Korey and Jim and bid them "good journey."

"Aaaah," said Lara.

Evey set Rachel on Roswell and climbed up behind her.

On Roswell's rump Evey had painted in red: California OR Bust.

"Boom!"

Patrick and Henry turned from Korey and ran.

They sprinted to Korey's old position, aimed their rifles and waited.

Gene sat in the saloon, his hands tied behind his back and his feet also secured.

The captured American flag fluttered above the saloon as the morning breeze started in.

"Okay, git outa here!" hollered Beau as he swiveled his gun and blasted the silence and The Dry Gulch. Ginny swung around and fired into the north, again, again.

And, so here we go.

The old people lit the fireworks, the government circle shot to life like an electrical switch flicked on.

The ghost town of Irving, Kansas ... Oz pulsed in the early morning like an L.A. discotheque, while the CRUSHERS with the tattoos slumped toward The Dry Gulch like partyers turned away at the door. They made their way carefully down the slope and disappeared into the cavern, unable to hear even their own footsteps with WW III happening right above them.

Patrick and Henry fired automatic weapons supported by sandbags at Marv's position and Marv's team responded with a rebel yell and pop-poppop-pop.

Carroll awakened in the back seat of his SUV outpost and jumped to the driver's seat to get up to speed.

Alexa found herself pinned down, searching in the dark for her phone, and Trevor dived to the ground to escape the bottle rockets and big guns.

Mike Braxton, on the northern front opposite Cole and Mandy gathered his line and moved out as Freddy and Alan, at the east and west barricades, began to take heavy shelling.

Evey, walking Roswell with Rachel riding, stopped as they heard voices, screaming, someone in agony. She bowed her head and kept going, over rocks, carefully, slowly.

Braxton got within reach of the northern bunker and tossed a grenade, which heaved Cole and Mandy up and over the sandbags.

A bullet thumped Trevor's thigh. He fell hard, on his nose, in the dirt.

Marv spread his team out to flank Patrick and Henry.

Henry lit two cigarettes and gave one to Patrick.

He raised up again, laying down a line of dust and rocks pretty much in the direction of the advancing troops.

Patrick stood to shoot and spun like a top as a round took his right shoulder.

A burst and another covered Beau and his big gun. He swung and swiveled wildly, then rolled out onto the ground, where Addy and Greta lay. Ginny worked all the harder to cover all sides until she fired no more.

Bullets whacked the saloon walls, going in one side and out the other, and the old people brigade lay on the wooden floor and also in the kitchen and out back. The blood dipped slowly toward the leaning porch out front.

Patrick and Henry stood back-to-back to shoot forward, right, left, behind as the rest of the battlefield lay silent, smoking.

Lara, Evey, Korey, Jim, Brooke stopped and looked back and saw nothing.

They kept looking.

"Oh! There!" said Lara.

And it was the saloon on fire and they turned and kept going, as Brooke's Special Team film crew kept shooting.

As Carroll's engine roared to bring him to town, Mike Braxton walked around town, turning over the bodies. He went everywhere.

"They're not here," he said to Marv, out of breath.

"Who?" said Marv.

"None of them," said Braxton.

Back to the howling old owl in the woods
Hunting the horny back toad
Oh I've finally decided my future lies
Beyond the yellow brick road

— Elton John

When your time comes to die, be not like those whose hearts are filled with fear of death, so that when their time comes they weep and pray for a little more time to live their lives over again in a different way. Sing your death song, and die like a hero going home.

—Tecumseh, Shawnee Chief

FIFTY-ONE

When you try to write a story, they say you need to get your characters in trouble and then get them out, that's what a story is. But when you are writing about real people they pretty much do that themselves.

The CRUSHERS made their escape, out of The Dry Gulch, into a small town where they mixed with the locals who did not know what was happening over in Irving, though they heard the noise. Because the press, for a while camped near Irving, had long been chased away. Evey found a place for Roswell for the time being, and tables in the little café, as Lara of course swallowed her pride once again and called Prince Hope for help.

Hope brought the red Suburbans Brooke and the others had left in Mayfield. Jim asked if he could take one and meet them in Minneapolis.

"I just got something I need to do."

Jim pulled the dusty red Suburban up to the old mailbox, unaware of anyone anywhere, of the F.B.I. sitting on the red Suburbans in Mayfield, of being followed. There was nobody in his rearview mirror, nobody nowhere.

Looking out over the old battlefield, and up on the hill, the Iowa state mental hospital, Jim could not believe he was here again. There was Bloody Pond where he had sliced the throat of the soldier, there was the farm house, in a million pieces, the glint of the graveyard fence in the sun, three large skeletons, parts of Rick's SUV.

He and Danny, sitting in the Bumfuck café, had long ago said they were going to get this guy out of prison. He was in there for writing. For writing a letter to the editor and he shouldn't be. It stuck in Jim's head because something like that happened to Jim's brother in northern Minnesota.

He wrote a letter to the Hibbing paper about logging and about bears and he got called names and rocks thrown at his car and he ended up leaving town. Jim was not a good writer. He used to like to listen to Max and his stories.

And Rick and Skylar and the soldier and so many others had died right here.

But the poor guy was still up there in prison.

So, Jim was going to get him out. He fought the urge to pull into the lane and walk around the old battlefield and rather pulled away, down the Iowa dirt road, toward the mental hospital on the hill, his AR-15 on the passenger seat, his pistol in his belt and his knife in his hand as he steered.

Jim parked and looked at the building.

After a while he noticed a face in an upstairs window.

He got out and the face went away.

He heard a car headed up the gravel road behind him. He watched the black and white sheriff's car with the top white light flashing pull up the drive and stop. The deputy talked a bit on his microphone, put on his hat and got out.

"You can't be here," he said.

"I'm picking up a friend."

"What's your friend's name?"

"Uh … Bill, Billy."

"These don't have any friends, or family. That's why they're here. For their own good."

"That's not what I heard."

"You're gonna have to leave."

"I don't think so," said Jim.

"You don't? Jesus Christ. Really? We're gonna do this?" said the deputy, reaching back into the car for his radio mic and pulling his pistol, keeping an eye on Jim.

"Yep, Zeke."

"Zeke? Really? What are these tracks out here? Bigfoot? Too big," said the deputy.

"They look like clown tracks to me," said Jim, smiling as the deputy continued to talk on the radio.

Jim heard "Ten Most Wanted."

Jim looked back and the deputy now squatted, held his gun with both hands and pointed at Jim.

Jim pulled his own gun and the deputy shot, missing. Jim returned fire and hit the deputy in the shoulder, spinning him around, knocking him to the ground.

He heard sirens. He ran to the deputy, kicked his gun out of the way, knelt down and checked his shoulder. He took off his belt and strapped it as tight as he could around the upper arm. He set the deputy up against the car and told him to stay put.

"I'm leaving, you'll be all right, there's more of yours coming."

The deputy just stared at Jim, clutching his arm, his teeth tight.

"Here," said Jim. He took off the belt and retied it, wound it around.

"That's a little better, shit you'll be okay."

Unmarked black cars stopped at the entrance to the hospital quarter section.

Jim sucked his lips and peeked over the top of the sheriff's car. The radio squawked like chickens in the shed with a fox.

"James Hedlund," said the voice in the megaphone.

Jim pressed himself against the police car.

"Officer Blount!"

"Yeah!" shouted the wounded deputy.

"I'm hit! I'm all right."

The news that the deputy was wounded seem to cause a commotion down below of doors and movement on gravel, in weeds.

"Jim! This is Mike Braxton."

Jim recognized the name.

He fired over the heads of where he thought the sneaking agents would be, on the left, on the right.

They returned his shots, plunking the police car and the red Suburban.

Jim saw a face in a window on one of the high floors.

He raised up and rested his pistol on the hood of the car and fired, again, again.

He wished he had brought his rifle with him from the passenger seat of the Suburban.

The windows of the cop car and the Suburban exploded in an avalanche of shots from down below.

Boomboomboom!

The sounds echoed out over the corn and the flatness. A blue jay cried out.

Jim reloaded with a clip from his shirt pocket. He smelled pigs, had to pee, just let it go, and raised his head to shoot.

Others appeared beside the face in the upstairs window, a man and a woman wearing white. Jim spotted a few lonely cars parked in the weedy lot behind the building. He needed a way out of here.

He fired and fired, click, click.

He spotted the deputy's eyes on his own pistol, in the gravel. They both dived for it, the deputy crying out in pain. Jim sprawled out, got the gun and crawled back to the car fort.

Bullets flattened the tires on the squad car: boom! boom! boom! boom!

And then the Suburban, both sitting there like old elephants.

Jim looked, trying to see what was happening. He saw more cars, deputy cars, fire trucks, an ambulance. For a moment he pressed his hands against his ears against the sound. A helicopter flapped somewhere he could not see.

A vision of Butch and Sundance flashed.

Jim drew his knife, took a deep breath.

"Fuck it.

"You'll be all right," he said to the deputy, still sprawled out in the gravel as he ran around the car.

He charged with the knife and the empty pistol at the lead car, the one with the guy with the megaphone.

"Aaaah!" he yelled, not able to think of anything better.

Braxton saw him coming, down the lane.

"Hold your fire!" he shouted into the megaphone.

Jim thought he was yelling at him. He kept coming, yelling as much as he could. It was farther than he thought.

Braxton climbed over the hood of his car and ran at Jim.

Before Jim could swing the knife Braxton hit him with a shoulder in the stomach. They rolled together. Jim struggled with the knife, having lost the pistol in the collision.

Braxton gained position and knelt in Jim's back, pinning his arms behind him. He handcuffed Jim as a dozen men rushed up, yanked Jim to his feet and rushed him away.

Jim hunched in the back seat of the unmarked black F.B.I. vehicle, breathing hard, sweat dripping into his eyes, smelling his own piss in his jeans. The fighter in the dressing room after the bout. He'd been here before.

Braxton rode shotgun and talked on the radio while another agent drove.

They talked with each other, a little on the wounded deputy, what road to take. Braxton looked back at Jim, not speaking, turned back around.

Jim, sat out of breath, adrenaline rushing through him, sweating, feeling cuts on his face, his arms, something in his leg pulling.

He heard the gravel as they pulled away. He squinted into the bright daylight. His head swiveled back and forth, as he tried to look down each row of corn. They skirted around Bumfuck. Jim looked behind to see stern silhouettes in the next car, gravel smoke.

Jim was relieved to see that the two F.B.I. agents spoke but a little, that he would not have to talk or be interrogated. Braxton seemed either fascinated or annoyed by Iowa. He looked and looked out his own window, for something, meaning, escape. Braxton talked on the car radio about something, cryptic. He exchanged a meaningful look with the driver agent and silence followed.

Jim was still excited, flushed, enjoying the trip.

They found the Interstate, heading north.

Jim, still handcuffed behind his back, leaned forward awkwardly and looked out at normal life, only feet, inches away, wondering what it was like, as if it were outer space, another planet, that he could not survive there in that atmosphere. Look at those people, driving, laughing. Normal things were now inaccessible and wondrous. The adrenaline rush was gone and Jim felt sad, but he bucked up, sat as straight as his numbing hands would allow against the back seat and would not let them see him ... cry?

Wondered a bit about the others, what had become of them, where they were gathering to have breakfast and laugh and talk, but mostly about himself. He was hungry, his cuffs dug into his wrists and his shoulders and back ached.

He saw the signs for "Entering Minnesota," Owatonna, Faribault, Bloomington ... joined the fast city traffic, saw signs for downtown. He always liked it here in this moment, feeling a part of something, and then came the green sign for where his old prison sat. A sick feeling entered his stomach, like bad milk. It's just there and there's nothing you can do about it. His jaw got like a spasm or a charlie horse.

Jim remembered being a kid. He didn't want to, the thoughts came on their own, like dreams you had no intention of having. He was in grade school, coming in from the cold to the warm, in middle school, a fight on the playground, a girl he wanted to talk to, Patricia ... high school, certain classrooms, lunch room, smoking in the restroom just like the song, out in the parking lot, skipping school to go drinking and hunting ... working in the woods, construction ... the group home. Why did he do that? He wondered and he guessed he just did it for the hell of it. All that CRUSHER shit. Killing the guy at Bloody Pond. *Damn.*

Braxton looked around at him. Jim looked again and saw at least two cars following them.

He felt alone, wow, don't do this, Jimmy, and he fought between sadness ... big sadness and defiance, bravery, with sad kicking bravery's fuckin' ass.

They hit hard, the entrance drive dip into the prison, "Walmart Civilian Public Service Center."

Jim glanced quickly for the protest, the signs, the attack to free him. He saw people climbing out of cars, normal life. An actual shiver ran down his spine and he could not feel his fingers.

Braxton and the other agent got Jim out of the car like they do, and into the familiar grey halls and walls, now joined by more agents, more guards.

Not much talking.

None at all around Jim. He was now gripped by familiar prison guards. Braxton had worked his way to the front of the growing line.

They stopped. There was commotion up front.

They crowded down the long narrow hall and he saw through the long windows the rec yard below with the new big wood thing taking up most of the fucking room.

There was discussion at the front of the line, stairs or elevator.

Somebody motioned and Jim's hosts ushered him up and stuffed him in the elevator to go down, two floors. Jim faced front, smashed between five, six prison guards, maybe an agent or two.

The door opened and Jim was shoved out first. The rest of his entourage awaited his arrival, Braxton, the only one without stoic face, red in the face and wide eyes; Alexa, Trevor, Marv, with scrapes and bruises on their faces, whom he did not recognize.

Jim thought about his own cell. He would get a shower, maybe even cigarettes, something to eat. He would be able to check out his own cuts and bruises and get some sleep, figure the rest out later.

Someone opened the grey steel door to the rec yard.

No. Wait. Wait. Not this, not yet. I don't want to walk, I want to eat, smoke, sleep.

Well, okay, whatever, he thought. He swiveled to talk to the guard behind him.

"Can I get these off?" he said, meaning the handcuffs. If he was in the rec yard they take off handcuffs. The guard stared right through him and Jim turned back around, kept walking.

A guard in front and who knows how many behind, they led him to the steps.

"What?"

On the platform a giant awaited.

Jim's front guard stopped at the steps and nodded and somehow from all his schooling and television he knew where to go. He climbed the steps, carefully, not without effort with his hands behind his back, but I got this, I can do this, I'm a good worker, I'm good.

He made the platform and looked at the giant looking at him. He walked toward him and stopped at the trap door. He knew what this was. He had walked around and around it for hours. But this was not right. This should take years and years, not now.

The giant wore guard clothes, black and dark blue, a Vikings full-face snowmobile stocking cap. Something hung at his side in a hand.

Jim turned, toward the wall and the hall and the window.

He saw an argument, Braxton, arms waving, yelling, some others holding him back.

Jim sucked his lips, then just as soon flared them out. Fuck them, he said in his own head. I was never one of them anyhow.

At the bottom of the steps a short, fat guard with one foot on the bottom step and leaning on the wood railing read from papers in his hands. Jim couldn't hear, but he did recognize "James Kristian Hedlund."

The giant offered the thing in his hand to Jim.

A Packers full-face stocking hat.

"Fuck you," Jim thought of saying and didn't.

He shook his head, "no, man."

Jim thought of everything right then. He had to. All the shit in the car he had already thought about, but there was more. He wanted to give them the Pussy Riot look of that defiant, beautiful Russian dissident being led down the steps by the guards, so smart. Actually had showed Jim the video on YouTube and Jim had thought, wow, someone like that woman really existed and he felt excited by the possibilities of the world when a second before there was nothing.

"Smoke?" he looked at the giant and the giant shook his head, no.

Jim saw more commotion in the window.

The giant grabbed his arm and pulled him towards, to stand on the cutout in the floor. The dangling thick noose bounced in his face, thumped his nose.

Jim looked at the one guard now standing almost at attention at the bottom of the stairs, two more at the door.

The giant with black-gloved hands forced the rope over Jim's head, scraping the nose and yanked it tight.

The door shoved open. Jim saw a hand on the door knob and someone rushing inside.

And then a loud sound, like the crack of wood at twenty below at night, or a rifle from a deer stand or a barricade.

And then dark. And then nothing.

He kicked and swung and gurgled as he struggled, he blew snot and tears and blood out his ass. He fought like hell as fucking long as he could.

Jim's green eyes glared straight-on at those dead faces in the window, as the man kept running toward him, but he was already gone.

Note from the narrator:

Discovered by the C.I.A. on the walls of a MEN's restroom at a restaurant near Beverly, Indiana, just off Interstate 80, on the sidewall of the farthest stall, to the east, written in Black Magic Marker:

"From the real files of the F.B.I. and C.I.A., the ones without the black Magic Marker: 'We murdered one hundred witnesses to the John Kennedy murder.'"

/United States Government: Memorandum/

Patrick, Henry

I think I'm an all right guy.

— Todd Snider

FIFTY-TWO

He sat outside, in the thick black dirt, in the roses, in the sun.
The Pres'dent played with his toy soldiers, drawing lines in the soil, mounds, ditches. He moved tanks into line, more soldiers over here. Over here, a giraffe.

Back here, he slides back, digging a ditch with his knee, black cars marked "F.B.I.," and ones marked "C.I.A."

He flicked over soldiers with his fingers and made shooting sounds with his mouth that he had practiced. He moved into position the bobblehead named Prince Hope that someone had sent to him.

Bam. Pow. Shoosh. Pow-pow. Da-da. Tthth, pffft.

"Aaaah!"

He looked around him, over his shoulder, up at the high windows with curtains, out on the lawn, heard the yelling sounds from the front fences, the occasional gunshot-like sound that was only fireworks.

The Leader Of The Free World moved the F.B.I. and C.I.A. cars fast, throwing up dirt, zooom! nyoooowwww, rmmmm!

For a moment the blank look left the face of The Chief Executive, The Commander In Chief as he glanced back over his shoulder with a wry grin.

Note from the narrator:

> Discovered by the C.I.A. on the walls of a MEN's restroom at the Elkart, Missouri Interstate 80 rest stop, written in pencil into the concrete block over the middle urinal:

"From the real files of the F.B.I. and C.I.A., the ones without the black Magic Marker: 'We murdered all those people at Waco and at Oklahoma City.'"

/United States Government: Memorandum/

Jefferson

Note from the narrator:

Discovered by the C.I.A. written with a silver tweezers into the sink of a MEN's restroom in Pisgah, Missouri:

"From the real files of the F.B.I. and C.I.A., the ones without the black Magic Marker: 'Nobody died at Sandy Hook.'"

United States Government: Memorandum/

Korey

ARGO: What is the long, hard night that America must go through that you've spoken of?

SAHL: She has to hang on through a period of the military and the C.I.A. with a blank check trying to sell fascism. If she can hang on long enough, Americans may yet live in the country in which they were born. And that is the country structured by Tom Paine and Tom Jefferson. … And the renaissance will be that a ground swell of public opinion will flush out the rascals because the C.I.A. has infiltrated every area of our national life. I'm afraid that the country they subverted best was the United States.

— Mort Sahl interview with Perry Adams,
underground newspaper *Argo*, 1968

FIFTY-THREE

"There's all this new shit, man."
"That's not right."
"It totally is."

Korey and Washington riffed their Lebowski routine, which they did all the time. Even here, at Jim's funeral, standing over Jim's grave, not far from Geronimo's grave, in the pauper's cemetery. They just did it, standing by themselves, behind all those over the grave, on a beautiful day in the city.

Dude. Hey. We're talking about unchecked aggression here.
Forget it, you're out of your element. These freeking amateurs.
I'm talking about drawing a line in the sand.
Has the whole world gone crazy? ...

Lara and Evey let go their red balloons.

Ike and Frida from Brooklyn tossed in lumps of dirt.

Hope from Arcata stood by, something like at-attention, along with Alice, Charlie, Cheryl and Dave from Rapid City.

Lara talked about Jim's life. Evey hugged Rachel close against her leg and all stared into the hole.

They wore disguises, old people clothes, white hair, toilet paper stuck to their shoes, provided by Prince Hope, and rented old people cars. Hope couldn't be there, he said, but he sent along money for breakfast and his "best wishes" to Jim and his family members, from Hibbing, who had also sent their best wishes and flowers to the service at the funeral home.

A police car drove slowly through and Ike flipped the car the bird after it was gone.

"Yeah!" said Korey. "Fuck them!"

"Good, Korey," whispered Lara, "awesome."

"What *are* we gonna do?" said Frida.

"Evey?"

"We're goin' home," said Evey.

"They'll find you," said Ike.

"Yeah," said Evey. "Yeah, they will."

"We should quit," said Lara.

"We can't," Evey said.

"We're wanted. We can go to court and prison, probly for life or hang."

"I didn't know they hang," said Ike.

"Evidently," said Cheryl, subtly nodding at the casket in the hole, "they do."

Evey put a hand over Rachel's ear and pressed her head more tightly against her leg.

"I thought it was injection," Ike went on.

"Yeah, I don't know," said Lara.

"I guess they do it all."

Evey sat at the edge of the grave, dangling her feet over, and then Lara eased herself down. Korey and Washington came up and plopped down with them and the others sat, forming a circle around the rectangle open grave.

"Over there's Geronimo," Evey nodded toward the knoll and the tree.

She talked a little about Gerry and how they started.

"This is a very complicated case," Korey whispered, sitting hunched over, cross-legged, yoga-style, his grey mustache tickling his nose.

"Stop," said Lara, staring at Korey.

"So," said Ike.

"What is the role of the super hero in society?"

Lara and Evey looked at him like what the bloody hell?

"No, really," said Ike.

"I'm serious. What about Geronimo. We started all this, you did. Doesn't it still mean the same thing, after all?

"Just askin', ya know."

Evey drew in the dirt with a stick.

"Yeah," she said.

"Save the world," Ike mumbled.

"When we're fifty what are we gonna think about us then?" said Evey.

"Fifty?" said Lara.

"Yeah," said Evey, "what if we do though?"

"That's too long," said Lara.

"Yeah, but what if we do?" said Evey as Rachel put her head on Evey's lap and watched all the other CRUSHERS in the circle overlooking the empty air, the open space of Jim's grave.

What in God's name are you blathering about?

Washington whispered, thinking nobody heard.

I'll tell you what I'm blathering about. I've got new information, man. New shit has come to light.

Lara, Evey and the others sat in silence in the dirt, like old people do at funerals, heads down, listening, as Korey and Washington went on and on and on, Rachel slept in Evey's lap, and a faint rainbow appeared over the downtown buildings.

"It must be raining over there, man," said Charlie, pointing, but nobody really looked.

"Not here."

"Nope," said Alice, "not here. Not here at all."

Lara walked alone.

The others tossed their wigs into the grave and allowed the waiting impatient grave diggers to fill in the hole. They headed over the lawn to the restaurant nearby where Kaitylyn used to work, but nobody said that. Lara said she wanted to walk by herself and would join them later. Where do you think you'll be. I don't know, said Evey. Okay, that works, said Lara.

She walked through a quiet neighborhood and sat in a large park and strolled over a freeway, missing Kaitylyn, C.I.A. agent or not, missing Jim, Skylar, Rick, Joe, Ariel, Zim, Max, Morgan, wondering about Prince Hope and the guy in the mental hospital in Iowa they had tried to break out, and her parents and her brother and sister, her high school soccer team, going back to school to study nursing and how it felt to be hanged.

Lara avoided many eyes, walked with her head down, imagining the screech of stopping tires and the squeaks of many doors and shouting. There she is! She recognized a street sign and headed down, found herself standing outside her granma's house, which had not changed.

That you? There's food in the fridge! I'm on my way to bowling! Good to see you! Thanks gram's.

Lara opened the refrigerator and stared and let it go shut.

She flopped onto the sofa, pointed the clicker and stopped herself. She opened the door to the basement, where gram's kept her wine. She found the light and clomped down, slowly.

Her eyes went right to a corner of the old gold sofa, where the contents of Actually's package, sent by F.B.I. agent Mike Braxton, formed a square, where her grandma had rearranged the mess Lara had left: The Actually Basement Tapes.

1) Actually, there's a town in Nevada, near Area 51, that is called Rachel. Just sayin'.

2) Terror is theatre... Theatre's a con trick. Do you know what that means? Con trick? You've been deceived. " - John Le Carré, *The Little Drummer Girl*, 1983

3) CRUSHER ... "C.I.A. puts acronyms in all caps" - just sayin'.

4) "There were no planes." — John Lear

5) The law of karma

And, again at the bottom was the fortune cookie.

The photo of agent Kaitylyn.

And an unopened envelope she must have missed after freaking out about Kaitylyn:

"If you ever really want to fucking win some day."

Someone had written across the envelope, had to be Actually. Lara smiled at her thought. Maybe it was a note from her granma she had slipped in where Lara would some day see it. Gram's did have an old black and white photo sitting on the fake fireplace of she and some friends at some kind of concert.

Lara pulled the papers from the envelope, set them in her lap and read them one by one.

She ran out of the basement, out the back door, jumping the little cement steps, falling, one knee in the garden.

She found them. She didn't know how, but she found them, all sitting together in the back room at Dunn Bros.

Lara, sweating, tried to catch her breath and also at the same time let them know about her incredible idea that she had got just now after reading the just now discovered new envelope hidden in The Actually Basement Tapes. (*Wait. That manila envelope came from the F.B.I., from agent Mike Braxton. He said it came from Actually and he had found it after going through the stuff of the dead CRUSHERs after the battle.*)

She put that thought out of her mind. The idea was just so incredible.

"Yeah, that *couuuld* work," someone said and then went back to her phone.

And others worked their phones or looked around or kept talking about other stuff.

Lara felt like, what? No, you don't understand, this is it, this is the thing, our new thing that we can do and we can actually win, don't you idiots understand, anything?

That's what she felt like.

What she did was suck down a big breath and play with Rachel and try to calm herself and be patient with these idiots. Because she had nowhere else to go on earth.

I was talkin' with my girlfriend, told her I was stressed, said I'm goin' off the deep end, she said god for once give it a rest.

— Todd Snider

FIFTY-FOUR

"Yeah, so, we're goin' back."
Dave from Rapid City announced.
"What?" said Evey.

Korey shook Dave's hand as did Washington. Others began the round of hugs.

"Yeah, you're not like really doing anything," said Cheryl.

"You're getting old ... er, er!" said Charlie.

"We got things we could still do," said Hope from Arcata.

"You, too?" said Evey.

"And Dunn Bros.," said Dave, "is, yeah, it's okay, but it's like not that great anyway. There's a whole world out there."

"Wait, sit down," said Evey.

"Please."

Evey looked to Lara as in, say something and it better be great.

"Well," Lara began.

And she motioned them to huddle in closer so she wouldn't have to yell, although the music and the other chatter gave them some cover. Lara smelled the coffee, heard the cars on the street whooshing through the remains of a quick rain spell, pressed her feet into the hard wood and scrunched up her butt on the chair, feeling a bit skinny these days, she felt the bone on the wood.

"Not to come down hard on you, but you can't just go home. You're wanted, probably, for certain. People died out there. I would say for sure they know who you are and are looking for you. That's one thing.

"And the other thing is, weren't you fucking listening to what I just said?"

She looked around the group. They were listening now.

At that point there was a big commotion as Brooke and her reality show production team clomped all over the wood floor and asked at the counter where the CRUSHERS were and everybody thought *WHAT?* and shut the fuck up.

And so they had to go all through them finding them in the back and saying hello and Lara was talking and sit down and what's this all about, why is everyone all quiet and huddled together and shit?

"They're heading out," Brooke whispered to Evey, "what's this about?"

Cheryl screeched her chair to get up.

Everybody looked at her.

"Just goin' to the restroom, chill people. No, I've got this gun hidden behind the towels and I'm gettin' it, now, to come back and shoot you all. That's totally what I'm doing."

They waited in silence until Cheryl returned and sat.

"You people are so crazy," she said.

"So, if we stay, we're goin' to Hollywood," said Ike.

"Yeah, we'll attack like a studio, a set … woah … Star Wars …," said Washington.

"Yeah we could do that," said Lara.

"But we're not.

"Listen. I think you're gon …"

Lara began to lay out her fantastic new plan and stopped.

On the wood floor, out in front, headed her way, came a familiar stomp, sixteenth-note tiny steps. She rested her hand on the Ruger on her hip.

Kaitylyn stepped up into the elevated room, standing deceptively tall in high black boots.

Evey and Brooke put a hand to their mouths as exclamation.

They all looked. Lara began to ease her weapon from the holster.

Slow is smooth and smooth is ...

"Excuse me, ma'am," Charlie began.

"If I can find you idiots here, they can," said Kaitylyn.

"They?"

Lara stood up.

"Who is that?" muttered Hope from Arcata.

"We're good, said Lara as she stood.

"You'd better go."

I quit. You don't ever quit. Yeah, maybe. But here I am. Is that okay? No. Yes. Maybe. What the fuck, Kaitylyn? ... someone mentioned Jim and they hugged and cried together.

Lara told Kaitylyn to get a coffee and sit in the other room while she told the new people about her.

I don't trust her. You don't know her. It's not your decision. Yes it is!

"Yes. It is my decision," said Lara.

"It just is."

Lara called Kaitylyn back. Kaitylyn took an open chair in the middle of the CRUSHER group.

"You can't stay, Kaitylyn," said Lara.

"That's the decision of the group?" said Kaitylyn.

"Yes," said Lara.

"No, it's my decision."

"All right, then," said Kaitylyn.

She stood and walked out, her short loud steps on the wood floor beating out rhythm to the banter and the coffee machines and the horns on the street.

"Anybody who wants to go before we talk about what we're going to talk about, go now," said Lara.

Everyone looked at the floor.

Chairs squeaked. Footfalls padded over the floor.

Lara looked up to see Hope from Arcata and Dave and Cheryl from Rapid City leaving.

They moved all their shit and took over a long table way in back, next to some windows that looked into the alley.

Lara sat at one end, Evey and Rachel at the other. Brooke, Korey, Washington, Ike and Frida from Brooklyn, Alice and Charlie from Rapid City filled the available wooden chairs.

Lara told them all about it, the package, The Actually Basement Tapes, and the plan he had given them.

She was relieved to see smiles around the table.

"The Battle of Wonderland," said Ike.

Note from the narrator ...

From "Not Exactly A Radio Show," a live podcast that traveled the circuit of Twins Cities bars for about six months, produced by former members of The Prince Hope Show:

... The 9/11 Museum was unveiled and opened a few years ago in New York City. Which begs the question, where will the Museum For Democracy be placed? It should be in Washington, D.C., we would think. Or, yeah, yeah, you're right ... right next to the 9/11 Museum in New York City.

I know, right? The Museum For Democracy will have a walkway from the 9/11 Museum and will have artifacts from Sept. 11, 2001 ... such as the TV tapes and transcripts telling us not ten minutes after it happened that it was done by Osama bin Laden. There will also be the missing video from the surrounding area showing the missile hitting the Pentagon. The Democracy Museum will also have artifacts from Nov. 22, 1963 – OKC, Waco, Wellstone, RFK, MLK, 9/11, Sandy Hook, Boston.

The Democracy Museum will have the tape of Dan Rather telling us the Zapruder film shows Kennedy's head and body lurching forward, it will have the bullets found on the street next to J.D. Tippit's body, the second and third unexploded bombs found inside the Murrah Building, the charred bodies of the children at Waco, the flight recorder of the Wellstone plane, the photos in the pantry of the Ambassador Hotel confiscated by the Los Angeles police, the real investigation into who are H. Wayne Carver, Gene Rosen and Robbie Parker, the real investigation into who really died or was injured at the Boston marathon.

And stuff like that.

Hast Du etwas Zeit fuer mich?
Dann singe ich ein Lied fuer Dich
Von 99 Luftballons

— Nena

FIFTY-FIVE

If you raise your voice when you're talking you've got a better chance of being understood, it feels like to me.

That's why blacks talk so much and so loud. That's all they've got. White people don't need it usually. And then the arm waving.

I feel like I should write this book. Yeah, I guess I want to, but more that I should. You ever feel that way about stuff? It's like it's not me writing the book, someone else is in control. I guess I've read where writers feel like that, like they are just taking dictation, I dunno, it's weird, anyway, you write what you know, huh. Thing is, I don't really know that much. I talk to no one. Yes, I have done some things, been a reporter, worked at a group home like the CRUSHERS, yeah. Anyway, so, is the world ending? I don't know. No one I talk to seems to know and I talk to no one, maybe just for that very reason. Sometimes I have these funny, at least I think they're funny observations. Not very fucking often, but sometimes. I saw one guy playing catch with another guy, tossing a nerf football and the one guy throws the ball, realizes the other guy isn't looking and he gives the international sign for oops, you know, shoulders up, open mouth, wide eyes, head tilted to get the ball to not hit the guy in the head. Oh, nothing. YHTBT. You had to be there. The biggest example of patriotism and courage in American history is the dozens of people in Dealey Plaza running toward the Grassy Knoll after

JFK was shot because they thought that was where the killers were. I watch a lot of YouTube.

Sometimes it feels to me it's better not to know all the innerworkings of something. Like a car. Isn't it nicer just to know it's running than to worry about all the details. Or a government or an organization. Or a book. I think knowing the author might ruin it.

I have just been noticing how highly suggestible I am. The hype for a big game. A hamburger, a new candy bar, the advice of someone on what is the best thing to do. Just almost right away I think that is the thing to do.

I've probly always had that, but I just now realized it I think.

Well, anyway, there's a lot going on.

Information, that's the key.

I don't know where that came from, just popped into my head so I wrote it down so I don't forget it.

The Beautiful Indian Maiden Heroine, The BIM (h) — Josie, Josephine Custer — is pursuing her lawsuit against the C.I.A. like mad. She is Ojibwe I think. She's Geronimo's sister and is getting her masters maybe and works at the same workshop where Geronimo and a lot of the CRUSHERs did. I probably already said that. There is a lot here that I've written and it would not surprise me one bit if I got something wrong. Just fuckin' sayin.

She is tall, slender, long black hair (geezuz god that hair), calf hide boots, all kinds of Indian things dangling everywhere and she carries with her, everywhere, a wry grin as if she just knows. I know I said that before but not one thing has changed.

And how do I know all these things, like how people feel and the behind the scenes at all this shit? I just do, don't worry about it. It's a story. My job is to write it and I'm worrying all about that, don't worry about it, your job is just read. That's all you fuckin' have to do.

Well, maybe it's aliens, that's making me write this, or the C.I.A., or the F.B.I. or the city council or the Easter Bunny. Don't you ever wonder about that?

If you go on YouTube enough, which I do I'm pretty sure, you could end up wondering if someone is shooting something into your brain and that's why you like certain things about characters in "Gunsmoke," or don't like certain things about certain characters in "Gunsmoke."

I just need to get this fucker done. Because if I don't get this done, I'm gonna die and be a ghost for a million years in this room looking at this computer and wanting to finish this and I can't. So here I go.

Fuck it.

Josephine Custer, Plaintiff

v.

The Central Intelligence Agency, Defendant

Complaint: That the C.I.A. intentionally and with extreme prejudice caused the death of Geronimo, a.k.a. Napoleon Ulysses Custer.

That's kind of cool. Well, good for her, I guess. Right in there pitching. She's got a lawyer. Guess the money came from somewhere.

I was actually able to sit in court the first day, U.S. District Court, federal, the big time. There weren't many others there. I would suppose that the lawyers involved expected it to be thrown out right away, but it wasn't, not really.

The scene? It wasn't Maycomb, Alabama. There were no fans in people's hands stirring the hot air, or people leaning over the balcony just to be a part of it. More just sterile-scary modern style, nothing cool about it, just get this over and get me out of here sort of motif, the 21st century version of 1984, no dust or humanity anywhere, and that's as far as I want to go, I don't really like thinking about it.

Josephine's lawyer started out establishing Geronimo's death and then the more tricky part that they wanted to put in there, was that he was murdered. A couple doctors testified and I didn't think they proved a thing, but the judge said, let's keep going, let's see where this goes.

And so they did.

Into the second day and the third. And they had me interested as well as quite a few others. It wasn't easy to find a seat that third day because the story made the papers, and I'll bet somebody wasn't too happy.

The evidence they had said, or they said that it said, that Geronimo was poisoned.

Then Ms. Coffman, Josephine's lawyer, kind of just said it. She said that the government wanted Geronimo to do an act of terror. He was disabled, but he was still pretty capable.

The police searched his room and found a 'manifesto.' And so, now the lawyer for the government is saying that Geronimo was a potential terrorist. What that has to do with killing him?

And then Josephine climbed to the stand.

She said Geronimo had an imaginary friend, who he called Marvin. That drew a lot of laughs, I'll tell you, and I thought, that's it, this is over, it's a joke.

And then, this shocked the holy shit out of me, I hadn't seen her for the longest time, the accusers or whatever you call them, Josephine, called to the stand: Kaitylyn Anne Bridge.

She was up there for a long time, through a couple of breaks and into the next day.

Well shit.

I wrote down everything I could.

I'm sure there's no C.I.A. actually in the courtroom, but they have at least four attorneys, maybe more in disguise, I don't even know. There were others sitting around on their side who looked a lot like lawyers, I thought. Some of 'em seemed to fidget a bit when Kaitylyn got up there. She was dressed nice, like in school clothes, maybe church clothes. Real nice.

Ms. Coffman: Please state your occupation.

Mr. Sanger: Your honor, we object. Ms. Bridge is under no obligation to answer that. It might be classified information.

Judge Bauermeister: The witness will answer the question.

Kaitylyn Anne Bridge: Criminal Investigator, Special Agent, C.I.A.

Ms. Coffman: And how long have you held this position.

Kaitylyn Anne Bridge: About four years, five years. Closer to five. Five.

•Did you administer medications that night?

•Did you purposely administer medications non-prescribed but rather meant to cause Mr. Custer's death? And under who's direction did you do so?

•I can't answer that.

•Please speak up.

•I said I can't answer that.

•You can't answer that?

•What kind of answer is that?

•You are under oath.

•I know, I know. I just can't.

•What can you say?

She looked down, calmly actually, then up at Ms. Coffman. Somewhere a door shut, hard, somebody cleared their throat and keys dropped onto the marble-like floor. In the middle of Kaitylyn's speech Josephine Custer burst out crying, trying to hold it back, but her tears came out in short coughs as she bent over and put both hands to her face.

•I was supposed to get him on the TV shows as a retarded young man with the plane ticket to promote the idea that there were planes that day, but he turned out to be so good and so charismatic that they could not take the chance that he would also find out the truth behind that day, so he had to be killed.

People gasped, papers fell to the floor, doors opened and shut, feet walked fast and the air sucked out of the room, like some stupid idiot fired a bazooka through the wall of an airplane at high altitude. Almost exactly like that.

•Once again, did you administer the medications and under whose direction were you acting? Your own or someone else.

•I would rather not answer that.

They let Kaitylyn go after that. I can't believe she wasn't arrested. She walked straight down the middle aisle and was not arrested, out the door, and I'm assuming she fucking ran.

I think it was after that she went to Dunn Bros., or maybe it was before, I don't actually know.

The next day in court, I was there again, and they called Kaitylyn back to the stand and she wasn't there. They called her name again, sent guys into the hall to look for her.

They proceeded, but if it's a murder and you don't have a main witness, don't really have any evidence because let's say the chemical analysis is inconclusive, or, all you have is a supposed motive and you have the term "C.I.A." loosely attached to it, what do you have?

Yeah, well.

She didn't really go berserk, that's not Kaitylyn's style really. She's more of the slow burn and then boom! Passive aggressive? Maybe. And me, personally, I don't think passive aggressive, if that's what this is, not saying, is such a bad thing, but that's just me. She had her service revolver and tons of CRUSHER weapons and gear, and costumes from when she and Lara were "underground" that one time.

What she did was go some place to think things over, see what her options were. She put on her Uncle Sam costume from something she and Lara did, went to Dunn Bros., a different one, got her favorite drink, her laptop and sat by the front door, her back to the wall, so she could tell who was coming in and who was going out, and watched the parade go by.

She typed to be doing something rather than staring, and thought about Jim. Goddamn it, hanging, what's that like? She touched her throat. Why did that happen? Who did it? A judge, I doubt it. Marvin? Carroll? Somebody else? Braxton, maybe. Did they have that kind of power, maybe.

Jim, the one person she ever really loved, never told him, never told anybody, now she would join him, wherever he was, wanting to prove herself to Lara, she realized CRUSHER was right all along … about some things.

Stop.

She told herself. Nobody could probably tell, her sitting in her Uncle Sam hat and beard and jacket, pants, big shoes, starting to lose it, but she was.

Just stop.

She saw she had typed "Just stop."

She wasn't the only Uncle Sam in the café, and that was kind of weird, but then again not that weird for this Dunn Bros.

In comes Alexa. And now she spots Trevor over there and in a car on the curb, Marv. And she can look anywhere she wants because she's this person in an Uncle Sam's costume and who would question that person for fucking lookin' around too much. No, really.

And Alexa stands in line for coffee and Trevor is seated by himself at a nearby little table and they go into their routine.

War!
Hooh!
Good God Y'all.
What is it Good For?

And of course everybody looks at the loony people and some laugh and thinks it's just a crazy cool part of being in the big city.

Alexa sits down with Trevor.

Personally I really don't know what it is, just something they do that maybe they think makes them not really C.I.A. agents. Who knows? It is kinda cool. Loud.

She, Kaitylyn, touches the gun on her hip. (Why do they always do that? Do they think maybe they forgot it, the gun. I don't know.)

Marv is still in the car, not the little e-Car, more of a real C.I.A. or F.B.I. car, something nobody else would buy.

Our Uncle Sam remains sitting at her personal table in the far corner working on her laptop, gun on her hip, doing her work, thinking about what to do with her life, watching three C.I.A. agents in front of her on her right and her left, and in the back of her mind wondering what those other three Uncle Sam's are doing in this particular Dunn Bros. at this particular time of day working on their laptops.

To be doing something Kaitylyn types CRUSHER, to get her thoughts going, the way she typed it in her reports and also in the CRUSHER meetings with Lara and the others.

She recalls how it was she who suggested the name in some late night planning meeting at the group home and then to Marv and the others.

Kaitylyn believed she was doing this "for her country" as they say.

She remembered the endless meetings and discussions about Geronimo, about CRUSHER, about what they were going to do with Geronimo and then how it all went to kaput as her grandmother used to say. They had to get rid of him. He was actually too good for their own good.

She was working at the group home that night and the one designated to take care of night medications. She worked in the office where the meds were kept in a locked cabinet, closed the door like you were supposed to do, at least halfway and began putting the meds in the little paper cups, checking things off in the med book. Geronimo had his metformin, clonazepam, and was taking some hydrocone at that time, and maybe Wellbutrin? She knew them all by heart at the time. And then she shoved the door closed all the way with her foot.

She then reached into her pocket for the baggie she'd been carrying around all day, that Alexa had given her as Trevor watched and Marvin sat by in his desk, watching, marking something down in a book after he saw the baggie had been transferred into Kaitylyn's possession.

Geronimo was one to know for certain what he was taking and he would make sure you gave him the right pills and he would tell you if anything was wrong.

So, Kaitylyn had come up with the idea that it would have to be in the Gatorade he also took and that's what she did, removed the capsules from the baggie and poured them into the Gatorade that she removed from the little refrigerator, something Gerry also demanded, that he get Gatorade with his meds and his own refrigerator. He had his guardian, his sister Josie, make sure they got it for him.

She added the capsules that contained the drugs that would put Geronimo's heart rhythm into a chaotic stage during the night, and another which would make his high blood pressure medication ineffective, and he would have an induced heart attack and presumably fall from bed onto his floor where he would be found, already dead, by night staff during the hourly (or so) regular checks, which is pretty much what happened. Except that Geronimo struggled to his door and called for staff and then collapsed on his chest and face, broke his nose and bled all over the hallway carpet before the night staff came around about a half hour later. She said she thought she heard something — which was Gerry's calling — but "I thought it was the TV."

She loved Gerry. She did not know "exactly" what the drugs were and she was never told "exactly" what would happen. She was only ordered to administer the drugs in the baggie on the next night that she worked at the group home and she was to make sure she was the one to give out the meds that night, which she did.

"It's for the greater good," Alexa had told her when Kaitylyn said "no way" she was going to do that.

"I'm telling you what they are doing," she said. "I'm basically organizing this whole group, getting people to join the group, getting someone to lead the group, that's enough. I'm not going to kill anybody. No way. Kill? Are you kidding me?"

"Kaitylyn."

Trevor sat down next to her. They were all in the Minneapolis office, on the nineteenth floor of the old IDS building. She had heard of people being hung out windows by her feet. She read about that on the internet when she spent a long time researching the C.I.A. and the F.B.I. and finally decided it would be cool to maybe get on the inside and find out how things really worked and maybe she could do some good, and then when she got the assignment that she had, a real revolutionary group and it was kind of her project, along with Alexa, Trevor and Marv, but they just coordinated things, she was on the inside. Well, that sounded really fun.

"It won't kill him," said Trevor.

"It won't."

"You just said it would," said Kaitylyn.

"Yeah, not really, but it won't, right?" Trevor looked at Marv.

Marv kind of shook his head, but just a little. He was lying.

"Yes, it will, you just said that!" said Kaitylyn.

Alexa came over and sat on the desk. She sighed and looked out the window and Kaitylyn felt like she was falling and she had to stop herself. Sometimes she got that, ever since grade school and it scared the crap out of her each time.

"It's going to knock him out," said Alexa.

"He will need to be transferred. He won't be able to make his appearances. (He was going to be on the Prince Hope Show and other local media.) The whole thing will kind of just go away. People will forget about him, that's what needs to happen."

"Conspiracy theories," said Trevor.

"They are tearing this country apart. Gerry got sucked into this. We are trying to get him out. He's being used by people who want to bring this country down. We're fighting against all that and you are helping us. You are literally saving your country, and Gerry, too."

"Cognitive infiltration of extremist groups."

Marvin read with his finger a memo from Carroll.

"Yep," said Trevor.

"That's exactly what you are doing, dear," said Alexa.

"But it's up to you, honey."

"You can choose to turn your back on your country," said Trevor.

"Or you can do your family proud," said Marv.

Trevor and Alexa nodded.

Kaitylyn recognized the mention of her family as a message to remind her of what she was involved in and with whom.

"Med time."

Gerry: How are you tonight?

Kaitylyn: I'm fine. What're you watching?

Gerry: Spiderman.

Kaitylyn: The first one?

Gerry: Three.

Kaitylyn: There's three?

Gerry: More, '77, '78, 2002, 2004, 2007, 2014. You got my Gatorade?

Kaitylyn: Wow, I didn't know that. Yep, here.
Gerry: Thanks, night.
Kaitylyn: Goo night.

They were looking for her, she just now realized it.

That whole schpiel that they did was to let Kaitylyn know if she was in here that they were here. They did that almost all the time in the office. They thought they were cool, the superstars.

And they were good. Pretty soon they would start walking around, checking every single person without them knowing, and every single Uncle Sam in the place and then they would go to the next Dunn Bros., and the next. And they would find Kaitylyn and they would kill her or threaten to kill her mom and dad and her sisters and Kaitylyn would live the rest of her life in a cubicle or teaching third graders and knowing how the world works and not being able to tell anybody.

That's what they did. That's who they were. They were so good and so smart. Why were all the good people so stupid, she thought and she so wanted to be good.

Kaitylyn took a deep breath. She closed her laptop, touched her sidearm, ran her hand down the smooth metal, Glock, Austria, 9mm, $500. She knew because they made her pay for it herself, so she would appreciate it, she guessed, maybe. She knew everything about the gun. She'd been through many weeks of training at Langley as well as the shitty CRUSHER stuff at Camp Sweaty. It was conceivable she could walk up to Alexa and Trevor, take them and then get to Marv before he realized what was happening. She yanked her hand away, wiped her sweaty palms down her blue pants, got up, smoothly, slowly, avoided Trevor's stare and walked, not ran, out the front door, past Marv and down the sidewalk, and then she ran.

Note from the narrator ...

From the assorted musings found by the cleaner, Jake the intern from St. Olaf, in the log book of Crawfish Cabin at Anderson's Resort on Lake June Bug in northern Saint Louis County, in the Minnesota Arrowhead.

July 2, 1995

I know.
They did OKC.

Have you heard about Terry Yeakey?

Jenny

That I would be good even when I am overwhelmed
That I would be good even if I lost sanity
— Alanis Morisette

Well, I look out my window
and I watch the cars
and I swear I'll do some damage
some fine day.

But I would not be convicted
by a jury of my peers,
still crazy, after all these years.
— Paul Simon

Kaitylyn got a gun.
— *What Ike said when he heard what happened in court.*
That's just what I think she did, definitely.

FIFTY-SIX

Prince Hope looks out his window. Sees Uncle Sam walking, a small Uncle Sam, with pants dragging. He writes something down. He's got two legal pads going on his two bare knees, one a list of new bits, the other a planned Farewell Tour of Minnesota and western Wisconsin.

Kaitylyn Uncle Sam sat on the bus bench across from Prince Hope in his window and The Lonely Lutheran Lunch Club & Bookstore.

She cried and nobody saw. She was in disguise. She missed Jim. She killed Geronimo. She betrayed her friends, Lara, Brooke. Rick died! Skylar died! They are chasing her! Her parents saw the thing in the paper about the thing in court and her friends from high school. God damn.

"Aaaaah!"

Somebody walking behind her heard her crying she was crying so loud in the middle of the city and if it were Minneapolis nobody would have heard, but this was Saint Paul and it was pretty quiet and pretty much the biggest thing happening was the crying Uncle Sam on the bus bench with the prison advertising.

"God dammit!"

Prince Hope looked up from his two legal pads on his bare knees. And then down again to his work.

He was trying to come up with a catchy ending phrase for his new farewell tour.

Do your time, remain on good behavior, keep in touch with your probation officer.

Watch your carbs, be vegan, or not, whatever you think is best, stay in Minnesota.

Be Lutheran, Do good things, Keep plodding forward. (If it helps, lean a little, it might help.)

That was too goddamn long. He circled, underlined and crossed out.

He would look up soon at the gunshots and then down again to his work.

Kaitlyn drew slowly the gun from its holster because it wanted to be out of there. It was not meant to be trapped in a holster. It was hand-crafted by studious, simple people for certain purposes and it was not let free to be what it was.

Jim, the one person she ever really loved, never told him, never told anybody, now she would join him, wherever he was, wanting to prove herself to Lara, she realized CRUSHER was right all along. She had really meant it when she talked with the others through the night at the group home in the beginning. Her reports were excellent because she believed in what she was doing.

She aimed it at Prince Hope's window. Lowered it, aimed with two hands at the couple seated in the first window booth by the side door and they both ducked. The others in the window pointed at them because they would duck, then sit up, then duck again. She aimed it at the intersection, at cars, at the bus driver and passengers as they wheezed off. She aimed it at the cop that pulled up in front of her with his lights flashing and she shot him through the window as he turned to get out, blowing out two windows and his left lung. He fell face-first, sprawled, in the street.

She took off.

Prince Hope looked up, saw Uncle Sam sprinting away and the policeman "X" on the pavement. He scribbled a quick note and ambled for the stairs.

Lara, Ike, Frida, Korey, Evey, Brooke, Charlie and Alice sat in Lara's grandmother's basement, on the sofa and some metal chairs and one good chair from the kitchen, planning the new project. Rachel was visiting her grandfather in the nursing home.

They had heard about Kaitylyn.

"Where is she?" asked Frida.

"Nobody knows," said Lara, tying her hair back.

"Oh, no," she said as she got a text just then, from Kaitylyn.

"Am I a REAL CRUSHER now?"

Lara read it to the group.

"God," said Brooke.

"This sucks," said Korey.

Lara furiously punched her phone with her thumbs.

"What're you gonna tell her?" said Evey.

"Asking what she's gonna do now."

They waited.

Lara's phone buzzed.

"What'd she say?" said Alice.

"You'll see," said Lara.

People go on like they don't know what's going on. People write songs, sing songs like they're not gonna die. They are gonna die. I don't understand why everyone isn't running around screaming waving their hands over their heads.

They know they are gonna die, everything goes black, they are dropped into a hole and dirt poured on their faces and they write songs. What the fuck!

Prince Hope found the note taped to his podium as he stood alone in the theatre on the stage. He'd gone there on a Sunday to practice though he never practiced. He thought it might not be a bad idea this time.

He searched the seats for her. He looked to the first balcony, the second.

Korey and Washington walked fast, past the theatre where Prince Hope stood inside on the stage, presumably alone.

Drizzle appeared on Washington's glasses. Korey's tongue, for the hundredth time today, found the gap where his tooth should have been.

They crossed diagonally, against traffic, hopped up and walked along a concrete railing, another street and there they were, at the old C-store. Korey went right to the post office kiosk.

"I knew it," he said, running his finger down the updated Ten Most Wanted list behind the glass frame.

Kaitylyn was now No. 4, behind Chuck The Impaler, Nadia Simpson the black federal judge impersonator, and Roger Klebsbach the Norwegian Black Knight of Eveleth. Lara was 7, Brooke 8. Korey was No. 9 and Evey wasn't even on it.

Prince Hope began his monologue, going from some loose notes. His glasses teetered on the edge of falling right from his nose. His hair was pretty much everywhere. He wore shorts he had worn to bed and sandals as well. His shirt was white and freshly pressed, sleeves rolled to mid-forearm and unraveling as they saw fit. His dark eyebrows nearly blocked his view.

"And that's the news from my home town," he said.

"What do you think, Kaitylyn? Did it work for you?"

"It was fine."

The voice came from up above. He stepped away from the podium to try to see.

"I never really liked you," she said.

"Yes, I know," he said.

"That was me.

"Uncle Sam."

"Yes. Why don't you come down where we can talk."

"I don't want to."

"Yes, I understand. I don't much like it here, either. I've nowhere else to go, though."

"You would rather be fishing alone on a boat."

"Yes, I suppose. I don't really fish, but the boat sounds nice. I plan to retire someday and that's really all I'm going to do, every day, all day."

"Sounds depressing."

"Yes. It keeps me working. Scares the shit out of me."

Kaitylyn stood, appeared in the front row of the first balcony.

"There you are."

"Why didn't you just turn us in?" she said.

"Sometimes you sound like you like us, and sometimes you sound like you would like us all to hang."

"Like Jim," he said, "yes, you've pretty much captured me. It's complicated. I don't know. I'm still working on it."

"Keep working. You'll get it."

"Thank you. Yes, I will."

"I've got to go now. Would you mind turning your back?"

Prince Hope did that. He heard many quick, short steps, and then it was quiet.

He turned back around, checked his notes, and began again.

"Well, it's been another long week …"

Korey and Washington hurried past on the sidewalk.

"Wait," Korey said.

He went to the window, pressed his nose against the glass and circled his face with his hands.

"What's in there?" said Washington.

"I dunno. I see … somebody's in there, on the stage. I can't really see. I think it's a ghost, no shit, really. You can't be in there, on Sunday! He must have died, died maybe just now and there's his ghost. We need to check the papers."

"Let's go," said Washington.

"Cops'll see us. You can't be just lookin' in there."

"Fuck it," said Korey as he pulled away from the window just as Kaitylyn came around the corner behind them and ducked her head into the drizzle and pulled her jacket tight around her.

Mars ain't the kind of place to raise your kids,
in fact it's cold as hell.
— Elton John, *Rocket Man*

FIFTY-SEVEN

FADE IN:

INT. [office in local C.I.A. HQ office, Langley, Virginia.]

Three agents meeting in the room. Quickly joined by Agent 004.

AGENT 004

It's warm in here, too warm.

Whattya got?

AGENT 002

Got?

AGENT 003

We was just talkin'.

AGENT 001

TV stations, radio, they're all on board, movies, magazines, the whole bit.

AGENT 002

Newspapers. Newspapers, too.

AGENT 004

Yes, but ...

(AGENT OO2 cuts in.)

Yes, go ahead.

AGENT 002

What we got? We got plenty, boss. We got these suckers, see?

AGENT 004

Good plan, boys … umm, and uh, girl.
Carry on.
(He leaves, in a hurry.)

AGENT 003

Hey, how 'bout those Dodgers, huh?

AGENT 002

Yeah.

AGENT 001

Forget that, we got to get to work. We told him we had something.
C'mon, follow me.

I still watch too much TV, but once you get hooked, ya know.

Lara's grandmother has died, heart attack. She gave the house to Lara, so Lara has a place to stay and all the CRUSHERS with her, I suppose. But Lara won't be doing much these next few days except plan the funeral and cry and sleep. And it's raining, has been now for a couple of days.

Prince Hope's show has gone to shit. His public radio contract did not get renewed for his Farewell Tour, so he's thinking of doing it anyway on his own. He'll just have to pay for it himself I guess. I wonder if he can still rent the same theatre across from his restaurant. Maybe, I guess.

You know, I go out walking sometimes, in the woods. You don't have to go too awful far around here to hit woods. The other day I stopped and closed my eyes. It was so quiet. I said hello to my relatives, some friends, some enemies. I say I will see them some day. Maybe I believe that. And I just wait for that something. That insight. Maybe I am this close to doing the right thing. Maybe I'm right at the edge of the cliff or the mountaintop and they are all just rooting for me to realize it and yahoo!

Nothing really comes to mind. But it's a beautiful day. If you like rain.

Kaitylyn's wandering the town like a homeless person, thinking of making her fame, her mark, putting her name in The Cretin-Derham Hall of Fame as a murderer.

Korey continues to be impatient with the planning stages of the next project and practically has the Twin Cities painted a new second coat with The C.I.A. Sucks and The Hell With The C.I.A.

Brooke has taken Kaitylyn's place as Lara's second in command. She has joined a health club and teaches hot yoga under the name Mary Lou McGonagall.

Evey seems to me to be fighting to hold it together. I don't think she has ever really recovered from killing the first Rachel. She goes out to the old place occasionally, with Rachel II. Roswell is out in back, plenty of grass ... and then her father's declining health, his new obsession with puzzles.

Ike, Frida, Charlie, Alice have learned how to make it through a day, knowing how much input Lara will allow with planning the new project, getting food for them all, checking the internet in the library about what's happening back in Rapid City and in Brooklyn. Ike's taking karate to get ready to survive prison, Charlie, taekwondo. Alice and Frida take long walks on the river, laughing and talking and planning their escape and how they will live forever in the little woods along the Mississippi.

And now, Prince Hope's Lunch Club & Bookstore has burned. The fire started at night. It was quite the scene in downtown Saint Paul. I guess Hope ran over there in his pajamas and sat on the bench across the street in his bare feet, watching it go, big crowd, big blaze. He borrowed a cigarette from someone else standing there, staring. He had notes in there for his Farewell Tour, that's what bothered him the most, is what I heard. Geezuz, what a deal. Lara said he could move in with her, but he said he still had the house off Summit, the lake cabin and an apartment in the old IDS, his CDs, so.

And the prison writer, Billy. He is still there. Still locked up for that one letter to the editor, presumably, still pretending ... we assume, to be at home, writing to friends and family, not mentioning the state hospital lockup ward in Bumfuck.

Note from the narrator ...

> From "Not Exactly A Radio Show," a live podcast that traveled the
> circuit of Twins Cities bars for about six months, produced by former
> members of The Prince Hope Show:

Susan's out of donut holes at the bakery and Dan has no more hamburger
buns at the café. What a goddamn coincidence. Of course. Russia did it.
You can't find your keys.
Russia took 'em, what else could it be.
Russia ate your homework. Russia made you late for work this morning.
Russia spilled red wine on the new white sofa.

Your car won't start. You have to pee very bad while trapped in traffic on
the freeway. You miss the last-second shot to win the game. Your pants
won't fit, the toothpaste tube is flatter than flat, the milk is sour and mother
in law has decided to visit for the whole month of January.
Yep, you guessed it, Charlie. The Red Menace.
Red Dawn and Reagan was right. Boris is hogging the bathroom again.
Olga ate all the red M&Ms.
Russia is spraying chemtrails all over your blue sky and polluting your
rivers so that you can't even eat the fish.
Russia did Fukushima and Sandy Hook and Boston, 9/11, Waco,
Oklahoma City and San Bernardino.
It's the Russians, Stupid. They are under your bed.
They are on your roof, they are in the back seat tossing spitballs at your
head as you drive along mountain passes.
Those god-damn Rooskies.
Taiga Turkeys. [tie-ga]
Moscow Marmots.
There's always somebody trying to steal your lunch money ... spying on
you when you dive under your desk and ...
It's always ... Russia-Russia-Russia.

Note from the narrator ...

> From the assorted musings found by the cleaner, Jake the intern from St. Olaf, in the log book of Crawfish Cabin at Anderson's Resort on Lake June Bug in northern Saint Louis County, in the Minnesota Arrowhead.

September 1989

I see some have been writing about history here.

Well, how about the Berlin Wall, Tiananmen Square?

Our family has been putting out an annual newspaper for our Christmas letter, for years.

Sometimes we write about movies and have our own movie reviewer.

I would like to ask those who read this later to please rate these movies, and if this catches on, maybe others can leave us more movies to rate.

Enjoy.

West Side Story
Mary Poppins
Star Wars Return of the Jedi
American Grafitti
Vacation
Jaws
The Godfather
E.T.
Back To The Future
Ghostbusters
Rocky
Close Encounters of the Third Kind
One Flew Over The Cuckoo's Nest

Ann Francis Broulliet
Chicago

Do you recognise this fine upstanding young man receiving his Master's degree from London University? This is Zacarias Moussaoui, just months before Hollywood demonized him as the surviving "911 Terrorist", and charged him with (1) Conspiracy to Commit Acts of Terrorism Transcending National Boundaries, (2) Conspiracy to Commit Aircraft Piracy, (3) Conspiracy to Destroy Aircraft, (4) Conspiracy to Use Weapons of Mass Destruction, (5) Conspiracy to Murder United States Employees, and (6) Conspiracy to Destroy Property. No hard evidence of any crime because he is innocent of all charges. But, as we shall see in part two, the prison shrinks and their drugs finally convinced Zacarias to plead "guilty".

Do I hear you protest that this could never happen in America, land of the free? Sorry, it just did ...

As stated earlier, government-selected 'patsies' have rather more than subliminal color coding thrown at them from a television screen. For these men and women (at least those who survive), have to stand up in a court of law and, eventually, make a full confession about a crime they did not commit, or simply mumble "guilty" a few times. Just how this is managed will be explained in part two of this series, probably ready about one month from now.

— Joe Vialls ... was a conspiracy theorist and internet journalist based in Perth, Western Australia.
He claimed that major incidents such as the Port Arthur massacre, terror attacks in Bali and Jakarta and the 2004 Asian Tsunami were the work of Israeli and American secret agents gained a measure of notoriety in Australia, America and Indonesia ... After a period of illness, Vialls was reported to have died at the Royal Perth Hospital in Western Australia on 17 July 2005 of a heart attack.

FIFTY-EIGHT

Steve,
Just returned from HEB run, not Boerne but Helotes, think is its name, Kelly likes the diversity and layout, liquor store next door. The funny old men are mainly not much fussing now. I always take the back seat, let Mike talk. They had someway got into the Mayans. I seem to know more than they there. I have always heard the Spaniards destroyed the Mayan records. My sense is remnants of the civilization still lived before this last wreckage. Mike and Kelly had thought all Mayans then long gone. Well, who was sitting on these records, tablets. At present all this is being very slowly studied, such as the Mayans knew astronomy. It is helpful Kelly knew the Mayans knew astronomy some way. Mike B. wants no such disorder of course.

Hard for me to not push these matters a bit, see how far. And, Kelly knows of this of ancient ruins had means of placing multi ton stone, which would be difficult now, all we have is cranes etc. Still no comment then from Mike B., and being Mike and Kelly were discussing "time" in their accepted history, I tossed in, Mike, it is in fits and starts. Mike wanted to discuss the linear, mystery of the linear. With the linear, Mike B. can pontificate. Naw, Mike, fits and starts, there are famines, there are wars. Mike, have you heard of this ancient computer contraption found in the ocean? I have seen it on television. Bill, Mike cut in, what are you saying? Mike, I am saying officialdom does not want us to know. If I used another word than officialdom, I know this time I did not use "the rulers." I just went enough to irritate Mike B. Mike respects authority for his own reasons. Kelly less so. I said there is all this all over the Earth unexplained in a purpose, denied. Look, take the pyramids. Then Mike B. cut me off, denial of the mysterious history of our species. He said he knows more about anthropology than I do, he studied thus, it was his major. I said, aw, hell you do not.

Steve, look at photos of the pyramids. They were supposed to only have copper tools, and consider even in lack of manpower/food constructing these necessary enormous cranes. I believer we have today no such cranes. Besides, tedious jobs. These pyramids in Egypt are enormous. And, pyramids are all over Earth, some yet buried.

And so. We don't have to be impressed by officialdom and authority. They lie. Just what is their problem.

Don't recall saying Trump is less evil. Trump is whelmed, having got into more trouble than he had thought to. I have not been much interested in him. He is ignorant, and MSM give him bad press. Now, Debbie Lusignan sees him as rather the stupid menace. But less dangerous, not inside officialdom at this time. Hillary and Obama are dangerous to Earth.

Many people within Alternate News respect Trump, sympathize, hope he will be let live, perhaps mainly because he wants no WW III. That, perhaps Trump is stout enough to learn as he goes, respect China, respect everybody. After all, he did instantly see 9/11 while murderous is inside, was fake, being he had built skyscrapers. Now all these years we have the 9/11 Wars. Yes, Obama is worse. Obama whom I had liked slowly did shock me with the murderous drone madness. You cannot explain why kill all these goats and children of poor people. I was living with our mother and Kelly would come in and I would complain why this drone bull shit, and not one time did he attempt to say why. Now this is no joke. My siblings are programmed. Now, I will never shut up. I keep looking. Am loyal. Good grief, they have kept me afloat, and now I have daughter and grandkids in touch. Coming during summer.

I have said, Alternate News is gone more murky. But there are some stout people. But one must be interested. I be looking, it does not bore me.

There be the kind in men which is possessed by demons, as they like to say, and is afeared of the pack and they be of him. He lives by notion in his head or his body and by which if it ain't demons it be too apart of them living in town. These kinds of men be apart of each other too, but they will come together, as like as is not, from their need and from sheer curiosity. They are curious men.

Females of the sort have a bad time, not being very able to set out by themselves, and they generally do not show themselves too much or else they just turn to witchcraft. Like as not they can't tell or trust a lone man when they see him. Or even tell themselves. I guess they go crazy.

Wayne was one of these, and she was lost and did not know about it. It is hard for me to reconcile with a female what tried to kill me. It is a strange world that is so crowded or scared it sets Cain upon Cain and Abel upon Abel. Yet there will be adventurers and ever surviving curious strain that hardly can know what they chase and what they outrun, but they go on looking for their kind or cousin. The information that everybody is cousin you don't learn in a school, but it ain't just everybody together that gets chased off into the desert of his head and told to be fruitful, in sake of further truth that man and life is all right, is the right thing, God is Father and all there is, too. Comprende. You are lonely in the desert but glad to look. Though when I first got to the water hole there weren't nothing in me felt good, and I was not sure I wanted to live, because I was shot bad, and I drunk, and it was middle of winter in New Mexico Territory and cold in my buffalo coat and only a little snow drizzling over that puddle of ice kept that hole from drying up. This is how I come to know Elizabeth.

Not at first. There weren't nobody down that way cept the miner and I knew it and was glad of that, because it had been hell getting away and I was going to die or I was going to live and I did not need the help either way. There was enough roof of what was left of the adobe to keep me and the horse and I had a little horse that could last in the winter by hisself, and I decided to live because two lost Indian ponies come down to drink and I shot them so they wouldn't run away with my horse, and I sat there that winter eating the cold horse.

Further Out,
    Bill

Geoffrey,

Please tell Woody hello for me.

Thanks for telling me you did get that about our poor chickens, and if I understand also the other one, without any text from me, but from this Chad rather political news report, which I never read. Yes, indeed, these two pieces were glued to my email.

I get a lot of this crap, sometimes they address me as Wild Bill, for years, decades.

I am sorry what our pigs suffer, our chickens, our wolves, but seriously I cannot know if these are C.I.A. who think I am important to their shit someway. I want them shot.

Reminds me, when I was in Boulder, you a little kid, and Mike Blackbird had found me a place to stay, had given a chest of drawers, was it, to this old hippy who had a bedroom extra for me, where Sissie gave birth. And I worked one day out of - damn, forget what they called this, employment for a day - Austin and Berkeley also had this - the one in Boulder and I and some younger hippies worked in this chicken factory, one day. There would be three chickens in a cage and the weak one dying slowly under feet of the two stronger. There was much waste, always a bunch of escaped chickens running about, and toward latter part of that day these flower children had gone callous, took to grabbing these loose chickens and tossing them alive at one another, in glee. Well, to carry a chicken or two all one had to do is turn them upside down, holding them by their feet, their brains immediately went numb.

Do you have any pot, for Woody, any jazz? You once told me this helps him.

Our next weed is only now planted, said to be good seeds. Funny, it is Kelly's nature to be secretive.

Presently I am running through my pills again. Will have to get drunk, today and tomorrow, before we get back to HEB where I buy Approdine (like olde Actifed) (neither be prescribed for asthma, but the MDs know nothing of this since 1944), but now times because some kids know how to cook speed from this type stuff I show my driver's license. Wish I had speed on hand. I may have to get very drunk on much wine which will give me the runs, both days before Monday. I have two said pills in my wallet for ride in. Not getting severe yet, I take a hit in order to work out. It is a boring drama.

Yeah, states maybe having this type hillbilly who make corn liquor and may be illiterate include Arkansas, their Ozarks, Kentucky, Tennessee, West Virginia, East Texas Big thicket, at minimum. Always they were distrustful of outsiders and illegally made corn liquor, and now days they grow weed. Really, when I was age ten I wanted to go up there somewhere and live. I am connected, lazy or no, yet by now I love New Mexico. Seems I came there. But I love that mountain music. Talk about dancing. On these videos I see these little kids dancing. And, USA white man culture turned in on itself. There is a question.

This classical music station in Cedar Rapids at times has ancient variety unto stuff I am surprised they call it classical. Yet, classical is that ancient, and I dig the Spanish and the exotic. The Irish. Scotch Irish, these old mountain people in the USA are plenty Scotch Irish. But like I said, see their faces, strains of Africa and Cherokee. Just free people....Prefer to live free in their mountains. Do not care to live in cities.

Guess I will go see more of these mountain folks. Alternate USA news has slowed, too many fake shitasses. Oh, they can arrest Hillary any moment. Or we shall see. I think we don't verge on World War III like last week, maybe. Lucky to have Putin. Forget slow death MSM.

I have on liver and onions. Trick is do not cook crisp. BE wanted his crisp. Very funny, one day I told him we others prefer beef rare. He said we should have told him. Anyway, liver, Mike and Bonnie wish to never eat it. Mostly I have slurped it down raw for B-complex but lately I know how to fix it.

Further,

Bill

PS I have not had cordial relations with Ann, since we disagreed over 9/11, and I do not know has she published anything since she got SWAGGART published. If I misspell SWAGGART.

Of present conversation, she in her book gave some information on these people with their corn. They did not all work very hard, as thus far is claimed in friendly material I have been reading. In SWAGGART, many of these guys got too drunk to work. Whatever did the poor wives do, leave them perhaps. Or drink too. Keep some pigs, chickens, and feed their kids I presume.

Well, growing their pot now, they have more money, and can toil in their fields better. I mean, at least on pot one can do it, not fall down in the hot sun.

Geoffrey,

Yesterday by time I was drunk again, I did a short email to you about encountering these audios/videos about different Appalachian peoples, as I have been enchanted with hillbillies well before puberty. But one of these uninvited junk things got stuck on my letter to you. You might tell me did you even get that email. I could not get rid of it, did go on and pass it at you. Indeed, this morning I observed I had also tossed it at my list of readers, possible readers. Just now was talking with Madrea - I call her Saturday - she has not heard of this before.

Generally I ignore these petitions and other uninvited, for it can be C.I.A.. Maybe by now you hear, C.I.A. can read my Postings or watch me through my laptop.

And so on. Trump was never expected to win. I understand he did not expect to but was growing his business. Now, he is inexperienced, ignorant of deeper states, even terrified. Certain humanitarians wish him to survive, and keep peace with Russia, China. Dig it, Trump early knew 9/11 was inside. His information of building skyscrapers is empirical.

Abolish the C.I.A.. Explain to him we do not need a fatter military. Fairly incredible Trump's otherwise ignorance. Welp. can a seventy year old rich egomaniac pull himself together to see what has to be done?

Naa.

I am still rather asthmatic, juniper is less but oak is pollinating all over without a big rain, so I continue to need decongestants and plenty alcohol.

I recall being asthmatic hitchhiking to New York and entering mountains of Tennessee, was it Kentucky, and the asthma cleared out. On little sleep. Maybe age of twenty.

Bits I have not told. At some point, in the South, I stood hitchhiking and this old black guy came along. We communicated, he would see a car coming and shy off from me in case the automobile should stop to pick up this young white guy. Or were I no nigger lover. Then, he would come back and we talked more. I cannot recall the general conversation.

Anycase, let me see can I get this note at you without the rabid death of C.I.A. trying to bother with Bill.

Love,

Bill

Jeff,

I habitually reread my Postings with morning coffee, was surprised to come upon last evening's drunken note to you. Without memory of it, I have studied it. Drunk, for sure.

Jeff,

I wonder can you very well follow all this. I hope an amount of logic lives.

Guess I can carry on, lap-top in pasture of cows. Somebody has to do it.

I have presently no plan to break law by puny man.

Yours Further,

Bill

I had been thinking, time to write you again, but have lacked subject matter, for you aren't fascinated as I am with the police state, strange drama.

Where I sit with laptop looking out this window is a pasture, beyond the cedar post fence, where Kelly's longhorns often are, sometimes deer too. Rather a peaceful and safe place, but I get bored, drunk, have ailments, asthma lately but work out anyway so I don't get bad off. Just now finished my bit of ax on oak routine. Use a decongestant to mix with drinking. Oh, no mix ax or weights with drinking, but right after exercise, add drink to endorphins.

But when we do this HEB and liquor store run, I am too nervous to talk with pretty women, just want to get my stuff and get out. Try to remember what to get. I have always been rather this way.

Anyhoo. Perhaps you noticed my last Posting to Steve, or I might talk about this morning's Debbie Lusignan (Sane Progressive) show with this genius (very likable) technocrat, I should have got his name, Japanese I think but his English is entirely American, about cyber warfare, Part One. Cyber combat has taken place, USA and Iran, there was damage. Debbie knows little enough and I know very much less. But her guest has been busy since the eighties or some point way back already.

Cyber warfare is destruction and can wreck a nation's economy but is this not nicer than bombing poor people? I say so. Looks like times be changing.

USA no longer has any gold in Fort Knox, I think, Jeff. I but pick stuff up over decades. Nixon took us off gold, I think. China has taken in much gold some way. To say, USA needs more war, the petro dollar is crashing. Libya like Iraq had gone off the petro dollar. USA prints paper now.

JFK was killed because he had caught on, wanting to dismantle C.I.A. and leave Vietnam.

The Masters of War are in control now, who are crazed, irrational. Putin is rational.

USA has 200 or so military bases in other countries. Nobody else does this. Without war,

USA crashes like never before. Obama was simply intimidated. We have got to have these 9/11 wars, punk.

Then let us witness.

Oh well. It is in TG. Probably I will be alive. Got grandkids, amazing.

Yours Further,

Bill

Caryl,

I read both the Victor articles. I have lived in California, though not since the later nineties. Yeah, it is a while back already. Mostly their Berkeley area. There was always some mad activity.

Texans are more laid back, thus far. I have a short novel my publisher of limited means did do, along with the TG novel. THE EMERYVILLE WAR, purely non-fiction. Can be ordered from Amazon Books, I think it would amuse you.

Yes I have used inhalers, off and on since maybe age ten. We saw an MD and purchased one for me just lately and besides the hassle, it was the weakest I ever had. Besides USA medicine became more of a crime against humanity, too expensive. I prefer booze and decongestants, marijuana, psychedelics.

I see I am waking up, having wine, from ax work and bent over dumbbell curl for my hook.

In my personal case, I keep on saying, alcohol mixes supremely with my endorphins. Keeps me younger. Very funny Mike B. set out from his research to tell me drink gives me asthma, as past year somewhere he set out from his research to tell me of 9/11, any mass can penetrate other mass, if, velocity is sufficient, leaving out incredibly no airplane goes a million miles an hour. Mike B. is a mad man, a scientist then mad scientist.

Glad you like classical music. It is so wide, ancient. In Prairie I got it on a TV station, but cannot here. I do get on TV the jazz station, play it during the day, and yes Kelly/Janus got my TV up again. Needed a receiver. Meantime I sleep with classical, off an old cheapest radio at my bed, get this very good Cedar Rapids station, brings in largest variety that can possibly be called classical. Wish these liberals working there would not talk so much, like they think their listeners are mostly lonely old folk having insomnia. But it is great anycase.

Love,
Billy

Caryl,

Thanks for these couple of articles from Victor, which are nicely written, but rather milder than what I am looking at. In the first one for example he says Hillary got the numbers and Trump got the logistics, while I understand he actually got the popular vote as well, but that the popular vote was rigged for Hillary. He just won anyway.

As you know, I follow certain Alternative News, many voices by now but a couple you know of is Debbie Lusignan, James Kessler. The have means of telling the voting was rigged for Hillary. Besides, the awful stuff about Hillary, and too Obama. That meanwhile, many well known Republicans wanted Hillary in. Trump is a "loose cannon." Won't join the club.

The war business is horrific, insane, but I guess, the further out, plain insanity, is the coming pedophilia scandal. Incidentally, Debbie Lusignan has not got into the pedophilia. She is an old Truther, has only brought 9/11 up a couple of times, to speak of 9/11 Wars, while she has tried not to get enraged and leave her main business of rigged voting and police state at this time.

Kessler, Robert David Steel, others many are giving pedophilia commentary - it is expected to blow up any minute. Obama and Hillary and Bill Clinton. Any day now. Next month maybe. When there is this much smoking there is flame. Oh, a couple names, Ron Paul, Jesse Ventura, who be old Truthers, talk of much other, haven't joined the clamor on satanic international pedophilia. Or not yet I have heard.

Caryl, I too, am astounded, the numbers, people in high positions, and not types who might fondle or molest a kid only, but who in these rituals may murder them and sometimes eat them. For this to be so, all is stranger than we have known.

I always want to know why is it, how come. How can it be.

While past week a hero of mine from before my knowing of James Kessler, is Cynthia McKinney, old Truther, ex congresswomen from Georgia, ran for President for the Green Party, does many things, was guest on Kessler's The Raw Deal. Our friend Jim wanted her to speak of what she knew on the pedophilia. She spent the hour laying out some background. Kessler caught on, impatiently, it was funny. She did though speak of the Lolita Express, that Hillary went several times and Bill went many times. She did agree to come back soon.

I was back into Bigfoot, and Extraterrestrials, before settling into present quarters. I can enjoy a laptop in those places. I believe in both sorts, know the numbers. But past year or so out here the wrecking civilization keeps a bashing, lambasting. One matter to wonder at mind control of my siblings, but then, there comes more, more upon us. I have to get hold of my mind and, stop fussing with my siblings.

Today on dog walk Mike B. and I had this on alcohol and asthma, because he had gone on line to learn about asthma. No shit, but he means well, people worry about my drinking. He found some technical shit how alcohol can cause asthma. I had never heard such, but leave it to the doctors. Mike Blackbird wants sugar... pie, candy, cookies, is not an actual drinker. I told him drink is long known to help asthma. He could not pause to hear me, would not shut up about information to the contrary from the web. Fantastic. I tried a moment of outflanking his crap, by admitting I drink for other reasons besides asthma. Drink even not taking decongestants to go synergistic with drink, off season of juniper. Help us all.

Love,
Billy

Caryl,

What I believe is governments lie since before USA came to be. USA lied about slaughter of Indians etc., treatment of negroes etc. Atom bombing of Japan etc. Hebrew Holocaust etc. Hitler simply needed his work camps. He should never have taken on Russia and his war went badly early.   Archeology is not honest. Clearly we have had advanced technology before the pyramids even. Anthropology is not honest. Clearly we have had human species in the forests besides our own. These being are well adapted in ways we are not and do not need our technology.   Clearly we have visiting or involved with us extraterrestrials.

Love,
     Billy

Bill,

I'm with you on the pyramids. I watch Ancient Aliens and so forth. There is a lot we don't understand, scientists, artists, and the rest of us. As to Trump: He is using more drones than Obama, he is arresting more brown people across the USA. He is bringing back private for profit prisons. This is bad. Stay alert and keep an open mind.

Keep the pace. S.

Steve,

With this laptop I have a back section for MSM news, Washington Post and so on. It is dull and more fake than I have before seen. I cannot hang in there. I wonder where from you hear this of Trump and drones and prisons for profit already.   You should understand I have placed no hope in him. My favorite intellectual Debbie Lusignan has been against him. What personally I have noticed is his ignorance. Like with the pipeline polluting Indian land. For cheap shit, what call it, shale oil? He is ignorant. Certain individuals in area of "Alternate News" have some desperate hope in him. They hope he can survive and mature at age 70. It is true the established want him dead. It is true the C.I.A. own MSM and want him dead. I have to consider where possibly have you heard he is more into drones than Obama who set the precedent. It is so early. Certainly Obama never struggled with Guantanamo, prisons for profit, war surpassing any before him, never ary break in 8 years, kids and goats gutted per day, in many countries who had not been hostile to USA. Personally, I took shock my siblings at 9/11 are gone blank.

All now is Post 9/11. I get out of bed early and look at these other intellectuals. This morning one person was saying after the JFK killing and charade it took fifteen years for people to wake up to it, and now we are there with 9/11, people waking up what the fuck. Oh, I have this bleeding elbow again. Blood on walls, my sheet. Had not known wherefrom this and now I scraped it again, these trailer door jams. We have planted some pot, should help. I drink so much now. Both tranquilizers mess up my reading. What a world. I am retired from work, que bueno. Har har. You too. The experience with Mike this morning was our strangest so far, see note to Geoffrey preceding this one. Before Kelly delivered your art card I wondered should I have bothered Geoffrey so early with this one. But Mike is tough. While I am mystified how he came on at me with this of a need to stake out our pieces of Blackbird acres, I wonder he is coming to his senses perhaps. My guess is he needs a mission. Glad you can follow what I said lately, the pyramids. Fake history. Extraterrestrials, drawn clearly on ancient walls of Earth. Broken cities where anti gravity fitted multi ton stone neatly honed. Funny how long all this takes. Who is in charge? Why, nobody is in charge, sir. Perhaps you would like to be in charge, sir? Janus had this surgery in Dubuque today. She had had a tear duct plugged up. I did ask Kelly while she sleeps now how could this happen. He said something about her having had cataract surgery earlier, maybe there was an error. I retorted something. He said: sometimes we have to take chances. Ah. Not me yet. I may return to hearing the extraterrestrial stuff early mornings. The other materials have been sounding less drastic. But I cannot see how can that remain.

Further Out,
Bill

Note from the narrator ...

From the assorted musings found by the cleaner, Jake the intern from St. Olaf, in the log book of Crawfish Cabin at Anderson's Resort on Lake June Bug in northern Saint Louis County, in the Minnesota Arrowhead.

May 29, 1994

My name is Ron Larsen and I am here with my family. It is our first time here. It's late at night and I hear sounds outside. Which is fine. I can get used to that. I want to tell people about Fr. Larry Rosebaugh and Fr. Roy Bourgeois and how they tried to tell people about the killing in El Salvador by entering Fort Benning and playing a recording of Oscar Romero.

What is that noise outside?

I'll be right back.

It is no concern of ours how you run your own planet. But if you threaten to extend your violence, this Earth of yours will be reduced to a burned-out cinder. Your choice is simple: Join us and live in peace, or pursue your present course and face obliteration. We shall be waiting for your answer; the decision rests with you.

— Klaatu, *The Day The Earth Stood Still*

FIFTY-NINE

Kaitylyn thought as she walked in the sun and the rain, the day and the night, avoiding everyone as best she could, eating in the soup kitchens, sleeping in the shelter, the parks, that actually wasn't so bad, so peaceful. She usually could sleep anywhere, but she couldn't sleep on the bench thinking someone would grab her at any second, but still, not bad, the city, the park, the stars, right in the middle of the action and the weather is nice.

She thought of what she should do. Whom should she kill? She thought of it all the time, probably muttered it as she walked, she was too busy to really notice if she was talking to herself. But she was a real revolutionary, she knew that, for certain, no doubt about it now. She should kill Braxton, the F.B.I., and she would. That fuck. Fuck the F.B.I. One day she decided that. She knew where the F.B.I. office was. There was an elevator and she would walk out into the office ask for him and shoot him.

Or she would kill Alexa, Trevor and Marv before they killed her. She constantly watched for a car that could be theirs.

How about a judge? More police? Soldiers?

She sat, alone, on a bench, somewhere in Saint Paul, not far from her old high school, her old neighborhood, the home where her parents still lived, her sisters with their families, all pretty much right here.

And here she was as well.

Everyone all together as it should be.

She saw Geronimo and Jim, Lara, Braxton, Carroll, Marv, Alexa, Trevor, all driving past and staring … sitting in the window seats in the bus.

She thought a cigarette at this time would be appropriate. She got up and walked across the street to approach the group of boys on the corner.

"Can I get a smoke?" she asked and received one.

"Light?"

She got that too, turned and walked back to her bench as the boys all watched her.

Kaitylyn enjoyed the cigarette down to the end, closing her eyes at times, imagining herself holding someone else's hand and leaping, going over the cliff into the wild blue yonder. It scared her as it excited.

She dropped the cigarette onto the cement, ground it out with her shoe, then got up to pick up the nub and drop it in the trash right there.

She sat back against the bench and almost relaxed for a while.

The sudden bark scared the boys and they ran in a group toward the lights of the gas station.

The bus came and went. Cars stopped at the light intent on getting somewhere not noticing Kaitylyn.

The boys went home deciding not to tell.

Near morning time a man headed downtown approached the bench seeing something in the faint light.

Kaitylyn stretched out, taking up practically the whole bench.

The man, disgusted, scolded her that this was not her bed.

"Hey, c'mon.

"Hey, lady.

"Lady?"

Note from the narrator ...

From the assorted musings found by the cleaner, Jake the intern from St. Olaf, in the log book of Crawfish Cabin at Anderson's Resort on Lake June Bug, near Ely, in northern Saint Louis County, in the Minnesota Arrowhead.

June 22, 1993

"They" burned people ALIVE at Waco

Jessika

Even if among us there is sin, untruth, injustice and temptation, at least in certain places, somewhere on the earth, there are men who are holy and exalted; to make up for it, those men have truth and justice … so it has not been lost to the world …
— Fyodor Dostoyevsky, *The Brothers Karamazov*

It's a Barnum & Bailey world, just as phony as it can be
But it wouldn't be make believe, if you believed in me.
— *It's Only A Paper Moon*, E.Y. Harburg, Billy Rose

SIXTY

Lara and Brooke and Evey and Rachel, and the others sat in their old people clothes in the back pews of the church. Kaitylyn lay in the box in the front and her family hunched in the pews close by.

After the service Kaitylyn's father stopped on his way out, following the minister and the others and the casket. He leaned over to Lara.

"My daughter was a good person."

Lara figured he was telling her or asking her or just hoping.

"Yes," said Lara.

"I know who you are," he said, reaching and shaking Lara's hand.

"Oh, we're not really any…," said Lara.

"From the auxiliary," said Evey, "for the lunch."

He smiled just a little and nodded, pulling out of the pew to rejoin his family, then he came back and told them that Kaitylyn had left a note, asking to be buried next to Jim and Geronimo, "in the Potter's Field."

"Or as close as possible," he said.

"That's what she said."

The stars were so vivid, right there and so many, geezuz.

The dominant smell was baking cookies and he remembers the feel of the soft something on his seat, felt the metal as he leaned to look out the

343

window and then there was no spacecraft, he was by himself, floating, and he heard them talking and he thought, laughing.

Billy dreamed … about a Russian race horse named Roswell and aliens with clown feet that they were self conscious about which made them favor the night and going on a moonshine run with the guys down the hall to Rachel, Nevada. … and going all over the universe … and the aliens were trying to tell him something and they were serious but he couldn't stop laughing and so they took him back, perturbed with him, he thought.

He dreamed that he woke up and wrote to his family and friends to tell the truth about where he was. And they were happy that they knew where he was and they were going to come get him and get him out of there.

"Can you do that?"

"Yes, sure, we're on our way.

"We'll need to get the pickup fixed, first."

"Okay."

Billy went to the window to sit and wait for his relatives and friends to come to the state mental hospital just outside of Bumfuck, Iowa to attempt to free him from incarceration, presumably for having written a letter to the editor that some thought dangerous.

He sat there for a while and not seeing any dust on the county road, got the idea that maybe since he would be leaving he could write another letter to the editor. He'd be long gone by then.

Dear Editor,

9/11 truth brings it all down, just like the truth about the JFK murder and others — topples the Trump statue, the U.S. military, defense contractors, big media, bankers, criminal corporations, stops wars.

And, even if it looks very bleak at the moment, try to gain hope and a reason to smile through your day by recalling the Wobblies, the anti-war activists of the early 1900s, the peace movement of the 1960s, and Jill Stein and her recent heroic Presidential campaign, the Berrigans and hundreds like them, Dorothy Day, Frank Cordaro, who has been working at this since the 1980s.

We take hope and pride in remembering that we walk with them. What good does it do? Did they stop war? Stop all of this? Maybe not, but maybe it's a long relay race and we have to run our leg of the race and pass the baton. Our race is being run, we can be certain of that and that's a good thing, an important thing.

9/11 truth is important even much moreso than the truth about the JFK murder. It is an event much more volatile in our society and more powerful. It will bring down the lying media and politicians and generals. And we will then be able to build up a just society. That is our hope and that is a goal worth basing our lives in.

Billy Blackbird, Bumfuck State Hospital, Iowa

(As a result of the publication of this letter in *The Clarion Call*, he was escorted from his room cell by two unsmiling short stout ladies with flour in their hair, told to collect his things, up the grey cement stairs to another floor, another room and told, "might as well get comfortable.")

In South Africa we had truth commissions and people told the truth after apartheid was over, and at least people came to understand their own history a little better.

... these people in the United States who really know the truth about all that has happened — can't tell the truth, because then nobody would pay their taxes, nobody would care about the military budget anymore, and everyone will get thrown out of office.

We have a government that changes hands on the surface every four years and every two years and every six years, but which in reality isn't that much different from the previous one, and is still pursuing the same interests at the expense of the needs of people.

... in the long run we would be better for it. We would be more a mature country and more understanding country and better able to safeguard ourselves in the future if we knew exactly what went down in '63 and in '68 and the government would fess up to it and we could examine it and study it in detail, we would be much better off in the long run because then we could move forward confidently and try to prevent such abuses in the future. ... only in that way can we recover our respect as a people and move forward much wiser and more confident about where we should be heading in the future.

— Douglas Horne

SIXTY-ONE

Dunn Bros., too hot, Lara decided.
So they were meeting at an outside table at Caribou on Grand Avenue in Saint Paul.

Korey walked up to where Lara sat drinking what looked like straight whiskey. He smelled the recently passed shower and heard the bells chime at the Basilica, but not really, he was interested in what Lara was doing. They were supposed to have a meeting here, but this looked like more of an afternoon party.

"I'll have what she's having, Jack," said Korey.

"This isn't whiskey," said Lara, "Mountain Dew."

The waitress waited not giving anything away.

"Mountain Dew," said Korey.

"Hey. It's Brooke the spy."

Brooke sat in a flurry of material and panache. She was now constantly in disguise.

"I really can't see how this is gonna work."

She fluffed her southern belle countenance.

"Yeah, I been kinda wonderin' about that, too," said Lara, elbows on the table, taking a rather long sip.

"So, whatta we gonna do?"

"Kill ourselves," said Brooke.

"Don't say that," said Lara.

"Yeah, yeah, okay, that was bad, I'm sorry."

"Sorry about your granny," said Korey.

"De nada," said Lara.

"What's that?" He pointed at the papers on the glass table.

"Nothin'."

"See it?"

She pushed them over, getting something wet on them, dabbing it off.

Korey read: Some day if you really want to fucking win.

"It's actually from Actually," said Lara.

He kept reading out loud: *the law of karma, pre-programming, passport, manifesto, drill scenario.*

Korey took a drink from Lara's glass as he read over the papers. He stretched an arm around Brooke, inviting her to slide over closer. She stayed pretty much where she was.

"Yeah, The Actually Meter doesn't really work," said Lara, downing the rest of the drink and crunching the ice.

"The what?"

"Oh, it's something where you put it on your computer and that one place where they film you on the top, that hole? Well you put it on there and you film them right back and you can see them, who's watching you, it doesn't work."

"Oh," said Korey.

Korey pushed the papers back into the edge of Lara's table bubble.

"I get it," he said.

"You see those?" he looked at Brooke.

She nodded a yepper.

"Actually gave you, us, those?"

"Yes he did," said Lara.

"But it came from the F.B.I.?" said Korey.

"Well, they sent it to us after Cicely, all his stuff, you know. They do shit like that … sometimes."

"They do?" said Korey.

"They sent us Morgan's hands," said Brooke.

"That's creepy shit, creepy people, the F.B.I.," said Korey.

"Yeah, buddy," said Lara, tipping her glass way up to get the drops.

Korey said thanks for his Mountain Dew. Brooke told the waitress just water.

"You should send up 99 drones and make 'em think there's an alien attack," said Korey.

"Sandy Hook 'em, Boston, Tucson, Aurora. There's a lot a shit you could do. Operation Enduring Freedom, call it that and then show how it's all fake."

"I know what you could do," said Brooke.

"What?"

"Well, you could have the C.I.A. find you again, arrest you, torture you and then tell you to go do something, you and Washington, and then you don't do it, and make them look silly, and then just keep doing that, arresting you, torturing you, and getting away. It'd be something to do."

He drew his arm back from her chair and groaned. It must have been sore, the arm.

"Yeah," he said. "We could do that."

"That's not half-bad," said Lara.

"Yeah, I don't know," said Korey.

"Not that, what you said."

"What I said? It's pretty much just what Actu …"

"Yep, we could actually do that. Most of it. We still have some of the gold money, but we might need more. I need to talk to Evey and my gram left me something. I could get a job waitressing, or Walmart, somewhere. It could work."

She pushed her glass away and pulled paper and pens and notebooks from her purse.

She assumed her familiar pose of pen over yellow legal pad, inviting, requiring input.

"Yeah, I don't know," said Korey.

Brooke half stood, pulling her chair with her to come around closer to Lara.

They talked lightly, Brooke pointed at the yellow pad. Korey couldn't really hear because some people next to them had started to talk loud.

"I know what you could do!" he said.

"Shhhhh," they both shooshed him.

He turned his chair toward them, scraping on the cement.

He suggested Brooke go sit on The Stone Arch Bridge and have the C.I.A. come arrest her.

"And then you could film them, your show, your people, they still around? and then show that and everyone would see what the truth is, what they're really like."

"Yeah, yeah I guess I could do that," said Brooke.

Korey squeezed over closer, right into Lara's chair, to see what she had written across the top of her yellow legal pad.

He read out loud: "CRUSHER In Wonderland."

Note from the narrator ...

> From the assorted musings found by the cleaner, Jake the intern from St. Olaf, in the log book of Crawfish Cabin at Anderson's Resort on Lake June Bug in northern Saint Louis County, in the Minnesota Arrowhead.

October 4, 1999

From the best TV show ever, as we enter upon the new century, perhaps to our demise, maybe to great things:

Be open to your dreams, people. Embrace that distant shore. Because our mortal journey is over all too soon."

"They say dreams are the windows of the soul — take a peek and you can see the inner workings, the nuts and bolts."

"Today, a belated apology to the much maligned Chicken Little. It turns out you were right — the sky is falling. The National Space Administration informs us that Uncle Sam's Com-Sat 4 satellite is in a rapidly decaying orbit. That's their way of saying a ton of angry space trash is heading back home at fifteen thousand miles an hour.

"What does that make me think of?

"Makes me think of a triceratops, innocently munching a palm frond when out of the sky, whammo, a meteor sucker punches old mother Earth. Next thing you know, that triceratops, along with a hundred and seventy-five million years of dinosaur evolution, is nothing but history.

"To that unsung triceratops and all its kin, here's a song for you ..."

Chris In The Morning
Northern Exposure

Samantha "Sam" Howard
Mendota Heights

When Švejk subsequently described life in the lunatic asylum,
he did so in exceptionally eulogistic terms: 'I really don't know why
those loonies get so angry when they're kept there. You can crawl
naked on the floor, howl like a jackal, rage and bite. If anyone did this
anywhere on the promenade people would be astonished, but there it's
the most common or garden thing to do. There's a freedom there which
not even Socialists have ever dreamed of.
— Jaroslav Hašek, *The Good Soldier Švejk*

Where are the Snowdens of yesteryear?
— Joseph Heller, *Catch-22*

You set people very discreetly against one another. They destroy each
other. You don't destroy them.
— Daphne Park, MI6 Controller

SIXTY-TWO

You are driving your car, and you are a young man, in Minnesota, Nebraska, or Iowa, and you hear the song It never rains in California, by Albert Hammond on the radio, and you think, well, one, you love the song and you are into it, though you have no idea of California or even Kansas, and you think, not consciously, but you think, what would it be like to right now be Albert Hammond, the comfy life of having written that song and having this young guy from Iowa, Minnesota or Iowa driving along hearing it ... and that's it ... that's as cool as it gets ... but Albert Hammond doesn't get that. You get that, bubba, you. You get to imagine, and that's the greatest thing.

Rang true, sure rang true.

They're mostly chill, but still, they're gonna die, they know that.
They meet again at a different Caribou.
Korey on phone: Has to be Caribou, no matter how frikking far you have to go. Goddamn, is this how the Sandinistas did it? No shit? Really?

"... uses the Hegelian dialectic (create thesis & antithsis to cntrol synthsis) to create, manage and perpetuate conflict."

Korey is sitting at the table, waiting for the rest, reading from The Actually Papers.

And this time the whole bunch walks in, Evey, Lara, Brooke, Ike, Frida, Alice, Charlie and some new ones, the new F.B.I. agents, Korey says to himself.

And they are talking way too loud, Korey says and not maintaining any sort of protocol.

Just as soon as they all get settled, he gets up and walks out.

"Where you goin'?" says Lara.

Korey waves his hands and shakes his head, goes for the door.

Lara knows he lately has these panic attacks, fight or flight, and thinks to follow him, but lets him go, gets everyone in close to start planning.

"Okay," she says, running a finger down her list.

"Brigades. T-shirts ..."

People nod. She makes check marks.

Korey walked around the block. He didn't really feel like walking. He came back and sat on the sharp brick ledge by the restaurant front door, keeping his head down.

The CRUSHERS strolled out after the meeting, talking now quietly, lighting up, not noticing Korey right there, the last one Lara.

"So," she said as she sat down next to Korey on the thin ledge.

She showed her list, he scooched over on the hard sharp brick.

"I think this is really going to work," she said.

"You do?"

"Oh, yeah, we've got some great ideas, I don't see what could go wrong. It's going to be big, get lots of attention. We're gonna score big points. Here let me show you what I've got for you."

Korey looked at the yellow legal pad.

"Yeah," he said, "that's pretty cool."

Brooke moseyed along the Stone Arch Bridge, the sidewalk on the east side. She headed for the spot Korey had told her about, where if she sat there, on the top and waited that the C.I.A. would come and arrest her.

She wore the new project T-shirt: "Hielten sich für Captain Kirk," with a photo of the Starship Enterprise Bridge and all the actors.

She was being followed by The Secret Team, the film crew for the reality show that Prince Hope had hired. Since Hope's lunch club had burned who knows if he was still paying them, but maybe, who knows? They didn't have the four red Suburbans any longer, just one white van. Brooke was also set up with a camera in her blouse that would record what the C.I.A. said to her. When they took her wherever and talked about what she should do for them they would put that on TV and the world would know the truth about the C.I.A.

She found the spot with the light blue gum stuck to the top of the bridge railing thing where Korey said it would be. *That's the place. Just do it. I know it sounds crazy, but it works. Trust me.*

And she told him no it doesn't sound any crazier than most of this other stuff, so yeah, absolutely, I'll go there.

It was a beautiful day and she almost hoped she didn't get arrested by the C.I.A. for a while. There were lots of people out, joggers, walkers, bikers.

The white van couldn't just sit there blocking traffic so they had to park back off the bridge down a ways in the parking lot by the river, but they could still kinda see her.

She talked to some kids and their young parents, she watched two people in a kayak down below, she smelled leaves burning, and watched a walker talking to himself and smiling and then the phone on the other side of his head. What would it be like to still be running the group home, she thought. For Geronimo to not be dead and Kaitylyn, Jim, Max, Ariel … Zima. What if they were still all working together and planning to go out tonight. Her heart sank and her stomach hurt. She got a little dizzy and she had to lean on the stone bridge. With a degree in psychology, she could be going to grad school now. Maybe Korey would be, hmm, I don't know. When she graduated from Wayzata she knew just what she wanted to do, help people. She felt she hadn't done that. How did she get off the track? She was a total revolutionary, total outcast from her family, wanted by the law, F.B.I. Top Ten, according to Korey's latest report. Is that helping? She found a rock and threw it into the air as far as she could. Yeah, maybe. The answer has to be yeah, or she was jumping right now. Right now.

She looked for little e-Cars and people in black suits. Some young boys drove by and hooted. The look Brooke gave them must have done the trick because they had not come back. She was not carrying a weapon. She remembered what Korey said: Don't jump. It's a fucking long ways and hitting water hurts a LOT more than you think it would, even feet first. Don't.

She sat there what she thought was an hour. One of the guys from the van walked up, trying not to look at Brooke, just out over the river, but talking to her out the side of his mouth, pretty secret and hush-hush.

"Whattaya think?" he said.

"About what?" said Brooke, looking right at him.

"This. Stay here? This working?"

"Yeah. A little while more," she said.

"You got it," he said and walked back toward the white van down the hill in the parking lot by the river with a couple of the guys sweating inside and another one sitting at the picnic table right there.

She was getting kind of a pain in her back from sitting there. She got down to stretch and stand, to look around and saw someone coming on the sidewalk that she thought she should know.

It was Korey's friend, Washington. Brooke knew him from Oz. They had never really talked that much, but he seemed nice, she thought.

She watched him as he walked toward her. He wore a white T-shirt, jeans, tennis shoes. When he got close he smiled.

"Hey," he said.

"Hey," said Brooke.

"You didn't go to the meeting?" she said, meaning the planning at the restaurant where Korey walked out.

"Nah, I didn't go to the meeting. Nice day, what you doin'?"

"Just waitin'."

"For the C.I.A.?"

"Yeah! How did you know?"

"Oh, we did that, right here, it works."

He turned to look both ways on the road.

"Nothing yet?"

"Nope."

"If you jump it hurts," he said.

"Yeah, that's what ..."

"Well, see ..."

"Where you goin'?"

"I don' know, just walkin', nice day."

"You back working at the store?" asked Brooke.

"Nah, they wouldn't take me, say I'm bad news."

"You're probly wanted," she said, "maybe murder, not much you can do. You ever think about jumpin'?"

She nodded toward the river.

"Sure," he said, "who doesn't? That's what all these people are doin', walkin' here, thinkin' 'bout jumpin'."

"Oh, do you think so? I don't think so."

"Yeah, maybe not."

"Projection," she said.

"Yeah, projection."

"But, yeah, it's not going to end well for you," she said, "me neither."

They stood in silence for a while, looking around, hearing the talk of the walkers, and the water, saw a plane, smelled someone cooking hot dogs.

"Nice day," he said.

She just nodded and leaned on the bridge rail, not a rail, more of a stone top where it's flat and you can sit.

"They might not be coming," said Washington. "I s'pose sometimes they don't."

"Yeah."

"We could try something?" said Washington, picking a little twig from the stone top and flicking it at the water. They watched it float down and lost it, never saw it get to the water, too far down there.

"Wait," said Brooke, touching her shoulder in the spot where it started all her cameras rolling.

"I'm not the C.I.A. if that's what you're doin'," said Washington.

"Okay," said Brooke, still filming.

Washington turned to lean on the stone top thing toward the water.

He whispered to Brooke to do the same because there's some guys in a white van down there watching us.

Brooke said, okay, tied her hair back in like two seconds with a rubber band she pulled from thin air and looked out over the water.

"Like I was sayin'," said Washington, now in a Minnesota gangster accent.

And he told her his plan while she kind of twisted her back to be able to film him while he talked. She raised a hand way up over her head to signal to the guys in the production truck that they might want to get up off the picnic table and start doing their job.

Because you can never know these days who is in the C.I.A. and who isn't, is how she was thinking as she listened to Washington lay out this plan that she was pretty sure he was making up right there, but still it wasn't that bad.

Korey had his notes from Lara on the recipe cards that he was s'posed to not ever lose. Ever.

It was Military Appreciation Week in Shandler Park and Shandler Park High School, The Bombers, was joining in the celebration. Students were to wear camo one day and military uniforms one day and one day they were wearing their The Bombers T-shirts depicting a B-52 dropping its bombs, "We Are Bombers."

So Korey was supposed to write graffiti, to "bomb," all over the school grounds in the bomb theme, to exaggerate, to make it obvious that the bomb theme was weird, to show that the bomb theme was offensive and weird and WTF?

He rode the bus and got to the high school early in the morning and he had his spray paint and his sidewalk chalk in his backpack. The birds are chirping and the cars are starting to run. He dug into his pack for the salted granola bar he was saving for lunch.

He walked fast, he was nervous, to his first spot, on the long, low cement boundary that goes around the whole big school block with the line of trees that are all the same, all the same height and he got the cap off and knelt and sprayed in red: bomb, the bomb.

He scooted along on his one knee, dragging all his other shit in the plastic bag with his other hand behind him, getting the one knee of his jeans all dirty: bomb-bomb-bomb, bombbombbombbomb.

Korey heard a motor and in the low light he saw someone chugging along the sidewalk … riding a mower.

Korey stood and folded his hands behind his back to face the man and the loud machine.

"Who are you!" the man said, stopping the machine right by Korey.

"Dude. The fuck? You're mowin' now? How early do I have to get here?" Korey thought.

The mower blade was running and it was spraying rocks and leaves all around.

Korey backed up.

The guy was dressed in like janitor clothes that you might see an actor on TV wear who was portraying a janitor or a delivery guy in the 1950s, all tan, brown shoes, with a tan hat and a nametag.

Korey had pretty long hair and he was dressed probably like some of the crazier kids at the school, so the janitor was maybe used to seeing guys like Korey.

The man switched off the machine. It took awhile to shut down and they waited.

"Oh, I'm s'posed to do this," said Korey.

"Bomb Days, you know. I'm in the club."

"What club?"

"Ummm, The Bomb Club."

"Bomb Club?"

"Yep."

"Oh, okay."

He switched it again and the blade revved up as the motor roared and the leaves and branches flew. Korey put up his arm by his face.

"Bye," the guy waved.

"Bye," said Korey.

Korey spray painted all the way around the block and when he ran out of spray paint he started to write on the sidewalk with his multi-colored box of chalk. He was on his hands and knees and saw serious shoes walking toward him and stopping. He looked up the legs and the suit to see a serious man looking down at him.

Korey sat back on the walk to look up.

"Hello," said the man.

"Hello," said Korey.

"You must be The Captain," he said, nodding toward Korey's "Captain Kirk" T-shirt.

Korey looked at his shirt.

"Oh," he said as he looked back up at the man, who was now leaning over to offer his large, strong, hairy, old hand to Korey to get up.

"You're early," he said, hustling Korey toward the school.

"We can have coffee and chat while we get ready for the convocation in the auditorium.

"Everyone is excited, Captain."

He smiled down at Korey, who had yellow and green sidewalk chalk smudged around his face.

***

Lara's mission was in White Bear Lake at The Run For The Apples 10K, 5K, 3K Disabled Walk, 3K Non-Disabled Faster Walk, 2K Children's Fun Run, 3K Children's Competitive Run For College Bound, and 1K Old People Thing, on Saturday morning.

She is to plant fake bombs at the end line, the finish line and it will be a bunch of smoke and at first everyone will be scared as shit, but then Lara will step through the smoke and say, "see it's not really a bomb," and then everyone will say and think, oh we understand everything now, not only about this, but about our whole fucking country and its history, even going way back.

That was the plan, definitely the plan. She had her Gatorade, roman candles, bottle rockets and sparklers and smoke bombs in green, purple, red, white.

She got all her stuff out. She was bent over, on both knees, on the sidewalk, setting it all up, in a line.

"What *are* you doing?"

A woman holding a clipboard and wearing a new yellow sweat suit, who could have been, probably did have, four other jobs to go to after this, librarian, mental hospital head nurse, downtown intersection traffic cop, and Hogwarts instructor for defense against giant cockroaches, appeared next to Lara, causing Lara to stand.

"Umm, nothing. How are you?"

"This doesn't look like nothing," said the short stout woman with a fresh new hairdo.

"Just celebrating I guess," said Lara.

"You guess?"

She checked her list with a yellow fingernail.

"You're not on the list," she said.

"No, probably not," said Lara, "last-minute you know, I should have gotten signed-up, next year."

"Yeees, but this is this year. Just what are you planning to do? This does not look good."

She walked slowly, somehow making her yellow tennis shoe heels click on the sidewalk, around Lara's stuff in a circle.

"In fact," she stopped.

"You know what it looks like?"

And Lara knew at that moment that she had made her point. The woman now knew what she should have known before, that the bombing at that one other running thing was not a bombing at all and that she should change her life while there was still time.

And in the meantime …

Prince Hope went over to the F.B.I. building on Nicollet.

He went up the elevator to the twenty-third floor.

He asked to speak to an agent and was asked to sit down.

Hope looked around at all the F.B.I. things on the walls, the dead agents, the agents who had done wonderful and great things, new agents, old agents, photos from Facebook of agents and their cats.

"Hello, I'm Mike Braxton."

Like a giraffe in a china shop, Hope followed Braxton through a break in the front office counter to Braxton's office, back down a long hall.

It was quiet in there with no smells.

"I would like to report the F.B.I. burning down my building," said Hope once they both got situated and staring at each other.

"We don't really do that," said Braxton, looking up, keeping his pen touching his yellow legal pad, but not really writing anything.

"How about the C.I.A.?"

"Okay," said Hope.

"You could do like Josephine Custer did and take them to court, just an idea."

"Yeah, I guess I could do that."

Prince Hope then met with Josie Custer, The BIM (h), at Dunn Bros. on Nicollet or close by there.

"Yeah, that didn't really work," said Josie.

"No?"

"No."

So, yeah, they both went, together, to meet with Braxton, going up the elevator all that way pretty much in silence, except The BIM (h) smiled at about the eleventh floor, and Prince Hope had bad thoughts that he would have had to confess if he was still doing that.

"Have you considered entrapment?" said Braxton.

"Yeah!" said Josie.

"We, you could get back at the C.I.A. for a lot of things, throughout history, like The Bay of Pigs."

"They didn't really do that," said Braxton.

"Nice try," said Hope.

"Yeah," said Braxton, "I read, so."

… *I happened to be at this meeting,* just sayin', not to brag, but they asked me, so that I would know all the ins and outs for the book.

"You could be in the book, if we do this," said Prince Hope to The BIM (h).

"I already am," she said.

"How's that going?" she said to me.

"Not great," I said.

And, yeah, so then Braxton asked me if I can use all those quotes that I use and stuff from other people?

"You can do that?"

"Yeah, I guess," I said.

And they all sat in silence and I knew what that was, and I held off as long as I could, but I just couldn't stand it and I broke. I talked.

"It's not really plagiarism," I said in a big rush.

"I try to explain to people. It's the culture, the whole zeitgeist, immersion, like that."

"Yeah, I guess, but," said Braxton, writing something down.

"The zeitghost as well," said The BIM (h).

"*Thank* you!" I said, so happy somebody got it.

"I like your hair," I said.

"You've said that."

"I'm going to use that," I said.

"I figured you would," she said.

"As I said, have you considered entrapment," said Braxton.

"I don't think so," said Hope, looking at The BIM (h).

"No, we had not," she said.

"Well you're in luck," said Braxton, already getting up.

He grabbed hold of a whole file cabinet, grunted to drag it over the carpet. He hurried into another room, bringing back armfuls of manila envelopes.

Braxton let them fall onto his desk.

The BIM (h) and Prince Hope scooched their chairs closer, picked up the folders that had fallen to the floor, and began fingering through the envelopes stamped with various official sounding names: "Murder," "False Flag," Outright Hoax," "Nobody Died," "Burn Down," "Deceit," "American Idiots," "Smoke?" "Mirrors!" "Big Secret."

At just about that time, Evey and Rachel were in South Saint Paul, at an elementary school that Evey didn't really know the name, but it was all one story, brick, smack-dab in a neighborhood and it looked like it would be perfect, is what she thought.

Evey had her AR-15 under her arm under a long coat under a long box of donuts that she had this last-minute idea and was in Kwik Trip just walking around, and was going to say she was bringing them for her daughter's class for "Wednesday Hump Day Is Donut Day" if anyone asked.

Rachel was with her because she was good cover for hanging around an elementary school with an automatic unlicensed weapon and she had nobody to stay with her and Rachel did not like to stay by herself out at the farm with just Roswell who if the F.B.I. or robbers came would just keep eating grass.

Lara had shown Ike and Frida how to purchase real weather balloons online and gave them the CRUSHER credit card with not CRUSHER on it, but something else, something secret. They got a bunch of them, in all the primary colors, and it came with a helium blower-upper attachment. They worked in Lara's grandmother's basement.

"Nice," said Lara one afternoon when she came down the stairs and saw the whole basement filled with balloons. So one night they got them out into the back yard, each one tied to the ground with the pinion accoutrement.

All they had to do was go around and flick the attachment thing and the balloon would take off with "UFO" hand-painted on each balloon.

Inside the house Frida was on the computer with the notice of the alien invasion ready to go to all the newspapers and radio and television in the whole Twin Cities.

And then when everyone realized it was just balloons, that would teach them, don't try this, C.I.A., if you were thinking about it.

"I don't get it," Ike had said to Frida as they were getting the balloons ready.

"Yeah, but it is pretty cool," said Frida, and they had kept working.

***

Charlie called the *Water Dale Concubine* and said he was Cheap Boat and spelled it out and said that was what he wanted to be called. Who is this? Cheap Boat. Jesus Christ, whattya wanna say? If you want the Swap Shop number … Not Swap Shop! I have some valuable intel about … bombs, running event, balloons, and there will be a shooting of the congresswoman. What's her name? I don't know, this is sports. In Water Dale when she talks at the shopping center at 1 p.m. Yeah, okay, buddy. Call us again next week.

Korey sat in the principal's office.

He could see out the curtain the desk where the secretary frantically worked the early morning phone and also dealt with students coming in with problems and teachers ducking in to say hello and pick up messages and leave secret messages for other teachers.

Korey looked around the office at all the photos covering the walls. He could see that the walls were a pale yellow, but just barely. There were a lot of photos and every one had the principal with a bomb, a photo of himself holding a paper mache bomb or showing the new Bomb mascot T-shirt, the Bomb mascot costume one of the students wore at all the games, or some town or visiting dignitary and they are both holding bombs and smiling.

The secretary brought him coffee on the run.

Korey felt his gun inside the fancy holster inside his pants and he liked it. But, it was itchy when it got sweaty and made it hard to sit.

The secretary came back with a handful of little creamer cups.

She noticed the bulge in Korey's pants and smiled.

"Nice weapon. Glocks rock, love 'em, fit the hand."

She held out her left hand with the fingers clenched and she gritted her teeth.

"Is he here?" somebody said.

"Really? In there?"

A teacher came in, having to duck to get into the door.

"Captain?" he said.

Korey kind of nodded.

"I'm Kyle Connnneally. I teach American History and coach boys basketball. We are just so glad to have you here. And I, personally, would just like to thank you for what you have done for our great country."

"No problem," said Korey, rising to a squat to shake Kyle's hand.

Evey and Rachel stood by the front door, kind of milling around with the other parents and children and kind of not. Evey did not want to poke anyone in the back with the gun barrel, for one thing, for another thing the other parents and their children looked kind of pretty crazy to be truthful.

So Rachel pulled the fire alarm.

It was right there.

She had never been in a school before and she had never really been this close to this many loud people and she felt kind of like cows must feel when they are being pushed into a chute to go in and have their throats sliced and their insides taken out, kind of like that and she needed out of there.

"What does this do?" she said.

And the second she said it, Evey, in slow motion, opened her eyes and … her mouth wide … and raised a hand and turned and … yelled … "NOooooo!"

She reached the alarm, just after Rachel's hand had been on the alarm and those turning, all they saw was Evey's hand on the alarm as the bell was blaring and the hall lights and room lights and parking lot lights flashed.

Rachel must have ran.

"She did it!"

Nine perfect darlings in black shoes pointed at Evey with her hand still frozen to the alarm like a tongue in winter on the slippery slide.

Everyone was yelling. The lights flashed. The bells rang like not continuous but blaring and like a fire truck trying to get through traffic, which is just what was happening a few blocks away as EVERYBODY was headed to "the element'ry."

"It's a gun!" somebody yelled.

"No! Yes!" screamed Evey with her one hand up, trying to clarify, the other still holding the rifle and also the box of donuts.

"It's not loaded!"

"Not loaded?" somebody screamed.

"And here's donuts!" hollered Evey.

"Donuts!" some people yelled.

"It's all fake, mostly, not the donuts, eat, eat 'em up, yeah, stick your face right in there, there ya go."

Evey stood in the passageway, kind of trapped, absolutely, opening the box, offering them to the screaming people and also trying to remember her manifesto she was going to read to make her point.

"And then Rachel pulled the fire alarm just as we were going in to do all this cool educational shit," she said.

"Fire!" somebody finally yelled.

And so they ran.

Charlie and Alice took the bus to Water Dale, jumped out and ran to the strip mall, excited to see what was happening because of Cheap Boat.

They found a few people standing around a podium and one TV camera setting up with a young female reporter getting her hair ready with her compac.

Charlie and Alice figured they were late, that the ambulances and cops and everyone else had already left.

"Shit," said Alice and they ran a little faster across the parking lot.

"It's fake," said Charlie.

"What's fake?" somebody said.

"The shooting?" said Alice.

"What shooting?" said the reporter.

"That's just it," said Charlie.

"It didn't happen?" said Alice. "It's all fake."

"What's fake!" said the cameraman.

He started to film and focus on Charlie's T-shirt, which showed the Captain Kirk and the Starship Enterprise Bridge and all the actors with the caption: Hielten sich für Captain Kirk.

"The bandana!" said Charlie.

"For one thing?" said Alice.

"The manifesto the police found," said Charlie as the cameraman continued to film.

"I am Cheap Boat, by the way, that's my thing I want to be called by. So whenever I call, that's what you call me. I called this in," he said.

"The drills? Beforehand?" said Alice.

A crowd began to gather as it was getting closer to the time of the scheduled short talk of the congresswoman to announce something happening with the strip mall. A black SUV pulled up and a well-dressed woman got out of the passenger seat along with three or four young men in suits. The reporter went immediately to the woman with her microphone. The cameraman left Charlie in mid-sentence to follow.

"This is crazy," said Charlie.

"It's happening again?" said Alice.

"They are re-producing it all, déjà vu like they had in the '60s."

"It's a portal," said Alice.

"What about the bandana?" the reporter asked the congresswoman from Stillwater.

"And the manifesto!" hollered the cameraman, his face red, the veins in his temples bulging.

"And the drills!" screamed the reporter at the congresswoman.

"God! Dammit!" screamed the cameraman.

"There's no blood!

"How do you explain that!"

The congresswoman stepped back. Her goons stepped forward.

Charlie and Alice tiptoed away, and right there was a coffee shop.

They sipped The New Twin Cities Coconut Kiwi Latte and had Nice Cream, which is actually strawberry and lime ice cream, and watched nine police cars slam to stops and throw the cameraman and the reporter to the cement, handcuff them behind their back, yank them up and throw them into the squad cars.

The lady with the clipboard stopped circling Lara's shit on the sidewalk.

"I know just what this is," she said.

"And it's not good. This is not that kind of an event.

"It looks as though you ... might ... be ... a ... redneck. This looks to me like a redneck celebration. This is not that."

Lara was now not really listening to the lady with the clipboard in the yellow sweat suit. She was squatting by her bag because there were still some things she had forgotten to put out.

She found the tennis shoe, with the firecracker duct-taped to the bottom and "ISIS" written on the rubber in blue pen, set it next to the sparklers. She dug more and pulled out the pressure cooker and set it next to the tennis shoe, and then found the boxcutter and laid it carefully by the pressure cooker. She stuck her head almost inside her bag until she was convinced she hadn't forgotten anything else.

She stood.

"Oh!" exclaimed the lady.

"Terrorist!"

"Exactly!" said Lara, pointing two fingers right at the lady.

The lady pulled on the lanyard around her neck and found a whistle.

"Tweet! Tweet! … TWEET!" she puckered her cheeks big and blew it, but it didn't sound like tweet.

It was echoed by other so-not-tweets from over there, there, and there.

Police in yellow vests rushed in to cordon off the area with squad cars and yellow tape.

A police car ran over a dummy in the street as a smoke machine filled the air with white and black clouds and volunteers with industrial size ketchup bottles began filling the street.

A young man carrying a backpack in one hand ran down the street chased by a policeman. The young man turned and shot the policeman dead with his finger.

Lara looked up to see a passport fluttering down from the sky and landing at her feet.

Lara: This is bullshit.

Somebody: There's juice. Everybody gets juice, get your juice. You got it coming. In the refreshment tent?

Lara: Juice? Really? I like juice.

At 9:30, the perfect time, Ike and Frida set to work releasing the balloons, slowly, one at a time and then they got so excited they hurried around as fast as they could and there they were, all the dark spots rising straight up, into the sky, over the Twin Cities, signifying something-something.

They went inside to watch the news to see if they would say something about the UFOs over Minneapolis-Saint Paul.

They got there late, just in time for sports.

"Shit," said Frida.

And then, Sancho, the tall even when sitting handsome co-host, smirked at his co-host Jennifer with a smirk. She smirked back in that knowing way.

"And now," said Sancho, "as we reported in the opening of the news hour … we have opened the phone lines asking what people are seeing out there, if anything … and we have been getting some answers."

Jennifer: Well, Sancho. Some think it is an advertising gimmick for a new cologne, some for nose tweezers from the 1950s.

Sancho: Talking blue donkeys.

They were fed pieces of paper from off-camera.

Jennifer: Fart balloons. Where you can send your farts somewhere far away …

Sancho: And when it explodes you fart on somebody far away.

Jennifer: Some kind of stupid CRUSHER thing, Russian ninja ballerinas, retired, really old.

Sancho: Condiments, blown up, and a lot of our listeners have reported seeing Osama bin Laden, Lee Harvey Oswald, Cruella deVille,

Jennifer: James Earl Ray, David Chapman, The Big Bad Wolf, a Cheshire Cat, Sirhan Sirhan and Mohammed Atta.

Sancho: And that's it for tonight, the, the, the, the that's all folks…That's the news and we are outa here. Have a good night, it is what it is …

Jennifer: Good night and good luck.

And so it goes.

That's the way it is.

Sancho: Stay on the same page, step up to the plate, good to go, take it to the next level, at the end of the day,

Jennifer: Bring something to the table, have a good day, it is what it is, on so many levels, it's time to wake up, your toast is ready, the bus is here, the world is on fire.

Evey and the others streamed out of the school to the designated safe spot place. They began counting off in their designated number, code name that every parent and child had memorized for in case of attack. They all stood in a line, Evey with her open box of donuts, now about half, and her rifle under her coat. She saw it coming toward her. This was one of her buttons, her triggers. She did not like it when things went around the circle or down a line and she knew soon it would be her time. It freaked her out, since she was little and whenever it came to her everyone looked at her as of course they did with everyone but Evey did not really like attention, though at times she craved it. "Red Bull 94Bdash12Alpha," "CoolJackNinerNinerNineFourer," … here it came to Evey. She took a deep breath and said, "Hump Day!" … the next person stared at her and waited. Evey nodded to her to say, that's it, go, go.

And the woman shouted: "Big Dog!Little Dog!One-er, One-er, Pyle! Gomer!"

After it went away, down the line, the person next to Evey, Big Dog, turned to Evey and said "you have donuts?"

"Do we give our real names now?" said Evey.

"Not yet," said Big Dog.

"Okay, Hump Day," said Evey, sticking out her hand.

"I'm Rachel's Mom."

They both ate donuts.

Evey's arm was getting tired and she dropped it a little. Big Dog took the box of donuts to help.

"You have a rifle under your jacket?"

Evey started to explain.

"You must be here for Rifle Day," said Big Dog.

"Umm, kind of. Yeah, I guess it is Rifle Day."

"Cool," said Big Dog as the safety bell rang.

"Yeah, cool," said Evey.

Korey waited in the principal's office listening to the morning announcements in the speaker on the wall as he watched through the window the secretary giving the announcements from her desk behind the front counter in the outer office.

The secretary now was dressed as a Cruise Missile and was surrounded by members of The Parent's Auxiliary, wearing bomb buttons and mushroom cloud hats.

The secretary announced the auxiliary and they sang the national anthem over the speaker.

The principal then welcomed everyone to the annual Bomb Days Celebration and asked the teachers to begin bringing their students "in an orderly manner" to the gymnasium for the convocation.

A small group of students with nametags that read Bomb Day Committee walked into the outer office and were directed to the principal's office by the secretary. They came in, sheepishly, heads down, afraid to make good eye contact. One said they were there to escort Korey to the convocation. They went the back way through the empty girls and then boys locker rooms to the back door of the stage. They put Korey in a metal chair and left, giggling.

Korey sat alone in the metal chair, behind the curtain, on the dark stage.

He listened to everyone loudly gathering in the gym filled with metal chairs.

The curtain slowly rose. The light from the gym began to fill the stage area. Korey saw that his line of metal chairs was full of people on this side of the podium and the other.

Everyone sported bomb buttons, students, teachers, on-stage minor town dignitaries, The Bombers T-shirts, firecrackers went off sporadically here and there and each time were greeted with a smattering of applause.

They stood for The National Anthem. The principal spoke, one of the Bomb Committee persons spoke, as well as a member of the VFW, DAV, Special Olympics and Northrup-Grumman.

The principal walked up to the podium, took a deep breath, extended an arm towards where Korey sat.

"And now, everyone … The Captain!"

The whole gymnasium as well as the upper balcony exploded as Old People and Other Parents stood and cheered. Hundreds of paper mache bombs dropped from the ceiling.

Firecrackers cracked. A line of elementary school children along the north wall, allowed to come over to attend the convocation but not sit, twirled red, white and blue sparklers.

Korey put up a hand acknowledging as he walked all the way across the stage to the podium.

Korey reached where he was going and everyone sat.

He took a deep breath, looked down, nodded at the principal, the minor town dignitaries.

"Thank you," he said.

"It is The Bomb!

"Bomb Day!"

He raised both fists into the air and everyone stood again and cheered for another five minutes.

Again they calmed and sat and Korey took a deep breath, looked down, nodded at the principal, the minor town dignitaries. He looked toward the ceiling, breathed deep, let it out.

"Yeah!"

And everyone stood again and cheered.

This went on for twenty minutes.

And then, from up in The Old People And "Other" Parents Section In The Balcony a sound was heard, a recording, perhaps from a cellphone or maybe something else, loud enough for Korey to hear: WAR! ... *Hooooh!* Good God Y'all! ... What is it good for!

Korey stared out into the crowd.

Korey thanked them, put up both hands and waved to them all as he walked all the lock-step way across the stage to his seat.

As he sat the Northrop-Grumman spokeswoman shook his hand.

"Very good," she said.

"Thanks," said Korey, continuing to stare, his hands clenched in fists, trying not to grab his gun that was in the expensive "Fully Loaded" holster shoved down the front of his pants.

He tried to understand what was happening. He had this urge. He wanted to stand up and start shooting everyone. He sat there, both hands over his crotch, smiling, nodding, sweating.

Brooke and Washington sat on the stone cap railing at The Stone Arch Bridge facing south probably.

"What's your idea?" said Brooke, holding up her hand and squinting to look at Washington.

"What?" she said.

"Burn our bridges? Ha. I'm so funny. Actually ...," she said, looking down at the ancient stone.

"Oh, just that white van," said Washington.

"Don't worry about them."

"Well, I was just thinking," said Washington, "we could do the C.I.A. right back at them, do what they do. But we need a name for the operation, something-something and then 'PRO,' like that."

"I know," said Brooke.

They sat and watched cars and runners and walkers go past.

"FUKTHEMTELPRO," said Washington and then they both said nothing for a while, just watching everything around them.

"I don't know," said Brooke, "I can't think of anything."

"I know," said Washington, "I can't either."

"Yeah," said Brooke.

Note from the narrator ...

From the assorted musings found by the cleaner, Jake the intern from St. Olaf, in the log book of Crawfish Cabin at Anderson's Resort on Lake June Bug in northern Saint Louis County, in the Minnesota Arrowhead.

June 9, 2002

All you need to know about 9/11.

Norman Minetta heard Dick Cheney say:
Have you heard anything to the contrary.

All I gotta say.

Peace out

We did not catch a fish, not today, not yesterday or the day before, maybe tomorrow?

Marcia McCarthy
Anoka, Minnesota

*To AnneFrancis in 1989

Titanic
Forrest Gump
Harry Potter
Men In Black
Shrek

To be hopeful in bad times is not just foolishly romantic, it is based on the fact that human history is a history not only of cruelty, but also of compassion, sacrifice, courage, kindness — and if we do act, in however small a way, we don't have to wait for some grand utopian future. The future is an infinite succession of presents, and to live now, as we think human beings should live, in defiance of all that is bad around us, is itself, a marvelous victory.

— Howard Zinn

SIXTY-THREE

Lara, dejected, left her grandmother's house, also now CRUSHER HQ, walked by the old group home in the dark, the workshop, across the Saint Thomas campus touching only grass because she could, crossed the river and walked to the White Castle on Lake to pig out.

She headed inside, with all the people of the night now having their say.

All the way she had walked thinking about how weirdly and finally awfully the big new project had gone and also about a YouTube she had just watched about hospice nurses and how they had seen evidence of life after death.

Lara had been thinking it was probably just lights out, there is nothing.

Someone had said that and Lara had started to try to accept it. But now she didn't know. She would like to think that all the people she knew who had died got what they wanted, what they really deserved, heaven, some version of Iowa.

She stared up at the menu but she already knew what she wanted. She saw the counter person was there but only now looked down.

"I'll take ten … Actually?"

"Hey, Lara. You said ten … ten *what*?"

"Is that you!"

She leaned over the counter and touched him with just her fingertip.

His nametag actually said ACTUALLY. She touched that too, ran her finger across the raised letters.

He smiled. "They call me that here, too, crazy, huh?"

"Yeah ... crazy."

She stared and looked behind her.

"What the fuck!" she leaned in and whispered.

Actually hurried to announce he was going on break. He grabbed Pepsis for them and led her to the farthest booth.

Lara was still staring, her mouth half open.

"Are ... are you an angel?"

She had to say it, had to.

"I've got so many questions if you are," she said.

"My grandmother thinks so," he smiled.

"No, god no, I'm not dead."

He sucked at his straw like a newborn.

"I am so thirsty, we been busy."

He removed his castle hat and set it down on the table, showing his sweaty, matted hair.

"So, what's new?" he said.

Lara started to tell him everything at once ...

"How are you ... here? You know?"

"Oh, yeah, well ..."

Actually explained to Lara that at Cicely they had charged the government troops to allow Morgan and Mollie to escape, that was the plan. He got hit and went down.

"And I just pretended to be asleep. I told myself that, just die, go to sleep, it's over, ya know?"

Lara nodded while sucking at her straw, eyes wide.

"And then I didn't die. They just left us there, didn't bury anyone and I thought, man, I am actually gonna live. If I can just stay in this pose and not move 'til dark. It was hard, cuz I didn't really fall in a comfort'ble position, but anyway, yeah, I did it. And at night, I ran."

"Why didn't you tell me?" she said.

"I wanted to live," he said. "I found out lying there how bad I wanted to live."

"Oh, yeah," she said. "I get that."

"But I been payin' attention."

"Okay," she said.

"We tried your plan. It didn't really work, though, but thanks anyway."

"What plan?"

"The plan in the envelope. The F.B.I. sent them to us, your plan.

"The Actually Basement Tapes? It was written on the envelope. Helooo."

She tapped him on the head.

"I didn't send anything, prepare anything and I know I haven't ever written "The Actually Basement Tapes" on anything in my life."

Lara had to think about that.

She watched out the window over Actually's shoulder.

"So," she said, "the whole package came from Braxton."

"Who?"

"The F.B.I., Mike Braxton."

"I heard that name I think, maybe, while I was on the ground," said Actually.

"Wow," she said.

"He's good.

"Well, it still didn't work."

"I do think the F.B.I. murdered your grandma," he said.

"You heard? With what? Old age?"

"No, with whatever she had," said Actually.

"Not the F.B.I.," said Lara, "the C.I.A., those fuckers."

"I don't think the C.I.A. is in the U.S.," he said.

"They're not allowed."

"I know, right?" she said, tipping her cup for ice.

Once you accept your own death, all of a sudden you're free to live. You no longer care about your reputation. You no longer care except so far as your life can be used tactically to promote a cause you believe in.
— Saul Alinsky

SIXTY-FOUR

The CRUSHERS sat on the screened front porch, able to see out, but nobody could see in. They gathered on Lara's grandmother's comfortable chairs and benches, holding in their laps plates of salsa and eggs, drinking coffee, hearing the cars go by and the city beginning to wake up.

Lara perched on the grey wood floor, her legs crossed, her back against the door to the grey cement steps out front. She had her yellow legal pad in her lap, her full plate and coffee to the side. She wanted to wait for them to finish, but they were taking their sweet time.

"Listen, I met Actually."

"Actually?" somebody said.

"Really? No," said Evey.

"What? Wow, woah," said Brooke.

"A real ghost. I always have wondered about that."

Korey hadn't heard what she said. He was trying to mind-speak with Alice *what in God's name are you blathering about?* to see if he could get her to smile, Lebowski-Talk having been officially/unofficially banned from meetings.

"What?" said Lara. "No, not a ghost."

Lara told them all the story, going back to The Battle of Cicely and then meeting Actually at White Castle.

"He's going to join back up with us, but not really be with us," she said.

"Umm, I'm sorry, I wasn't listening," said Korey.

"Actually," whispered Brooke. "He's not a ghost."

"Not a ghost?" said Korey.

"Yes," said Lara.

And she talked about an idea Actually had for a new project.

"No," said Evey.

"Yes," said Lara.

"We are going to try … one more thing."

"Yeah, right, I don't know," said Brooke.

"I think maybe we need to start thinking about escaping and getting the fuck out of Dodge," said Charlie.

"Really?" said Lara.

"Yeah," said Ike.

"We been talking, and …"

"Then quit fucking talking," said Lara.

"I'm in charge and you can shut the fuck up and listen."

They watched her chest as she took a deep breath, held it and let it out slowly. They shut the fuck up.

"So, here's the thing."

And she told them about Actually's idea that they ask the people to support us and not the C.I.A.

"We send out these massive messages all over everything.

"The next time there is a phony something we will be there on the spot, in C.I.A. uniforms and tell people that it's not real and we'll tell the truth about it in 'the electronic media.' Nobody would believe a 'conspiracy theorist,' but they would believe the C.I.A., go figure, but it's true, right?"

She used air quotes, twice, even though they had been banned and Alice nudged Charlie in the side.

"We use something called SecureDrop. Actually will set it up. Can't be traced to us or to them. It's safe."

"There is no such thing," said Charlie.

"It's all very confusing," said Alice.

"Yeah, we could do that," said Brooke. "Or, how 'bout this? We could be The People Who Are Out There, like there is this legend that we exist,

CRUSHER, and some believe in us, but most don't, but nobody can find us, wanna do that, huh? … instead?

"Huh?"

Well … There is a place.
Like no place on Earth.
A land full of wonder, mystery, and danger!
Some say to survive it: You need to be as mad as a hatter.
And if you come to understand this mad place, the others will tell you
that you are entirely bonkers.
But I'll tell you a secret.
All the best people are.

— Alice

SIXTY-FIVE

Well, it's been another long week in Wonderland, my home town, at the end of the empire.

Prince Hope put one foot up on the wooden chair at almost the center of the stage. The audience settled in like a flock of wood ducks, puffed their feathers, subtly sniffed their own underarms and got comfortable.

"I smell the brimstone and I look around for you."

Hope began his story, about a small town C.I.A. agent, Henry, who worked in his home town.

"In high school he took an aptitude test in Mr. Crosby's *Non-College Preparatory More For Something "Technical" Class* that told him he would be a Magician.

"Hmm, he thought. How am I gonna manage that?

"And he went home and tried to make his sister disappear and he put a neighborhood cat into a trash can and tried to make it reappear in the tree.

"And he went back to school the next day and asked Mr. Crosby if he could retake the test and it came up Magician again and again the next time."

Hope told how Henry tried magic in his neighborhood through the rest of high school and then somehow just migrated over to the C.I.A. booth set up next to the Magician's booth at the next school career fair

— alphabetical order, it was a small fair — and he just got started in the C.I.A. Even he didn't know quite how it happened.

But it did. It just did.

"And now he was bored in the little town in his little office on main street. He did the regular C.I.A. things, hiding stuff, putting other stuff where it shouldn't be and making people suspect everyone else, sitting in the back row at church and writing down what the minister said as well as everyone else he could hear around him.

"He sat on a bench and sat real still and tried to talk to dogs through his mind and he never really got that good at it. Henry even tried putting a transparency over his parents' television set where all they could ever see was a beautiful sunrise no matter what the sound said about all that was happening in the world. Ernie eventually figured it out and said to Ethel, what's this?

"Well," said Hope.

"It's a tough job.

"We just want to do our part, to help guys and gals like Henry, on the front lines."

Hope then in one practiced swipe tore off his white suit revealing a black suit with white shirt and black tie over his red tennis shoes.

"I would like my assistant to now come on-stage."

Josephine Custer, tall, elegant in a matching black suit strode right up to Hope, smiling, waving her arms around and up and down like a *Price Is Right* product model.

Hope then explained that "as you know" the C.I.A. was going through some tough times "as everyone thinks they are liars and scumbags."

Josephine made some model gestures and pointed her knee with her toe raised.

"We hope that you will find it within yourselves to help support the C.I.A.," she said.

As The BIM (h) motioned elegantly toward the back of the theater Hope explained that there would be a table set up in the entry after the show.

"A White Elephant sale, a rummage sale ..."

"As well as a bake sale," said The BIM (h).

"You can also sign up to sponsor a C.I.A. agent overseas," said Hope.

"In El Salvador," said Josie, showing a large poster to the crowd.

"Venezuela," said Hope.

"Cleveland," said Josie.

"Des Moines," said Hope.

"Or right there in your Twin Cities," said Josie, holding up a large color poster of a big building on Nicollet Avenue.

"And that's the news ...," said Hope walking right to the edge of the stage, front and slightly off-center, "from Wonderland ... where all the ..."

After the show Hope and Josie hustled down the aisle and through the crowd to get to the table where there was rhubarb pie, apple strudel, baklava, bear claws and cannoli, cherry pies, cinnamon rolls, needles and truth serum, thumb screws, temple screws, waterboards, MK-Ultra flash cards, a used tiger cage, and in an array of sizes, white elephant statues made of the tusk of elephants "from Cambodia, Vietnam, Thailand and the Congo."

Under a plastic cover marked "please ask attendant to view" were samples of C.I.A.-grade cocaine and opium.

Behind the table were giant posters of the places around the globe where the C.I.A. had agents and where you could sponsor an agent in the field.

Hope and Josie had to hurry to take care of all the business.

A woman waited in line not patiently to talk to Josie.

"You are not C.I.A.," said Alexa, leaning over and pointing in Josie's face just as soon as it was her turn.

"Kind of," said Josie, pointing to her C.I.A. flag pin on her lapel.

Alexa wore a black suit with white shirt and black tie, just like Josie's.

"No, you are not," said Alexa.

"How would you know?" said Josie, trying to see around Alexa to the next customer, who was holding one of the larger white elephants.

"Excuse me," said Josie, "are you here to purchase an item?"

Trevor appeared next to Alexa, his face burning red, two fingers pointing.

People had begun to notice. Prince Hope paused his sale of an ounce of C.I.A. coke to watch.

Trevor pointed right at Hope, didn't say anything, more like pouted with his lower lip.

"We are C.I.A.!" Trevor hissed.

"No, you're *not*," Josie smiled and waved a hand.

The people standing around smirked, giggled and laughed out loud, putting their hands over their mouths.

"They think they are C.I.A.," people said. "Astro-NOT!"

"Looney Toons."

"I suppose you think we didn't go to the moon either," somebody said.

"How come we don't have a body, by now, if you really exist? Scientists don't even study you, you're so fake."

"I s'pose you made all those crop circles, too?"

"How come nobody has seen them then, in all these years?"

"What?" said Alexa, stomping one foot in frustration.

"What!" said Trevor, throwing up his arms.

"Prove it," said Hope.

Trevor grabbed a young man in the crowd, threw him to the floor, put a cover over his face and began pouring water through the cover into the man's mouth as the man fought and screamed loud.

Alexa leaned in to talk to a young woman next to her, telling the young woman that when she heard the song "Dancing Queen" by Abba she would take a knife and murder the king of Ethiopia.

Alexa then grabbed one of the thumb screws and jerked someone out of the crowd and squeezed the device until blood spurted.

By that time police officers had begun to stream into the theater entryway from three doors. They grabbed Trevor and Alexa, handcuffed them behind their backs and dragged them outside to the squad cars on the curb, lights flashing.

Note from the narrator ...

From the assorted musings found by the cleaner, Jake the intern from St. Olaf, in the log book of Crawfish Cabin at Anderson's Resort on Lake June Bug in northern Saint Louis County, in the Minnesota Arrowhead.

July 25, 2017

False Flags are as American as apple pie.

Obama lied about Osama and everything else. He did not prosecute Bush and Cheney because he is in on it.

John Barbour film, if you still can by the time you read this, rent it on Amazon: The American Media and the Second Assassination of John F. Kennedy.

Sun, water, moon, bugs, fish, it's all here in Minnesota. I sound like an advertisement, but ITS TRUE!

Jeff Bennett
Las Cruces, New Mexico

Why don't you love the people?
Why don't you struggle for the people?
Why don't you die for the people?

— Fred Hampton

SIXTY-SIX

B^{ix,} These days I await some action, and I have been waiting all my life. People know I am unhappy and misfit thus think I am biased, yet it is they who cannot connect 9/11 Wars. Do they imagine we fight Syria because Assad "gassed his own people." How explain Iraq, Afghanistan, Libya. They work to believe how many jerks with box cutters? Four airplanes. Oh well.   Down in there somewhere. Must have entered an abandoned mine shaft. Oh well. Eh, 16 years. Many murders now, added to the 9/11 victims. Many disappeared.

Past year, where I go, much on uncounted Clinton murders. I don't follow it, just notice it has no end. Next is Pizzagate. I don't follow it, it has no end. Internationally the satanic pedophilia is uncounted decades, I had some sense already. OK, arrests are to be made. Maybe not, the wrong people have more money, more military. Sure, I know there is friction inside US military, probably inside the F.B.I. and C.I.A. Past week I am not getting enough action. I drift off into Appalachian folk videos, or Nova videos: The Secret Life of Plants. Had past year not been enjoying Ufology or Sasquatch or previous civilizations proven, hoping for action on the child abuse and murder, to expose our rulers for their greater evil.   I did say to Caryl, all this past cover up of extraterrestrials and higher technologies clearly in schizoid nation and present world history is related, nor did we get to the Moon as reported. Too much radiation belt back then. Possibly we have, by now, via secret space program, but I think extraterrestrials have the Moon. Been hearing, technical developments on the Moon's dark side. But are they friendlies or pillagers. We know there are diverse groups.   My hero Debbie Lusignan disdains Trump, and she is nearly always correct. Others of intelligence hope Trump can get himself together. Hell, this jerk is a 70 year old jerk. He is being threatened. What has set him apart is he wishes peace with Putin. While mostly they who want Trump impeached or shot are made ignorant, in fear of death, of Putin. Who wins? Likely not a 70 year old jerk. USA is a murderous police state.   I am glad I get to sit here at my window upon natural world and drink. Retirement is good. If without a cheery woman.

     Further Out,   Bill

Note from the narrator ...

From "Not Exactly a Radio Show," a live podcast that traveled the circuit of Twins Cities bars for about six months, produced by former members of The Prince Hope Show:

The "Dan Rather Award For What Passes For Journalism In This Country" will be presented next week.

The coveted bronze statue of a mockingbird will be bestowed at the Lincoln Center For The Performing Arts.

Engraved on the statue:
"His head could be seen to move violently forward."

It's no use going back to yesterday,
because I was a different person then.

— Alice

SIXTY-SEVEN

The numbers rolled into place: 5:00 a.m.

Brooke was already awake, listening out her window to the birds beginning to chirp, thinking about stuff, any stuff at all that came into her head, going way back to grade school then right up to yesterday.

She heard doors closing, low talking, running sounds on the grass, kids getting home from being out all night. Wouldn't want to be them today.

She heard steps, on the porch, into the screened porch.

Now banging, hollering.

Geez, we paid the garbage bill, wow, chill. She threw off the blankets to get up and talk to them.

"Open the door! Law enforcement!"

She stopped on the steps.

What?

She heard banging on the back door, hurried to the window and saw black cars and black SUVs and one robin's egg blue tiny little car parked all up and down their street.

Brooke rushed to double-lock the door when it burst open.

"What is going on!" shouted Lara, now standing on the steps, pointing.

"Leave her alone!"

She headed back upstairs for her weapon.

Three large men in full combat gear stormed the steps and dragged her down.

Note from the narrator ...

From "Not Exactly A Radio Show," a live podcast that traveled the circuit of Twins Cities bars for about six months, produced by former members of The Prince Hope Show:

... The United States is not a police state. And you would be a fat Communist soccer-lover wearing lederhosen and a tiny Bavarian hat with a feather and tight jacket and knee socks with buckle shoes who does not fit in with the rest of the family at Thanksgiving dinner if you thought so. There are not police everywhere. You do not have to go to where the police put you in order to hold your sign and have your freedom of speech like a Bolshevik perched atop a potato crate like a stranded nanny goat. This is America.

There are not thousands and thousands of people making their living off of the "War on Terror," in Homeland Security, the border patrol, the U.S. Army, the airport box cutter-shampoo-bazooka up the wazoo-finder guys, the video game industry, the bullet industry, the casket and handcuff and Easy-Bake Oven secret spy camera industrial complex.

It's just not a police state.

The police are not shock troops protecting the rich against the poor.

It's not.

Say it.

It snot.

And in the night one family camps in a ditch and another family pulls in and the tents come out. The two men squat on their hams and the women and children listen. Here is the node, you who hate change and fear revolution.

Keep these two squatting men apart; make them hate, fear, suspect each other. Here is the anlage of the thing you fear. This is the zygote.

For here "I lost my land" is changed;
a cell is split and from its splitting grows the thing you hate
"We lost our land."

…This is the thing to bomb.

This is the beginning — from "I" to "we."

And the great owners, who must lose their land in an upheaval, the great owners with access to history, with eyes to read history and to know the great fact:
when property accumulates in too few hands it is taken away.

And that companion fact:
when a majority of the people are hungry and cold
they will take by force what they need.

And the little screaming fact that sounds through all history: repression works only to strengthen and knit the repressed.

— John Steinbeck, *The Grapes of Wrath*

SIXTY-EIGHT

Geoffrey,
    My siblings may be too old to change. They are in their seventies. Hard to say about you, or Gunter, in your early fifties. But this happens. One prefers to not deal with it. One may prefer to not know, in fact.   I am not that way. Sure, a decade and a half back I questioned 9/11, then began getting information. JFK official story I never had believed, or MLK, Malcolm, Bobby. At this time it is incredulous people close to me can still hope to think that two airplanes wrecked the World Trade Center complex, inclusive of Building 7 across the street. Then the 12 feet or so hole in the Pentagon, no airplane pieces....Most fantastical the too narrow a ditch outside Shanksville, Penn. In there somewhere. Must've gone into an abandoned mine shaft.   That Trump is suddenly a dangerous egomaniacal love starved buffoon, I spoke of it today, and Kelly took heart. Jumped in with something about the Russians, and I assured him I still don't believe any of that. Fake shit, anybody can hack anybody, is words simplistic enough to cut out that shit. Kelly's impulse still is to run off, but I had already agreed to give him a lb. of pintos, and he calmed it then. Kelly is still good at smiling. Mike Blackbird is just going to be blank. He is a scientist out here, non political, so what he votes, Democrat of course. My siblings believe Obama is better than Trump. They will keep this. In

their seventies, eighties, zero connect to 9/11 Wars on civilians. They never speak of the civilian bombing, Obama never missed one day in his 8 years. Putin is bad. Trump is bad. Obama is good. Son, said our late B. E. to me - we USE that oil! That would have been the first USA attack on Iraq. The next one, my father had some dementia.   Oh, lets see, I need to remember what I think better, in these years. There is too much known fact, for my siblings and people to not know better than they now do, ten years from now. Perhaps, Obama and the Clintons and the Bushies will never go to prison. Because, USA is a police state. It is proven in court the F.B.I. murdered Martin Luther King Jr, though never yet has the trial made Main Stream News. It is well proven Oswald did not kill JFK, but Mossad, C.I.A., F.B.I. and LBJ have become proven the ones who did. James Kessler and friends have proven that NOBODY DIED AT SANDY HOOK, a book that began selling well and then Amazon Books jumped to ban it. It sells now at Moon Rock Books. James Kessler organized Scholars for 9/11 Truth, and he and friends have certainly proven 9/11 was done by the Bush family and C.I.A. and Mossad and Neocons. Nobody has had to prove the official 9/11 account is not possible. Airplanes can't do that. There were no airplane parts there either, and so what, mini-nukes were used, and I keep forgetting how many days or weeks at Ground Zero there was molten steel and concrete in the ground.   Geoffrey, do you wonder why I obsess, for 16 years counting. People do put it to me. But I say, how for sixteen years counting do all of you prefer to not speak of all this. THAT...is how I obsess. What the hell is UP? SOMETHING IS WRONG!   Recently, in an email, Bix remarked "how simple it is," 9/11 Truth. There was a single step forward. Normally he is not moved to talk about it.   It is unpleasant, people feel small, let us be nice, see no evil, speak no evil, hear no evil.   I say there is more to it. This is a phenomenon. Years back already, on the Larry King show, Jesse Ventura was saying: Why can't we talk about it? I have neither read nor heard anyone try to answer the question. Why can't we talk about it? Perhaps any conjecture is too horrible....any possibility too horrible? Might be, but it can be deeper, while people cannot freely wonder.   Surely it is not going away. Our constitution is wrecked and most people have not known it is. More people are disappeared. More locked up without trial. Our news media is no damn good. Trump was not wanted, voting was rigged for Hillary, Trump won even so, and the MSM went uglier. He was being slapped

around and next in claim Assad was "gassing his own people" again, Trump the boy had to get some praise and he did a poor act on his sympathy for killed kids and he had a few rounds lobbed in, illegally, killed folks. That Assad had gassed his own people again appears to be a false flag. Google some latest Ron Paul if you have time. There are others, Debbie Lusignan. Ron Paul put it well, Assad is popular, he with Putin were beating the terrorists, Assad is not crazy. But who cares? Hitler or somebody said if a lie is repeated long enough people begin to believe.   I see there are some people in "Alternate News" who want boy Trump to do better. His enemies will get him. Lately he has thought about striking North Korea. I will not be following his doomed career.   Lately I became aware how as Hillary has these ugly facial expressions that only her enemies wish to show, same with boy Trump. He, too, has grotesque facial expression. This is already used in cartoons. What a president.   Love,
                    Bill

QUOTE REMOVED BY ORDER OF DHS, UNITED STATES
DEPARTMENT OF HOMELAND SECURITY. [DHS US2FA]

Note from the narrator …

From "Not Exactly A Radio Show," a live podcast that traveled the circuit of Twins Cities bars for about six months, produced by former members of The Prince Hope Show:

If you stand for the national anthem.
You Might Be An American
If you stand for fighter jets flying over the stadium.
You Might Be An American
If you stand for the bombing of children.
You Might Be An American
If you recite the pledge of allegiance to bombing children.
You Might Be An American
If you recite the latest from the TV Nightly News as if it were the truth.
You Might Be An American
If you pay for bombs that kill children.
You Might Be An American
If you pay for soldiers who kill children.
You Might Be An American
If you hate immigrants coming into your town.
You Might Be An American
If your great-grand-parents were immigrants coming into town.
You Might Be An American
If you put your neighbors in cages because they are too poor to live without stealing because you have taken far more than your share.
You Might Be An American
If you can walk around Walmart with your eyes open for more than seven minutes and still believe you and your neighbors are the hope of the world.
You Might Be An American.

Well, I've walked these streets, a virtual stage, it seemed to me.
Makeup on their faces, actors took their places next to me.
— Natalie Merchant

SIXTY-NINE

Lara and Brooke stood together out in back of The Walmart Public Safety Complex by the green and black Dumpsters, their hands tied behind their backs, their feet bound as well.

They faced a firing squad from the various units lead by a guy in a grey uniform and a nametag that said "BOB, How May I Help You?"

"Kuss mein arsch," said Brooke.

"They don't get it," said Lara.

"Right?" said Brooke.

"You guys know any Tracy Chapman? On your phone?"

"Who's that?"

"We tried," said Brooke.

"Yes, we did."

How many peers do we have. The thought jumped into Brooke's head and she did not know why.

"Truth is stranger than fiction," said Lara, looking straight ahead.

"I know, right," said Brooke.

A young, hip woman with piercings and tattoos came out of the store to throw something away, talking over her shoulder to somebody back inside.

"At least it's an ethos," she said.

"I know who you guys are," excited, she pointed at Lara and Brooke.

"Ohmygod!"

"They do get it!" said Lara.

"Success. Fire," said Brooke.

"No, there's a fire, right there."

Somebody's cigarette had started some paper. Somebody stepped on it.

"Love you."

"Love you too."

Someone with a name badge stuck his head out the door and said, "Those are going to have to go back to Sporting Goods." And two of the firing squad people looked at each other and rolled their eyes.

"Duh."

"Yeah, duh."

Brooke scooted over to be able to hold pinkie-swear fingers with Lara.

Trash hung high in the trees between the building and the river, like ghosts, plastic bags, toilet paper, oily rags, a diaper, a faded, torn CRUSHER T-shirt, Nothing Is Fucked. The breeze picked up and everything waved like the flags of the damned.

"Now fire," said the firing squad leader.

Lara flew back, her arms out. Brooke dropped to the side, next to her, her head in Lara's lap. Crows screamed and flew up out of the trees. A semi driver honked his horn and the squawk of a drive-up window could be heard way over here.

The workers had another cigarette and went back inside.

A small bird, nervous, flitted on the Dumpster, then hopped down to sit for just a moment on Brooke's knee.

Through the day the blood in their mouths and noses and on their shirts dried and caked. Their bodies stiffened and the sun shined down hard. Cats began to venture closer over the hours and the smell made it difficult for the smokers on their breaks. Finally, somebody covered them with cardboard boxes that had to be broken down anyway to make more room in the Dumpster.

Alice, Charlie, Ike and Frida stopped for gas in Nebraska.

They got out and stretched.

"I got it," said Alice.

The others slumped inside for snacks, moaning, bitching.

"How many more miles?"

"We just got started, dude."

Alice wiped with her hand the dirty back window to show the sign that said "Hollywood OR Bust."

Kory gunned it up the hill and stopped the red Suburban outside the mental hospital.

They grabbed their guns and got out.

"It's open," Washington said and they went inside, up stairs, rifles at their chests, leaning against the wall, being very careful for snipers and other things.

They walked down the shiny tile halls, looked into each room, up more stairs, every room. Their footsteps echoed.

They made it all the way, through every floor, every room, until they were at the top, looking out the last window down on their vehicle and out at the corn.

"There's nobody here," said Korey.

Evey sat in the stands at the elementary school track meet.

She wore her father's TWINS cap.

Blake sat next to her.

He nodded toward Rachel, getting ready for the fifty-meter dash.

"She was born to run," he said.

Evey did not smile.

"I think you're right," she said.

Roswell stood in the back yard at the farm, head down, eating grass, wearing a blanket that looked Native and kind of like a dancing alien, a dancing Ojibwe alien.

And something glinted, way over there, in the sky, toward the sun, way up high.

To be fucking continued.

About the Artist

Lisa Rouleau is a direct support professional working in human services. Damara Jean Rose Allen is a ninth grade student. Both live in Cloquet, Minnesota.

www.ingramcontent.com/pod-product-compliance
Lightning Source LLC
Chambersburg PA
CBHW071150250626
47159CB00001B/43